Shetland map

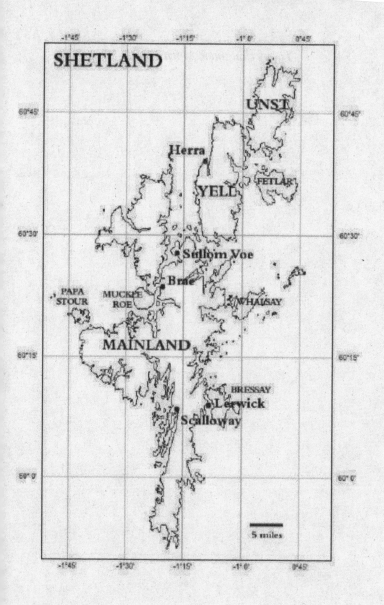

To my daughter, Marnie.

wrestin treed (n): a piece of knotted thread used by witches in their spells

Wednesday 19th October

Low Water Scalloway 03:34 BST 0.5m
High Water 09:53 2.2m
Low Water 015:48 0.5m
High Water 22.08 2.3m

Moon: New, 0.3%

Sunrise 07:51
Moonrise 08:00, 122 degrees
Sunset 17:43
Moonset 18:09, 233 degrees

The knotted cord tumbled out from under my pillow. I didn't register it for a moment. I was tired, after a morning of clearing undergrowth and an afternoon of college lectures on regulations for discharge of hazardous substances at sea. I'd cooked tea on my little stove, dangled a string for Cat, read a book as the autumn sunlight dipped down behind the hill, then gone for a brisk walk to warm me up before bedtime. I'd boiled the kettle, taking it off the gas ring at the first squeak of the whistle, filled my bottle, and slipped it under my pyjamas. I'd drawn the faded navy curtains along *Khalida*'s long windows, visited the toilet in the boating club, and brushed my teeth on deck. I'd loosened my dark plait so that my hair fell in curls round my shoulders.

My bunk was the traditional captain's starboard quarterberth, a long rectangle reaching back under the cockpit. The pillow was tucked under the downie at the open end. I pulled it out, and the cord fell from it like a snake striking.

I stood for a long moment looking, my heart thumping, while Cat pounced on it, rolling on his back on the wooden floor, and kicking it with his hind legs. It wasn't any cord I had aboard, but a fine grey twine, with five knots along its length. I stretched my hand down and eased it from Cat's claws.

It was about sixty centimetres long, and the knots were simple half-reef knots – or, I amended, looking closer, three were the correct right-over-left and two were half-grannies. I knew what it was: a wrestin treed, the old folk would call it, a witch-token, made by five people, a knot each, and an evil-eye charm muttered as the fingers tied. I found myself looking up at *Khalida*'s curtained windows as if there were eyes outside, watching to see how I reacted to their malice. One of them had come into my home and slipped this piece of malevolence where it would dissipate its poison into my head.

If I believed that kind of thing, I told myself. Seven years ago I'd sailed with

i

a Venezuelan who swore by it, and one of the other crew had almost given him a heart attack by slipping a knotted cord under his pillow; but I didn't believe demons could harm me at the calling of a knotted piece of string. Human malevolence was different. I slipped forward to the forepeak and screwed the catch tight, then came back aft and slid home the bolts that would keep the washboards closed in the wildest of ocean storms. Nobody would come aboard my ship this night.

I picked up the cord again. I wasn't sure what to do with the thing. Eventually, I said an 'Our Father' before undoing each knot, and a 'Hail Mary' as my fingers worked on each one, then a final 'Glory be'. The cord lay fluid in my hands. I never wasted cord – aboard ship, ropes are cut only in the severest of emergencies – but I wasn't going to use this one to bind a loose shackle or whip a rope end. I set light to it in the sink, washed the ashes away and went to bed.

I lay in my narrow berth and considered, chin propped up on my arms, the candle flickering gold beside me, and Cat purring in the crook of my neck. I'd only been in Scalloway for a month and a half. I knew my class at college, of course, and our lecturers, and Kate and Peter, whose garden I was helping clear. I'd chatted to the woman who ran the local shop. I hadn't yet been to a dance or concert, and I hadn't had a disagreement with anyone, so who disliked me enough to leave that unpleasant gift? I couldn't think of a single person, let alone five of them.

Furthermore, they'd dared to invade my space, my *Khalida*, my home, my sanctuary. She was my companion on soft nights with the stars hanging above us, my fellow voyager when the wind blew up and she was tilted over until the waves washed her lee window. She was my adventure and my safety. She was my self, now I was marooned ashore, one of a class of pupils in the busy North Atlantic Fisheries College. She reminded me of who I was: Cass, the mast-climber, who'd helmed tall ships in the black velvet of tropical nights. Cass, the planner, the decision-maker.

Cass Lynch, the captain of her own ship.

ill (n): moral wickedness, evil; to do ill (v) to do evil, deal harshly with

ill-viket (adj): malicious

Chapter One

Wednesday 26th October

High Water Scalloway 05:49 BST 1.4m
Low Water 011:53 0.7m
High Water 17:57 1.5m
Moon waxing gibbous 73% of full

Moonset 1:31, 253 degrees
Sunrise 08:09
Moonrise 15:43, 102 degrees
Sunset 17:28

You'd have heard the door slam over the sea in Faroe. Cat froze at my heels. I hesitated on the other side of the garden wall, my hand on the old-fashioned door knob. If the household was in the middle of one of those daughter/parents rows, they wouldn't want the gardener waltzing in. Then footsteps clattered down the flagstone path. Cat leapt nimbly into the ditch and skulked among the long, yellowed grass. I stepped back just as the door flung open, and Annette tumbled out.

Yes, there had been a row. Her cheeks were scarlet, her eyes flashing. The wind caught her scarf as she came out of the walled garden into the sea air, and pulled one end upwards. She grabbed at it, swore, then realised I was standing there. She bit her lip, doubled her scarf with elaborate care, threaded the end through, and pulled it around her neck, grimacing as if it was too tight, then at last stood straight up to face me. Her eyes went first to the long scar running along my cheek, winced away from it and moved up to meet my eyes. 'Hiya, Cass.'

'Now then,' I said, traditional Shetland style. *Noo den, lass, foo's du?* How are you, what's wrong? But we weren't on those terms, and I didn't want to be nosy.

She shuffled one foot, as if she wasn't sure what to say. She was one of those china-doll girls, with a smooth complexion, groomed brows, and perfectly separated eyelashes above velvet-brown eyes. Her lipstick was

1

glossy, a dark plum colour. She was dressed in her usual purple jacket, with a black velvet beret tipped to one side on her blonde hair. Her black skirt trailed lace like the streamers on a jellyfish. It was all too artificial for a windy morning in Scalloway.

She glanced down at Cat, slipping out of the long grass, his plume of a tail lashing, and her brow cleared. 'He's a bonny cat.' She bent down to him and put out her hand. 'Here, puss.' His yellow eyes looked at her with disdain. He didn't do casual caresses. She said, almost to herself, as if she'd suddenly had an idea, 'He's a bonny, healthy cat ...' She moved forward on her hunkers, brought her other hand forward, as if she was about to grab him, and Cat hissed and backed away.

'He doesn't like being picked up,' I said.

She turned her head up with a look I couldn't read, a mixture of defiance and apology, then stood up. The petulant frown returned. 'You ran away from home, didn't you? When you were much younger than me?'

'Sixteen,' I agreed. I didn't want to encourage whatever daft ideas she was brewing. 'It wasn't thatna good idea. It's a tough world out there.'

'But you managed.'

'I lived aboard tall ships, with someone else to do the cooking, and no money worries. Bed and board taken care of, at the price of climbing a mast or two daily.' Whatever else she did, I'd bet my last shackle Annette wouldn't run away to sea. For a start, nobody made sensible outdoor gear in her favourite Goth black with lacy frills, and her sleek hair wouldn't last five minutes in the wind.

She fiddled with her scarf again. As it slipped, I saw there was one deep scratch and several smaller ones on her neck, as though she'd picked up someone's cat, and it had fought to get away. No, the marks looked too big, too indented, with the shadow of a bruise around each – dog's claws? They had two pointers, Dan and Candy, a pair of soft lumps. I couldn't imagine them going for anyone's throat. She saw me looking and pulled the scarf up to cover the marks. Her cheeks reddened. She looked away from me, and reached into her pocket for gloves, put them on carefully, finger after finger, then sighed. 'They don't understand!' It came out as a suppressed wail. She drew a ragged breath, then continued, 'They're suffocating me. Why shouldn't I go out and meet people, if I want to? If I think they can help me?'

'No reason,' I agreed. It wasn't any of my business, but although what I'd heard of the rows with her parents sounded like typical teenage angst, she was eighteen, past the most dramatic stage, and well old enough to be leaving home. 'Why don't you get a flat for your gap year, and do what you like?'

'I'd have to get a job first,' she said.

From the look on her face, she wasn't going to do that, not when Daddy was willing to keep her. She must have seen the thought, for she said, defensively, 'It's not that easy. My degree's going to be research-based, so I'm waiting for something in my field, as useful experience.'

At her age I'd cleared tables and washed dishes while I waited for another ship. She drew an angry breath. 'Anyway, I think I'm old enough to decide where I can go, and who I can see.'

And you know perfectly well, I thought to myself, *that it's someone you shouldn't be seeing* ... There was something strung up about her, as if she was determined to come to what she knew full well was the wrong decision. She glared as her father's dark-grey BMW slipped out of Ladysmith Drive and turned left towards Lerwick. Then her face smoothed to uncertain and young. She turned her eyes towards the sea, bit her lip, then looked back at me. Her hand went back up to the scarf. 'Cass, do you ever feel as if you've lived before? Like, you know, another life?'

'Reincarnation?' I shook my head. 'Do you?'

'Sometimes.' She tugged at the scarf again. 'This – it's choking me.'

I wasn't thirty yet, but she was making me feel like my own grandmother. 'It's not any good running away,' I said. 'I didn't run away from. I ran to. I needed the sea. Listen, if you'd like to come and talk, you know where I live?' I turned and pointed along the shore, towards the marina that jutted out in front of the glass and tiles of the Fisheries college. 'That's my boat, *Khalida,* the little white one with the sails still on. Just give a shout from the marina gate, and I'll come and open up.'

She looked relieved, as if she thought I could solve all her problems. 'I'll maybe do that.'

'Any time,' I said. 'I'm in most evenings.'

Her eyes went from my face to over my shoulder, and flared in alarm. I turned my head. Three girls of around Annette's age were coming along the sea road towards us. They were dressed in that steampunk style, leather and flounces mixed together, in shades of grey and black, like a Victorian photograph. The style extended to their make up of spiky eyelashes and black lipstick. I'd seen them hanging around the corner just short of the shop, indistinct through a cloud of tobacco smoke, victims of the recession. Shetland used to have jobs for anyone who was willing to work, but now the council was slashing front-line troops, and people who had jobs as home helps, care-centre workers and office staff were clinging on to them. Furthermore, the first casualty of the Education Department's rush to save five million pounds had been the secondary department of Scalloway's Junior High School. Now all the teenagers were taken by bus to the big school in Lerwick, and the small army of cleaners who used to meet the home-going pupils had been made redundant.

These girls knew Annette. The tallest of them was giving her a hard glare from under her dye-black fringe. Annette looked back, pleading at first, then her eyes hardened and her lips set in a straight line. The tallest girl lifted one hand, and rubbed her thumb against her first two fingers in the universal 'money' gesture. The other two sneered.

Annette's chin went up. Without saying goodbye, she swung around and set off along the sea front towards the shop, shouldering through them. Her heeled books clacked on the pavement. I watched her go for a moment, then glanced back at the other girls. The tallest girl's hand fell slowly. Her look would have stopped a seagull in flight. The black, glossy leather, the grey frills of skirt, the poised attention of the turned heads, gave them the look of a trio of hooded crows sizing up a dying sheep. They were an ill-viket trio. If I was Annette, I'd be watching my back.

I had a garden to clear. I turned away from the sea, and pushed the heavy wooden door open. Cat slid out of the ditch and bounded in ahead of me, plumed tail held high, showing the paler grey underneath. The starving kitten I'd found on the hillside three months ago was now a glossy young cat, slate grey on his back, with darker guard hairs, and pale stripes leading down to a grey-pink belly and neat white paws. At Brae, he'd slept happily on board while I was out, because he'd had my friend Anders' pet Rat with him. I'd tried leaving him on board alone when I'd first come to Scalloway, but he'd clawed gouges in my woodwork in his efforts to get out. When I left the hatch open for him, he'd bounded along the dock and wriggled under the wire fence to follow me. Now he charged around Kate's garden with Dan and Candy while we worked; otherwise, he came to college. On classroom days, he curled up in my lap, and when it was an at-sea day, I left him with Nate, who worked in the college café. It was fine and warm in the cupboard off the kitchen, to say nothing of the occasional bit of fish, so I hoped he'd still want to come home to an unheated boat as the temperature dropped.

Inside the gate, the flagged path stretched up between sycamore trees to the old house, grey stone, and built with that early eighteenth century square look, like a house drawn by a child: steps to central porch, with door in the middle, two windows each side, three on the next floor, a rectangle of tiled roof, a chimney stack trailing smoke at each side. At least, that was how I'd drawn houses; I wondered if my friend Inga's toddler, Peerie Charlie, drew houses like that, or if his drawings were of modern Shetland houses, made of coloured wood, with triple-insulation picture windows, a small turbine by their side, and solar panels on the roof.

This house had belonged to the last of the lairds, the Scott family who'd dominated Scalloway life for five centuries. It had been sold after his death to a couple from England, and I'd seen the notice in the shop: 'Wanted, person for active gardening, through October, hours to be arranged.'

Naturally, I'd asked my pal Magnie about them. He'd phoned an old whaling crony in Scalloway, and got all the information. 'The man's Peter Otway, and they're been up here for ten years or so. He's in his mid-forties. He's the manager o' the RBS in Lerwick, and they rented there, then when this big house came on the market, they bought it and moved to Scalloway. The wife's called Kate. He must be fifteen year younger as what she is. They hae just the one lass. They came up when she was just out o' the primary school. He's one o' these folk who's involved in aathing. You ken. He's in the Rotary, and the Masons too, I've no doubt, though I wouldna ken meself, and he gengs oot wi' a squad at Up Helly Aa.'

The Lerwick Up Helly Aa, the biggest of Shetland's fire festivals, involved a thousand guizers with flaming torches. It was men only, you needed to have lived in the town for five years, and getting into a squad was strictly by invitation.

'The manager o' the bank, that's aristocracy in Lerook.' Magnie's voice gave the town name its full blast of country scorn. 'He's been right in the heart o' organising the new museum and all.' This, as it involved seafaring, was more acceptable.

'The Shetland Bus Museum?' I'd seen it from the road, a big, red-wood building, but hadn't yet been inside.

'The *Scalloway* Museum,' Magnie emphasised. 'It has the whole history o' the place. 'There's a prehistoric ard, and a Viking bracelet – well, a replica, the Edinburgh museum took the real one – and stuff about witches, and the herring fishery, as well as the story o' the Norwegian men.'

I should have remembered that what a Shetlander doesn't know about his own history's not worth knowing. 'I must go and look,' I said. The Shetland Bus men were my heroes, young Norwegians in fishing boats who'd run arms and radio parts into occupied Norway, and brought refugees out.

'That you should, lass. They're done it brawly well. So he was involved wi' that as well. The wife doesna work, she does painting, bonny peerie pictures o' flowers, in these bright modern paints.' Magnie himself had a weakness for the pictures his mother favoured: Victorian prints of a child with ringlets holding a kitten. 'So she's decided to get the gairding in order afore the winter sets in? It's a great, rambling area just filled wi' trees and brambles.'

'Active gardening, right opposite where *Khalida*'s moored, and at times I can fit in around the college,' I said, and dialled their number.

'What gardening have you done?' was Kate's first question, once I'd introduced myself.

I'd thought out my answer. 'None,' I replied promptly, 'but spending my life at sea means I'm quick to learn and very good at following orders. I'll do far less damage than someone who only thinks she knows about gardening.'

She laughed out at that, and we agreed on me doing as much of the heavy clearing as I could before Bonfire Night, the first Saturday in November.

Inga had found it very funny, 'Given that you've done your best to stay away from the land since you got your first boat.' In spite of that, I was enjoying myself. I was used to fresh air, and the occasional shower of rain didn't bother me. Working for Kate got me outside, away from the strip-lighting and recycled air of the college, away from the constant admonitions-for-two-year-olds: *Have you washed your hands? Don't use two when one will do!* The only notices aboard ship were serious ones, so the constant visual drivel was getting on my nerves.

Kate was standing in the doorway, a dog at each side. Everything about her said 'county' – the dark brown cords, the green bodywarmer over a jumper and polo shirt, the scarf held round her neck with a cameo clip, the green rubber boots. They didn't keep horses here, but you could bet she'd grown up with them, and could back a horsebox into a tight space as easily as I'd back a dinghy trailer. Her shoulder-length hair was bright and glossy as a newly fallen conker, and held back with an Alice band, sixties style. She had an outdoor complexion, with faint red veins running under the skin, and hazel eyes. One look told you that anything she organised would run like clockwork.

Her eyes were on the gate, but looking beyond it, to where Annette had gone. The dogs saw us first; Candy, the black and white one, bounded forward from a standing start, leapt over Cat, turned in a circle, and began sniffing at his back. The male, Dan, rose more slowly, shook, and strolled forward to greet us. Then Kate turned and focused on us.

'He's not quite right yet,' she said, watching Dan. 'We still think it was food poisoning. Maybe we're about to find a half-eaten dead sheep in the wilderness. He even refused his walk last night. Peter was talking of calling the vet out, but we decided to see how he was in the morning.'

She straightened her shoulders and came down the steps. 'All set for another hard session of undergrowth clearing?'

'All set,' I agreed.

We were clearing a patch of ground where the Japanese roses, tough as herring-gulls and spined like sea-urchins, had flung their suckers up through the grass for two yards around the parent plant. I'd come to enjoy these land colours: the primrose leaves held out from the rain-black stems, the shiny damson-red hips like miniature pomegranates. Here and there a bird had torn one open to show the yellow flesh and seeds within. There was a clump of autumn crocus among the central stems, veined violet globes on transparent stems, the petals shut against the cold.

It was satisfying work: the feel of the root giving, the speed you could clear a group of suckers when first one, then another, and another came free, and you had a whole bush in your gloved hand. Cat scampered about with Candy, leaping over him, pouncing on leaves, chasing trails of grass as they pulled through with the roots, and retrieving the jingly ball that Kate had bought him. It was covered with tinsel, and flat enough for him to carry in his mouth, so when you flung it, he'd play with it where it landed for a bit, then bring it back to be thrown again, just like a dog. Candy would join in that too, and where it was a good throw she usually got it first, but Cat would be on it before her if it went only ten yards, and bringing it back while she circled round him. She'd tried, just once, to pick him up like a puppy, but he wasn't having that one.

When we'd cleared back to the centre bush, Kate headed off with the barrowful of suckers, while I raked the brittle bluebell stems and gave the grass a last stamp, for luck. The bonfire was at East Voe, on the other side of the harbour, so she had to pile the suckers into a salmon feed bag in the back of her estate car and drive them over. The burning space was already piled high with old chairs and pallets and what looked like a shed roof. It would be a good blaze, come a week on Saturday.

'Coffee and tabnabs,' Kate said at last, leaning the emptied barrow back against the wall. It was part of our routine, a ten-minute tea-break and a biscuit to give us energy for the next onslaught. Cat, Candy, and I followed her into the kitchen, where the oil-fuelled Rayburn glowed gently, with the kettle tickling on the back burner, and Dan's brown and white length sprawled out in front of it. The room smelt of warmth, coffee, and dog. Kate moved the kettle to the hotplate and fetched the biscuit tin while I got out the mugs and dished coffee into each, and Cat curled up in his bubblewrap box by the Rayburn. Then we sat down one each side of the wooden kitchen table and relaxed.

I'd taken to Kate straight away. We'd not become mates during our tea-breaks, the age difference was too wide, but I'd learned a lot about her. She'd grown up in the Cotswolds, and her mother had been very proud of her garden: 'She had real green fingers, you just gave her a root and it'd grow.' She'd met Peter at a function in the children's home she'd volunteered at; he'd been one of the trustees, and they'd caught each other's eyes while one of the other trustees was making a particularly pompous speech, and somehow that had been that – 'Although it took him nearly a year to get over me being almost twice his age – he was just twenty-three, and I was in my late thirties.' She'd learned to entertain businessmen, instead of the hunt set – 'Slightly less interested in the quality of the wine, and thought a pretty presentation was more important than a quantity of good, filling, warming food.' Her face had softened. 'And then Annette came along. She was the most beautiful baby, with a head of golden curls –' Nothing had been too good for their child: a black Shetland pony called Ricky, dancing lessons, the baton-twirling club, private tutoring for the subjects she found hard in school. She'd got reasonable Highers, and was waiting for her university place. 'So we can get back to our bachelor days!' They still seemed a pretty stable couple (in so far as you dare say that of any couple, these days), in spite of the age difference. He was out all day, of course, but made the six-mile drive from Lerwick for lunch, and rarely stayed late in the office. His evenings were devoted to the museum, or socialising at the Rotary and the Legion, while she painted in her wooden studio hut by the house. She was a regular exhibitor in Bonhoga gallery out at Weisdale, and I'd managed to hitch my way over to see her recent show. That had been flowers, as Magnie had said, and most of them had a red dot on the label.

Equally, she'd learned about me: brought up in Shetland, the only daughter of an Irish oil worker and a French opera singer. When I was a teenager, Dad was asked to oversee a new construction in the Gulf, and I'd been sent to Maman's elegant town flat in Poitiers. I'd hated it; I was homesick for the sea, for my fellow sailors, and I'd emptied my bank account and run back to Scotland, via a berth on a Russian ship, *Mir*, in the Cutty Sark Tall Ships' Race. After that, I'd wandered the high seas on tall ships, and taught dinghy sailing in Med resorts. I'd crossed the Atlantic with my lover, Alain – but I didn't talk about that, nor about his death on the way home. My weight of guilt was lifting, slowly, but it hadn't gone yet. Then I'd found my *Khalida*, lying neglected in a Greek marina, sailed her to Norway, and come home at last to Shetland, and reconciliation with Dad, with Maman, who were now themselves mending their sixteen-year separation, while I took the qualifications I'd missed as a teenager, so that I could be an officer on a tall ship.

Kate stirred her coffee and took a second Kit Kat. 'Did you meet

Annette on your way in?'

I nodded.

Kate sighed. 'I just don't understand it. We used to get on so well – she was such a sweet little girl, and of course being the only one she got buckets of attention. We used to do everything together. I thought she'd always listen to me, at least ...' She got up and went to the sink, face turned away from me. 'I think it's a boyfriend, and one we wouldn't approve of. What really worries me, Cass, is these uneven moods, flaring out at the least thing. I'm afraid she's taking drugs. You can see she's not happy, guilty-looking ... do you think it could be that?'

'I don't know much about the drugs scene,' I said. 'It's not something you see much in the sailing world. Well, for a start you can't afford them, because any spare money goes on the boat.' I'd got £4,000 from the job as skipper of a replica longship for a film. If I could live on £3,000 for this college year, the last thousand would go on a new suit of sails for *Khalida*. 'And then you have to be alert at sea, you need all the senses you've got, and none making you see things that aren't there.' On a moonlit night, alone on deck, with the sea in a great saucer all around you, it was easy to see things. Once I could have sworn I saw the ghost of a long-gone square-rigger, with tattered sails and dead men pulling on the ropes. Then the moon went behind a cloud, and I was left alone on the sea that glinted like coal, wondering what was out there, until the moon returned to show empty water.

'There's a big drugs scene in Shetland, among the young ones,' Kate said. She began twiddling her Kit Kat paper into a silver cup. 'I'd hoped Annette was too old and too sensible to be drawn into it, but you never can tell. Parents always say that: "We thought our child was too sensible." It just takes the wrong company.'

'Do you have any idea,' I asked, diffidently, for after all it was none of my business, 'who the wrong company is?'

She shook her head. 'There's a boy from the college who seems rather keen on her, fair-haired, rather protuberent eyes, quiet. James something. He's phoned a couple of times.'

'James Leask,' I said. That explained how Annette knew I'd run away to sea. He was on the engineering component of the rather mixed course I was doing. 'He wouldn't lead anyone astray, nor be led himself. He's one of the quiet, stubborn ones.'

She nodded. 'That's the impression I got too. She met up with him a couple of times this week – let me see, on Saturday, and then they went out for a meal at the Scalloway Hotel on Monday. So I was hoping ...'

I thought, but didn't say, that maybe Annette had a reason for feeling suffocated, if she was watched as closely as this. When I'd been

Annette's age, Dad had been busy with his new oil installation, and Maman had been in Poitiers. I'd been on board *Sorlandet* all summer, then on a Caribbean beach teaching dinghy sailing all winter, and neither of them who knew who I met, or how often, or where. They still didn't, but at least bridges were being built. 'James wouldn't do drugs, I'm sure of it.'

'Anyway,' Kate said, 'she's off to some party at Hallowe'en, and that's what this latest row was about.' She gave me a sideways look, as if she was trying to assess whether I was a rabid anti-Hallowe'en fundamentalist. 'Peter thinks it's all going too far, dressing up as devils and witches, and skulls everywhere, all that. He was disgusted with that silly Hallowe'en play – did you see it?'

I shook my head.

'It was just a bit of fun,' Kate said. 'It was about this village where the dead came alive every 31st October. It was the minister's son, Nate, that got it together for the Drama Festival, last March. He played one of the dead, a zombie, and she played one half of a honeymooning couple, and he carried her off. It was very silly, and they played it for laughs, and got a trophy for being the "most entertaining". I thought it was harmless, but Peter was angry about it, said she should have shown us the play first.'

'I know Nate,' I said. 'He works at the café in the college, and looks after Cat on days I'm at sea.'

'Peter doesn't like him.' Kate sighed. 'He's turning into a *Daily Mail* reader. He says the boy has a brain that he's wasting, and no good ever came of someone taking a job that was beneath their intelligence. Then he starting going on about Branwell Brontë, when I could have sworn he wouldn't even have known who Charlotte was.'

'What had Branwell to do with it?' I asked, amused.

'Search me. Wasn't he supposed to be the really clever one who was going to make the world sit up, then he died a drunkard, and the unimportant girls became famous?'

'I'll take a good look at Nate this afternoon,' I promised, 'and tell you if there are signs of a neglected genius.'

'You do that.' She tilted her wrist to check her watch, and stood up. 'Back to those suckers. I'm getting so excited about this garden, Cass. You know how there's the remains of terracing? Well, I was standing at the door, yesterday evening, just looking, and the sun caught something red among the roses – a withered paeony leaf. It's like digging on a treasure island.'

I wouldn't have gone that far, but I did wonder how the bulbs that the suckers brought up with them would look in spring, a drift of snowdrops

10

under the roses, a yellow ribbon of daffodils down each side of the flagged path, and bluebells making a sky haze under the sycamores.

We worked away until the click of the wooden door told us it was lunchtime. The dogs went barking forward. Peter came striding up the path towards us, a black plastic bin bag in each hand. 'Hello, girls,' he called. 'You're making good progress.'

He said that every day.

'Peter!' Kate said, as if she was surprised to see him. 'Is that really the time?' She said that every day too.

Peter didn't look like a banker, which I supposed was just as well in the present climate, with 'banker' being synonymous for 'scum'. Even with the dark grey suit and old school tie, you'd have said a naval man, or an explorer, or an entrepreneur. He was just into his forties now, with thick fair hair combed back from a broad forehead. He had level, sandy brows, blue eyes, and a rather beaky nose over a firm chin. Like Kate, he had a ruddy, outdoor complexion. He gave the impression of someone who'd make a good naval officer: efficient, decisive, ready to act quickly in an emergency. I'd have put him as watch leader without hesitating.

Kate uncramped herself from under a lichened flowering currant, and went over to kiss his cheek. He flourished the black bags at her. 'A present from an admirer.'

'Mine, or yours?' Kate unknotted the top of one bag. 'Oh, the lamb! Fantastic. I'll get it in the freezer straight away. How about you, Cass, could you use some lamb?'

I would have loved some. 'I don't have an oven on *Khalida.*'

'You have a grill, though. Come into the kitchen, and I'll sort some chops out while you wash your hands.'

By the time I'd stowed the barrow, cleaned the tools, and got the last of the grime out from under my nails, she'd spread the meat out over the table. The room was rich with the pink smell. Cat was stretching up a table leg, whiskers forward and grey nose twitching.

'Do you eat kidneys?' Kate asked. Her hands were already cleaning them, creamy-white fat peeling away to show the dark red oval beneath. 'Peter and I don't touch them.'

'Fried kidneys would be a treat,' I said. 'Thank you.'

'Here, then.' She put them into a freezer bag, then into a Co-op carrier. 'And some soup bits –' she added a neck and several legs '– and a few chops. And your pay.' She held out an envelope.

'Thank you,' I said. 'We'll eat well for a week on this.'

I passed Peter on the way out. He was frowning, his mouth twisted downwards, but when he saw me, his face re-arranged itself into his usual cheery good humour. 'Thanks for the work, Cass. See you next time.'

But his voice echoed from the dining room as I let myself out. 'Kate, I've found out who it is that Annette's got herself entangled with –'

It was none of my business. I closed the door on the name.

Chapter Two

Cat and I headed home for lunch. I was moored up at the westshore marina, right next door to the college. There were fifteen berths on each side of a long pontoon, protected from the long Atlantic rollers that washed straight into Scalloway harbour by a solid breakwater. Good luck had me up tucked on the inside, behind a wooden-masted Colin Archer ocean-crosser which protected me from the worst of the winds.

The scenery was good. My stern was thirty metres from the shore that formed Scalloway's curved seafront. Looking out of the cockpit, there was a vertical bank of rough grass, with chocolate brown heather on the left, and a tangle of rose bushes and yellow-leaved montbretia on the right. There were three or four houses at the top of the bank, backed by dark green pine trees, then the hill, chocolate dark with heather, and topped by a radio mast. The shore ran along the jumble of sheds and slips used by the Shetland Bus men and past the youth centre and shop, buildings that had once been herring curing stations. It ended at Burn Beach, with the square eighteenth-century front of the pink Haa above it. A street of coloured houses led along to the castle: a cream former inn where Sir Walter Scott once stayed, then grey stone, powder-blue, Minoan-red, creamy yellow, pale green.

In front of the coloured street were three stone houses, each built above a buttress jutting into the water, one square buttress, two curved. The last of them had been a smithy, and it was said to be haunted. The water below it was where they had put witches to the test: bind your arms and throw you into the water. If you sank, you were innocent, though unfortunately dead; if you floated, the Devil was holding you up, and they took you up the Gallow Hill that I could see from *Khalida*'s cockpit, garotted you, and burned your body to ashes. Scalloway was the last place in Scotland to burn witches.

Past the smithy was Blackness Pier, a great space fronted with tyres, and above the pier, in a space of its own against the green hill of East Voe, was Earl Patrick's castle. It was sand-brown, with four rows of windows topped by a great chimney. In its day it had been a Renaissance chateau like the ones along the Loire where my Maman performed in

13

operas by Rameau or Lully, the composers of the Court of the Sun King. There were pictures inside showing how it had been, with tapestries on the walls, and wooden panelling, and a great fire blazing in the hearth. Now it was bleak and bare, dominating the town like a reminder of what the power of the lairds had meant for ordinary Shetlanders: wood from the tidelines to be diverted 'for the Lairdis works', the extra work of cutting and drying more peats for 'the Lairdis fires', and taxes, taxes, taken in fish and wool and butter. It was the taxes that had been Earl Patrick's downfall; his cousin King James, son of Mary Queen of Scots, hadn't minded the way he'd mistreated his tenants, but objected to him pocketing the taxes levied in the king's name. He'd been executed in Edinburgh in 1615.

Below the castle, modern Shetland fought back. The descendants of the men who had fished for the lairds had their own boats now, parked alongside the pier, where they could offload their catch straight to the green sheds of the auction room, linked electronically to the big fish market in Lerwick, and to buyers all over the world. There was a salmon processing factory here, and a brown square tower of ice plant, to fill the holds of these trawlers with ice before they went to sea. The boats here mostly caught whitefish, cod, haddock, and whiting; the big pelagic trawlers, who went down to Ireland, up to Iceland and across to Norway, were moored in Lerwick and Whalsay.

A long finger of sea went behind the castle. I couldn't see it from here, but it too was modern Scalloway, another marina filled with little motorboats and tall yachts. A fleet of wooden houses, navy, red, and dark brown, held the overspill of Scalloway folk from this old town of Scottish-looking houses among sycamore trees.

I opened the washboards and went below. After I'd wrapped the meat up in newspaper and stowed it below the waterline to keep cold, I heated up the last of my pot of stock-cube soup. Real lamb soup tomorrow! Cat scoffed some of his fish, and washed his whiskers, then we headed along the twenty yards to the college.

We walked straight into trouble: Antoine, the college chef, was on the warpath. He came bursting out from the café, in his chef's apron and white hat, brandishing a rolling pin as if he was going to brain me with it. 'Cass Lynch, you come here, immediately.' He paused in mid-eloquence to kiss me on each cheek, French-fashion. 'Come and see what that animal of yours has done now.'

I sighed and followed, hoping that the latest outrage had happened at a time when I could give Cat an alibi. I reckoned that most of the thefts Antoine blamed him for weren't his doing, but, cats being cats, I couldn't swear a hundred per cent that he was innocent. I suspected that Antoine didn't really believe he'd committed them either. He just enjoyed the chance to make a good scene in French.

They were busy clearing away the debris from today's lunches, and preparing for tomorrow. A girl was loading plates into the dishwasher, her face flushed. Nate bent over a bucket of fish; a little pile of fillets lay on one side of the steel draining board, a heap of heads and backbones on the other. His long, dark hair was shoved up under a cap. He looked up as I came in, and grimaced sympathetically, then drew a finger across his throat.

'There!' Antoine said, pointing dramatically. The damage wasn't hard to spot. The greaseproof paper on top of a tray of plaice fillets had been pulled aside by a set of efficient claws, the fillets had been nosed among, one or two pulled out of the tray, and it was a fair suspicion that at least one was missing.

'When did it happen?' I asked.

'Not half an hour ago.' Antoine flourished the rolling pin. 'I set the plaice aside so that we could clear the tables, and then have a cup of tea once all the customers were gone. A proper tisane, not your horrible strong English tea, with a spoonful of honey in it, real French honey that I brought from home, in spite of the airport madness. I do not overwork my staff.' A sweeping gesture warned them they were being talked about; he returned to English. 'I do not overwork you.' When he turned back to me, Nate rolled his eyes. The girl made an 'oh yeah' face. 'We hear nothing, nothing, then suddenly there is a clatter.' His rolling pin indicated a fork on the floor. 'I shouted, because I remembered your cat stealing before, and then I looked, and there was no sign, just the door open a little, and this. Now it will all have to be thrown out, these beautiful plaice.'

'That seems an awful waste,' I said. 'Can't it just be washed? Cooking will kill any germs.'

Antoine sniffed. 'And look at those clawmarks. That is definitely cat, and I ask myself, what cat is around the college?'

'Several,' I cut in. 'There's that big black and white bruiser from over the road, I've often seen him hanging about on the slip. There's the ginger one from Ladysmith Drive. He comes down the hill every morning about nine o' clock.' I joined him in the drama, flinging an arm out towards the marina. 'Half an hour ago, Cat was curled up on a bunk aboard *Khalida*, washing his whiskers after a good meal of the little fish I catch for him.'

'You catch fish for him?' Antoine's tone expressed deep scepticism, in spite of having seen me doing it, when he'd come out of the back door to flap a discloth.

'Off the end of the pier,' I asserted. 'Those little ones that hang around there. He loves them.' Boiling them up made *Khalida* smell for the rest of the day, but Cat liked them so much better than tinned cat food that it was worth it. 'And also, look at the size of those claws. You know very well Cat is just a baby. Those were made by a beast at least this long.' Getting into the spirit of the debate, I indicated a size which would have done credit to a young puma. Nate stifled a grin. 'And how would he have got in here? Through that open window?' I pointed at the narrow upper window, which was propped outwards on a metal stick. 'He is a very little kitten, you know.' My hands made the size of the average hamster. 'He could not jump up there.'

Antoine snorted. Given that he'd seen Cat jump-scramble up to my shoulder, it was maybe too obvious an exaggeration. 'Beside,' I finished, with the air of one clinching the thing, 'he's a friendly little cat. If it had been him, he'd still have been here, ready to talk to you.'

Antoine snorted again, but seemed to be conceding Cat's alibi. 'Well, if he was really with you on your boat this last half hour … but do not let me catch him in here again.'

'You haven't caught him in here yet,' I pointed out.

'Well, make sure I do not. We had a visit from those health and hygiene people, and they would not like a cat making himself at home here. Nate had to put him in his pocket, at high speed, and smuggle him out of the back door to the janitor, while Sarah –' he indicated the girl '– put his dish into the sink and hid his box.' I grinned. Antoine saw he'd given himself away, and shooed me out. 'Off you go. We have work to do, and you have classes to attend, and already you are late.'

I allowed myself to be shooed. I had just reached the café when one of the biologists came in, a tall woman with dark hair, swept up to show pearl earrings. She wore a businesswoman suit, grey with a narrow paler stripe, the colours of Cat's coat, and shiny, long-toed boots. She nodded to me, and went on to the counter.

Nate came out from the kitchen, his professional welcoming smile turning to sourness. 'Now, Rachel?'

It was obvious, seeing them together, that they were brother and sister. They both had dark wavy hair, the same long, narrow nose, and high cheekbones. That was an odd setup, I thought, the sister up among the lecturers, and the brother washing dishes. I wondered if she'd got him the job. If so, his tone said he resented it.

Hers was equally brusque. 'Is Antoine there?' She flicked a glance at me, as if she was reminding him that there were students present.

Nate inclined his head towards the kitchen, but she made no move to go through the door. 'Go and get him, will you please?'

Nate gave her a murderous glance. I was at the door into the foyer now, and just about to go out, but a crash of glass made me turn. Nate bent to the floor and picked up the stem and shattered bowl of a wineglass. He turned it in the light, and gave a twisted smile, then set it on the counter. His dark eyes met hers. 'Still breaking things, are you?'

'You know very well,' she retorted, 'that I was nowhere near it.'

'Oh, yes,' he agreed smoothly, 'you certainly didn't touch it.' He picked up the glass again. 'But it's broken.'

'Nothing to do with me.' Her voice was made ragged by uneven breathing. She took a step back from the counter, then turned and hurried away, brushing past me as if she didn't see me. Behind the counter, Nate watched her go, smiling and turning the glass in his hand, so that the jagged edges splintered the light.

When I came out, two hours later, Nate was waiting. He had a plastic bag in his hand. 'A present from Antoine,' he said, falling into step beside me. 'The fillets he said would have to be wasted.'

'Very nice,' I said. 'Thanks.' I had every intention, as Antoine knew full well, of eating most of them myself, giving only obviously tooth-marked bits to Cat, who'd slipped out halfway through the class on dealing with an airlock. When he'd returned, he'd spent the last of the session washing his whiskers. 'And thanks for looking after him.'

'No problemo.' Nate turned his head to look at me. Without the cap, his hair fell in waves to his shoulders. If it was cut short, it would be a mass of curls. He had a thin, agile face, dominated by his eyes; they were dark too, staring at me in a way I found uncomfortable. I tilted my chin and stared back, and the moment drew out, becoming a duel. I wasn't going to look away first, but I could see that he'd now taken it as a challenge, and wasn't going to be beaten. I kept looking, raising my brows slightly as if I was amused, and in the end it was he who blinked first, and turned his head away.

I smiled, and looked back at the bag in my hand. 'We'll eat well tonight. Thanks.'

'He's a clever little cat.' Nate gave me another dark, glittering glance, then nodded ahead at the Otways' garden. 'Do you see much of Annette?'

Branwell Brontë, Peter had called him, the talented one everyone expected to go far, except that here he was, well through his twenties, washing dishes in a two-bit café for nautical students. So what was he doing with all that talent? Getting to the highest level of fantasy computer

17

games, drawing intricate pictures of motorbikes, smoking dope, and thinking universal thoughts so deep that the rest of us couldn't possibly understand them? He had that superior air I'd noticed in people who take drugs. I liked him, but I wasn't going to discuss Annette with him. 'I'm the hired help,' I said. 'I don't mix much with the family.'

'It's just that I'm worried about her.' He grimaced. 'We're not particularly mates, but we got on fine during that play we did – did you see it? A Hallowe'en one, about zombies. I had to carry her off.'

'No,' I said, 'I didn't see it, but someone was just telling me recently how good it was.' Maybe that was where his energy went, on directing plays and acting in them. 'What makes you worried about her?'

'Well, it's just ...' He gave an artistic pause, gripping his underlip with his top teeth. 'See, I was out for a walk, I often do that, late at night, when I can't sleep. I just go out, around the castle, and down to the Blacksness Pier, then back along New Street. So, three, no four, days ago, I was out, and I'd just got to the old smithy when I saw this girl on the pier. There was only a crescent of a moon, but there weren't any clouds, so it was bright as day, with that silvery light, and I could see her, clear as anything, staring down at the ripples on the water. I was going to call out, you know, I thought she was going to jump, but then I was afraid to, in case I startled her and made things worse. Just as I was thinking I'd really have to do something, she moved away from the water, and came fast up the path towards me. I just had time to duck into the little lane by the anti-German inscription, opposite the Smiddy gate.' He paused to draw a much-needed breath. 'As she passed me, I saw it was Annette. Her hair was all over the place, and she looked as if she'd been crying.'

He paused again, but I didn't say anything.

'And then I realised she'd been looking at the witches' ducking stone, you know, where they put them to the test.' His dark eyes gleamed at me. 'You know about that?'

'Yes,' I said.

He jerked his head backwards, as if he hadn't expected so brusque an answer; as if he'd wanted to re-tell the story and see how I reacted.

'Maybe,' I suggested, 'she was thinking about how horrible it must have been for those poor women.'

'They were witches, though. They confessed to all sorts of things – meetings with the Devil, casting spells, having a familiar.' He looked along the pontoon at Cat, who'd got tired of waiting, and was trotting to the boat by himself. 'You'd have been in the frame if you'd lived back then, you and Greymalkin.'

'They also happened to be women who challenged the existing male hierarchy by surviving without a man.'

18

HIs smile was unexpectedly charming. 'Like you.'

'So,' I said, cutting that one off, 'you think that Annette's a bit depressed?'

He shook his head. 'I don't think it's anything as simple as that. She came out into the light as she passed me, you know, under the streetlight, it shone on her face and head, and I noticed –' He let the silence hang, looking from the sea to my face, as if he was judging how much I'd believe. Finally, he came out with it. 'I noticed what looked like claw marks around her throat.'

Claws ... 'Maybe she was playing with the dogs, and got a bit rough.'

'Maybe. But then ...' He looked over his shoulder, then his voice softened to a sly whine. 'What if the Devil was loose in Shetland?'

His tone sent a shudder down my spine, but I wasn't going to let him scare me. 'Nonsense.'

His gaze shifted back to the sea again. His voice hardened to venom. 'You saw that glass shatter. Today, in the canteen. Rachel was nowhere near it.'

'Certainly not near enough to touch it,' I conceded. 'But why are you blaming her? Things just fall sometimes.'

'They "just fall" a lot more often than sometimes when Rachel's there. She's done it all her life. Light bulbs go phut, TVs flicker, glasses break.' He jerked his chin across at the Smiddy. 'She'd have been on that ducking stone.'

'Thank goodness we live in a more enlightened age.'

'Sometimes.' He leaned closer to me. I felt his breath warm on my cheek. 'What are you doing on Hallowe'en?'

Whatever it was, it wouldn't be anything to do with witches. 'Going to the All Saints' vigil Mass,' I said tartly. 'Thanks for the fish, Nate.' I unlocked the marina door, eased it open with its usual squeak, and closed it between us. 'See you tomorrow.'

I was conscious of his eyes on me as I strode along the pontoon. I swung myself aboard, raised a hand, then waited until he'd begun to walk along the shore before I took the washboards out and went below. His voice was whispering still in my ear: *You saw that glass shatter* ... Rachel had certainly been too far away to touch it. I hadn't been watching Nate's hands, though. He could have dropped it – but why should he?

What if the Devil was loose in Shetland? 'Nonsense,' I repeated to Cat, and busied myself putting the kettle on.

Chapter Three

It began to rain off and on as dusk fell, but by bedtime it was clear again, the moon shining like a frosted lantern behind thin clouds. The wind was rising from the north west. Little wavelets slapped against *Khalida*'s stern, and the wind tugged strands of my hair from its plait as I headed out for my evening walk. I was used to more exercise than this round of garden and college was giving me, and after an evening spent aboard, with the candle lamp shedding an amber circle my notes and books, I was glad of a breath of air to help me sleep.

Cat lifted his grey nose as I got up, but didn't stand. I was glad of that. I felt like a good long tramp without having to worry about my little shadow. Nate's stories had set up an uneasiness in my mind, so that I found myself glancing out at the dark water beyond my oblong windows, until I scolded myself and drew the curtains shut. I pulled on my sailing jacket, gloves, and hat, and headed out into the night.

The air smelt of seaweed, of wet leaves and grass. I strode out along the west shore road, past Norway House, the dark red hut where the men of the Shetland Bus had stayed in the war, past the rusting slip where they had launched their boats. I paused to bow my head at their memorial, and marvel again at their youth. Their headquarters, with its carved wooden door, was fifty yards further, then I walked between the shops of the main street, former herring sheds on the sea side, and, facing them, houses with old-fashioned windows and front doors opening onto the pavement. Just past them, above Burn Beach, was a skip in the car park which was always worth casting an eye over. There'd been a notice in the shop that this would be the last one, due to council cost-cutting, so it was filling up quickly. Someone had flung in a snakes-wedding of blue nylon rope, a good thirty metres of it, but it looked too worn to be worth untangling. I went on past Mary Ruislip's Garden, furred now by yellowed montbretia leaves, past the ironwork gate of curving plaice with goggle eyes, past the lavender blue wood of Seaholme, to the first of the coloured houses of New Street. The street lights cast a circle of orange in front of each one. On my right, below the Smiddy, the coal-black water rose and fell, as though the sea was breathing.

20

Usually at this point I turned up Smiddy Closs. Today, though, I wasn't sure I wanted to pass the witch's garden behind the first house. It stretched right back to the big white house at the top of the hill, two sides of a square of low sycamores around tussocked grass hanging down from old steps and a rockery. At the lower end was a thick wall, which was all that remained of the house. There were the broken poles of a square-meshed fence, but the only barrier now was the iron railing to help older folk up the steep hill.

Magnie had told me about it. 'It was afore I went to sea,' he'd said, 'and I'd got work laying pipes to the Coonty. We had to dig in this gairdin. Well, this wife came out as we were digging, and said, 'Boys, you'd maybe better no dig ower deep in here, for the house used to belong to a witch, and I'm aye been told there are twa babies buried in it.'

I glanced up at the darkness and shuddered, then headed forwards, alongside the coloured houses. My footsteps echoed on the flagstones. I was just level with the green house when I heard a shout in the night, swirling on the wind, then an angry voice. I paused for a moment, not wanting to run into a drunken quarrel, but the sound wasn't repeated. Young men, high spirits. All the same, I slid into the little steps that led down the water and spent a few moments admiring the lines of a long-keeled yacht that someone was restoring on the far side of the pier: a lovely curve from stem to stern. She'd hold her course in waves halfway up her mast. When I was sure all was quiet, I came back into the lamplight and strolled on once more.

The Chinese restaurant around the corner was open, spilling tantalising smells into the night, but we'd gorged ourselves on fresh plaice, Cat and I, and it wasn't hard to walk past it. The castle's jagged gables were floodlit in orange so that the shadows stood sharp and sinister against the stonework. Next to it was the wood-clad side of the new Scalloway Museum, with its glass porch and double logo on the corner, the stylised castle on its promontary echoing the real one beside it.

New Smiddy Closs, just opposite, would bring me back to the water. I passed below bushes planted among gravel onto the flagstoned path. The textured concrete stones were slimy with algae, but I trusted the grip of my boots. The green mesh fence on my left gave way to whitewashed wall, belonging to a solid old house whose small-paned windows were set back in metre-thick recesses. It was the first of a cluster set around an irregular courtyard known in the village as the 'Spanish closs', because of its pantiled roofs and angled doors. The entrance to the closs was a low gate set in a wide arch. A glass oval, held with rusty bars, shone white light over the inside of the close. I heard the 'snick' of a closing door, as if someone had come down just before me, though I hadn't seen anyone.

I was halfway down the little flight of steps above the archway when I saw the body lying sprawled in the entrance.

It was a girl, young, with blonde hair spilling from her sweatshirt hood. She lay in a tumbled heap, as if she had crumpled from standing, her fashionable boots tucked up under her flounced skirt. Her right hand stretched out towards a carved front door, as if she was pointing. I crouched beside her, picked up the outflung hand, and laid two fingers on her wrist. Nothing, and the hand had the chill weight of a dead animal. I replaced it as it had lain, then loosened her scarf and laid my fingers on her neck. I felt the rough line of scratch under them, and my heart missed a beat. I turned her head to the light.

It was Annette. Her face was death-white, and set in an odd expression I couldn't quite read, something between shock and guilt, like a child caught with its hand in a biscuit jar. Oh, Kate, Peter, their beloved baby with golden curls. I eased her head down, tucked into its hood, as it had been. Then I stepped back and thought. What was my quickest way to get help?

It wasn't easy. The Scalloway sub-police station had been closed in the last round of cuts, and the policeman's house sold off, so I couldn't knock at his door. I needed the Lerwick police, but I didn't have their number, and 999 had become a last resort for isles residents. Just this summer a tourist guide on the island of Mousa had had difficulty getting help for an injured visitor because the island doesn't have a postcode, and the central office in Inverness wouldn't let her speak directly to the coastguard. All the tourist guides had now been issued with the island's GPS co-ordinates, just in case.

I looked around the little close. There were four doors. Number 1 was just behind me, a plain wooden door. I tilted my head up to the windows, but there were no lights. Number 2 was the wooden door Annette was almost touching, carved with four oblong panels in a line down the centre, each with a wooden flower, and great cylindrical hinges, like the ones on my Poitevin granny's wooden china cupboard. There was a frosted glass window on the right of it, with green-painted wood around it, and as I looked at it I thought I saw movement behind, but there were no lights.

Door 3, in the angle past me, was a plain door with a glass panel, and Door 4 was set slantways under a low, narrow roof. There was a curving step in front of it, and a little window under the roof. Glory be, just as I looked at it, a light sprang up in the darkness. It must have been the bathroom, for I heard water running as I walked towards it. I knocked. There was a long pause, then, just as I raised my hand to knock again, I heard footsteps, a cough, a voice, 'Coming – joost a minute.' The door eased open, and an elderly man with a shock of grey hair stood in the doorway. He passed a hand over his head to smooth his hair down, and looked at me in surprise, then his gaze went past me, over my shoulder, to Annette.

'My mercy, what's happened?'

'Do you have a phone book?' I asked. 'I need to call Lerwick police.'

He stayed on the doorstep, peering over my shoulder. 'Is your friend bad hurt? The wife at Number 1's a nurse in the hospital, only she works shifts, the way they all do, so she might no be hame.'

'I need to phone the police,' I repeated, holding tight to my patience. 'I need a phone book.'

'Should we maybe put a blanket over her?'

'No!' I said. It came out more sharply than I'd meant. I added, gently, 'I'm afraid she's dead. We need to call the police. They say not to touch anything.'

He shook his head, then began to close the door. 'You stay there.' Through the last inch he said, 'I'll get you the phone book.'

It seemed an interminable wait, with the bitter wind curling into the close, and the dead girl lying there. I stood listening to the noises from inside the house: a light switching on, another, a drawer being opened, a glasses case – I could see his fingers unfolding the earpieces, polishing the lenses with that light blue pinking-edged cloth. In my peripheral vision, a shadow moved behind the frosted glass of Number 2's window. I turned my head slightly, tilting it downwards as if I was looking at Annette, and thought I could make out someone standing in the dark, motionless, with a pale blur of face looking out at me. Behind the closed door of Number 4, another drawer opened and closed, then the footsteps padded to the front door again. It opened a crack, and the phone book came out, suspended in air.

'Thank you.' I carried it over to the light above the gate, found the number, and dialled.

It was answered straight away. 'Police Scotland, Lerwick office, good evening.'

I recognised the voice. 'Sergeant Peterson?'

'Cass Lynch,' she retorted. 'How can I help you?'

'I've found a dead girl,' I said, 'in Scalloway, in the Spanish closs.'

I heard the click of computer keys. 'Don't touch anything, Cass. We'll be right over. Where exactly are you?'

I explained, and said I'd stand at the end of New Smiddy Closs to guide them.

'We'll be with you in less than fifteen minutes,' she promised, and put the phone down. I leaned against the wall, looking at Annette. The way she was lying didn't look right to me. The crumpled look, yes, that was right enough, as if she'd fallen all of a heap, but there was something very melodramatic about that outstretched arm. Her handbag was dropped beside her, one of these fashionable little rucksacks, and I wondered about that too. If she'd been taken by a sudden seizure, I'd have thought she'd have gripped it, or that it would be closer to the body, dropped as she herself dropped. Then, there was something about her coat, as if someone had pulled it out, then rumpled it back ... in short, it looked to me as if someone had checked inside her handbag and pockets, then taken her arm and made it point at the carved door. And if someone had interfered with the body, then the chance of it being a natural death was receding. I cast a quick look sideways at the frosted glass window with the shadow still behind it, and decided to stay at my post.

Only twelve minutes had gone when I heard the soft whisper of a car drawing up. I ran up to meet it. It slid quietly to a stop beside me, without flashing lights or siren, and Sergeant Peterson got out. 'Well, Cass?'

'Down this path,' I said.

'That's fine. Sit in the car, and I'll get your statement once I've had a look.'

I was glad to get out of the cold. I huddled into the warm seat, and prepared to wait.

I'd met Sergeant Peterson before. She was tall and fair-haired, groomed like a businesswoman. Her eyes were the green of sea-washed glass, and as indifferent as a mermaid's. I suspected she was ambitious, and wondered she hadn't been moved to somewhere more active. The main crimes in Shetland were drink-driving and, recently, street scuffles. The thought reminded me of the noise I'd heard. It had come from somewhere up towards the castle, I was sure, although the wind could blow noise from unexpected places. It had been a man's voice, the same man speaking twice, rather than an argument between two. I hadn't recognised the actual voice, just the angry sound.

The warmth of the car was soothing. I eased my gloves off, and paused. My right hand was gritty with a reddish dust. I rubbed it between finger and thumb, then lifted my hand to my face, and sniffed. Yes, it was the fine, red ash from a peat fire. The texture and smell were unmistakeable. Where on earth had I got that from? I tried to recall if I'd touched anything in the skip, but I couldn't see how I could have got peat ash on my hand from there. I'd been wearing gloves all the way from *Khalida* until the Spanish closs, where I'd taken them off to feel Annette's pulse. I tried to recall my movements. I'd taken her outflung hand up in my right hand, and felt her pulse with my left. Once I'd done that, I'd checked her neck with my left hand. Then I'd put my gloves back on. I could only have got the ash on my hand from Annette.

Whatever she'd been doing, wherever she'd been, it was somewhere with a peat fire.

heksi (n): a witch

Chapter Four

Thursday 27th October

Low Water Scalloway 00:39 BST 0.6m
High Water 06:52 1.4 m
Low Water 12:52 0.7m
High Water 18:59 1.5m
Moon waxing gibbous

Moonset 02:53, 262 degrees
Sunrise 08:12
Moonrise 15:55, 93 degrees
Sunset 17:25

I woke at seven. The hills were still black, but the heavy sky was marbled with milk-grey streaks of light. The wind had risen; *Khalida* jerked at her mooring ropes, making her fenders creak against the pontoon. Even in this sheltered space, the slate-mauve ripples flowed like a river. I'd tied the halyards so that they wouldn't rattle against the mast, but they thrummed in the wind, each gust giving a vibration that could be felt right through the hull. A glance out of the window showed me long, white crests rolling in to break on the pebble shore of the Minister's Beach. It was just on high water.

I wriggled out of my berth, wincing as my bare feet touched the icy wooden floorboards. I boiled the kettle and took a cup of drinking chocolate back to bed, leaving the gas ring on low, with a clay flowerpot over it – the poor woman's central heating. Cat swarmed out of the propped-up forehatch to his preferred toilet on the shore, then returned, his fur cold, and smelling of seaweed. I stroked him absently.

Poor Kate, poor Peter! I hadn't seen any signs of violence, only that shocked look, but I hadn't examined Annette's body. She could have been struck on the head, stabbed, strangled … I remembered the scratch marks I'd seen, and heard Nate's voice: *What if the Devil was loose in Shetland?* I shook the thought away. I didn't believe in a Devil that came down to earth and attacked people. A human hand had wielded whatever weapon had been used.

But why should anyone as young as Annette have murderous enemies? The three crows had given her a basilisk warning stare, but I didn't see a group of teenagers resorting to this kind of murder. I wondered if Kate had been right about drugs.

I'd done my best to give details last night, under Sergeant Peterson's indifferent gaze, with the other officer taking notes. No, I hadn't known Annette particularly well. I worked for her mother, gardening. The last time I'd seen Annette had been that morning. I didn't mention the row with her parents; I'd let them tell that in their own way. We'd passed as I was going in, she was coming out. We'd said hello, that was it. Sergeant Peterson gave me the sort of look that made it clear she didn't believe me, and started on my movements for the evening. I'd spent the evening aboard *Khalida.* Yes, I'd been alone. I didn't think she'd accept Cat as an alibi, and she didn't. I'd gone out for a walk, to warm up before bedtime. I hadn't seen anyone around, but I'd heard shouting, in the direction of the castle. No, I couldn't distinguish words, but it was a man's voice. I thought I'd heard only one voice. It had been midnight before I'd finally been allowed to crawl into my berth.

Now I set my memory to work. Annette had been worried about something, to the extent of talking of running away from home. She'd complained about her parents stopping her from meeting people. Her soft wail came back to me: *If I think they can help me.* I remembered her air of defiance, as if she knew the help she was taking was something she shouldn't be doing. There had been a pause, then she'd put her hand up to tug her scarf away from her throat, and begun to talk about reincarnation – *do you ever feel as if you've lived before?* I wasn't sure if that had been part of the same conversation, what she was wanting help about, or if it was a new one. Then I remembered the words I hadn't stayed to overhear. *Kate, I've found out who it is that Annette's got herself entangled with ...*

Peter would tell the police the name, and they would investigate. It was none of my business. I hoped that the DI sent from Inverness (Shetland pub fights and drink-driving didn't warrant a criminal investigation department) would be Gavin Macrae. We were edging our way to a tentative – no, I couldn't call it a relationship. An undeclared interest in each other, that showed itself in the occasional phone call, carefully not in a regular slot, although it was moving to as often as once a week. It would take more than attraction to smooth a relation-ship between a roving skipper with Alain's death in her past and a respectable DI who lived in the family farm with his brother and mother. Maybe if I got a post aboard a tall ship, I'd be respectable too. Second Officer Lynch. First Officer. Captain. I'd be spending my time at sea, of course, which might make a relationship difficult. I sighed and got up.

By now the heat from my improvised radiator was warming up *Khalida*'s small cabin, and condensing the long windows. I had a basin wash, scrubbed myself with the towel to warm me up, and dressed in several layers, then laid a cloth over the prop-leg table to protect my varnish, and made a pot of porridge. One of the benefits of this living attached to the land was fresh milk; it was going to be a shock going back to UHT when I went wandering again. While it was cooking, I grilled the last two plaice, and put one down for Cat.

Outside, the sky was overcast, long skeins of grey wool cloud with lighter streaks between, grey-blue to the west, pale rose to the east. I chopped the leek and turnip I'd bought yesterday at the Meat Co, peeled and grated the carrots, then put them all with the lamb neck and shanks into my largest pan, added water and a handful each of barley, dried peas, and lentils, and left it to simmer. There would be real mutton soup for lunch.

Going outside was like walking into iced water. The wind was glacial, and my hands were frozen by the time I'd checked all the mooring ropes. I reached back in for my gloves, then slid the cabin washboards into their slots and pulled the hatch closed. Cat's fur was blown in partings as he paused on the pontoon to wait for me.

I wasn't quite sure what to do with the morning. I should have been heading for Kate's garden, but there was a police car parked in front of the house. I made for the college instead. There wasn't an official library, but you could always find an empty classroom for studying in. I'd just spread out my diagram of the inside of a diesel engine when my mobile rang. It was Gavin.

'I thought I'd let you know that I'm at Inverness Airport, checked in for the 09.50.' He had a Highland accent, lingering on the final 'ss'.

'You've heard all about it, then.'

'Sergeant Peterson told me all you told her. She wasn't very pleased with you. I'm hoping you'll be more forthcoming with me.'

I quoted one of his own proverbs back at him. 'The roe is swift enough without setting the dogs on her.'

'Would that be a yes?'

'Annette was worried about something,' I said. 'She'd had a row with her parents about going out at Hallowe'en. I wanted to let them explain it, instead of me making it sound worse than it was. Kate's been kind to me.'

'And the row was worrying Annette?'

29

'No.' *Suppose the Devil was loose in Shetland ...* I explained my morning thinking. 'But I'm not sure if the reincarnation thing was to do with the worry.'

'I'll be in Scalloway around midday. They've given us "the old museum" as an incident room.'

'On the seafront,' I said, 'A grey stone building, with a good view of the marina, so Sergeant Peterson can keep an eye on me. Very handy for the shops, too – coffee, tab-nabs, pies, that sort of thing.'

'I'll want to talk to the parents first, so we can leave them in peace, and I'll organise my team, then I'll come along to your *Khalida*. Shall I bring a chip supper?'

I sighed. 'There's no Frankie's here.' Awards declared Frankie's, in Brae, one of Britain's best fish and chip shops, as well as the most northerly, and I wasn't disagreeing. No Frankie's was one of the down sides of moving to Scalloway. 'There's a good Chinese, though – at least, it smells good. Lemon chicken, for preference.'

There was a bing-bong in his background, followed by an automated voice. Gavin ignored it. 'Lemon chicken. Rice or noodles?'

'Egg fried rice. Cat'll like that.'

'Chopsticks or knife and fork?'

'We have both aboard.'

'Then I'll see you later.'

I laid the phone down, and went back to the insides of engines. I'd only got as far as the cylinder head (via fuel tank, primary filter, fuel lead, secondary filter and injector, elementary stuff) when the phone went again. It was Kate. 'Cass, I was wondering if you wanted to come over. I know it's a bit cold –'

'It wasn't that,' I protested. 'I didn't think you'd want a stranger around today. Kate, I'm so sorry.' I couldn't think of words. 'So very sorry.'

'It was you who found her, they said.'

'Yes.'

'Come over, Cass, please come over. I don't know what to do here. Let's go out into the garden, and you can tell me about it, and then maybe I'll believe –'

My throat tightened. 'I'll be right over.'

It was Peter who opened the door and motioned me in. 'Kate's just –'

He made a kitchenwards gesture.

He'd grown old overnight. His brisk walk had turned to a sleepwalking daander, feet placed unevenly as if the floor had grown unsteady under him, and his head was bowed over, bending his back like an old man's. There were black circles under his eyes, and his fair hair was uncombed. He caught sight of himself in the hall mirror and paused, peering, as if he knew something wasn't right, but couldn't make out what. Then he lifted one hand and smoothed the fair hair back. Finally he turned to look at me. His eyes were blazing in the greyness of his face. 'Cass.' His voice had sharpened; the words tumbled out, with an impatient edge to them, as if they were taking him from what he really wanted to say. 'Kate's in the kitchen.' He gestured again. 'I'm just going out.' His hand fumbled among the coats, as if he was searching by touch for his own waxed Barbour. His cap lay on the hall table, one of those leather ones with the fur ear flaps standing up. He crammed it on his head, and whistled for the dogs. I heard a thud from the sitting room, the patter of paws, and Dan and Candy came flurrying along the hall and sat at his feet, waiting. Dan was allowed to run free as far as the main street, but Candy had to have her lead. Peter's fingers fumbled the familiar catch, then he frowned, put his free hand in his pocket, and drew out a bunch of keys. He looked at them for a moment as if he'd never seen them before. As he weighed them in his hand, the rage within him exploded. He raised his head to look at me. 'That boy.' His voice was venomous. 'I'll see he gets brought to book for this if it's the last thing I ever do.' He gave a sharp nod and hurried out of the front door.

Kate came along the passage just as the door slammed behind him. She too had aged. Her whole face had shrunk away; there were black shadows under her eyes, and her chestnut hair was too glossy against the white of her cheeks.

We went out, and down to the bottom of the garden. Above us, the fissures between the clouds became creamy-grey, then pale blue. By eleven, the sun had come out. There was no warmth in it, full in the wind like this, but in our sheltered corner it sparked lines of yellow along the green whitebeam leaves. We worked in silence; I didn't know what to say, and didn't want to seem to be forcing confidences. We filled one barrow, then a second.

'She went out,' Kate said abruptly. I glanced at her, then focused on my hands, clearing the brown umbrella leaves and frothed seed pods of lady's mantle. 'About ten o'clock. I didn't know she'd gone; I was in my studio.' She made a vague gesture towards the wooden hut at the side of the house. 'Peter heard her go. He said it was about ten. Just before he took the dogs out. Candy was raring to go, but Dan wasn't quite right, so he didn't go as far as he usually does, but even so he was away a good half hour, and she still wasn't back when he came in. Well, he wanted to go and find her. We quarrelled about that. He was furious, he just wanted to go up there and march her home, and I said he couldn't do that, she was too old – and then the police car came, and the officer said – she said –'

Up where? I wanted to ask. *Who?* – but I couldn't. She began tearing one leaf into segments, separating it neatly along the vein, re-living every parent's nightmare. Already the sky was darkening again. 'Then they began asking about money – what money she should have in her purse, as if a random thug would kill someone for money, here.' Her voice was shaking. 'Cass, you saw her.' It was the question she'd been psyching herself up to ask.

'She'd fallen in a heap,' I said. 'She didn't look as if she'd been in pain, or frightened. I couldn't see any sign of injury. She just looked as if she'd fainted.'

'They said that since you'd identified her, there was no hurry for us to go over – they said they'd get us for the formal ID later, once they'd taken her away from there.' Her voice went bleak. 'I wanted to see her. To hold her. I couldn't believe it.'

Above us, the sky closed over, and the rain began, great cold drops flung at us like bullets. I stood up, and slipped my hand under her elbow. 'Time for a cup of tea.'

She unfolded upwards, stiff as an old woman. I took my hand away, and followed her up the path to the house. She put the kettle on the hob with shaking hands, and looked around the kitchen as if she'd never seen it before, as if she didn't know where to find mugs, the pot, tea, milk.

'Sit down,' I said. 'I'll make the tea.'

She slid into a chair and huddled in silence as I joined tea, pot, and water. I poured her mugful, added two spoonfuls of sugar, and set it in front of her. Her hands came up to clutch it as if she needed the warmth. 'Who would do such a thing, here? Who?'

I couldn't give an answer to that.

Do you ever feel as if you've lived before? 'I don't suppose,' I said slowly, 'that she'd got entangled with something mystical?'

Her head came round sharply, mouth turned down, eyes dismayed. 'What makes you ask that?'

'It was something she said about past lives. It sounded like she was thinking about reincarnation.'

'Ohhh.' She let out a long breath, relieved, then caught herself up and talked almost at random, hands clenching and unclenching on the handle of her mug. 'One of those New Age groups, you mean, with people seeing space ships, and being channelled from Iris Reticulata, and thinking the pyramids are an alien powerhouse, all that rubbish?' Generations of squires who'd bossed their Church of England vicars rang scornfully in her voice. 'But surely she's too intelligent for that. Her place at Edinburgh is to study science.'

'I don't know if intelligence has anything to do with it,' I said. 'Conan-Doyle was tricked by those ridiculous fairy pictures, because he wanted to believe. And look at those awful Victorian ghost photos. You wonder how they can ever have taken anyone in.'

'I wouldn't like to think of her getting mixed up with something like that,' Kate said. Her voice was bitter. 'Someone enticing her to get involved with it.'

'I'm not sure if it was that,' I said. 'I think it was the past lives thing – you know, reincarnation, memories of being someone else.'

'An Egyptian princess, or a medieval lady,' Kate scoffed. 'Always one of the higher-ups, you notice, never the third under scullery-maid. Annette wouldn't – she wouldn't have –' Her eyes filled with tears, then she turned away from me and began to sob and shudder, gasping for breath.

I sat beside her, watching the rain drops fling themselves at the window, and making soothing noises that the rattle of the rain drowned out, until at last she blew her nose again, and stood up. 'Well, you'll need to get off to college now. Can't have you missing lobster-breeding, or the correct inflation of life rafts, or whatever it is today.' Her voice was restored to normal, though I could hear the effort it took to keep it that way. She reached for my envelope, but I put up a hand, palm forward, to stop her.

'We hardly got anything done today. I'll earn it next time.'

'Tomorrow,' Kate said. 'Tomorrow would be great.' Her voice was steady now. She even managed to smile. Englishwomen didn't break down.

'Great. Usual time,' I agreed. I hoped my voice made it clear I'd forgotten her tears already. 'Come on, Cat.'

I'd just left the gate when a police car drew up behind me. Sergeant Peterson came out of one side, and Gavin out of the other. He was brisk and alert-looking, russet head high, looking around him with his sea-grey eyes. He wore his green kilt, with the plain leather sporran, and his green tweed jacket. I paused, but he just nodded his head in recognition, and knocked on the wooden kitchen door. Poor Kate ...

The wind buffeted my hat as I went back to the boat, and the waves rumbled at the low tide mark. *Do you ever feel as if you've lived before?* Christianity didn't believe in it, but Buddhism did. You worked your way slowly up the wheel of life, going up if you did well in one life, going down if you did badly. It explained those sudden flashes of déjà vu, and the way some people seemed to have always good luck, and others bad. Karma. There'd been some interesting cases, with children too young to have read about it talking of their former lives. It didn't feel showy enough for Nate, but I wondered if quiet, serious James Leask, the boy Annette had met up with at the Scalloway Hotel, would be interested in stories of reincarnation. Yes, he might be. I could see him working his way through the *Fortean Times* magazine, then going through the internet references to make his mind up on this classic poltergeist case, or that UFO sighting. Once he'd decided he did believe it, he wouldn't be shaken; but I'd never heard it mentioned at college, and believing you can live more than one life would be a good stick for his classmates to beat him with.

The winds tugged at the pontoon, sending little ripples slapping against the plastic floats. I tightened the halyards again, then went below. The cabin was blissfully warm, and the soup smelled wonderful. I fished the bones out and cut the flesh off, gave some to Cat with the rest of his plaice, and put the rest in a bowl. I'd add some to my soup each day. Then I ladled out some of the broth and sat at my little table, blowing on each spoonful before eating. The flesh was delicious, and the lentils, peas, and rice had turned into a filling sludge at the bottom. It wasn't quite up to the standards of the soup at Nesting Up Helly Aa, so thick you could stand your spoon up in it, but it was pretty close. I finished off with a mug of tea, washed and dried my bowl, then pulled on my gloves and jacket again. I had a class to go to.

Chapter Five

The yellowed clouds were building to the west; the wind snatched my hair from under my hood and whipped it against my cheeks. There was the tin smell of snow in the air. We had practical this afternoon, so I put Cat straight to Nate. I could see he'd heard: his face was drawn, and he greeted me with a grave nod. 'You've heard about Annette. It doesn't seem real.'

'I found her,' I said, 'in the Spanish closs.'

'What happened? Was it a heart attack?'

I shrugged. 'I don't know any more.'

'But it was you that found her?'

I nodded.

'It doesn't seem real,' Nate repeated. 'We all feel it. Most of the students were at school with her.'

There was a subdued feel about the class that afternoon. I didn't imagine the sideways look I got from Jeemie, usually the loudest person in a class, with a jolly laugh that could well drive a future wife to braining him with the nearest blunt instrument. Today, instead of making his way over to share this morning's Facebook joke, he kept apart from me, as if my finding the body might contaminate him, and the rest of them bent over their engines in strained silence.

'My' engine was in the far corner. I unscrewed the bolts that held the injector in, and eased it out of its chamber. *Khalida*'s engine was about as similar to this Yanmar as a Shetland pony is to a racehorse, but the fuel line was laid in the same way, with the rocket-shaped injector at the end, and as I worked I could see my friend Anders at my shoulder, and hear his voice: *If you have to force it, you are doing it wrong. Pause, move your spanner and try again, gently.*

I missed Anders. He'd been a casual friend when I'd brought him over to Shetland as engineer for the replica Viking ship being used as a film set. We'd lived together aboard *Khalida* from March until August; shared meals and swapped stories of our days – him in the engineering firm of Malakoff in Lerwick, me doing week-long courses for beginner sailors up at my home town of Brae. He'd comforted me when I'd had nightmares after being shut in a horrible Neolithic tomb. When he'd been gored by a bull, his mother had jumped at the opportunity to whisk him away from my contaminating influence and back to Bergen, where she could feed him proper meals and introduce him to a nice Norwegian girl. That had been the last time I'd seen him: handing over Rat in Bergen under his mother's hostile eye. It still felt odd to wriggle into my berth without a last 'Good night' to and from the forepeak, to get up into an empty boat in the morning. He'd kissed me before he left Shetland ... but I wasn't going to think about that. He was younger than me, and stunningly handsome, and I was a footloose skipper with a scar across her cheek. He was a Lutheran too, a regular churchgoer, and I was Catholic; that would be bound to cause trouble. Besides, there was Gavin Macrae ... I wondered if a psychiatrist would say I was fostering this dual attraction in my subconscious so that I didn't have to commit to either of them. I shrugged that one away. Anders was in Bergen, and Gavin was here.

It was at that moment my phone bleeped. Speak of angels. It was a text from Anders: *Read Shet news wht r u mxd up in? Doc said ystrdy shouldr officly healed + can rtn to work. Shl I try Malakoff?*

He would be so suitable, Anders. We could take *Khalida* off to the Caribbean together, then go on to Australia ... but I couldn't say 'Yes, come' unless I was sure that was what I wanted.

I grimaced at the phone. It would be three o'clock in Norway, time to stop for a hot chocolate. He'd be sitting with his pals in his dad's yard in Bildøy, in his green overalls, with Rat on his shoulder and his mug in his hand, handle outwards. For a moment I missed him so much that it hurt – but Gavin was here, talking to Kate. I'd see him later. Each of them deserved a whole heart.

I sighed and pressed 'reply'. *Nothing to do with me I just found body. Glad u better. Taking college engine apart over and out.* Over and out was our shorthand for 'I'm about to go up the mast, so won't be answering the phone for a bit.' I couldn't think about Anders just now.

The nut stuck. *Pause, move your spanner, try again.* It still wouldn't move. I could hear Anders' voice murmuring over my shoulder. *Tighten it, just a little, then try.* That trick worked, and I was just easing it round when a shadow fell over it. It was Kevin, a quiet, sandy-haired guy who always arrived late. Being last today had landed him with me as a partner.

'Hi,' I said.

He gave a nervous bob of the head and sidled round to the front of the engine. 'Aye aye, Cass. What're we doing the day?'

Our lecturer had told us last Thursday that today would be the fuel system, and our homework had been to look at the diagrams. I nodded at the injector. 'The fuel system.'

He looked blankly at my line of nuts, washers and piping. 'What's all that?'

'The fuel line from the secondary filter to the injector.' I fitted it back together and screwed it in its place. 'There, you take it apart.'

I watched him as Anders had watched me, and heard myself using his words: 'If you have to force it, it's threaded wrong. Move your spanner and try again.' Kevin's hands were trembling so that the spanner was slipping on the nuts, and now I looked at him, he was paler than usual, his freckles standing out against the skin. 'Are you okay?'

He shrugged the question away, then hesitated, hands stilling on the spanner. He gave me a sideways look, then finished unscrewing the nut. He lifted it out and began to ease the fuel pipe upwards. 'It's Nan. Me great-granny.'

I waited in silence.

'She's ninety-three, but not doiting yet.'

Doiting was the Shetlan for losing your memory.

'She lives in the upstairs o' the big black and white house up on Castle Street. She has home helps and all that, and two days at the Walter Gray.' The Walter and Joan Gray Eventide Home was Scalloway's church-run care centre, just opposite the slip where the wartime Norwegians had repaired their boats. Walter Gray had been a radio operator in Canada; he'd received the telegram to say that the murderer Crippen and his mistress, Le Neve, were on their way across the Atlantic, pursued by Inspector Dew, and he'd been one of the first to know the *Titanic* had sunk, through a telegram from the *Carparthia*. Shetlanders get everywhere.

'And on the other days,' Kevin said, 'I go up in me lunch break to make her some soup for her dinner, and speak about what's all doing.'

I nodded. That explained why he was so often late for class.

'For all she's ninety-three, and her eyesight maybe no so good as it was, she's no doiting,' he repeated. 'We have some fine chats, me and Nan.' He lifted the fuel pipe out and laid it beside the nuts, then began unscrewing the injector. 'But the day, she was awful upset. She'd had this bad dream – well, I thought it was a dream, then I remembered –' His hands stilled on the nut. He gave that sideways bob of the head again. 'It was you that found the body, wasn't it?'

'Yes,' I said.

'Just down from Nan's, in the Spanish closs.'

I nodded.

'I didn't tell Nan about it, though she'll find out soon enyough, when the wife that comes to do her shopping comes in. She was that upset about

37

it all that I didn't want her to think –' He came to a dead stop, gave me an uncertain look, as if he was checking that I wasn't laughing at him, then finished, in a rush, 'She thought she'd seen Auld Clootie.'

Nate's words echoed in my head. 'Auld Clootie – the Devil?'

'Or the ghost of Black Patie – you ken, Earl Patrick, him that built the castle.'

'What did she say she'd seen?' I asked.

'Well,' Kevin said. He sat back on his hunkers and prepared to make a story of it. 'See, we usually have a bowl o' her own soup, an' I get a pie to go with it, and we heat that in the oven while we eat the soup. She kens when I'm comin', so she has it all ready, so we have time for a cup o' tay afterwards, an a chat. So I kent there was something wrong when I came up the stairs and there was no smell o' soup. For a moment I thought –' I saw it in his eyes, the darkened hallway, the long stair, fearing what he'd find at the end. 'I called out, "Nan!" and she replied, "Is dat dee, boy?", sounding awful nervous. So I called back, "Yea, Nan, it's me," and then I went in. She was in her usual chair, by the fire, wi' her taatit rug over her knees and her stick by her, but sitting awful huddled, as if she'd been there all morning. So I got the soup on, and the oven, and asked her if she wanted to just eat where she was. Well, that got her up and to the table.' He laughed and imitated her. "Boy, when I'm no able to eat my meals at a table wi' the family du'd better book me space in the graveyard." So we ate the soup and once there was a bit more colour in her face, then I asked her what was wrong. And she said, just like that, "I'm no long for this world, boy, for I'm seen Auld Clootie in the village last night, just as clear as I see you."

Kevin paused to take a swig from his water bottle. 'I said, "What d'you mean, Nan?" and she told me the whole story. Just as she was going to bed, she'd gone across to the window, to see if there was any rain coming up the voe, so that she knew whether to have her window open or shut. Well, she looked across at the castle, and she saw a black creature coming towards the house, "tall, he was," she said, "and black as the inside of a chimney, with his horns and his tail, and a misshapen hump on his back, and a cloud of evil around him, and the hounds of Hell at his back, and if it wasn't Auld Clootie then it was the ghost of Black Patie, and it's no better luck to see him. And there he came, slowly, and looking up and around, I saw his face, as if he was seeking another victim to carry off." She didn't want to do anything to attract his attention, so she just stepped backwards and backwards, out of the room, and closed the door behind her, and went into the living room, where the curtains were shut tight, and sat by the fire with her rug. She'd stayed there all night, and all morning, till I came, and I was right worried about how cold she'd gotten, but once she'd had the soup inside her, and a cup o' tay, her colour cam back.'

'What time does your nan usually go to bed?'

'Half past ten, on the dot.' He went back into his nan's voice. '"I'm aye gone to bed then, since I was a married wife, and there wouldn't be half of this carries-on and divorces if aabody else did that same."'

I was silent for a moment. His story told, he sat watching me, expecting me to make sense of it. I could make a start. I remembered the way Annette had lain, as if she dropped all of a heap – or had been dropped. 'Do you think that what she saw was maybe someone carrying poor Annette's body to where I found it?'

'I wondered that. Would the time be about right?'

'Bang on.'

'Then I'll call in on me way home and tell her you said that.'

I smiled. 'Me saying it'll cut no ice with anyone as tough as your granny. Tell her about poor Annette, and let her work it out for herself.'

'Oh, no, she approves o' you,' Kevin said. 'I'm telt her all about you being at the college. She used to sail herself, Nan, wi' her faither, and they won cups at all the regattas, until he got over old and had to give the boat up. She can just see your boat from her cludgie window, and she aye looks to see if you're home, last thing at night. She says it's awful fine to see the gold glow o' candlelight from your window. She misses the old days, you ken, with lamps and candles and fires. She kens fine the hydro is more convenient, but it's no the same, for her. In fact ...' Suddenly, he blushed scarlet. 'She said if ever you were passing she'd like fine to meet you, or if I brought you for lunch one day.'

'I'd like fine to meet her,' I said. 'And you tell her about Annette. It wasn't the Devil that did that. He's no loose in Scalloway yet.'

I spent the rest of the lesson brooding about that snippet of information. A misshapen person, a tall person with a dead girl on one shoulder, coming from the castle. The inference was clear. It was the castle that Annette had visited at dead of night. *Why shouldn't I go and meet people, if I think they can help me?* But what sort of people would be meeting in the ruins of Scalloway Castle so late? I could hear Kevin's nan's voice answering: 'Nobody up to any good, you mark my words.'

I was heading for the canteen to collect Cat when I heard a burst of laughter from inside the kitchen, that uncertain kind of laughter when someone's being pleasurably scared. It was yesterday's three crows, folllowed by Sarah, the kitchen girl, all coming out in a flock, dressed in their leather and grey fantasy wear, with full warpaint. Nate was behind them.

'... claw marks,' he was saying, 'on her throat.' He stretched one hand menacingly towards the short-haired lesser crow, fingers crooked. 'As if the Devil had gripped her. She'd meddled with what she didn't understand, and a demon came to get her.' His hand closed on the girl's throat. She gave a protesting shriek. 'And then,' Nate said, suddenly catching her off balance and hoisting her over one shoulder in a fireman's life, 'it carried her soul off, like this!'

He spun her around, then set her back on her feet, his face serious. 'I'm telling you, the Devil's come to Scalloway.'

Chapter Six

It was just after four when I left the college. I stepped out into a grey murk, then suddenly there was sunlight from the black sky, magnifying every grass tussock's shadow, making the fence posts and tall ditch grass into a ragged comb across the road. The light was harsh and yellow, as though before a thunderstorm, the bleached hill grass brightened to pale gold. It could have been a summer evening ... then the clouds closed over the sun, leaving a slanted shaft falling on the east hill. The light was dimming already. The tide was halfway in; along the westshore, sandpipers stabbed the dark seaweed with slender, curved beaks.

I clambered aboard *Khalida*, mechanically checked her ropes, then went below, closing the washboards after me, and sat down in the corner seat. I'd put the kettle on in a moment. I leant my head against the varnished bulkhead, and closed my eyes – then, before I knew it, the long windows were darkened, and my mobile was ringing. It was Gavin.

'We're at the marina gate,' he said. 'Can you let us in?'

Us? I thought. I creaked up and headed along to let them in: Gavin and Sergeant Peterson. I motioned them ahead of me onto *Khalida*, reached into the locker to turn the gas on, then lit the hanging lantern and put the kettle on the stove before I closed the washboards again.

'Sorry,' I said. 'I fell asleep after college. It'll soon warm up, with the gas on.' I motioned Sergeant Peterson towards the corner I'd just left. 'Sit down.'

Gavin had a white carrier bag which was filling my cabin with a wonderfully savoury smell. He reached for the anti-slip mat to lay below it. It was strange and familiar to see his green-jacketed arm stretching to the right place, his countryman's hand laying the mat out and setting the carrier bag on top. 'Lemon chicken, as requested, and egg fried rice. Are these the plates to use?'

'Let me give them a dry first.' They were stored in the fiddled shelf above the cooker, and the top one was always damp with condensation. Gavin sat down in his usual place, without fuss, as if it had just been yesterday that we'd shared a Frankie's fish supper at Brae. The lamp sparked red lights in his russet hair, and brought shadows under his eyes, as if he was short of sleep. He looked straight at me and smiled.

'Good to see you again, Cass. Let's eat before we do the official stuff. The sergeant and I have been hard at work all afternoon.'

'Sounds good to me,' I said. I doled out the plates and found eating irons while Sergeant Peterson opened the boxes: lemon chicken, those little orange-brown worms of beef, and something with prawns and dark mushrooms. There were two boxes of rice and one of noodles. Cat's whiskers twitched. I chopped one slice of my chicken up for him, ladled a generous helping on my own plate, then sat on the engine box to enjoy it.

One of the things I liked about Gavin was that he didn't feel the need to fill silence with chatter. We ate to the noise of waves tapping the hull, and bubbles rattling in the kettle until its low hiss turned to a shrill whistle, and I rose to turn it off. 'Coffee, tea, drinking chocolate?'

'Coffee,' Gavin said. 'I don't expect to be in bed for a good while.'

'For me too,' Sergeant Peterson said. 'Thanks.'

I filled the percolator and set it between them, made myself a drinking chocolate, then sat back on my box, nursing my mug and waiting. Gavin nodded at Sergeant Peterson, and she took her notebook out. 'Official stuff?'

'Go you,' I said. Cat jumped up on my lap to wash his whiskers.

'Well,' Gavin said. 'Let's go back to how you found the body. What did you touch, to ascertain that she was dead?' He was on duty now. His voice lost some of its Highland lingering on the 's', the precision of the final consonants.

'Her hand first,' I said. 'I lifted the hand that was stretched out towards the door, to feel the pulse, and there was none, so I laid it down again and tried her neck. I had to loosen her scarf to do that, not much, just enough to slide my fingers in. I was pretty sure she was gone, but I wanted to double check. And then – yes, I felt the scratches on her neck, under my fingers, so I turned her head to the light, to see – when I'd met her, in the morning, I'd noticed the scratches, and I wanted to know if it was her.'

'Did you replace her as you found her?'

I nodded.

'Did you touch anything else?'

'No.'

'Her bag, her jacket?'

'No. But I wondered – there was something odd about the way they were lying –'

'Someone with gloved hands had handled the bag, and the purse inside.'

'She wasn't wearing gloves,' I said. 'Not yesterday morning either. It's not really been cold enough yet – last night was the first time I've had mine on.' I remembered Kate saying the police had asked how much money she should have had in her purse. 'Was there anything missing?'

'Her mother thought she wouldn't have had much money on her, and nor she did. Her bag had all the other things you'd expect: tissues, make-up, old bus tickets, a cinema ticket. Nothing unusual. No keys, but the house door isn't locked, so she wouldn't need them. We thought, from the way her jacket was lying, that someone had searched her pockets too.'

'But what for? What might she have had that someone else would want?'

Gavin spread his hands. 'There was money in her purse, and credit cards, so it wasn't robbery.' He paused for emphasis. 'Except that she'd taken £100 out of her account yesterday, at the Cashline. That money wasn't in her bag, nor in her room, and we can't find that she bought anything in town.'

'I asked the obvious places,' Sergeant Peterson said. 'Clothes shops, jewellery, hairdresser. Nothing.'

'A hundred pounds,' I echoed. To me that sounded riches beyond imagination, but I didn't know what a banker's daughter considered small change. I paused, stroking Cat. He sat up straighter to let me scratch behind his ears, then curled up, tail over nose. 'Have you done the post-mortem yet?'

'It's tomorrow. I can tell you informally that there's no obvious cause of death.'

My mouth fell open. 'None?'

'She wasn't struck, stabbed, smothered, or poisoned with an irritant poison. There are no external signs of anything that would have caused death. That doesn't mean she didn't, say, inhale fumes, or drink a poison that didn't cause vomiting.'

Inhale fumes ... 'Did you notice the ash on her hand?'

He smiled. 'Noticed, drew a diagram of where, took samples for analysis.'

'Maybe she brewed something over a fire.' I had a sudden picture of witches standing around a cauldron. 'Listen, there's something I found out today.' I told them what Kenny's great-granny had seen.

'A tall, misshapen figure coming from the castle,' Gavin repeated. He looked across at Sergeant Peterson. 'Investigate that, once we've finished here. Door-to-door, focusing on that time. Tomorrow, we'll look at the castle. Find out about keys, and if anyone's been in today. Make sure it won't be visited again until we've been in.' He was talking to her as I'd talk to Anders, the captain giving orders, and I felt a pang of jealousy.

43

Then he turned back to me. 'Can you describe those scratches you saw yesterday morning?'

It seemed an odd request, since he'd seen them himself. 'What I saw – ' I visualised it, standing outside the garden door, with the wind tugging at my hair. 'It was on the right side of her neck, her left. I didn't see the other side. It was just a glimpse as she was catching her scarf. There was one long scratch, and several shorter ones. I thought she'd maybe been playing with a cat that had gone for her, then I realised there was like a bruise around them, a darker indentation, like dog's claws. They have two pointers.'

Gavin and Sergeant Peterson looked across at each other, a spark of understanding and interest that excluded me. Sergeant Peterson leant forward. 'How old would you say they were?'

'Not fresh, there was a scab on the scratches. The day before, or earlier than that.' When had Nate said he'd seen her with scratches round her neck? 'You should maybe talk to Nate Halcrow. He told me he'd seen the scratches on her neck three or four days ago.'

'Nate Halcrow,' Gavin repeated. His eyes met Sergeant Peterson's again, and she nodded. 'Were they friends? Why was he talking to you about her?'

'He was worried about her. I'm not sure if they were close friends, but they'd acted together in a Hallowe'en play. You'd need to ask him. He'd seen her by the water, one night, and he was worried she might be suicidal.'

We were caught in a circle of lantern-light now. The long panes of *Khalida*'s windows let in only the silver gleam of the marina lights. I stood up to draw the curtains across on their elastic, to shut the cold and dark out, keep the warmth in. The gold glow intensified without the silver to dilute it, gleaming on Sergeant Peterson's fair hair, picking up gold flecks in the varnished wood. She drained the last of her coffee and set the cup on the table. 'Do you know where he lives?'

I shook my head. There was a rattle against the window, as if someone was throwing pebbles. I remembered I'd smelled snow earlier. It would be a cold night.

'Number 2,' she said. 'The house her hand was stretched towards. If she was carried there, someone wanted us to think she was beseeching him for help, or pointing to him as her murderer. Which would you go for?'

I shrugged. 'It could be either.'

Gavin leaned towards me. 'Were the clawmarks you describe definitely part of the scratches?'

'Yes,' I said. 'They were at the top of each scratch, as if the claw had

44

dug in, then trailed down her neck.'

'There were new marks on her throat.' Sergeant Peterson made an abrupt move, as if she didn't want him to say this to a suspect. Gavin's eyes flicked across to her; he nodded. 'Don't repeat this, Cass.' I liked the way his voice lingered on the 'ss' of my name. 'She had marks around her neck, made either just before her death or just after, indented, bruised claw marks.'

'But she wasn't strangled?'

Gavin shook his head. 'Was it light enough for you to see her face – her expression?'

'I could see it very clearly.' I could see it now. Gavin waited, then, when I didn't speak, made a gesture with one hand.

'I don't want to put words into your mouth. By the time I saw her, all the expression was gone. She looked peaceful.'

I was glad, for Kate and Peter's sake. 'She looked – not frightened. No, maybe a little frightened, but more shocked. Not terrified.' Not as if something horrible had stretched a clawed hand out towards her. 'More as if –' The same comparison kept coming back. 'As if she was a child caught taking sweeties in a shop. Surprise, guilt.' I spread my hands. 'I'm sorry, that's the best I can do.'

'Surprise, or guilt,' Gavin repeated.

The words suddenly raised an echo. *Claw marks on her throat, as if the Devil had gripped her* ... 'Nate knows about the fresh marks,' I said. 'He was telling the other kitchen worker and her friends.' I remembered the shadow behind the frosted glass, the closing door I'd heard. 'I bet it was him who came out to look, then went back in quickly when he heard me coming. He kept watching.'

Gavin nodded, as if he'd already worked that out. 'And left you banging on doors to get a phone book. That's not the act of a friend.'

'No,' I agreed. 'No, it's not.'

'Maybe he was the person who searched her bag and pockets. We need to find out what someone was looking for.' He rose, and brushed a stray grain of rice from his kilt. 'Make him our first interview tomorrow, Sergeant.' He turned back to me. 'Her mobile was in her pocket too. The last call she'd made, at 21.43, was to Nate Halcrow's house.'

There were snow flurries throughout the rest of the evening, rapping against the windows and on the fibreglass roof. The wind was a good force 6 now, and *Khalida* rocked in her berth. Across the pontoon, somebody's halyard had worked loose, and was banging against a metal mast. I sighed and hauled on my jacket and toorie cap. A loose halyard meant frayed ropes, and I'd be grateful to a fellow-mariner who tightened mine.

I swung onto the boat nose-on to *Khalida*, hauled the rattling rope down and wound it tightly around its cleat. My feet had just touched the pontoon again when I heard a voice calling my name. I looked up and around, shielding my eyes from the snow with one hand. Across the water, on the shore road, a figure raised a hand, then began walking towards the marina gate. He was muffled up in an old-fashioned parka, navy, with fur around the hood, so I couldn't see who it was. I walked along the pontoon to the gate, but didn't unlock it yet.

When he got to the gate he flung the hood back. It was James Leask, that had met Annette for a meal in Scalloway Hotel the Monday before she died.

'I wanted to speak wi' you,' he said.

It was too cold to stand shouting at each other through a mesh fence. I unlocked the gate and motioned him towards *Khalida.*

He stood in the middle of the cabin, looking around, while I re-lit the lantern. 'This is bonny. My folk hae a motor cruiser, but it's aa' fibreglass inside. This is lik a home, wi' the wood, an' the books apo' the shelf.'

'Have a seat,' I said.

He eased himself down in the bulkhead corner, where Sergeant Peterson had sat. I still thought of it as Anders' corner, and it gave me a queer pang to see James' fair head against the mahogany, except that he had thicker hair than Anders, with a wiry texture, and none of Anders' dazzling Norse god looks. Instead of the reckless Viking raider, only happy at the prow of his ship, you could see the Norse settler who came over with his steatite bowls and Eidsborg whetstones, his wheat, sheep, kye (and looking at James, probably his mother too) – all he'd need to make a new life. His slightly bulging eyes were a clear, pale blue, and his eyebrows were low-set and dark, giving him a serious look. He wore a boiler suit under his parka, and a faint smell of sheep came in with him. He was sensible, reliable, the very best type of country Shetland man, that could turn his hand to anything, but for someone as lively as Annette, boy-next-door was stamped on his forehead.

I made him a traditional tea, adding an extra teabag for the pot size, and leaving it on the ring to stew before pouring it. He eyed up the tarry colour appreciatively and sloshed some milk in. 'That's a good cup o' tay, that.' He cupped his hands around it. 'I'm fair starved wi' that wind.'

'It's no' warm,' I agreed. I offered him a ginger nut from the plastic

46

tub tucked behind the starboard fiddle. He shook his head.

'I'm just had me eight o' clocks.' He paused, drank some of his tea, then set the cup down, still gripping it as if the cold was deep inside him. 'Cass, I cam aboot Annette.' He looked down at the floor, then up at me. 'I dinna ken if what I'm got to say is o' any use in catching wha' did yon to her. I'm no' used wi' meddling wi' dat kind o' a thing. I towt at if I browt it to you, you'd ken. You're courting wi' dat policeman wi' da kilt, so if you towt you should, you could tell him. If it would help catch – whaivver.'

I'd forgotten the way Shetlanders said 'courting' for folk who were going out together. I stored that in the back of my mind to think about later, and said, 'Tell me about it.'

'I met up wi' her,' he said. 'I aye liked her, at the school, she was that lively. Dramatic-way, I suppose you'd say. She seemed to live life as if it was much more interesting than what I was doing, feeding the sheep and kye, and sailing the Shetland model at the Interclub regatta. I suppose in a way, that's part of what made me sign up for this course. I wanted some o' that excitement an aa.' He twisted the mug in his hands. His voice roughened, like the sea dragging itself out of a crack in rock. 'Maybe I thought that she'd notice me if I was a seaman, travelling all over the world.'

He finished the tea and pushed the mug away, then leaned towards me. 'I'd see her about in Scalloway, from time to time, and I'd say aye aye. Then, ee' day, I was going up one of the lanes, an I saw her coming towards me. She was dat upset she wasna looking where she was going, and I had to catch her to stop her walking straight into me. Well, I walked with her along to the hotel and took her in for a coffee. She was wearing a scarf, but just loose aroond her neck, not the way they all wear it these days, with the end doubled, and she kept it on, even though she took her hat and coat off. Then, when it slipped –' He paused, and looked sideways at me. 'You're heard about these marks apo' her neck?' His voice hardened. 'The whole place has heard. Nate's made sure o' that.'

'I saw them, yesterday morning.' Was it really only yesterday? I seemed to have lived years since then. 'Scratches, with a bruise around them.'

'Well, that's what I saw. Fresh, they were, as if they'd been done no an hour before, and the darker mark where the claw went in just beginning to colour.'

'What day was this?' I asked.

He thought for a moment. 'Saturday. It was Saturday, because I hadn't planned to be in the village, wi' it no being a college day, but then Mam decided she fancied a different sort of roast for Sunday lunch, and she sent me in to get a piece of pork from the butcher. It was the middle o' the efternoon. Anyway, Annette wouldna tell me anything that day – well, I didna really ask, she was that upset. I phoned her later, and we agreed to meet up for a bar supper on Monday. I hoped she'd tell me what was wrong then, once she'd calmed down and had time to think it through.'

The lantern guttered with a hissing noise, then went out, leaving his face in darkness. I fished behind the fiddle for another tea-light candle, picked the old one out with a spoon and dropped it in the sink, then lit the new one. The gold glow bathed James' face once more.

He looked as if he'd hardly noticed the interruption. 'She told me, that second time, that she was really worried about something someeen wanted her to do. She wouldna tell me wha' it was, or what they wanted, but she said it wasna wrong exactly. She said that several times, so I could see that it was wrong, and she didna want to do it, whatever it was, but she was frightened about what would happen to her if she didna do it.'

He looked directly at me. 'I bet you're seen some queer things. All the old men who'd been to sea, they were willing to believe in things that don't seem ordinary.'

'I saw a mer-horse once, off Fiji,' I said. 'It had a head like a horse on a snake's neck, with a brown mane, and great, blind eyes. I didn't put it in the log, but in my own head I'm sure of what I saw, and it's not anything in the natural history books.'

He gave a long sigh. 'Yes, that's what I meant. Well, Annette, see, she had this thing about having things around her neck. That's why her scarf kept slipping, because she wouldna pull it tight, and she never wore choker necklaces, or high-necked jumpers, or anything like that, never, so long as I'd known her, and if anyone put their hands near her neck, you ken, playing in the playground, she'd scream blue murder. Some o' the boys in my class were just awful for teasing her about it, until they got a talking to from the headteacher, and gave it up. Well, she thought – ' He paused, took a deep breath, then said it steadily, watching my reaction. 'She believed she was the reincarnation o' a witch who'd died here in Scalloway.' He jerked his chin towards the cockpit. 'Up on the Gallow Hill there. Before they burned them, they strangled them, with a cord. It was kind o' merciful, I suppose, instead of burning them alive. She said she kept dreaming of being hustled up the burn beside her house, with her arms tied, and everyone laughing and jeering at her, and then of the big pile of peats, and being tied to the post, and the smell of peat reek filling her mouth. She was nearly in tears just thinking about it.'

'What did you say?'

The sensible crofter answered. 'I telt her it was worrying about it was bringing the dreams, and if she made her mind up and telt them she'd have nothing more to do with it, then the dreams would go. But she wouldn't. She said that what she'd promised to do would exorcise her, and then she could forget all about it.'

He paused and looked around, as if he was afraid of being overheard. 'She wouldn't say who it was, but I think I ken. I dinna get on wi' Nate dat well, he's a bit o' an odd fish, an he has a sister. She works to the college. Rachel, Rachel Halcrow.' He took a deep breath. 'She's a heksi.'

I'd never heard the word. 'A heksi?'

'A witch. See, she's aye had an odd reputation. She was older than me at the school, she'd left by the time I came into first year, but folk still remembered, ones that'd had an older brother or sister in her class. Things used to break around her, and there was one time in Chemistry when a fire started, just by itself, with her nowhere near it.'

I remembered the wineglass that had broken in the canteen, and Nate's voice: *Still breaking things, are you?*

'Annette woulda heard those stories too. I reckon she went to Rachel for help, because she'd ken about witches, and now Rachel's taking the chance to get her into her coven, that meets up on the dark nights on Gallow Hill. Then she refused after all, and Rachel killed her, outside her own house.' He rose, jerkily, and pulled his hood up over his fair hair. 'I'd need to go. That was what I was wanting to tell you. I don't want to think about what cloored Annette, but I'm certain that Rachel's behind it all.'

He pulled back the hatch, lifted the first washboard, and was out over the second one and lost in the darkness, in the flurrying snow, before I could stop him.

49

Chapter Seven

Friday 28th October

Low Water Scalloway 01:29 BST 0.6m
High Water 07:42 1.5 m
Low Water 13:41 0.7m
High Water 19:51 1.6m
Moon waxing gibbous

Moonset 04:12, 272 degrees
Sunrise 08:14
Moonrise 16:06, 84 degrees
Sunset 17:22

I woke at seven, and stretched out one hand to haul the curtain back. The cold air sent a shiver down my arm. Below the sea wall, the beach-stones were outlined with snow in the long slope down to the water's edge. The tang on the shore was frilled with ice. There was a triangle of snow in the pavement angle on the far side of the road, and a frosting of white across the grass hills. A combed-out skein of cirrostratus cloud spread across half the sky: more wind coming.

It had taken me a while to get to sleep last night. I hadn't thought of Nate's house also being Rachel's. *Folk said she was a witch ...* The smash of the glass falling behind the café counter echoed in my head. Poltergeist activity, although Rachel was older than the usual adolescent focus of unexplained power surges, falling objects, and mysterious fires. The Scottish nanny had been older too, Carole Compton, she'd been twenty, twenty-one when she was put in prison for fire raising. I knew about her because of a Brazilian boy we'd had on board the *Sorlandet* at the time of her trial. His home village had had a series of unexplained fires, so he followed the case avidly, and he was full of similar tales, which he shared with his whole watch on dark nights out at sea.

Fear was what had spawned the witch hunts: the male fear that women who'd been put so nicely in their place, with even the clothes they wore belonging to their father or husband, had a source of power that would let them get their own back. They'd picked on women who were outside the accepted round of children and tea parties, women who had an important place in the women's community as midwives and healers, and given them a sinister reputation, the black side of white magic, with charges too outrageous to be believed. I glanced out at the Gallow Hill as I dressed. I had a vague memory of a poem we'd studied in school, *Auld Maalie*, a child asking her mother what they were doing to the old woman as they dragged her up the hill. The last women who'd died there, had they been dancing on the Sabbath? I'd need to go along to the museum and find out more –

Suddenly there was a rattle on the cabin roof. I looked out and saw hail balls bouncing off the pontoon, the size of my little fingernail. The sky behind was still blue, and the hail was blowing across it like columns of grey smoke. Soon the road was white. Then the real snow began, drifting flakes from a Christmas card. I looked out, and couldn't believe it. We hadn't left October, and there was winter spread before me, in the snow-glazed hills, the grass tussocks bent under their white shadow, the cobalt sea tumbled over with long white crests. The castle wore a white cap, and the little turrets had disdainful eyebrows over the latticed windows.

When I came out of the shelter of *Khalida*'s cabin, the cold struck me like a blow. I'd dressed for it today, with my sailing thermals under my jeans and warmest jumper, but the wind searched out the cracks between glove and sleeve, cap and cheek, scarf and neck, and stung like a wasp. The air was thrumming with the noise of taut rigging being plucked by the wind. I checked my halyards, then headed off towards Kate and Peter's house. Cat came out onto the pontoon, turned tail, and slid back below through the forrard hatch. It wasn't a day for cats to go walking.

There was no sign of Kate in the kitchen. I waited for a moment, then took a step into the living room, rapped on the door, and called her name. There was silence for a moment, then a call from upstairs. I retreated to the kitchen and waited as a bed creaked. Footsteps edged along the upper hall. I heard Kate's voice: 'Cass, is that you?'

The living room mirror reflected me standing there. I'd pulled my hat off as I'd entered, and my hair curled in a dark cloud around my face. The mirror was one of those old ones that makes everyone look as if they're underwater; my skin was greenish white, with the scar crossing it like a blade of seaweed. I looked like the witch of the *Little Mermaid*, the original story, which had gripped me with fascinated horror as a child, or like Medusa with her snake hair. There were Michaelmas daisies in a vase, filling the room with their bitter smell. The lilac petals were browned and falling.

'Hello,' I called up.

She hadn't dressed yet, Kate, whose scarf and Alice band always contrasted smartly with her round-necked jumpers, whose padded waistcoat matched the grey, brown, or green of her cords. I felt that sense of wrongness you'd get if the captain came up on the bridge in his underwear. Her dressing gown was a man's housecoat, scarlet silk with a thirties Paisley pattern, like something from a Noel Coward comedy, worn over a white nightdress, and she'd thrust her feet into Damart slippers. She hurried down the stairs, pausing halfway to tie the dressing gown around her. 'Don't go, Cass. I'm up, I was just –'

The kettle was already on the Rayburn; as I moved it to the hottest part, over the fire-box, my brain caught up with my senses. This cream box of glowing warmth, this cosy kitchen, smelled of oil, not of peat. I opened the firebox door and saw only the little flame of the burner.

I'd assumed that Annette had been working with the Rayburn at her house before she'd gone out, but now I thought about it, that was nonsense. Even if it hadn't been oil-fired, it would have been riddled and the ash removed in the morning. When you wanted the fire to stay in all night, the fuller the ash-pan, and so the less air from below, the better. No, she'd been working with a peat fire or stove that was being lit only for the evening, clearing the cold ash before lighting the new fire. She'd dusted her hands off, but not bothered to wash them – no, the fastidious Annette would never have left her hands dirty. She hadn't washed them because – My imagination stuck there. 'Do you have a peat fire, as well as the Rayburn?'

Kate shook her head, every gesture weary. 'Just the Rayburn, and the radiators, and Snow White's box.'

'The what?'

The ghost of a smile crossed Kate's face. 'It's what I call the fire in the sitting room. It's one of those electric ones that looks like a real fire, but it's inside an iron and glass box, like Snow White's –' Her lips moved on the word 'coffin', but no sound came out. Then her her sorrow welled up and overflowed, great gulping sobs interspersed with apologies; she pulled a large, green-edged handkerchief out and buried her face in it, then blew her nose. 'Sorry, Cass. It's all been –'

I hoped my expression showed my sympathy. I couldn't think of what to say; but she didn't need me to say anything, just to listen.

'We had to go, last night, to identify – I thought it was going to be awful, and it was, but not as bad as – That wasn't our Annette, always so lively, and changing expression every two seconds. I knew then she was really gone. She was a waxwork of herself, so still, with nothing on her

52

face at all. It wasn't even as if she was asleep. She was just gone.' She took a sip of tea. 'I'd never seen a dead person before. I was too little when Grandma died.'

She needed someone with her, I thought, not just the hired help, no matter how well we got on. She needed someone who could hug her and let her cry, someone to tuck her into bed and sit beside her, and bring her sweet biscuits and cups of tea. 'Kate, is there a friend I could phone for you, someone you'd like with you?'

She shrank back into her chair, shaking her head. 'You're fine, Cass. I don't need anyone else.' Her voice quickened. 'We don't really belong here, you know. It's a time like this you feel it. Oh, everyone's being so kind, but we're outsiders. It's kindness to strangers.' Her voice changed suddenly, became alarmed. 'Did Peter go out?' She began to twist the cup around in her hands.

'I haven't seen him,' I said, 'but Dan and Candy aren't here.'

The turning cup stilled. 'Then that's all right. He won't – ' She peered sideways at me, then shook her head, as if chasing a thought away. When she lifted it again her eyes were clear, the mask of competent countrywoman back in place. 'Sorry, Cass, I'm making no sense today. I'll finish my tea and go back to bed.'

'Take another cup with you,' I said, 'and a hot water bottle. It's snowing outside, did you see?'

She looked up at the window. 'Snow? But it's only October.'

'It'll get mild again after it's over.' I hoped so; if it didn't, I was in for a long, cold winter.

'You don't want to work in snow.'

'I'm well wrapped up. I'll do a bit of stick chopping and bonfire trundling.'

She heard what I didn't say, that I'd be there until Peter came back, and gave an imitation of her usual smile. 'Thanks, Cass.' She lifted the cup, paused. 'If you hear the phone, ignore it. I've had three calls this week already – you know, the Indian voice saying my computer's interfering with Microsoft's mainframe. I told him I knew it was rubbish, but he was so persistent. Now I'm not answering.'

It was the last thing she needed. 'If they phone again, I'll sort them,' I promised.

I collected the barrow from the shed and set to. The corner we'd worked on yesterday ended in a hedge of monkshood, the Shetland delphinium, hip-tall, the leaves turned autumn red, the hooded flowers intense gentian blue. I could haul these up as vigorously as I liked, they'd still be back next year, but I didn't want to destroy the bonny patch of colour. Behind them was a clump of hemlock, its creamy frothed heads turning to green seeds. Monkshood and hemlock, witches' brews ... I hacked the lower branches of the sycamores above them, as Kate had done, and found frilled lichen on the stems, and spindly stemmed fungi. In France, the woods would be fruited with mushrooms: scrolled angel trumpets, and those bone-white ones that curved like a baby's skull among the fallen leaves.

It didn't take long to fill the barrow. I wasn't insured to drive their car, but I packed the white salmon-feed carrier into the back of it, and filled it up with several loads of sticks, ready to be taken to the bonfire pile of pallets, old couches, worn boards, hacked tree branches. The whole village would gather round on the east shore next weekend, with boxes of fireworks, then there'd be tea and bannocks or hot dogs in the hall. Kate was keen to get the undergrowth cleared now so that it would be burned on Guy Fawkes day. After that, my job would be over – but maybe she'd think of something else for me to do, digging borders or planting bulbs.

I was already worrying about firework night. The noise would echo round Port Arthur and into my fibreglass home, and Cat would hate it. I might ask if we could come up here. Dan and Candy wouldn't worry about bangs, for Peter often took them up the hill with his shotgun, after rabbits or the wild geese that were overwintering here now. Or, if it was a night for it, we could just sail out to sea and heave-to two miles offshore. I could sleep in the cockpit, with the tiller under my hand ...

The snow kept up all morning, the sky suddenly darkening, then the white flakes falling until the clouds had shed their load, and the sun shone again in a blue sky. The flakes swirled outside the windows, clinging to the glass in blotches and sidling downwards as if seeking a way in. When I went into the kitchen at last, numbed hands tingling in the warmth, the glass was so clean that everything outside seemed clear yet tiny, as if you were looking at it through the wrong end of a pair of spyglasses: the jumble of sheds that had been used by the Shetland Bus, the street of coloured houses, the castle, sand-brown against the whitened hill, with a line of snow along each gable wall.

I was just leaving when the phone rang. I snatched it up, and waited, Kate's white face before my eyes. These bloody fraudsters ... The Indian voice spoke, with a caricature accent. 'Is that Mrs Otway?'

'I'm a neighbour,' I said briskly. 'There has been a death in the house, and Mrs Otway is extremely distressed, so I would like to to take her number off your list immediately. Don't call again. Thank you.'

I put the phone down. No peat fire in the house. I'd brooded about that one as I'd hauled and sawn. It didn't quite make sense. Annette'd gone out at ten, and not been long away – it hadn't been eleven when I'd found her. She'd gone – *somewhere* – lit the fire there, then gone straight out again. An old person, maybe – she'd gone just to light the fire, then left? But the Rayburn argument still applied. An old person wouldn't want her fire riddled, if it was to stay in all night, and if it wasn't, then there wouldn't be any point in lighting it this late. Maybe it had gone out, and had to be cleared. At this point, my memory of peat fires began to get shaky. I took out my mobile and phoned my old schoolfriend, Inga.

'Aye, aye, Cass.' Inga sounded harassed, and there were clattering noises in the background. I realised she was probably bang in the middle of dealing with children's lunch.

'Sorry,' I said. 'Bad timing. It was just something I wanted to ask you.'

'I kent you'd get mixed up in this somewye,' Inga said.

I glanced upwards, and spoke softly. 'She's the lass from the folk I work for.'

'Oh.' Her voice warmed. 'I'm vexed to hear that, Cass. It's always an awful thing when a young een goes like that, but worse still when you ken them.' She paused, as if listening. I heard Peerie Charlie saying 'I want a spik wi' Dass.'

'Joost a quick hello,' Inga said.

I knew Charlie would ignore that. I could picture him as if I was there. There were thunks as he clambered up to the window seat and got himself settled, little feet sticking straight out, then heavy breathing.

'Aye aye, Charlie,' I said. 'What's du up to?'

'I speaking to you on the phone,' Peerie Charlie said. Fair enough.

'I'm speaking to dee an 'aa. Then I'm going to hae my lunch.'

'I eaten mine.'

'You havena,' Inga said, in the background.

'I nearly eaten mine,' Charlie amended.

'I've got soup. It's going to be good.'

There was a pause, then Charlie said, 'Green spidey going to beat the Iceman.' Spiderman was his current thing, but I'd lost track of the baddies, as I'd not been over to baby-sit for the last two months. Charlie launched into an account of the latest news, Spidey-wise, punctuated by indignant 'Mam!' as Inga tried to get the phone back from him. Eventually she persuaded him to say 'Bye bye' on the grounds that pudding was coming.

'Hi,' she said. 'Did you say you wanted to ken something?'

'Peat fires,' I said. 'Why would you want to riddle one out after ten o' clock at night?'

Inga considered that in silence for a moment. 'If you were trying to light it, for overnight warmth, or if it wasna burning properly because it was choked up – you'd riddle it then. I canna see why anyone'd bother, this time of year. It's no that cold that you'd need it all night. You might as well let it die down and get rid of cold ash in the morning, rather as working with it hot. Hot ash flies aawye, much worse as cold.'

'An old person, maybe, with no other source of heat?'

Inga snorted. 'There's naebody like that these days. If their family hasna made sure they're got central heating or at least an electric back-up, their social worker or home help's sorted it. Na, lass, can't help you. Unless,' she added cheerfully, 'she was a witch welcoming home a vampire, or some other night creature. You never ken, in Scalloway.'

She went off to feed Peerie Charlie his yoghurt-from-a-straw. I could hear Kate moving in the bathroom, as if she was dressing. There was still no sign of Peter, so I supposed he was gone for the day. I set the kettle on the hotplate again, and opened a tin of tomato soup, best invalid food.

'Oh, yes, just what I was wanting,' Kate said, when she came down, dressed like herself again, though her face was still white and drawn above her bright scarf. 'Now you go, Cass, you have college. I'll spend the afternoon in my shed.'

'I've left you a carload of branches,' I warned her. 'But we're almost at the bottom layer of sycamores now, just ten yards from the lowest wall.'

'We'll make it before bonfire night,' she agreed. She managed a smile that was more like her own. 'Thank you, Cass.'

I scrunched off along the sea road. *A vampire, or some night creature* ... I'd been remarkably slow in the uptake. Kevin's nan had seen the misshapen creature coming from the castle, and what better place to hold some strange exorcism rite than Black Patie's Great Hall, where the witches had been condemned? I remembered the image I'd had of witches crouching over a cauldron. *Double, double, toil and trouble, fire burn* – Was that how Annette had got the ash on her hands, making the fire for some witches' brew designed to free her from the presence she believed was within her?

Chapter Eight

My soup was even better the second time around. After I'd eaten, I left Cat washing his plaice-smeared whiskers and headed back towards the town. The hailstones crunched under my boots and the wind stung my face. The kerbside snow was turned to ice by the wheels of parking cars.

Inside the shop, the staff had put on a Hallowe'en spree. There was a bucket with apples for dookin, that game where you had to pick one up from the water with your teeth, or you could put your hand in a bowl of green goo to fish for a prize. The women were all dressed as witches of a Gothic turn, festooned with black lace and those black T-shirts with a snarling ghoul on the front, and wearing black lipstick below their frizzed up hair. There were a couple of workmen in the queue at the till. 'Have a go at dookin for apples,' one girl teased, and the younger man reddened and shook his head.

I was chilled enough without getting my hair wet. I found prunes and an onion, to make a lamb recipe I'd learned from an Arab cook on board the *Christian Radich* – that would keep for tomorrow, and I could cook it in the flask, which saved my precious gas. We'd have fried kidneys tonight, with the left-over rice from yesterday.

I was just outside the shop door when it opened again, and a woman in a dark jacket hurried out, clutching two bags in red-gloved hands, and with her hood pulled down so far over her face that she didn't see me. She bumped into me just as I was turning to avoid her, and dropped one of her bags. We stooped together to retrieve her shopping, in a flurry of apologies, and I realised it was Rachel. I handed over two tins and a packet of fire-lighters.

'Cass?' She seemed uneasy, shoving the items back into the bag. The firelighters wouldn't fit, and she hesitated for a moment, then rammed them into her other bag, squeezing them beside a grey fake fur costume. 'Thanks to you. I wasna looking aboot me.' She glanced around the pavement at our feet. 'Hae I gluffed your little cat?'

Frightened, she meant. 'He's sensible.' I fell in beside her on the narrow pavement. 'One twitch of the nose out of the cabin, and he decided to stay at home in the – well, I couldn't call *Khalida* warm

57

exactly, but at least it's not snowing in the cabin.'

'Awful, isn't it no'? And it's only October. Guid kens what kind o' winter we're going to have.' She seemed as willing to talk as I was. I wondered if she was someone else who thought I was courting with Gavin.

'A fine, green one,' I promised. 'We'll get the cold over early, and have daffodils in January.'

She turned her head at that and smiled. 'You're an optimist.' She paused to swap hands with her shopping bags, and I took the chance to look at her properly. Yes, the resemblance to Nate was marked, the high, bony nose and sharp cheekbones, the fine, dark hair, though hers was shiny with conditioner, not greasy like Nate's – but then, she didn't work in the kitchen all day. She was wearing off-duty clothes, slim, dark jeans and a pine-green jumper with a round collar. With the plain jacket, they gave an impression of school uniform, a prefect from S6. All she needed was the blazer badge. Then I looked at her face, and the impression blurred. There were strain-wrinkles under her eyes, with dark curves beneath them, and lines running down from nostrils to mouth. Her fresh complexion was greyed under the powder. It was natural that she'd have been kept awake by police activity on the night Annette died, but she looked as if she hadn't slept last night either. Our eyes met, and I just had time to register the fear in hers before she dipped her head away. She took a quick breath, and found a conversation-making tone: 'How are you finding college?'

'Strange,' I admitted. 'Being cheek by jowl with the same people for so long.'

Her head turned quickly, mouth open. 'I'd a thought you'd be used to that. You're gone all over the world on sailing boats.'

'But that's different. You're out in the open air, not shut up in a classroom. And most of the people on the tall ships were paying passengers, on board for a week or two, so you knew you only had to stand even the most annoying ones until Friday.'

'What about annoying crew?'

'I summed them up as soon as possible, and put them on another watch.'

She nodded, smiling. Her breath was coming more evenly now, her college lecturer poise restored. 'And you're older than the most o' the students. Does that mak it harder, or easier?'

'A bit o' both, I suppose. And my mercy, some of them seem so young. We were told twice that we'd be working on the fuel system yesterday, but my partner still came in asking what we were doing.' I slanted a look from the corner of my eye, and decided to stick my neck out. 'That was an awful thing, yesterday, up at your house.'

'Dreadful.' She swapped her bags round again. The grey fur was trying to slither out. She tucked it back in, gave me a quick, sideways look. 'I don't actually live there now, I have a flat over that way – ' she tilted her chin towards Port Arthur, – '– but there was a funeral apo' Fair Isle, and the south mainland minister had a dose o' the flu, so Dad said he'd go and take it for him, and I said I'd come and keep Mam company. She doesna keep well, so we don't like to leave her on her own.'

'Oh,' I said, 'I thought Nate lived wi' your folk.'

She ducked her head away from me so that the hood hid her face. 'Ye.' Her voice was constricted. 'But he's a boy. You ken. Mam prefers Dad or me.' Was it Nate she had wanted to talk to me about? Her head came up again. Her voice gained confidence. 'So I checked it was fine wi' Lawrence and left his tea in the oven. I arrived about six, and made tea for Mam and me, then we just watched a film all evening. One o' the old ones, Cary Grant with two poisoning aunts at Hallowe'en. I thought it was right stupid, wi' the actors mugging all over the place, but Mam enjoyed it.'

Gavin could have asked her for this level of detail, but there was no reason she should give it to me. I nodded and waited.

'Nate came in sometime through it, an stuck his head round the door to say hello.' We had reached the sea front now, with the benches. She paused, put her bags on a bench for a moment while she did up her jacket, then picked them up again. The wind blew cold from the pebble shoreline. Down at the water's edge, a scurry of sandpipers dodged the waves. 'After that we just sat and chatted until it was bedtime – Mam's bedtime, that was just after ten. I helped her to bed. There'd have been water running, the curtains closed, all that. If poor Annette knocked at our door then, I never heard her.'

How we re-write the dead, I thought. *Poor Annette ...* Alive, Annette would have looked down on Rachel, with her schoolgirl jersey and her smooth hair pulled back in a bun. *So cool, not.*

'I sat by Mam's bed, chatting for a bit. Once she was sleeping I was just about to come home when I heard the folk outside.' Her tone sounded casual, but I remembered the shadow watching me from behind the window blind. 'I couldn't believe it, the police on the doorstep. Then they cleared back a bit, and I saw poor Annette.' A shudder ran through her. 'Lying there. It's awful, isn't it? That it should happen here, in Shetland, makes it worse somehow ... and her poor folk.'

'How about Nate?' I asked.

Rachel's head swung round to me. Was it just the cold that had drawn the colour from her fresh complexion, leaving the wind-sting scarlet of her cheeks like lipstick circles on a china doll? Her eyes were afraid, as if she couldn't bear to face the question, though she'd invited it. I realised I was older than her by three or four years, and pressed that advantage. 'Might he have heard Annette at the door?' Except that she hadn't knocked; she'd been dead when she was brought there.

She didn't look at me. 'I don't know what he's said to the police.'

'But that doesn't matter,' I said. 'You can only say what you saw and heard.'

'I'd have heard the front door opening – I'd have wondered who was coming in so late.' *And you did hear it*, I thought to myself.

'But you didn't look to see who it was,' I murmured.

Panic flared in her again. 'I would never look at Nate's visitors,' she said vehemently, then she turned to me. She flushed again, staring at me with those startled eyes, and catching her underlip with her teeth. She looked each side of us, as if afraid of being overheard, then gripped her shopping tighter. 'That's why I wanted to talk to you – to warn you.' She took a step closer. 'I heard Nate talking about you. If he invites you to his group on Hallowe'en, you don't want to go. You really don't. It's no' your kind o' thing.' She ducked her head away from me, stepped back. 'I have to go. Lawrence doesna like if I'm late.' Her eyes pleaded. 'Dinna tell him I spoke to you. Please.'

I put a hand on her arm, holding her back. 'Rachel, do you have a peat fire?'

The colour drained from her face. For a moment, I thought she was going to faint. Then she shook her head so violently that the hood fell back from her face. 'Mam's all electric.'

'Who are the firelighters for?'

Her breathing was ragged. My face was so close to hers that I could feel the warmth of it on my cheek. Her eyes fell to her shopping bag, with the red and black corner of the box of firelighters protruding from the grey fur. She shook her arm free. 'Lawrence likes a real fire.' Then she turned and scurried off along the Port Arthur road, clutching the bags to her like a shield.

I watched her go. Nate, Rachel. Rachel, Nate. Which of them was Annette's dead hand pointed towards?

James had talked of Rachel's reputation. *Folk said she was a witch. Things used to break around her* ... On the other hand, Nate had been right beside the glass. He could have pushed it, to upset her. I remembered the gloating way he'd spoken to her, the way she'd hurried out, poise shattered. I was beginning to wonder about Nate: Branwell Brontë, the clever one, the talented one, who was going to make his way in the world, but who was now washing dishes in a café. Old Mr Brontë had been a minister too. He hadn't valued his girls much, from what I remembered of the introductions to the novels. It was their aunt who'd been willing to set them up in their own school. *The boy* was the one expected to shine. There was still a good bit of that up here; I could think of half a dozen fathers who doted on their girls, but took their boys in their laps on the tractor seat as soon as they were knee-high to a marlinspike, gave them a little staff for helping with the sheep when they were big enough to fit into a boiler suit, and their own boat as soon as they could swim. How would a boy who'd been the centre of his father's universe take to a little sister who was more successful? Making her believe she was clumsy, *haunted*, would be a clever way of undermining her. I could just see Nate as a boy, dark eyes wide with innocence. 'Rachel just lookit at it, then it fell and broke. I'm faered o' her …'

Rachel had a fire, and access to peats. I wanted to look at the castle. If I was quick, I'd have time before afternoon class.

I turned and strode back along the street. The quickest way would have been through New Smiddy Closs, but I didn't fancy passing the entrance where Annette had lain. Instead I cut up earlier, through Smiddy Close, and past the witch's garden, a tumble of tussocked grass over steps and a rockery, with the remains of a house below. There was the green smell of moss from a grass-choked gutter. Halfway up the hill was a square of low sycamores around a green. A gossiping of starlings swirled around me as I passed the trees. On the other side was a lime green house with darker facings, t-shaped and running into the hill, so that the low roof on Braehead was only just above my head. The hilltop had a house with a stand of trees clustered around an ornamental well. I paused at the corner by Kevin's nan's house to catch my breath and look around me.

To my right, the castle towered against the grey sky, a turret jutting out on each corner, one on the second storey, one on the first. It was L-shaped, and this was the longest wall, an expanse of red-brown stone. The windows had been renewed, in spite of the Great Hall being open to the sky. The lower halves had wooden shutters, the upper were diamond panes: three windows below, two above, and two slit windows in the corner tower, to light the spiral stair. Within, I saw the flash of a camera. The gate was blue-taped. *Police, keep out.*

The new Scalloway museum was opposite me. It was a large, rectangular building. The front corner of the wall was the dark red of Norwegian houses, with a glassed corner where visitors could drink coffee or study records. I was surprised to see Dan and Candy waiting outside. I'd taken it Peter was in Lerwick, at the bank, without looking at the front of the house to see if his car was there. His work at the museum was important, of course, but nobody would have expected him to come in today. Kate needed him more.

I was just crossing the road towards the taped-up gate when he came out. That blind air of yesterday had gone; he walked briskly to the dogs and snapped them loose. He came along towards me, and stopped, the dogs at his heels. 'Hello, Cass. How's Kate doing?'

He was worried about her, I could see that, but the worry lay over something else. He looked as if a heavy weight had been taken off his shoulders. Yesterday's frown had gone, and his back was straightened, his eyes clear.

'She stayed in bed,' I said, 'and got up for some soup. She was talking of an afternoon in her studio.' What was he so relieved about? *She was really worried about something someone wanted her to do*, James had told me. Had Peter suspected she'd been up to something to do with the museum? *It wasn't wrong, exactly* ... Her father would have keys; was that why she'd gone at night, while he was out, to take something from the museum? I remembered him fishing the keys out of his pocket, and his sudden flash of rage. *That boy!*

'Good,' Peter said. 'I didn't mean to be so long. I'll see you tomorrow, Cass.'

He turned and strode away, the dogs following obediently. I watched him go, thinking. *Not wrong, exactly* ... then she hadn't been asked to steal anything. Borrow something, perhaps? She could persuade herself that wasn't wrong, if she was going to return it unharmed. I tried to remember what Magnie has said was in the museum. There was the Oxna bracelet, an elaborate gold chain crafted in Viking times. A young man had found it in the sand, and kept it for a wedding gift for his fiancée. I wondered if Rachel, or Nate, or maybe even both of them working together, had been going to do some sort of exorcism rite with Annette that involved her taking the bracelet. The Shetland Bus items – might they summon one of those men to battle with the long-dead witch?

The simple answer was straight in front of my eyes when I came past the glass-fibre killer whale to the castle's grey-painted gate: a notice saying that if the castle was locked, keys were available from the Scalloway Hotel and the museum. Annette hadn't been working mischief in the museum; the carefree way Peter was striding around the corner proved that. Whatever he suspected, he'd checked, and proved his suspicions groundless. No. She'd simply used his keys to take the key for the castle.

I was just laying my hand on the castle gate when there was a bustle out of sight around the corner, and then the creak of the heavy castle door. A number of officers in uniform came out, with Gavin dwarfed among them. You could see with one look that he was the officer in charge: there was a space around him, and all their heads were turned to his. I remembered that from the first time I'd seen him, that sense of space, like a sea-eagle in its eyrie, lord of all it surveyed, alert and watching over its domain.

'Impossible to tell,' he was saying to Sergeant Peterson. 'SOCO may be able to help, so keep it taped up for now, and take samples.' He looked up and saw me. 'Good afternoon, Cass.'

'I'm just being nosy,' I said, to forestall the question on Sergeant Peterson's brow. 'Was this where Annette's fire was, the one that got her hands covered in peat ash?'

Gavin began strolling away from the castle, motioning me before him on the red chip path. 'There's ash and charred peat in the fireplace of the Great Hall. Unfortunately, a week ago the local school came in medieval costume for a history project. They lit a fire for them, to make the room more cosy, and because the snow's wet it, we can't tell if it was from last night. There are no other signs of activity.'

We came out of the shelter of the castle wall, and the wind swirled into our faces. I turned my collar up against the drifting snowflakes.

'I'd offer you a lift home,' Gavin said, 'but it'd come under "waste of police resources". Sorry.'

I shrugged. 'No problem. It's not far.'

I paused in front of the Chinese to look back at the castle. It was beginning to make sense now. Annette had believed that she was haunted by a long dead witch, and someone – Rachel? Nate? – had persuaded her to a ritual of exorcism in the hall where Black Patie had condemned the witches. All she had to do was steal the castle keys. Then something had gone wrong. Annette had died. And so, to hide what had been going on, the strongest of the exorcisors had carried her body to the Spanish closs, where I'd found it.

No, that didn't work. If Rachel or Nate had been her helper, they wouldn't have brought her body to their doorstep – unless the hatred between them was so strong that each would risk detection to cast suspicion on the other. Maybe ... maybe.

I'd just come round the corner when three dark figures erupted from the little steps down to the pier. They were all taller than me, and before I could protest I was being hustled sideways into the little garden there and pressed against the knobbly mural on the wall.

Three to one. I'd find out what they wanted before I proceeded to violence. I knew the faces pressed close to mine: the hooded crows who had given Annette such a malevolent look on Wednesday. I didn't like them any better close to. Three pairs of black-fringed eyes glared at me. I leaned back against the wall, ignoring the stones that stuck out into my back, controlled my breathing and crossed my arms, as if I was entirely at ease. They couldn't hear my thudding heartbeat. I reminded myself that I was ten years older than them, and didn't need a daft disguise to give me confidence. I let my eyes travel down them then up again, with what I hoped was an expression of total boredom.

The leader was the tallest, and from confident tilt of her head, from the malevolence she radiated, I knew she was the one I had to deal with. My eyes were on a level with her white-powdered chin and dark plum lipstick, but I wasn't going to give her the satisfaction of trying to stand on tiptoe. Her hair was dyed purple, long at the sides, and cut in a ruler-neat fringe two inches above her plucked eyebrows. The combination of white-powdered face and dark line of fringe made it look like she was wearing a mask. She had a long, thin nose and narrow eyes, and mascara made her lashes stick out like the spikes on a sea-scorpion. Her clothes were extraordinary: a grey corset bodice, like a can-can dancer's, with a short scarlet kilt below it, and a frill of black net petticoat. Below it were fishnet tights and heavily buckled motorcycle boots.

The other two were just followers. Both were dumpy beside the leader's mast-slim grace, and even I could see that their uniform of full, short skirts and holed tights didn't suit them. One wore a black leather jacket and spiked dog collar, the other had a sea-green Victorian bodice, low-cut with a frill of lace, like some vampire's prospective victim, and a spider drawn on one cheek. I'd have put their ages at just-left-school. I could out-think and out-run either of them.

I turned my eyes back to the tall one, tilted my chin, gave her back look for look, and spoke in Shetlan. 'What's aa' this aboot?'

'As if you didna ken.' She had a low voice, like the warning growl of an unfriendly dog, and an accent somewhere between Shetland and the south of England, as if she'd had the first years of school on the south coast, then come up here.

'I dinna ken,' I asserted, and waited. Dog-collar moved her foot as if to kick me.

Being 5'2" in the seaports of the world teaches you to react decisively to unwanted attentions. I bent down as fast as if I was tacking my childhood Mirror *Osprey* in a race, and caught her ankle. I lifted it upwards so that she was caught on one leg, and pushed it hard away from me. She staggered, and had to grab at the wall to save herself from falling. I glared at her, and spoke softly. 'Don't try that again.' I turned back to the tall one. 'Well?'

The purple mouth turned down. She gave a snort of contempt, and turned on her followers. 'Back off. I'll give the word.' The narrow eyes came back to me. They were sea-green between the black lashes, and tinged now with curiosity. 'You really spent aa your life at sea?'

'Since I was sixteen.'

'Been to them places where they practise voodoo an all?'

'Haiti. Yeah.' The two followers gave me an uneasy look and edged backwards. I didn't add that the closest I'd come to voodoo was some daft for-tourists show they'd put on for our passengers, all white masks and whirling black rags.

The tall one thrust her face so close to mine that I could smell the powder. 'We don't need your sort around here. We got our own way.'

'I'm not interfering with it,' I said. I still wasn't sure what this was about, but decided to chance my arm. 'Unless you had something to do with Annette's death.'

Her eyes narrowed to slits, her breath hissed out. 'She got what was coming to her. She wasn't special.'

'She had the power,' I said. 'Passed down. She dreamed of how she'd died – before.' I paused for emphasis. 'Your leader thought she had the power.'

I'd struck home. The plum mouth contorted with fury. 'She deceived him.' *Him.* So it was a man we were looking for. The low voice turned sickly sweet. 'All scared smiles, and "Oh, I'm so worried".' The snarl returned, the dog preparing to bite. 'When all the time she was planning to put a stop to us. I could see that, even though he couldn't. He had to be protected from her – ' She broke off, as if she'd said too much.

'Trying to take your place,' I prompted.

But she was wary now. 'I was nowhere near when she died. I had nothing to do with it.'

I remembered my surmises about what Annette had been doing in the castle. 'He held the ritual without you there?' I said, incredulously.

Her anger flared again. 'Like I said, she was worming her way in. Thought she knew everything, just from a few dreams.' She caught at control over herself, and glanced over her shoulder at her followers. 'Right, you've been warned.' She took a step back from me. Her voice sweetened again. 'That's a pretty little cat you have, that follows you everywhere. You wouldn't want him to fall sick.' She turned her head to give her followers a gloating smile.

'Like Annette's dog,' Spider-Cheek added.

Cold fury filled me. Dan had been sick. *We still think it was food poisoning*, Kate had said. He and Candy were friendly dogs, and it would be easy to feed one of them a piece of poisoned meat, when they were loose in the garden. 'You poisoned him,' I said.

Spider-cheek smirked. 'We don't need poison. We got more power than that.'

The leader grew tall. 'We got power over sickness and health, wind and weather.' Her eyes said she believed it. 'You remember that, next time you go out in your boat.'

'So,' Dog-collar chimed in, 'if you want to keep your own little familiar, you better do as we say.'

'Like Annette did.' Spider-cheek made the money gesture again. Was this, I wondered, where her £100 had gone, in paying these grotesques to reverse the spell?

'I don't have any money,' I said. 'You leave my cat alone.' I jerked my head up, gave the leader glare for glare. 'Like I said, I've been in voodoo places. Two can play that game.'

There was silence that seemed to stretch out for ever. I wasn't going to break eye-contact first, not with this woman, and in the end she looked away.

'You keep off our turf,' she said.

She didn't wait for me to reply, but turned on her heel and strode off, her two dumpy followers scuttling after her. Suddenly, I was shaking with reaction. They were a dangerous trio, and I'd been lucky to escape unharmed. *He had to be protected from her* – I was no closer to the name of the leader, but I knew now who his most devoted follower was. She'd been jealous of Annette, that was obvious, and resented the dreams, the connection to those long-dead women, that made the leader interested in her. The way her anger had flared when I spoke of the ritual suggested that she really had been excluded. As Gavin had suspected, it had been just Annette and the leader … unless this girl had intervened, and caused Annette's death. *I was nowhere near when she died. I had nothing to do with it.*

The classic defence of the guilty. I wondered where she'd been that night.

Chapter Nine

The snow showers continued all afternoon, the sky clearing a bit more each time, until by six o'clock the sky was mostly clear, edged with waiting clouds. To the east the moon flared, like a chipped silver penny, and due south Venus blazed alone until the sky had darkened enough to show her company: Orion, with his belt and dagger, the hare nestling at his feet, Taurus with his red eye, and the ghostly cloud of Pleiades.

I'd hurried to college after meeting the three crows, and just made my class. Annette's death was yesterday's story; now my fellow students were full of what they were planning for tomorrow, the Saturday before Hallowe'en.

'I'm going oot guizin,' Kevin told me, as we crouched together over our engine, contemplating the little pump which came next on the fuel system. 'Aroond me freends ida toon.'

I took friends in the Shetland sense of relatives. 'I didn't ken you had family in Lerwick.'

'Me auntie and uncle moved there, so I hae a whole hush o' cousins. Me an me cousin Peter and a couple o' his pals, we're goin to put on fause faces and geeng aroond them aa'.'

'What're you going to dress up as?'

'I'm got an old Up Helly Aa suit of a wizard, that time we did an act about Harry Potter, and Peter's got a monkey suit, and his pals hae animals an aa', so we'll be the wizard Merlin and his performing beasts. We'll do a peerie act at each hoose afore they try to guess us.'

'Sound fun,' I said.

He gave me a sideways look, part curious, part wary. 'You'll likely be busy – I'm no' asking, mind.'

'I will indeed,' I agreed. His face closed against me. 'I'm been asked to judge a Hallowe'en party, round at Aith.'

It wasn't what he'd expected. He sat back on his hookers, eyes on mine, frowning, as if he didn't quite believe me. I added convincing detail. 'It was my pal Magnie, you ken, Magnie o' Strom up at Muckle Roe, that got me roped in for it. The mother o' one o' wir sailing bairns is running it, and he suggested Magnie, and Magnie persuaded the mother

67

I'd do a far better job.' I went into Magnie broad Shetland. 'Du kens, women ken far mair aboot costumes as a man at's spent aa' his life at sea.' Kevin gave a reluctant grin. 'So I got landed wi'it. I'll sail round tomorrow morning, help wi' decorating the hall or laying out the fancies, enjoy the party, sail back by moonlight' and be ready for college on Monday.'

His eyes went wary again. 'You'll be back here for Monday night, then.'

'If the weather's willing,' I agreed. 'Why, is something exciting happening then?' There was nothing obvious in my mind. Tuesday was the feast of All Saints, so I'd need to get to Mass in Lerwick, and Wednesday would be All Souls. My French cousins would be putting bitter-scented chrysanthemums on Papy and Mamy's graves, in the shadow of the eleventh-century church whose pillars sprouted almond-eyed warriors and snarling dragons. I liked to go to Mass then if I could, and pray for Alain, the lover whose death I'd caused. Prayers were all I could do to say how sorry I was. They weren't enough.

It was only when I was back on *Khalida*, making a cup of tea, that I remembered Hallowe'en. All my Shetland childhood, the Hallowe'en party had been the Saturday before All Saints Day, so I'd never really associated it with a particular date. Of course, Monday was the eve of All Hallows. *You'll be back here for Monday night, then ...* Did Kevin really think I was going to join a coven dancing around a bonfire for their big night of the year?

How big a night was it anyway? I switched on my laptop and googled 'witches hallowe'en'. A wardrobeful of costumes leapt up. Witches' festivals got me a page on Wikipedia, which explained the wheel of the year. I read it carefully, then sat back, thinking.

It seemed there were eight pagan festivals, linked to the sun and moon, and celebrating the change of the seasons, one for each change, then a height-of season one. I knew some of the names. The old Shetlanders had a Beltane fire at midsummer, and the young boys of the place had to leap the flames for good luck in the coming year. The witches' Beltane was the start of summer, followed by Lammas, the harvest festival, and then Samhain (pronounced sow-in, Wikipedia added helpfully), the Night of the Dead, around the end of October, considered by Wiccans to be one of the four Greater Sabbats. It could be held on a particular calendar night, or at the night of a full moon. I didn't need a tide-table, with the moon gleaming silver on the water and the waves reaching towards the top of the beach, to know that Monday would also be full moon.

I was just contemplating that one when my phone rang. It was Gavin.

'Shall I bring tea along, or can I lure you out for a meal?'

He'd bought the Chinese yesterday. I couldn't let him pay for me again, and my finances didn't stretch to the Scalloway Hotel. I did a quick calculation of the food aboard. I'd made a double portion of rice in the thermos flask. If I fried extra onions and carrots up with the kidney, and added the meat from the chops, they could stretch to two. 'Tea's just cooking, if you can eat kidneys.'

'Sounds good. How are you going to cook them?'

I hadn't visualised him as one of those fussy men who have to have their meals just so. 'Don't you trust my cooking?'

'I do. I just wanted to have the thought in my head to comfort me as I do paperwork. Remembering what I saw my mother chopping up as I left home is a great encouragement as I fight through the end-of-day Inverness rush hour.'

'Fried,' I said, 'with onions and carrots.'

'Rice or potatoes?'

'On board, rice happens by itself in a flask, with just one boiling of the kettle, while potatoes take twenty minutes of gas and fill the cabin with steam to boot.'

'That will be rice, then. Shall I bring a pudding?' Dash! He was beginning to know my weaknesses.

'I've got apples,' I said, austerely.

I could hear the smile in his voice. 'Something with lemon and cream.'

'Sounds good,' I conceded.

'What time would suit you?'

We fixed on six o'clock. I closed the laptop and began chopping onions and carrots, sliver-thin, as I'd been taught by the Danish chef on board the *Sorlandet*, my first voyage on her – what had been his name, now? It had been only my second voyage aboard a tall ship, and a golden one, with a brisk wind, and all sails set. Just thinking of it reminded me why I was here, at this college, with people who thought I was a witch: to belong under those tiers of white sails, with the great wheel in my hands. I'd have my own cabin aboard, instead of sleeping with the paying crew in the long row of berths that had to be tidied away by eleven. I'd be part of the dinners around the captain's mess, and the conferences at sea, to plan course and set watches.

I didn't see how Jimmy could think I was a witch. I went to Mass every Sunday, rain or wind, leaving *Khalida* at quarter to nine, and striding out up the hill. Sometimes I got a lift straight away; other times I had to walk a third, half, two thirds of the six miles to Lerwick before someone stopped to ask where I was off to. Maybe Scalloway gossip didn't spread the way it did in the country. Everyone in Brae would have known I went to church.

Maybe he heard only what he wanted to hear. It was nearly a century since women had fought their way to the vote, yet you still heard contemptuous jokes about blondes, or women drivers. Men still called women 'dear', and talked about 'girls', without meaning to be patronising, then complained we didn't have a sense of humour when we objected. In their heads, nothing had changed. Maybe they still felt threatened by a woman who was visibly doing fine without them, who didn't bow to their own idea that they were lords of the universe, and covered their uneasiness by deciding there was something wrong with her: a witch, a lesbian.

I scowled in the direction of Scalloway. Even the witches had to have a male leader, Nate or some other shadowy figure ... my hand stilled on my chopping knife. They didn't have to. If there was a coven of witches in Scalloway – or, I added in the PC part of my mind, peaceably practising Wiccans celebrating the turn of the seasons – there was nothing to stop them all being female. Maybe Rachel compensated for having to make Lawrence's tea on time by sneaking out at night to lead the ceremony to the mother earth goddess, along with all the other women whose days were set rigidly to a husband's timetable.

Just before six my phone bleeped. The text read *V sorry slower be along by half past. Normal for policeman. G*

Normal for sailors 2 kidneys not yet on stove. I turned the onions off so they wouldn't overcook, then spent the half hour re-stowing the sails in the forepeak. I'd be sailing tomorrow. Excitement bubbled up in me just at the thought of casting off these ropes that chained *Khalida* to her berth. We'd feel the wind again, and the swell of the sea. I refused to watch the clock for any man. Gavin arrived sometime about the time he'd said, after I'd finished laying the geneker out on deck, ready to hoist in the morning, and while I was busy re-coiling the rope to its furler. I saw him striding along the sea-front as soon as he'd passed the last building, the shed after the one where the government had done some kind of top-secret experiment in the fifties – heavy water, according to Magnie. Naturally it hadn't been top-secret in Shetland. I waited until he'd reached the dinghy slip before I went to the gate. 'Aye aye.'

'Halo leat, Cass.' *Hello to you.* He had a carrier bag in one hand, with a pudding-style box distending it, but no bottle; still on duty.

I'd had a shot at reviving the Gaelic that had been spoken all around me in my childhood Christmases in Dublin, with my dad's Mam and Da, and all my Irish cousins, particularly my tearaway contemporaries, Sean and Seamus, who'd led me into all sorts of trouble. Irish Gaelic was slightly less close to Scottish than Danish was to Norwegian, but I reckoned we'd communicate in time. 'Conas atá tú?' *How are you?*

'A long day.' He closed the gate behind him. 'But good news at the end of it for your friends.'

I paused by *Khalida*'s guard rail, looking at him enquiringly. He nodded and came past me in a swing of pleats, then turned in the cockpit. 'Annette died of natural causes.'

'Oh!' Gladness welled up through me. This was good indeed: no news coverage or press intrusion for Kate and Peter, no long trial, no constantly re-living how their child had met her death. I motioned him into the cabin. 'A heart attack? But she was so young!'

'Not exactly.' He sat down in his usual place, leaving the far end of the cabin free for me to manoeuvre round the cooker. 'The cause was a spasm the body goes into when someone else comes up suddenly and places their hands around the person's neck. It's a sort of shock. Death's unusual, but not unknown. We'll still be investigating the full circumstances, but we can release the body to the family now, and let their grieving go on.'

'So she died of fright?' I remembered what James had said of her phobia about having her neck touched. Had someone known that?

'The pathologist was more complicated than that. Essentially, yes. Whoever killed her probably didn't mean to. The Procurator Fiscal wants the story cleared up, but it's a case for the local force now.'

A rush of disappointment swept over me. It was an effort to keep my voice casual. 'So you're going home?'

His dark lashes flicked up, then veiled his eyes. His answer was as careless. 'I thought I might stay on for the weekend. There's no sense in carrying the paperwork home.'

To occupy my hands, I took down the lantern I'd blown out while I was on deck, and began to open it. I was just framing a casual invitation to join me in tomorrow's sail when there was a disturbance on the pontoon: a clang at the gate, followed by the stomping kerfuffle of a number of feet on the pontoon, and children's voices from above us.

'There aren't any lights on. She's not there after all.'

'She's a *witch*,' said a very young voice. 'I told you. She'll be flying her broomstick.' Across the table, Gavin frowned, his eyes flying to my face: *What are you not telling me?* His level brows rose, and his lips echoed, 'A witch?'

'She's not a witch,' said what had to be the voice's big sister, impatiently. I knew that voice: it was Shaela, one of my sailors from the summer in Brae.

'Mam wouldn't have let us come if she was,' said another girl. She didn't sound totally sure.

'Anyway, she's not in,' Shaela said. 'There's no light.'

'Sssshhh!' someone scolded. 'I saw her come in.' I couldn't recognise the whisper, but the sound was familiar.

'It's guizers,' I explained to Gavin. 'Children in fancy dress. I'll bring them aboard.'

I called, 'Aye aye' as I came up the companionway, so they knew who I was, and swung onto the pontoon. 'Were you looking for me?'

The moon cast a cold, clear light over the five strange shapes, two at waist-height, two just below my size, and a taller one at the back, an adult crouching down. That made sense; they wouldn't have been able to get on the pontoon without a key.

'Come aboard,' I invited them. They nodded solemnly, then filed after me to *Khalida*. Not speaking was part of the game; we had to guess who they were. Gavin moved to the heads space as they came in, head bent under the wooden lintel, kilt bright against the white paint. Squeezed in, the visitors were sinister, with their masked faces turning silently from Gavin to me. It took me straight back to my own childhood. Inga and her brother Martin and I had gone round the houses like this, in costumes made from our parents' old clothes. I'd taken one of Maman's dresses after she'd gone, and ruined it dodging in ditches. She'd never come back to notice.

I lit the lantern to see the guizers better. There was a collective gasp as the candlelight flickered gold over *Khalida*'s wooden walls, the bookshelves, the brass fish medallion. I could hear them forcing themselves not to ask questions. The witch with a green face and a black bin-bag gown looked the right height for Shaela. Beside her was a very small ghost with two eye-holes cut in a sheet, then a soldier in khaki with one of those black balaclavas, and a pink sparkling fairy with a Venetian carnival mask. Last in was a scarecrow with a blue mask under a battered hat, and straw sticking out of the ends of his jacket. He was the tall one, knees bent in the baggy breeks to give an impression of a child. The eyes glittered at me in the candlelight. The fairy crept closer to the witch, and took her hand.

'Shaela,' I said, looking at the witch, 'and your peerie sister.' I nodded at the fairy. 'I canna mind your name.' They took their masks off. 'I heard you speaking on the pontoon,' I explained, and turned to the others, trying to remember who Shaela's best pal had been. She'd usually sailed with a dark girl called Dorothy, but I would spoil their fun if I guessed too easily. I looked at the scarecrow, and named another sailor at random. 'Dawn?'

He shook his head, triumphantly. I turned my head to the soldier.

'Francesca?' A headshake, and a stifled giggle. 'Are you Dorothy, then?'

She nodded, and took the balaclava off. She'd painted her face khaki, so it still wasn't easy to recognise her. Now, did Dorothy have a sister? I looked at the ghost. 'And her peerie sis – ' He was shaking his head before I'd finished the word. 'Brother,' I substituted.

He nodded and untangled himself from the sheet. Now I had four faces turned to me expectantly, with that air of suppressed glee which suggested I was going to have difficulty guessing the scarecrow. I looked at him carefully. *Khalida*'s headroom was nearly six foot, and I reckoned that if he stood up straight he would be not much below the ceiling. I asked Shaela, 'Is he someone I know?'

She nodded and giggled.

'Does he come sailing?'

The scarecrow shook his head. 'He's too old!' Dorothy's little brother said, and they all giggled again.

'Does he live in Brae?' Shaken heads. 'Lerwick?' The heads shook again. 'Here in Scalloway?' Everyone nodded.

I looked at the scarecrow again. Kevin had talked about going guizing. 'Kevin?'

The battered hat shook so hard it almost fell off. The gloved hands grabbed it. I tried to think of the other members of my class. 'Jimmy? John?'

'He doesn't go to the college.' Shaela put the emphasis on the 'go'.

'He doesn't go,' I said, thinking, 'but is he there anyway?'

Shaela gave the scarecrow a guilty look. He stood up to his full height, and I saw the black hair edging the blue mask. 'Nate,' I said.

'He's my cousin,' Shaela said.

Nate unmasked, and looked around with interest. 'So this is what it's like aboard. I like all the wood. What would happen if you had a fire?'

I indicated the two fire extinguishers. 'And there's a fire blanket too.' I wasn't going to tell him the truth: between wood inside and fibreglass outside, she'd go up like a torch, and heaven help anyone who didn't get out of her within thirty seconds. I didn't like the way his mind worked – but maybe he'd just had kitchen safety drilled into him. *Annette had dreamed of being hustled up the burn with her arms tied, and everyone laughing and jeering, and the smell of peat reek filling her mouth ...*

'Well,' I said, looking round. The next bit was that I had to give them sweets or money. 'I wasn't expecting guizers, so there isn't a sweetie aboard, but have a ginger nut.' I unscrewed the biscuit tub and passed it round. 'Are you collecting?'

I didn't like this, Nate here, aboard, looking round at where I kept things. I fished in my jacket pocket for my purse and found two pound coins. 'Here.'

The small ghost tucked it solemnly in a black leather bag hung around his neck, like an old-fashioned ticket-collector's satchel. 'Thank you.'

Gavin had opened his sporran at the same moment, and passed over a five-pound note. 'Do you buy sweets with it?'

The small ghost was so busy staring at his kilt that Dorothy had to answer for him. 'It's for fireworks, for bonfire night.'

I remembered our other Hallowe'en ploy. 'Are you going kale-casting tonight?'

All the heads shook. 'Tomorrow.' Shaela grinned. 'We'll do it properly, wi' peats, but the older bairns have got eggs.'

'My big sister said,' Dorothy added. 'They bought a whole box of boxes from Tesco. They're all going out, the whole class.'

'Secrets,' Nate warned them.

'We used to kale-cast round Brae, wi' kale,' I said. Kale was a form of cabbage, dark green and so tough you had to boil it for twenty minutes before you could chew it. 'We had to steal it from Magnie's rig first, and he'd wait up with his shotgun.' That had been part of the fun, trying to be so quiet that he never spotted us, to loose off a volley of shots in the air.

The little ghost's eyes went round. 'Did he ever shoot you?'

I shook my head. 'We were very, very quiet. Then we'd take the kale and throw a few leaves in each porch, guttery roots and all, until we ran out. We'd save the gutteriest one for Magnie's house on the way home, and he'd send his sheepdog, Bess, after us.'

She'd never have hurt a soul, but she'd circle round us, as if we were sheep to round up. There was always one of us who got frogmarched into the house. Magnie's mam, Jessie, would shove a bucket of hot water at the unfortunate, and stand over them, arms folded, while they scrubbed the porch floor.

Shaela said to her little sister, 'You see? I telt you Cass is no' a witch.'

The sister set her lip stubbornly. 'There are witches in Scalloway, though. We learned all about them in school.'

'That's a long time ago,' I said. 'There aren't any now.'

I could see she didn't believe me. Her glance went up to Nate, as if checking what she could tell, then back to me. She took refuge in past facts. 'They used to burn them. There's a circle up on the hill that's all ash, right down.'

'No any more,' Dorothy said. 'Jim o' Shalders' Ayre ploughed it over. He said it was a superstition and a shame, and the women were poor folk who deserved a better burial.'

'But they still meet up there,' the sister insisted. 'You have to pass an ordeal to join, and they'll maybe consider me when I'm older.'

Behind her, Nate made an abrupt movement, as if he wanted to stop her. His eyes flicked to me, then away; he put his mask back on. 'Time to go, bairns.' There was a collective 'Awww'. The little ghost was looking longingly at my bed, running back under the cockpit.

'If your shoes are clean,' I told him, 'you can try it.'

'Quickly,' Dorothy said.

He didn't need a second telling. He dived into the space and cuddled himself down comfortably, head on my pillow, then rolled over on to his back and contemplated the ceiling. 'You can hear the water.'

'It's level with your ear.'

'Cool,' he pronounced.

Shaela began to put her sister's mask and hat back on. Nate made a movement as if he wanted them to file past him, but there wasn't room. He would have to go first. He went up the steps and out into the cockpit, then over the guard wires. Shaela and her peerie sister followed him.

The small ghost climbed out of the bunk. 'It's in the new museum,' he said.

'What is?'

'Ash from the fire.' The breath stilled in my lungs as if he'd punched me. He stomped up the steps like Peerie Charlie, one foot at a time. 'We went to visit it, wi' wir class, and there was a cauldron there, filled with ash from the witches, an a picter o' where they used to burn them. Up there.' He pointed vaguely out from *Khalida*'s cockpit, and explained, with small boy blood-thirstiness, 'They used loads o' peats and burnt them and burnt them till there wis only ash left.'

I came up the steps after him to make sure he got over the guard rail, and watched as the little party set off along the pontoon and out of the gate. Nate locked it behind them. I wasn't sure I liked the idea of him having a key. I'd get the padlock out for when I left the boat.

Ash ... you have to pass an ordeal to join ... I turned back to Gavin. He looked as if his thoughts were running the same way. *Not wrong exactly ...* to take some of the ash from the museum, ash that held the bones of long-dead witches. Someone had been going to exorcize her demons by trying to call up those ghosts, and her task had been to take her father's keys and get it.

I told him about James' visit last night, and my lucky bluffing with the three crows as I fried the meat, and we talked it over as we ate.

'There's plenty of talk in Scalloway about what goes on up the Gallow Hill,' Gavin said. 'If she'd been involved in a ritual, it could have included a "devil" appearing. If that person had "materialised" behind

75

her and put its hands round her neck, that could have caused her seizure. Then the perpetrators took fright and decided to get her body away from the castle.'

'But why to the Spanish closs?' The tender lamb had cooked beautifully, making a rich sauce with the onion juice. Cat's yellow eyes were round with hope, but I wasn't going to feed him from the table; he'd get the pan scrapings with his supper.

'Someone who knew Rachel's reputation, and wanted to implicate her.'

'Or Nate. The three crows talked about a *him*.' I frowned. 'Kevin's nan only saw one person. If there had been more, surely they'd have moved the body together, pretending she was drunk.'

'Perhaps one was keeping lookout. Perhaps they were trying to take the body to a car, only you came along before they could get it there, so they ditched it in the closs. I know the pointing arm looked posed, but it could just have flopped like that.'

'If the intention was to accuse Rachel or Nate, does that mean they weren't involved?'

'I'd usually say so, but that young man thinks he's too clever by half. I can see him thinking that kind of double bluff was a smart idea, to mislead us.'

'Or both of them could have been involved,' I said, thinking it through, 'one the main celebrant, who ran when Annette collapsed, leaving the person dressed as the demon with the body. So that person carried the body to their house to get them involved again, as revenge.'

'A witches' ritual – especially the sort of thing I think we'd be dealing with here, based on ideas from fiction and the internet – would normally involve several people.' Gavin made a face. 'Perhaps the leader told his followers to get back home and act normally, establish an alibi, while he moved the body away from the castle.'

I shook my head. 'You should have seen how mad those girls were, at the suggestion *he*'d done the ritual without them. I'd bet my last mooring rope they weren't there. And that the person Kevin's nan saw was the leader.'

Gavin's face was grim. 'Playing with power isn't good for anyone. If they'd been following the Dennis Wheatley version of Satanism, this man would have a band of devoted women at his beck and call. He provides the thrills, they give the adoration. He'd be thinking himself above the law. This girl who died so suddenly was expendable.'

This picture of a ruthless leader sent a cold shudder up my spine. But … *who was he?*

The pudding turned out to be lemon soufflé in little glass dishes, and it was delicious. After it, I offered coffee, but Gavin shook his head. 'I've planned an early night. I'd take tea, if you have it.'

I fished the teapot out from the bottom of the locker behind the cooker, and set the kettle on to boil. Once I'd set the mugs out, there was one of those awkward silences. We broke it together, with 'How's –' I made a you-first gesture.

'How's Anders?' he asked. His tone was casual. I gave him a quick look, but there was no sign of the complacent male in possession asking after a defeated rival.

'Threatening to come over,' I said. 'His shoulder's healed fine, he's had to go back to work and he wants some excitement. How's your brother?'

'Kenny's very pleased with himself. His ram took first prize at the local agricultural show, and other sheep took various rosettes, and the calf of his favourite Highland cow, Morag, she took the trophy for her class. Now he's sitting at night poring over grant forms to re-seed more land, so he can expand the herd. Mother's encouraging him. She likes the kye.' He leaned his russet head back against the fiddle of the shelf where I kept my cruising books, and yawned. 'Excuse me.'

'Have you been working solid these two days?'

He shook his head. 'That's a myth. When there's nothing to be served by overtime, they don't spend the money. But I was in my B&B, thinking.' He turned his head to look straight at me. 'What's this about you being a witch?'

'I haven't the least idea,' I said. 'Really I haven't. Jimmy, at college, was going on about it today – well, hinting, that I'd be busy on Monday, Hallowe'en. I can't think why. Surely the world's got past the idea that a woman living on her own, with a cat for company, is bound to be a witch.' Even as I said it, I knew it wasn't true.

Gavin shook his head. 'You would be surprised. Look at the rumours about Rachel.' His eyes flicked to the locks at the cabin washboards. 'You'll leave yourself an easily opened exit forward? I didn't like the way that young man's mind was running on fires.'

'I didn't like it myself,' I admitted.

'Could you move to a berth on the other side of the town?'

'It wouldn't help. All these marina gates are designed only to keep honest folk out. The number of times I've gone around the Brae gate because I've left my key on board and gone off from the pontoon in a rescue boat. If he wanted to get in to create mischief, he would.' I tilted my chin up. 'If he tries to set fire to my *Khalida*, I'll make him sorry.'

'I've managed to avoid arresting you so far,' Gavin said.

'I'll do it when you're not looking,' I promised.

He shook his head. 'Can you limit the damage to throwing him into the water?'

'He's a good deal bigger than me,' I pointed out, 'so I can't promise.' I paused, then asked, diffidently, not sure if this was confidential, 'Do you see him as your head wizard?'

He hesitated before answering. 'He's an intelligent man who's in a dead-end job, and ripe for mischief. I can see him enjoying creating his own universe where he's the lynch-pin. On the other hand, he's too obvious. His hair, his clothes, his manner, everything about him stands out. The men like that that I've come across hug their secret life to themselves, and become more ordinary in their everyday one.'

'Like James Leask.'

'Yes. Though I did think Nate Halcrow had that sense of superiority – it flashed out now and then while we were interviewing him. He could be, that's the most definite I can say.'

I let the silence last. It was strange to be alone together in *Khaldia*'s little cabin. Our elbows were almost touching across the mahogany table; his head was tipped back against the bookshelf, showing the long line of throat running down to his broad shoulders, his forearm strong under the blue shirt. A conventional man, for our age, still wearing a shirt, rather than a relaxed long-sleeved T-shirt under his tweed jacket, but the kilt itself was unconventional, even in Scotland. It had become wedding dress, Tartan Army dress, rather than the simple woven plaid of its origins. Traditional was a better word for him, someone who had a strong sense of the story of his community. He'd told me once that he'd worn the kilt all his childhood, and hated it; their mother had insisted that his great-grandfather's great-grandfather had died at Culloden for the right to wear the plaid. One year of wearing uniform trousers in the police had convinced him the kilt was warmer and more practical. His russet hair, the colour of a stag's ruff, was cut slightly long, and curled slightly – not as much as mine, which turned into a wiry mass round my head if I released it from its usual plait.

He turned his head, and our eyes met. His were the grey of a stormy sea, with dark lashes – like Alain's, I'd thought with a shock the first time I'd seen him, that sea-grey, wide-opened below level brows. They were good eyes, looking at me straight, and the warmth in them had my heart pounding with mixed longing and nervousness. I wanted to turn my hand and lay it on his, but wasn't sure how he'd react, wasn't sure if I was ready for that. The moment seemed to last a long time, just looking at each other, until I broke it by looking away. I hoped it was too dim, in the gold lamp light, for him to see the colour in my cheeks. The corners of his eyes crinkled as he smiled. 'So, what's happening tomorrow?'

'Tomorrow?' I echoed.

'When I arrived you were working on deck, and lit up like a bairn on Christmas Eve.'

I felt my heart pound again just thinking about it. 'A day on the water – we're going round to Aith, for their Hallowe'en Party.' It was twenty-eight nautical miles away, seven hours' sailing. We – *Khalida* and I – would start at first light, and be there before dark. Magnie had offered to come and fetch me, in his ancient mustard-coloured Fiat, but I wasn't going by road when I had my tough little boat with her sails bent on, and a good forecast. For this weekend, the Fair Isle weather station promised a southerly wind, force 3-4, backing on Sunday to a northerly, which was perfect; we'd have a wind behind us both ways. 'Would you have time to come?'

I regretted the invitation as soon as it was out. To ask him aboard for a long sail, in my own *Khalida*, was inviting him into my private world. But he answered as if it was the most natural thing in the world.

'I have a cartload of paperwork to do. When do you plan to get back?'

'I'll come by moonlight, after the party's over, and be back here for Mass.'

'That should give me time, on Sunday.'

We agreed on him coming to the marina at eight, to hoist sails. We'd have breakfast once we were under way. After I'd seen him to the gate, I'd walked slowly back to *Khalida*, watching him walk along the promenade in bars of orange light and shadow. Out of your sphere, Cass … yet putting himself within reach, without grabbing. Most men of our age would have felt entitled to grab … I didn't want that, but I didn't know if I was ready to reach out to him either. *A eligible parti*, Maman had pronounced him, *who will not wait for ever*. 'What's for you won't go by you,' I muttered to myself, and brushed my teeth with extra energy on deck in the moonlight, while the kettle boiled for my hot water bottle.

It was a glorious night. The orange streetlights along the promenade were dimmed by the silver globe of the moon, and the water gleamed milky-radiant, notched by the dark cones of the navigation bouys showing the path into Scalloway. The moon was almost due south now. To the north, the sky was midnight blue, with the stars blazing white: the bent-handled saucepan of the Plough, the long curved tail of the Dragon around the Pole Star. Hercules brandished his club above the Gallow Hill. A brighter star shone steadily just above the eastern horizon: Jupiter, king of the planets.

Just looking at the stars reminded me of nights at the wheel of the tall ship *Sorlandet* in the middle of the ocean, where the stars were company and pathway. When the light of the seven stars in the Plough had left them, Drake had been sailing around the world. The three stars of Orion's belt were even further away; that light had been travelling across space since the building of the pyramids. The dog at his feet, Sirius, was the Egyptian s' calendar. The second star of his dagger was the Orion nebula, where new stars were being flung into space. If anything could turn me into a romantic, the stars would.

At the end of the promenade Gavin turned to look back. One hand lifted; I waved my toothbrush back at him. Then he blended into the shadow of the buildings around King Olav's slipway, and was gone. I went below, and to my berth, and, eventually, to sleep.

cloor (n): a claw *a cat's cloors* (v): to scratch or claw
'Dinna touch him, he'll cloor dee.'

Chapter Ten

Saturday 29th October

Low Water Scalloway 02:10 BST 0.6m
High Water 08:24 1.6 m
Low Water 14:22 0.6m
High Water 20:35 1.6m
Moon waxing gibbous

Moonset 05:30, 281 degrees

Sunrise 08:17
Moonrise 16:18, 75 degrees
Sunset 17:20

I woke at first light, and stretched up to look at the day. It had clouded over again, the white sky blotched with clouds like grey and white fish scales. The biting cold had gone; it was a pleasant October day, a bit brisk for standing about, but perfect for going for a sail. There was even a warmth of sun on the wooden pontoon.

I dressed in thermals and mid-layer, set the engine running, put my life-jacket on, and went out to take off the mainsail cover and cast off all but one mooring rope. Gavin arrived bang on time, in his older green kilt, and what looked like hand-knitted socks. The little dagger in the top of one had a workmanlike wooden handle. He had a brown leather binoculars case around his neck, a large and a small carrier bag in one hand, and an olive-green waterproof jacket in the other. I suspected the bulge in the pocket might be one of those Sherlock Holmes caps.

'You look like you're going stalking,' I said.

He handed in the larger carrier bag. 'My best clothes for tonight. As to the stalking, my grandfather taught me to creep up to within fifty yards of even the most suspicious stag.' He brandished the remaining carrier bag. 'My grandmother taught me the fishing. Can I trail a darrow from your boat?'

'If the fish can swim fast enough to catch us.' I put the good clothes bag down below in my berth and took the smaller from him as he climbed aboard. 'Lifejacket.' I passed over the spare. He put it on without fuss as I slipped the last line and backed us out of the berth. Out in the channel, we were motoring straight into the wind, so I gave Gavin the helm and headed forward to haul the mainsail up. The rope was smooth under my fingers, hauling evenly, with the mainsail cars in their groove rattling up the mast. I tightened the luff with the winch, and tidied the halyard away, then straightened up, one hand on the mast, swaying to the feel of *Khalida* surging forward through the channel, the water curling white at her forefoot. To port lay the north end of the island of Trondra. A scatter of houses lay along the shore, the history of Shetland: two traditional Shetland houses, low and long, as the Norsemen had built them, with the house, byre, and barn all in a line, then an eighties bungalow, built with the crofter grants when oil came to Shetland, then a timber kit-house of the last decade's settled prosperity. Now, as the recession hit even here, each new edition of the *Shetland Times* brought another story of cuts: home helps, free music tuition, the pensioners' Christmas bonus, all being slashed in a desperate attempt to keep within budget and take no more from Shetland's oil-revenue rainy day fund. These wooden houses would be the last new-builds until prosperity returned.

Half a mile on, the middle channel to the west was open before us. I indicated it with my arm to Gavin, and he nodded, and turned *Khalida*'s nose to it. The boom fell over to starboard with a clank and rattle of mainsheet block; the mainsail filled. Gavin hauled it in, and jammed the sheet. I came along the tilted deck and unwound the jib lead from its cleat. The sail came free from its roll on the forestay with a flap, then tamed to a curve as I sheeted it in. *Khalida* surged ahead under the power she was built for, breasting the long Atlantic swell. I put the engine lever to neutral, and saw the surprise in Gavin's face as the pressure on the helm disappeared. He moved it towards him slightly, then away, as if he was checking nothing was broken. I smiled.

'She was built for sailing. She hates the engine. Now you'll hardly need to steer her.' At sea, once the sails were set right, I simply hooked a light chain over the tiller to keep it steady, and she could go for miles without a hand on the helm, letting me doze on the seats, or go below for a hot drink or a meal.

I switched the engine off, and there was only the shooosh of water curling under her forefoot, the creak as the wind eased momentarily then took up again. Gavin sighed, and sat down, cradling the helm in one hand. 'That's like home.'

I hadn't thought of his home being as free of traffic background, as filled with natural noises as my own, though I should have; he'd told me that he lived at the head of a sealoch, thirty miles from the nearest town. 'What do you hear, at your house?'

'The hens in the courtyard, and the kye in the field. The wind rustling in the birch trees, pretending to be the sea. The waves on the beach on a calm day. A skylark up above.' He smiled. 'Kenny tinkering with his tractor, or Mother listening to Radio nan Gàidheal.' He turned his head away from me and said, so casually that at first I wasn't sure I'd heard right, 'I was wondering if you might like to come and spend Christmas with us.'

I hadn't expected this. We had been moving towards each other so gradually. His face was still turned away, but his chest rose and fell more quickly, as if asking had been an effort. I leant back against the guard rail, taking long breaths of the sea air. The sun shone on my face and dazzled on the dancing water.

He shot a glance across at me, then returned his eyes to the horizon. 'Think about it. There's no hurry.'

I thought about it. It was a dozen years since my last family Christmas in Dublin. I'd kept going to Granny Bridget and Da Patrick and all the aunts and uncles and cousins for three years after I'd run away from home, until my plump Granny Bridget died, and then Da Patrick, not long after: 'He couldn't manage without her,' Auntie Bernadette had told me. I'd thought, aged nineteen, that soon I'd know how it felt to love someone so much that you gave up without them. I hadn't loved Alain that much. I'd felt I was being stifled. Maybe I was too independent. Maybe half-love was the best I could do.

Uncle Patrick and Auntie Teresa had taken on the family Christmas, but I hadn't gone. It wouldn't have been the same. I'd spent Christmas on some tall ship overwintering in the Caribbean, surrounded by strangers, until two years ago. That was the first winter I'd had *Khalida,* and I'd stayed in that marina in the Med, avoiding the relentlessly cheery turkey and trimmings meal and celebrating a day of not teaching spoiled teenagers. Last year I'd volunteered for the Christmas Day shift at the restaurant in Bergen, and spent the evening alone, until Anders had called in for a Christmas dram, and taken me up to his family. I hadn't thought about this year, with Dad and Maman's reconciliation. If they were together, it would be good to be with them … except that maybe this was my chance to love properly, to be part of a different family. I'd spoken to Kenny, when Gavin was out, or taking longer than usual to come downstairs. I could imagine their phone from the sounds around as we talked: an old-fashioned black one fixed in one corner of the hall, with pots and pans noises echoing from the kitchen, and a sheepdog padding in and out through the open door. Kenny seemed encouraging, as if he thought I'd be a good thing. His voice was like Gavin's, with the soft Highland 'sss', but he spoke more hesitantly, as if he was translating in his head as he talked. I'd like to meet Kenny. I hadn't spoken to their mother, who didn't answer the phone in case she had to speak the English, Gavin had said. I was uncertain about her; my Irish Gaelic wouldn't survive a rattle of Scots Gaelic, and nobody was ever good enough for a son –

Gavin's sea-grey eyes flicked back at my face. 'Mother speaks reasonable English, from watching the English TV. She just doesn't like speaking it on the phone. Kenny's fluent.'

There was something unnerving about the way he could read my thoughts, yet something reassuring too, as if I'd come to the end of running away, and I had just to turn and be myself. 'I've spoken to Kenny,' I said.

'So you have,' he agreed. 'You could have fun reviving your Irish Gaelic, to add to your other languages. Where were they from, your Irish grandparents?'

'Munster,' I said. 'Da Patrick was more used to the city, he had a building firm in Dublin, but Granny Bridget was a farm girl all her days. All her sayings were farm ones.' I could hear her voice in my head. *Everyone is sociable till a cow invades his garden. It's a bad hen that does not scratch for herself.* I scratched for myself, Granny, I told her in my head, and look where it got me, nearly thirty and with a boat for my love. *There are no unmixed blessings in life,* I heard her reply.

'Then we're cousins,' Gavin said. He tried letting the mainsail out a little, inched it back in, eyes steady on the fluttering ribbons. 'The Munster Gaelic is the closest to the west of Scotland Gaelic.'

I knew that. I'd looked it up on Wikipedia, wondering if I'd be able to talk to him in his own language. Tongues mattered. Maman had always spoken to me in French, Dad spoke English, Anders and I used Norwegian as our private language. Here in Shetland I had fallen back into the Shetlandic I'd used as a bairn, playing around the beach with Inga and Martin. Maybe I had too many tongues on land to know who I was there. This was my language, the swell and fall of the sea, and the creak of *Khalida*'s rig, and the sun dazzling white on the sails.

Christmas was a fair way away. I'd think about it.

Cat came up out of the cabin, nose stretched forward, paws on the step between the washboards, as if he was trying to remember what this was like, then, cautiously, he came out into the sun, crouched in a corner of the seat and curved his plumed tail round his front paws. He kept his head up, looking around. Gavin fished the darrow out of the carrier bag, leant over to ease the hooks and lead into the water, then began to unroll it, one-handed, wrist twisting in a figure-of-eight motion. The green line stretched behind *Khalida* in a shallow diagonal, still visible for several metres beneath the water. It was late for mackerel, but we might be lucky.

I leant back against the guard rail to enjoy the day. To the south and ahead were a scatter of green islands, named by long-gone Viking settlers: Burra, Papa, Oxna. The grassy hump of the Green Holm was a cable below us, shining emerald in the sun, as if it was summer still, and with a cluster of black cormorants, like badly rolled umbrellas stuck into the green grass. The tide was as high as it could go, so the smaller isle in front of it was underwater, along with the rocks marked by the north cardinal bouy coming up ahead of us, a yellow cone with two upward pointing black arrows at its tip. I looked at Gavin, and nodded my chin at it.

'There,' I said, 'that north cardinal. The clear water's above it, bear away a little.' I eased the sheet as he pushed the tiller away, and re-cleated it, then eased the jib. The diagonal of the fishing line veered away from us, then came back in line. *Khalida* slowed a little and rolled to the waves from her stern.

I turned my head for a last look at Scalloway. From this angle it was a Scottish East Coast fishing village, with the long street facing the sea, and the scatter of grey roofs among the browning sycamores. Past it, the sky was dominated by the five wind turbines on the hill. That was my Dad's solution to Shetland's recession: to erect a great chain of turbines, twice the size of these, on the peat hills in the central and west mainland. The electricity generated would be transported down to mainland Scotland by cable, and sold for between ten and fifteen million pounds a year. The council had embraced this fairy godmother with enthusiasm, and sent it straight to the Scottish Energy Minister for rubber-stamping, but now Dad's firm, Shetland Eco-Energy, was running into opposition. A good number of local people were unhappy, particularly the ones who would be living surrounded by turbines, and wildlife organizations like the John Muir Trust and the RSPB had come out against the plan. They'd had to down the number of turbines due to regulations about the nearness to houses, and objections from Scatsta, the oil terminal's airport. Figures of carbon dioxide offset and revenue seemed to vary with each press release. The substation and cable that the idea depended on was put back by five years. Now the main local opposition group had announced that they were going to seek a judicial review, to force the local planning enquiry that the council had side-stepped. Dad had been tight-lipped about it all last time I'd spoken to him.

What I minded most was the effect this was all having on the community. Getting on well with the neighbours you lived so close to was ingrained in Shetlanders, so people talked about contentious issues only within groups they knew shared their view. Now there was a windfarm supporters' group as well, and letters to the paper came mostly from the secretaries of the pro- and anti- groups, but within communities feelings ran too high, and people who'd been friends were now wary of each other. My friend Inga was one of the opposition group's officials, and we just didn't talk about it at all, even though I wasn't sure how I felt. Given I was a visitor who planned to sail away when my college course was ended, I wasn't sure I deserved a vote. I could see the financial advantages, assuming Dad's firm had done their sums right, and more importantly, I could see how Shetland, with its plentiful wind, could help the planet, if the most positive of the carbon dioxide sums were done right.

Against it, our moors were so beautiful, even in this dying season. I turned my head to the Gallow Hill. To eyes used to the changing blues and greys of sea and sky, it was a tapestry of rich autumn colours: the hill was a warm rose, the chocolate brown heather hazed over with dying pink grass stems. A burnt orange patch was the last bog asphodel flowers, a damp area overlaid with spagnum moss was coloured lime and pomegranate ruby. A drystone dyke bisected the hill, straight as if it had been drawn by a ruler. Parallel to it, a burn ran down to the pale sand beach, a twisting thread of green, with the flash of white where it tumbled over rocks. The water at the shore was overlaid with olive-rust seaweed.

Between me and the shore stretched the dancing water. I let out a long breath I hadn't realised I'd been holding. Ah, it was good to be in my element again. I let my body feel the movement of the boat on the water: the hesitation before the wave at her stern took her, then the rise as it came under, the surge as she slid along its back, then the fall as it slipped away from under her and rolled ahead towards the open sea which lay dazzling to the horizon. If I set *Khalida*'s nose to it, our next landfall would be the toe of Greenland, then America, two thousand miles of tumbling grey rollers away. I glanced at Gavin from under my lashes, wondering how he'd take being kidnapped on a voyage to America. Maybe he'd like it. Maybe he wanted a girlfriend who'd do surprising things. *Maybe he wanted me ...*

The north cardinal slid closer. I reached below for the chart and held it in front of Gavin, indicating where we were. A good skipper didn't take the wheel from the crew for the interesting bits. 'Once we're past this then it's a straight run through these islands.' I glanced at the log. Its electronic numerals read 4.2; a reasonable speed for this following wind, but we'd make better time soon. 'Then your course is a straight 270 degrees.'

Gavin glanced at *Khalida*'s compass and nodded. We came around the cardinal, then he set *Khalida*'s nose between the scatter of little islands. I tightened the sheets as she came up into the wind; she heeled to it, and the numbers on her log rose: 4.5, 4.9, 5.1, 5.3, 5.5. Now the water peeled back from her prow in a gurgle and froosh of curled water, and the white nylon curved taut from the spars. Our wake was arrow-straight behind us. Gavin's brown hand was steady on the tiller, his eyes narrowed at the horizon.

Langa came first, to starboard, two low, green islands joined by a strip of pale gold sand, and flanked by two rows of circular salmon cages. I could see the glitter and flash of fish jumping. Papa, the priests' isle, was almost opposite it, a bigger island with the ruins of grey walls and dykes on the green western end, and sheep still on the hill scattald of the rest of the island. People had lived there until the twentieth century, when life on the mainland became easier than life on an isle, and the car took over from the boat as transport. Hascosay, opposite it, had a house still, and a landing place. It was a summer cottage for a family who didn't mind carting water from the burn and using a generator for electricity.

As we came along the top of Papa, the island changed. To the east, there had been pebble beaches in sheltered bays. Now, on the side exposed to the force of the Atlantic, the soil had been washed clean from the rocks, leaving the grey mountain bones bare to the snatching sea. I glanced back at Scalloway, out of sight now, with the Gallow Hill protecting it, looked forward, then back again in a double-take. I was certain I'd seen something move right on the point of the hill, where the burning site had been. I reached into the spy-glasses holder just inside the cabin, and did a slow sweep along the top of the hill. Yes, there! A figure appeared briefly on the horizon, then blended into the hill again. Now I looked there were four, moving over the hill, converging towards the summit. They were all wearing camouflage colours, green or brown, and without the binoculars I'd have difficulty in picking them out. They were moving slowly between the twisting green line that showed the course of the burn and the straight dyke that bisected the hill, and there was something stealthy about the movements, a quietly determined progression towards the burning site. I focused on one of the figures. He or she was walking slowly, then stopping, bending down, and picking something up. There seemed to be a bundle under one arm. It was too far away to tell what, but I wondered if it was dry heather, to kindle a fire. *Sacrifices* ...

I tried to remember when you picked heather berries. The memory was a summer one, August, when Inga, Martin, and I had searched among the heather stems – not this late, I wouldn't have thought, with school back and the evenings spent between homework and early-bed-with-school-tomorrow, but there might have been some left, or those thin-stemmed brown fungi growing among the heather tussocks. Magic mushrooms, maybe.

Gavin let his darrow trail from the cleat, and lifted his own binoculars. 'Might they be bird people counting nests now the summer is over?'

It was a nice explanation, but I could see he didn't believe it, and neither did I. As I looked, one of the little figures straightened and turned to gaze seawards. It was looking straight at us. An arm came up to point. I covered the lenses of the glasses so that they wouldn't flash, and lowered them. 'They're looking at us.'

I turned my back to the hill, feeling absurdly vulnerable. A high-powered rifle could pick us off at this distance … but there was no reason why anyone should goshooting at us, and none of the little figures had carried a metal stick. All the same, I was glad *Khalida* was carrying us away from them. 'Do you suppose,' I said, carefully casual, 'that it was the witches preparing their bonfire for Hallowe'en?'

'It's not against the law,' Gavin said. He frowned across at me, the policeman hat gathering on his brow. 'You wouldn't consider staying in Aith until Tuesday? Or visiting Brae?'

I was afraid of the power of the elements, of storms at sea, of falling overboard in the clawing waves. I wasn't going to be afraid of some land fancy. I tilted my chin. 'They're not going to scare me away.'

Gavin nodded, as if he hadn't expected anything different.

'You can tell one of your police friends to keep an eye on the marina,' I conceded. 'Any sign of any fish on that line?'

'We're going too fast.' He began hauling it in. Cat stretched his neck, interested, and Gavin put out a hand to fend him off the hooks, without looking at him, as if he had to do this to the farmyard cat at home every time he wound up a line. I looked ahead at the friendly sea horizon, at the islands coming closer.

'Keep to port,' I said, indicating on the chart. 'There's a bristling of rocks on the Hildasay side, see, and only that one, tucked round the corner, on the Cheynies. See, the outermost rocks are almost in the middle of the channel.' They were dead ahead, almost awash with the high tide, but with a warning of white crests around them. 'I'll go make a cup of tea.'

It was good to be below in my little cabin, with the rattle of the water echoing around me. Cat followed me down and curled up in my bunk, remembering where the swell would bother him least. I buttered rolls and watched the islands slip slowly by as the bacon crisped and the kettle boiled. I wrote up the log, spun the dividers over the chart to see how far we'd come, and made two mugs of hot chocolate, put bacon in four rolls and took them up. Suddenly, as Gavin balanced his second bacon roll on the wooden thwart, without caring about a plate, and ate the first without taking his hand from the helm or his eyes from the horizon, I knew I needn't have worried. It was going to be a happy day.

We took hour tricks with the helm. When it was my turn to sit aft with the tiller, Gavin slipped his fishing line over the stern again and settled on the other side of the boat, eyes ahead, one brown hand dangling the line that made a V-arrow in the water. The ribbons on his socks fluttered in the wind. He moved about the boat as soft-footed as a cat, and didn't chat or fidget, just relaxed as if being on water was as much a part of his life as it was of mine. We sped over towards the rugged point of Skelda Ness, the bottom point of the triangle-shaped westside, then continued until we were half a mile off. In two hours we'd be off the red cliffs of Watsness, with the swell from the last windy days bouncing back to make it an unsettled place for a little boat. As it was, some of the long Atlantic rollers were as high as *Khalida*'s cabin – but it was so peaceful out there, with only the suck and curl of waves breaking, the occasional crackle of voices on the radio, the creak of *Khalida*'s spars as she leant to the wind. At one point a kittiwake came down from the cliffs to glide above us, then landed on the water and settled there, chin tucked in, black beady eyes watching us. In the air he could outpace us without even trying.

We made good time, with the wind on the beam. We were passing Vaila's square watchtower by eleven, and came through the Papa Stour channel on the last of the east-bound stream. There, in the curve of St Magnus Bay, we hove to. From being heeled over, with the waves rushing past, suddenly *Khalida* was bobbing gently among them, her sails set against each other.

'Now,' Gavin said. He paid out his line again, brows intent, then smiled at me over his shoulder. 'There. Have you a bucket?'

Already? I whisked below for a bucket, and by the time I brought it up Cat was darting a paw at a flapping mackerel, tiger-striped green, black, and silver. Gavin fished in his pocket for a little implement like a wooden truncheon, and gave it an efficient tap on the head. Another two writhed on the hooks in the water.

'Wow,' I said.

He looked up, smiling. 'I've impressed you at last.'

'You were lucky. You can't see a shoal of mackerel underwater.'

'Very true.' He drew out the knife from his sock, and turned the wooden handle towards me. It was thin-bladed, and lethally sharp, a

90

fisherman's knife. It was just as well *Khalida* was private property. 'Would you prefer them filleted?'

It was I who was on test now, but Granny Bridget's mother had followed the herring as a gutter girl. I cut the heads off, scraped the guts into the water, and gave Cat the tail ends to get him out of the way.

We had grilled mackerel sprinkled with oatmeal for lunch, Cat too, and an apple each. I'd just thrown my core overboard when Gavin stretched his hand over to my arm. 'Look.'

A great bird had flown up from the cliffs of Little Bousta, and was coming towards us, filling the sky. The huge wings seemed too long for the body between, and the flight feathers were spread like fingers. It came closer, closer, on one long glide, gave two slow flaps of its wings then rose higher. Its underfeathers were speckled with white, but the sun turned the rest of its body to bronze and gleamed gold on the clenched claws. It was huge. I reckoned each of those clawed feet would be the size of my hand.

'An erne,' Gavin breathed. His eyes were like a child's on Christmas morning.

The sea eagle spread its wings to glide downwards, reached out those claws, and grabbed a fish from the water, then flapped upwards, the fish twisting in its grasp, and flew back to the cliffs. Gavin raised his binoculars to follow it. 'Could it be nesting here?'

I realised I'd been holding my breath. I let it out in a long rush. 'I haven't seen a nest mentioned in the paper, but there's been one flying about these last weeks. A Norwegian one, they said, from the colours of the rings, not one of the Scottish releases.' The last Shetland sea eagle had been shot over sixty years ago, in a deliberate act of extermination. Now man was trying to restore what he'd destroyed, in a reintroduction of young Norwegian eagles all up the Scottish east coast. In time, they'd make their way back to Shetland, and once more these magnificent birds would be common on our cliffs.

Gavin passed me his binoculars. They were very good ones, I realised as I raised them to my eyes, the instrument of a serious nature-watcher. The bird had landed on a ledge of the cliff. I could see the yellow foot holding the fish, the hooked beak tearing the still-flapping creature. It lifted its head to look around as it ate.

I handed the binoculars back. We looked at each other and smiled, and I was tempted to say yes to Christmas there and then. Except that I'd be a stranger, and if it didn't work it would be too awkward, and would he expect me to sleep with him?

I leaned over and released the jib, letting *Khalida* free again. We were in my sailing territory now. I'd grown up here; the red cliffs of Muckle

Roe ahead on port, the green island of Vementry to starboard, were the gateway to my home waters.

The sky had been clouding over through the morning. Now the sun slipped behind the clouds and the rain came back. *Khalida* heeled to the stronger wind until her lee side touched the water, and waves washed the cabin windows. Cat disappeared to wash his whiskers properly in the safety of my bunk. I rolled part of the jib away, and *Khalida* came upright once more. The raindrops pitter-pattered on the sails before we felt their touch on our faces and bare fingers. The white clouds darkened to grey, the water gathered on the white fibreglass deck and ran in the hollow along the gunwales. Gavin hauled on his green oilskin jacket. I'd been right about the bulge in the pocket; it was a green deerstalker that looked as if it might have belonged to his grandfather. There were several salmon flies stuck in the band. I felt positively modern in my scarlet Helly Hansen.

By the time we reached Vementry, with the twenty-foot barrels of its World War I guns still projecting against the sky, visibility was down to half a mile, and Papa Stour behind us was lost in grey mist. It didn't matter; I could see the heather hills of Muckle Roe, still tinged with purple, on our left, and the white water around the Coo's Head rocks on our right. The entrance to Aith Voe was opening before us now, with the little cottage of Skeattelie half way up the hill. Another damp hour, solaced by drinking chocolate, and we were around the point, dodging the sea-serpent mussel floats which seemed to have doubled in the two months I'd been away. Home was Brae, up to the left; we turned down to the right and into the 'white city', the Brae name for Aith.

The population of Aith was only three hundred people, but its central location on the west side had given it the junior high school, attended by all the west side teenagers, with the attendent leisure centre. Now the JHS was fighting for its survival against the council's wish to centralise education – money again. It was the station for Shetland's west lifeboat; the high orange flying bridge jutted up above its massive pier. The buildings behind it included the red-roofed leisure centre, with a swimming pool and hot showers (I hoped it would still be open when we arrived), three clusters of housing estates as well as single houses in their own gardens, the old school, now become a charity shop, the church, a garage, and the community shop, housed in the old knitwear factory. Magnie had assured me that the designers of that grey, rectangular box went on to create Sydney Opera House. I wasn't sure I believed him.

I checked the number in the Shetland Marinas Guide and called to book a berth. The number turned out to be one of Magnie's cronies, and he was waiting for us: 'Aye aye, Magnie said you'd be. Now mind there's no starboard bow visible at the entrance, the salmon boys geed wi' the top o't. You can take the end berth on the seaward side. Just leave the gate open when you come up to the pairty.'

The marina here was much smaller than the Brae one I'd lived in all summer, only thirty berths, but well sheltered, with the rock arm cradling the boats from northerly waves rolling down the voe, and the high wall of the leisure centre breaking the south wind. We lowered the sodden sails and covered them loosely, to be dried as soon as the weather would let us, then puttered between the two cans and into the visitor's berth. Gavin stepped ashore with the lines as if he'd been doing it all his life. We secured her with a bow and stern rope and spring, then laid our jackets wet side out under the shelter of the cabin awning, and tumbled below into the cabin. Gavin took off his deerstalker and shook wet drops of hair out of his eyes. 'Did you mention a swimming pool? Have we time?'

It was just after half past four. 'I reckon so,' I agreed.

I put out a saucer of mackerel for Cat, wedged his escape hatch open, and patted my bunk invitingly, stroking him when he jumped up and curled into a ball. He couldn't come to the leisure centre, and I didn't think he'd enjoy the party much either. We dragged our wet jackets on again, took our party clothes and dashed up the road, dodging puddles and slithering in the wet. The roadside grass was sodden, and the gutters were running with water.

The leisure centre was impressive. Each junior high school had one built beside it, with a full-sized games hall, a fitness suite with enough black iron machines to stock any medieval torture chamber, and a swimming pool. This one was slightly shorter than the Brae one I'd used in the summer, three lengths to 50 m, and had a toddler pool and deep hot tub (with waterfall) beside it. There were pots of palm trees and tables for anxious parents to sit at, and a poster-colours mural of fish and seaweed on the end wall. The warmth was blissful. I left Gavin going up and down in a serviceable crawl, and sat in the steam room for five minutes, revelling in the heat, then swam twenty lengths very fast, not looking in his direction. I was breathless by the time I hauled myself out.

We were the only people in the pool, and I was grateful for Gavin's tact. It would have been uncomfortable to have him in the steam room with me, or stopping to chat with only the transparent turquoise water between us, or to be under the shower side by side, when we were both wearing only swimming gear. That would have been more intimate than I was ready for.

I supposed it was the party which made it so quiet, but I wasn't sure of that. There were only a thousand people on the west side, not a lot to sustain a centre like this. It had to cost a packet to run. There was the heated pool, for a start, and the white-uniformed staff. I wondered what would happen to them if the school closed, taking away their main weekday customers. Budgeting was all very well, but in a little place like Aith the school and leisure centre would be the principal employers, not just of teachers and gymnasts, but also of the folk who made ends meet by cleaning for a couple of hours a night. For a job like that, if you had to go to Lerwick to do it, you'd spend your pay in petrol. This little township, with its new housing estate and trim hall and well-stocked shop, wouldn't thrive without its school.

I gave my hair a thorough wash in the Shetland Soap Company's best heather-smelling shampoo to get the smell of chlorine out, wuppled it in a towel, and headed into changing room. There were had hair dryers, fuelled by 20p pieces, and a mirror. After drying my hair, I wriggled myself into my only dress, a black and flowered affair of a material Maman called 'georgette' which clung to my waist and swirled around my ankles. The strappy heeled sandals weren't going on till the very last minute, and I'd splashed out £1.50 on a pair of tights, instead of Maman's no doubt very feminine but horribly uncomfortable stockings and suspenders. I wasn't going to even think which Gavin would prefer.

She'd also insisted on leaving what she called 'maquillage essentiel' with me. I tipped the little pouch open and surveyed the contents. Foundation. I already had a healthy outdoor glow, as much wind burn as sun tan, which let me off the blusher as well. A fine guy I'd look with candy pink spots on my cheeks. I dabbed the brush in the powder, tapped it off as she'd shown me, and swirled it over my freckles. It didn't make any difference to them. The little palette of colours was more daunting. I went for the greys she'd used, and managed to add mascara without stabbing myself in the eye. I finished off with lipstick. I wasn't sure any of it was an improvement, and the bullet-straight scar across my cheek was as visible as ever, but at least Gavin would know I'd tried.

He was waiting in the foyer when I came out. I was glad I'd dressed up, for he looked magnificent in his scarlet kilt. He was wearing a long-haired sporran, in place of his plain leather one, and a black jacket with a double row of square silver buttons. The one at the top was different, round, and slightly larger. He saw me looking, and touched it. 'It's our house heirloom, given to my grandfather's great-grandfather's great-grandfather by Bonnie Prince Charlie himself. I'll tell you the story later.' He offered me his arm. 'Where's your party?'

Chapter Eleven

The Hall was a large building, harled with white chips, and with picture windows in a side extension. Inside, there was cheerful green wallpaper, set off by wooden skirting and halfway trim, and the original wooden ceiling. The photos in the foyer showed it was well used: the Girls' Brigade in a smiling row, a team of carpet bowlers, tables of five-hundred players intent on the cards in their hands, a birthday party, and the top table of a wedding, with silver hearts strung across the back of the stage, and the bride and groom smiling in the middle.

The Hallowe'en and Christmas Party of each village were run by a committee of volunteers, drawn from the parents of children who'd be coming. Aith, Magnie told me, had four sets of parents each year, two who had done it before, and two rookies. A fiendishly thick book with instructions, bills, and ideas from previous years was handed over, and the parents were left to get on with it, supported by their entire family rallying round to help.

Preparations were in full swing. There was the chink of plates and chatter of cheerful voices from the kitchen, and the smell of sausage rolls. Chairs were set out round the perimeter of the hall, and the walls were festooned with black and orange paper chains and cut-out pumpkins. A waist-high devil, complete with pitchfork, was chasing an equally small vampire and up and down the middle of the hall. A man in a knitted toorie cap and grey padded jacket was erecting a keyboard on the green-curtained stage, and a woman in a black eighteenth-century gown, hoop and all, was putting up posters for the corners game: a spook, a skull, a witch, a cat. Up in the rafters hung a badminton net filled with black and orange balloons. Memory rushed back: the balloons falling at the end of the party, and older bairns stamping them in a fusilade of bangs, while the younger ones rushed to rescue as many as they could. I'd been among the stampers, enjoying the balloons expanding to one side until at last I got that satisfying bang.

A young man with dark hair was halfway up a stepladder pinning up an adult-sized skeleton on one side of the proscenium arch. I recognised him, Lawrence Ratter. He worked at the college, on the practical side, something to do with grading fish. If I hadn't known he was a dyed-in-the-wool Shetlander, I'd have guessed he was Scots. He had high cheekbones and that taking-life-earnestly mouth. His flyaway eyebrows were dark over clear blue eyes, and his fine, dark hair flopped from a side parting. There was something imaginative about the cast of his face, as if he was meant to be a writer or a painter rather than a scientist. He wore an ironed white shirt, black trousers, and real shoes. If we'd not been at a party, I'd have guessed he was on his way to a funeral.

That old-fashioned look fitted in with what I'd learned about him from the chats we'd had in passing. He'd come and spoken to me a few times, asking about how I was getting on, and sliding the talk to voyages I'd done. He had an odd way of giving me advice about how to tie up the boat properly for a gale from a particular quarter, as if he couldn't quite believe that a woman could really do anything by herself. I could take it in passing, but if I'd been his wife I'd have thrown china at him until he gave it up.

Lawrence fixed his skeleton, then came down from his step-ladder and up to us. 'Aye aye, Cass. Thanks for coming.'

'You're welcome,' I said, and introduced Gavin.

Lawrence nodded. 'I'm already met the inspector, It's fine to see you here.' His voice was pure Burra. 'Did you come round wi' the yacht? Fine day for it – until the rain came over.'

I nodded. 'Grand. We were in the Rona when the rain set in, so we'd had the best o' the day.'

'Come you and have a cup o' tay, to warm up.'

My stomach liked the idea of a 'chittery bite' after the swim. I ignored it. 'I won't disturb the folk in the kitchen. I just wanted to check on what we have to do.'

'You need Janette for that, me sister. I'm just helping out.' *Ah*. If for some reason your man was elsewhere, then you took along a brother or cousin in his place, to help with the men's tasks: setting out chairs and tables, hanging decorations, and serving drink. Either Janette's man was at sea, or they'd split up. The divorce rate in Shetland was probably lower than down south, but I was still cautious about asking after anyone's partner. It was easy to put your foot in it.

He motioned us into the peerie hall, the side wing of the main room. It was set up with long tables around the edge, each labelled: Nursery – Primary 1-3 – Primary 4&5, with help – Primary 4&5 without help – Primary 5-7, with help – Primary 5-7, without help – Secondary. There were already a few pumpkin lanterns set on the tables, emergency-sail orange, with grinning teeth and slanted eyes. Lawrence gave them a dour look. 'Janette's man's away, so I said I'd step in. I dinna hold wi' encouraging all this witchy gear. It's gettin worse and worse – do you mind, now, when we were bairns, you dressed as all sorts of things, no just vampires and dat. An the neepie lanterns were all sorts too, no just devil faces.'

'I made a UFO,' I reminisced, 'with the apple peeler to cut holes all round it, then I put the round bits on cocktail sticks, and painted it neon colours.'

Gavin nodded. 'I made a stag's head with a particularly long turnip, and branches for antlers. I was very pleased with it.'

'Ye,' Lawrence agreed, 'and I did a Cheshire cat one year, wi' the grin. None o' this witchy nonsense.'

'And it was turnips, too,' I said, 'not pumpkins.' I'd never seen a pumpkin in Britain when I was young, only on market stalls in France in the October holidays. It had been turnips that we'd carved. Dad had scooped the inside out with his clasp knife and a spoon, then I'd carved the face and borrowed the augur from his toolkit to bore the holes for the string handle. I'd choose my costume from a book Maman had, *Jane Asher's Fancy Dress* – I could see the cover of it clear as print in my memory – and then we'd go into Home Furnishing in Lerwick to get the material, and Maman'd make it for me, bringing out her electric sewing maching from the hoover cupboard, and getting me to stand still while she pinned, then sewed, the way her own mother had made her clothes, as a girl on a farm near Poitiers. I'd won several boxes of sweeties which I'd taken home to share with Inga and Martin before Advent arrived, and sweets were banned. Maman had been very fussy about sweets: '*Ils sont mauvais pour les dents.*' It must have worked, because I'd had neither fillings nor a brace, unlike poor Inga, who'd suffered a mouthful of metal all through secondary.

The kitchen seemed full of people. It was a sizeable room, with a stainless steel table down the middle. There was a rank of fridges and freezers along the wall side, and a door leading to backstage; on the other side, below the windows, were a commercial-size gas cooker and a dish-washer like a stainless steel box. There was an assembly line of women around the table, their party dresses protected by pinnies. I could recognise the sandwich fillings at a glance: egg mayonnaise, tuna mayonnaise, cheese and pickle, corned beef and brown sauce. At the far end, a woman with a dark bun was taking a tray of sausage rolls out of one oven, and replacing them with pizza squares. When she lifted her head I recognised Rachel Halcrow. What, I wondered, what she was doing so far out of Scalloway? Three teenage girls dressed as witches were emptying packets of sweets into a cauldron. The work surfaces at the door were covered with filled trays of fancies: cake, chocolate squares, and angel cakes mixed with Hallowe'en specials shaped like spooks, cobwebs, or pumpkins, and iced accordingly. My stomach rumbled in anticipation.

'Janette,' Lawrence said. A younger woman with brown hair pulled back in a pony tail looked around from scooping egg onto buttered bread slices. 'This is Cass and Gavin.'

She dusted the egg off her hands on her pinnie, and came over to us, smiling. 'Thanks very much for coming. It's so hard to get judges, aabody's related to someone.'

'Thanks for asking us,' I replied. 'I'm really nervous. I mind how much work everyone's mams put into the costumes when we were bairns.'

'Some folk still do,' Janette said, 'but I think you'll find the most o' them are bought from Tesco or eBay. Anyroad, you just choose what you like best.' She was one of those people who rattled off instructions without waiting to see if you'd got them. 'There's a prettiest, a funniest, and a most unusual for each age group. You can add a 'special' prize for each class, if there's something good that doesn't fit those.' She handed Gavin a carrier bag of sweetie boxes. 'We got loads, just in case. Then everyone gets a sweetie, these.' She fished out a box of coca cola worm-shaped jellies. 'We do the judging first, then there'll be pass-the-parcel while you look at the lanterns. Those are just a first, second, third for each category. Then we have the lit lantern parade, and you give a first, second, and third for those – and then there'll be another game or two, then supper, before the raffle, if you could present the prizes for that.'

I was glad I remembered the drill for my own young days.

'We're got one o' the teachers to do the games, so just follow along wi' her.' Janette gave a harrassed look at her abandoned loaf of bread.

'We'll do that,' I said, and we went back around to the stage. The woman in eighteeth-century dress was checking through her props and laying them out on a chair: several packets of sweets for prizes, cards for the corners game, three large parcels, lists for 'Bring me', and blindfolds and rolled newspapers for a game I remembered as being very popular, where two contestants tried to whack each other. She looked up and smiled. 'Are you the judges?'

I nodded.

'Good luck,' she said. 'I'd rather do the games any day. They're all so good.' She picked up her radio mike and tapped it. 'I'll announce the age groups, then they go round in a circle until you've made up your mind.'

People were beginning to arrive now. A family-worth of mother, father, granny, grandpa and what looked like an auntie, all in traditional

Shetland knitwear, ushered in a Harry Potter (complete with cloak, glasses, and wand), a spaceman with a neon-green gun, and another vampire. The children rushed straight to their friends in a waft of black cloaks and flying sparks. A toddler had its powder-blue wooly-bear suit peeled off to show an elf costume. It staggered dangerously out into the centre of the hall while its mother gossiped with a friend. Then there was a clump of folk together, a group of young mothers with a miniature Spanish dancer, a Victorian doll with bonnet and ringlets, and a black balaclava terrorist. The boys, I noticed, tended to go for costumes which meant they could run around, shout, and fire guns at people. Inga and Martin's parents were anti-gun, and Martin always took full advantage of the Hallowe'en party to be a cowboy or a commando.

At last, Magnie came in, behind a small boy in a green lizard suit, whose father was carrying a dinosaur head, obviously home-made papier mâché over a wire frame, and painted with what looked like best antifouling. He still had that rolling seamans' gait even after ten years of retirement ashore. His face had been scrubbed till his cheeks were the red of a Snow White apple, his curly fair hair was sleeked back with grease, his chin shone, and the stripes of his Fair Isle gansey were blindingly white. His mother had knitted it for him just before she'd died, and he wore it only for dress occasions. It was a traditional 'all-over', with hoops of pattern in shades of blue on a white ground. He looked up at the stage. I saw him clock Gavin. His eyes narrowed. He paused a moment, considering, then stumped over to the steps, exchanging greetings with half the hall as he came.

'Now then, Cass,' he said. 'I see you're brought an extra helper. Now, boy. How are you keeping?'

'I'm very well,' Gavin said. 'And you?'

Magnie shook his head. 'Keeping out o' trouble. It's fairly quiet up at Brae without Cass.'

'It would be,' Gavin agreed gravely.

Polliteness duty done, Magnie turned to me. 'Well, Cass, are you decided who we're giving the prizes to?'

'Hae a heart,' I said, 'the party's no' begun yet.'

Naturally, it didn't begin on time. Janette popped her head out of the kitchen every couple of minutes to clock the number of people in the hall, and it wasn't until ten to seven that she gave the teacher the nod to officially welcome the folk. By that time I had worse butterflies than I'd have had at the helm of a four-master for the start of a Cutty Sark race. So many children, all dressed to the nines, all hoping for a prize ... I didn't want to disappoint any of them.

The pre-school and nursery group came first. Gavin and I went down onto the hall floor to watch as they walked round in a circle to music. The elf's mother gave him – her? – a sticky-out petals hat, popped her into a flower pot, and carried her round. A painted-face clown in a pompom suit stomped confidently beside an older girl dressed as a witch, with a froosh of grey hair and ragged black robes. He was followed by a miniature Charleston lady with rows of fringes, and a pink fairy with glittering wings. Both of those costumes were boughten, I reckoned. Then there was a soot-black chimney sweep, a chef with a paper salmon on a silver salver, and a vampire with a flour-white face and painted blood streaming down his neck.

'I like that one,' Gavin said. 'He looks just like the old version of Dracula, the silent one. *Nosferatu*.'

I'd never heard of it. I paused for a few seconds to contemplate the idea of Gavin as a film buff. All those long, dark winter nights – 'Shall we put him down for – what, funniest?'

Gavin shook his head. 'He's meant to be scary. We don't want to hurt his feelings.'

'Lawrence was right, you know,' I said. 'I don't think it was quite so witchy when I was young.' I looked up into the rafters. 'The balloons were just ordinary, all colours, not black, and we dressed up as all sorts of things. A good third of these are witches or vampires or such.'

'Concentrate, Cass,' Magnie said. 'Du's ower young to be reminiscing about the days o' dy youth. What are we geeing prizes for?'

'Prettiest. The flapper lady or the little flower – she's cute.'

'An unusual one,' Gavin said. 'The chef with the salmon, or the chimney sweep, both of those are good ideas.'

'The chimney sweep could be funniest,' I suggested.

It took us ages. We settled at last for the flapper as the prettiest, the sweep as the funniest, and the chef as the most unusual, then awarded the extra prize to the vampire, for being the scariest. He beamed at us and gnashed his teeth as he collected the sweeties, and I did an exaggerated jump. The lower primary class included a flowergirl in what looked like a dress she'd been made for an older cousin's wedding; another pink fairy (Harry's toy shop, I reckoned); Spiderman (Tesco); the Victorian doll, now surrounded by her box; and the green lizard wearing his dinosaur head. Being older, they got to walk on their own, and the circle got tighter and tighter, then huddled to a standstill until the teacher swayed down to take someone's hand and open it out again.

It was strange how natural it felt, to be standing side-by-side with Gavin like this, Magnie on my other side. Magnie smelled of Lynx, and Gavin of old-fashioned soap, Imperial leather or something like that, and it felt natural to put my hand on his smooth black shoulder as I leaned up to murmur a comment into his ear. We agreed at last on the Victorian doll, the lizard, and Spiderman, and dodged the feeding frenzy for the jelly worms.

The middle primary class were more influenced by TV and film. There was a Harry Potter group, with Harry, Hermione, a Death Eater, and Dumbledore, a pair of cardboard dominoes with backcombed and sprayed hair that I reckoned would cause a screaming match at bedtime, an old man crofter with boilersuit, staff, and toy dog, and Merida from *Brave* complete with bow and arrows. The biggest children were definitely going for the ghoulish side of Hallowe'en: there was a ghost pierced by a bloody sword, several *Twilight*-style vampires, and the three crones with pointy hats and green faces that I'd seen in the kitchen. It was only when she said 'Thank you' that I recognised Shaela, grinning out from under the green face paint.

After we'd done all the costume prizes, the teacher got them seated in circles, and the keyboard player started up pass the parcel tunes. We judges headed through into the peerie hall and contemplated tables groaning with pumpkins.

'It's no healthy,' Lawrence said, suddenly coming up behind us. He'd put on a squad suit, some sort of grey furry animal. I couldn't see what, as the head was hanging down his back. 'All this stuff about witches and ghouls, it makes evil glamorous.'

I was surprised he was taking it so seriously. I knew that some American fundamentalist churches were keen to ban Hallowe'en, but it had never seemed to be glorifying evil to me. We'd just had fun at the party, and went out kale-casting afterwards. I didn't think it had led any of my classmates to devil-worship. 'It's just a fun,' I said.

Lawrence shook his head. 'It causes trouble.'

'What sort of trouble?' I asked.

He gave me a long look, as if he was trying to judge how much to say. 'Rachel said she'd talked to you.' It was only then that I put this Lawrence together with the man Rachel had mentioned, her boyfriend who didn't like his tea to be late. Yes, I could believe that. Then he added, 'Annette.'

I stared at him. 'What do you mean?'

'She shoulda left this sort of thing alone.' He gave me a stern look. 'Have you talked to James Leask?'

I glanced over at Gavin, over at the Primary 5-7 (without help) table. He and Magnie looked to be discussing the merits of an elaborate lighthouse turnip, complete with red stripes and matchstick railing by its carved steps. 'Talked to him about …?'

'About Annette, of course. What she'd told him. I saw them walking

101

together the night before she died.'

I tried to remember what John had told me. He'd said they'd met at the Scalloway Hotel on the Monday night, but I was pretty sure he hadn't mentioned seeing her since. 'When,' I asked, 'and where?'

'Out along Port Arthur Road,' Lawrence replied. His costume's gloves were dangling from his wrists; he began drawing them on. 'I was late working, and when I came out I passed the pair o' them, walking the water side o' the road.'

The gloves he was drawing on took the breath from me. It felt as though it was suddenly silent in the hall, in spite of the squeals and paper-ripping rustles from the main hall, and the clatter from the kitchen.

'I didna hear what they were talking aboot,' Lawrence said, 'but I could see he was trying to persuade her to something, and she wasn't willing.'

Gavin turned his head then, and I met his eyes and glanced down at Lawrence's hands, then away. Lawrence caught the look. Suspicion flared in his eyes. He turned away, crumpling the half-on glove in his hand, but not before I'd had a good look at it.

We'd talked about someone dressed as a demon. I should have remembered costumes like the one Lawrence was wearing. I'd seen them in a hundred Up Helly Aa squads. I saw again the marks on Annette's neck, clawmarks, as though they'd been made by something gripping round her neck. There, dangling from Lawrence's wrists, were gloves that could have been designed to make a mark just like that – big, spread pads, with straggling fur on the backs of the hands, and at the end of the grey rubber fingers were broad, blunt claws, with a sharp needle-glint at the end of each, as if someone had inserted drawing pins into the fingers. We'd called them *cloors* in Shetlandic. '*Dinna touch wir cat, sho'll cloor dee.*' It had a thin, vicious sound. Great hands to grasp around a throat, cloors to bruise and scratch … was this what had attacked Annette?

Chapter Twelve

I didn't get a chance to talk to Gavin about it then. We presented the neepy lantern prizes from the tables, then there was a pause while each child collected its lantern and parents fumbled for matches. You could tell the smokers by the crowd around them. The teacher didn't try to make them parade this time. Once the lights were out they all stood still, and we dodged around them in the darkness.

My head was full of what I'd just seen: those glinting claws at the end of the hairy fingers. Lawrence said he disapproved of witches. In the dimness of the hall, orange-lit eyes and teeth leered at me. That could be good camouflage for a chief warlock, the upright citizen who was known to be a bit straight-laced about Hallowe'en. Beside me, a pair of slanted eyes had a scar like my own across one cheek, visible only because of the flickering tea light inside. Then there was Lawrence's connection with Rachel. James Leask reckoned she was a witch. But if she was involved, why shift the body to her doorstep, and arrange that pointing hand?

Hang on. I paused to admire a pumpkin cat's face, complete with eyes as round as Cat's, and pipe-cleaner whiskers each side of a huge, toothy grin. I'd taken it for granted Lawrence and Rachel lived together. Next to the Cheshire cat was one with a moon and a dozen little stars – we definitely hadn't given that child a prize yet, which was now one of my awards criteria. Given Lawrence's old-fashioned ways, perhaps she had her own flat. The lighthouse was gorgeous lit, with a small flashing torch inside, we had to give that a prize, even if it already had one. Supposing Rachel wasn't living with him, maybe he didn't know she was over with her mother. Maybe he'd been too busy covering what he was up to to ask where she'd be.

Gavin had almost completed the circuit; his kilted silhouette was only three metres ahead of me. I'd seen Lawrence and Nate together, and there'd been a marked lack of cordiality, given they were to be brothers-in-law. I could see Lawrence's upright work ethic condemning the use Nate had made of his talents and opportunities. *So*, I concluded, as Gavin and I met up, perhaps Lawrence was incriminating Nate without realising he'd involved Rachel too.

I murmured the theory to Gavin while we were sitting on the steps at the front of the stage and waiting, teacup in hand, for the men with filled tay kettles to reach us. Lawrence had sidled towards the other end of the hall, I noticed. The children charged through to the peerie hall to be served with juice and crisps; the occasional 'bang' from a crisp bag filtered through their squeals. All the adults sat in peace around the hall while the workers from the kitchen came around with trays of food, urging us to 'help yourselves'. I balanced two sausage rolls, a slice of pizza, and an egg sandwich on a paper napkin on my knee.

'The grease will go through to your bonny frock,' Magnie observed. He tugged a still-folded handkerchief out of his pocket. 'It's clean.'

I spread it underneath. 'Thanks.' Lawrence had doled out his kettleful of tea and gone back to the kitchen without a glance in our direction. 'So?' I said to Gavin.

He nodded. 'We did interview him, because of his connection with Rachel. I remember being doubtful about whether he knew she was visiting her mother.' He took a bite of pizza without spilling any tomato on his kilt or smearing it on his chin, and chewed and swallowed before continuing. 'He said that he did. My impression was that he hadn't known, but didn't want to admit that. I thought at the time he was just loath to admit he didn't know where his fiancée was, or even that she'd told him and he hadn't been listening, but maybe it was more sinister than that.'

I glanced around. Only Magnie was within earshot. 'And Rachel?'

'She couldn't remember who knew she was there. She supposed she'd have mentioned it to Lawrence – "Why would I not have?" ' He made it sound like Rachel's intonation.

'Because he disapproved of Nate,' I said. 'I remember us sitting chatting in the café once, and Nate coming to take the cups, and I noticed the atmosphere between them. I'd have put them on different watches straight away, if I'd been their captain. He'd have done his best to have her seeing as little of Nate as she could.' I hesitated, and took a cautious bite of sausage roll. I was feeling a bit nervous about the pizza; I wished I hadn't taken the thing, for I knew I'd get tomato on my face. Sausage roll was safe, except for the crumbs.

'We could refresh the two people acting together idea,' Gavin said. 'Rachel as the witch, Lawrence as the clawed demon who frightened Annette to death, and disposed of the body. Rachel would have had time to meet Annette after putting her mother to bed, but in that case, I don't see why she'd have gone back to the Spanish closs, unless your interruption left her only able to dive into the house. Would you eat that pizza if I turned away and talked to Magnie?'

I gave him an indignant look and took a carefully small bite. As I'd expected, a piece of onion instantly fell on the napkin. Gavin laughed.

After the teas there was the dookin' for apples, with the bairns forming long rows at two baby baths filled with water, and coming away with foreheads and fringes dripping, and a scarlet apple held triumphantly in one hand. Then, as a finale, there was the Grand Old Duke of York. The teacher in the eighteenth-century dress came down to take up a toddler, the older children formed pairs, and parents or siblings came out with the younger ones. Gavin held out his hand. 'May I have the honour?'

I curtsied with a swirl of material. His hand was warm as I laid mine in it. The musician struck up a chord and we were in, clapping as each pair danced up and down, following off and joining again to squeeze under the archway of hands. We were both breathless and laughing by the time each pair had had its turn of leading, and when he smiled at me, and released my hand, I wanted to lean against him. If we'd been alone then, we'd have kissed; but we were surrounded by people, and I stepped back, self-conscious, and made a play of watching the roof as the men undid the strings to let the black and orange balloons fall.

I'd counted on the party organisers to get me out of cooking an evening meal, and they didn't let me down. We wandered back to the marina just after nine, most comfortably replete, and with an ice-cream tub of leftover sandwiches and fancies to keep us going for the voyage back to Scalloway, as well as a thank-you bottle of wine. To save embarrassment, I changed back into my sea-going clothes in the ladies as we left. I'd just wriggled into my black Musto mid layer when Rachel came in.

'That all went fine,' she said. 'I'm glad I didna have your job.'

'It was hard!' I agreed. 'I ended up just trying to find someone who hadn't got a prize yet. They were all that keen.'

'You did well,' she said.

'So did the organisers,' I replied. 'The decorations were great, and the food was magnificent.' I indicated my ice-cream tub. 'We'll be eating this all the way back to Scalloway.'

'Oh, are you sailing back tonight?'

'It'll be a bonny night,' I predicted. I hesitated then launched in. 'I'd no' have thought Lawrence would have want to be involved in this kind o' thing.'

'I didn't want to be either,' she said, with feeling. 'I'm had enough o' witches. But Janette's man's at sea, so he felt we should come along instead.'

105

'He got into the spirit of it.' I watched her face in the mirror. 'That was a good costume.'

'The grey werewolf thing?' Her face didn't alter. 'Oh, that's Nate's. I knew Lawrence's squad hadn't done anything in the witchy line.' Suddenly I remembered meeting her outside the shop. She'd had a bag with a grey fur fabric suit in it. So who'd had the suit the night that Annette had died, Lawrence or Nate? It had been the day after Annette's death that I'd seen her.

'It looked good, anyway.' I zipped my black jacket up. 'Thanks for asking us, it's been a fine night.'

'Thanks to you for coming.'

I came out again, feeling more like myself, and found Gavin back in his green kilt and tweed jacket. 'The werewolf suit was Nate's,' I breathed at him as soon as we were safely clear.

'I thought it might be. Ratter wouldn't be one for dressing up in witchy clothes.'

'And I think Nate had it on the night Annette died. I saw Rachel the next day, with the suit in a carrier bag.'

The rain had stopped while we were in the party, and now the night was clear, with the moon turning the water to shining pathway between the black hills. A small, dark lump by the marina gateway expanded as we approached, and gave Cat's almost silent mew. I picked him up and stroked his cold fur. 'I'm sorry,' I said, 'but we brought cake back.'

I'd calculated the times beforehand: the flow at Papa would turn to westwards just before one o' clock, so we needed to leave here no later than ten. We had a cup of tea together in the flickering lamplight, and I allowed Cat a crumb of soft sponge cake with buttercream icing, then we put on our oilskins and went up to cast off. The westerly wind had not yet backed to the northerly that was forecast. We hoisted sail as soon as we'd passed the lifeboat pier, and I took the helm for the brisk reach to the Rona, then we tightened the sails to beat between Muckle Roe and Vementry.

The silence of sailing was good after the noise of the party, the soft curl of the waves around us, and the crash as they fell on the shore to each side, and the creaking of *Khalida*'s rig. A gold rectangle marked Dad's house on Muckle Roe. I should have phoned to tell Maman I was in Aith. It was a Freudian slip, I suspected; I was nervous about her and Gavin meeting. Above us, the stars blazed, with the Milky Way a river of stars whose brightness even the lambent disc of moon couldn't dim, and the occasional meteor from Leo falling in a white rush. I gave Gavin the helm as we came under the Vementry guns, and went below to make hot chocolate, working by touch in the dim light. Then, as we came clear

106

of the Rona and out into the Atlantic, the north sky lightened with a green phospherescence, dripping down from a curve, as though someone had drawn an arch in the sky with a watery paint brush. The distant singing noise in the air was eldritch enough to raise the hairs on the back of my neck.

Gavin's head was tilted towards the light. The green reflected faintly on his nose and cheekbones. 'Is that what I think it is?'

'The mirrie dancers? The aurora, yes.' I pointed above us. 'There's more, see, that misty white patch above us.'

'That's cloud, surely?'

I shook my head. 'Wait, and it'll clear, and reappear somewhere else. And do you hear them singing?'

We watched together, sitting companionably side by side on the up-tilted bench, faces upturned, as the white patch broadened to a zebra river running across the whole sky, shimmering and fading, then disappeared altogether and reappeared as a white light like distant car headlights, or wartime searchlights. It lasted a good half hour, then was gone as suddenly as it came.

I'd never felt like this before. It was the gentleness of the silence, feeling Gavin breathing beside me, his knee, his shoulder, his hand so close to mine that an inch of movement would have had us touching. My breath thudded in my breast to have him such an easy part of my world. He didn't exclaim, or point, or do anything that would have broken the night. We just watched, drank it in together, eyes cast up to the heavens. It was as though we were kneeling together at Mass – and it was like a Mass, with the glory of God's handiwork spread above us. When the light was quenched at last, we both gave a long sigh, as if we'd been holding our breaths, and neither of us spoke. I rose to put the mugs below and check the time, then tacked in a rattle of sheets to set us on our compass course to negotiate Papa Sound: 230 degrees true to the centre of the Holm of Melby, 295 degrees across to the middle of the bay, then 240 degrees to the sea. Subtract six to allow for the difference between true north and magnetic. I reached in for the handheld compass and handed it to Gavin. 'Have you used one of these? You just hold it to eye level. When we get to this island, I need a back-bearing of 120 degrees, looking straight over the stern.'

He nodded, and I fixed my eye on the circular cockpit compass as we turned. 240 – 250 – 290.' I held her steady. 'How am I doing?'

'120 – 125 – 115 –'

'Near enough.' We sailed on for ten minutes across the channel, then I swung her nose over and hauled the sheets tight. The compass swung to 245 degrees. 'This is the important one. I need to keep on a backbearing of 55 degrees on Forwick Holm, that lump of rock there.'

'The Independent Crown Dependency of Forwick,' Gavin surprised me by saying. 'We heard all about him in Inverness. Driving without tax and insurance on the grounds that Shetland had never officially been ceded to Scotland, therefore the UK rules didn't apply because he was driving a consular vehicle.'

'Our Sheriff sorted him,' I said. 'I don't know what century he thought he was living in. Nobody's independent now. How's my bearing?'

'55.'

I let the sails out a touch. 'We're avoiding the Huxter Baas, off that headland, and a couple of rocks off this one.'

'What would you do if you were on your own?'

I stood up, put one leg each side of the tiller, and my hand in compass-viewing position. 'Steer with my knees. And there's the simple ready-reckoner.' I tilted my chin at the white star of Muckle Roe light, five miles behind us. 'We can still see it.'

He laughed, and looked again. 'Spot on.'

Once we were clear of the point Gavin went below, and I heard the chink of metal as he put the kettle on. I held *Khalida* steady on her course until we were half a mile off the dark crouch of land, then turned her nose south once more. The wind was back on the beam. I took the hot chocolate and pizza Gavin offered, gave him the helm, reached a fleece blanket up from below, and curled into it and dozed for the next hour. He woke me at two, and I took over while he went below, without fuss, without comment, and stretched out on the settee, his jacket over him. The moon cast silvery lights and velvet shadows on his lashes and cheekbones.

I left him for two hours; I was used to catnapping, and knew my boat and my waters. We just had to keep pointing south for the next four hours. *Khalida* skimmed on, her sails set so that I needed only to balance my hand on the helm. The stars turned on their great wheel, and the moon followed her circle from just north of east to just north of west. When I went down to put the kettle on again he woke by himself, grey eyes suddenly wide open in the moonlight, then he swung his legs down and pulled his jacket on. I nodded at the log book, open on the table. 'Our course is 130 degrees, straight south-east. Just keep her steady as she goes, this distance off land. You'll see the Vaila light in half an hour, flashing every 8 seconds – red first, then white. That means we're there.' I put a cold finger on the chart. 'Then look out for the red sector of Fugla Ness, there, and aim for it. If the wind falls away completely, stick the engine on. There's plenty of fuel in the tank.' I yawned. 'Don't hesitate to wake me.'

He nodded, and I peeled off my oilskins and boots and slid into my berth. The water rattled at the hull as *Khalida* surged forwards. I was at sea again … I slept.

I woke at ten to six, in a grey dawn light, and wriggled forwards to look out. A headland that looked like Skelda Ness was abeam, and the scattering of islands that guarded Scalloway lay ahead of us. Our wake was still arrow straight on the water behind us, but I could feel our speed had fallen to less than four knots. We were making good enough time; there was no need yet to tear the early morning silence apart with engine noise.

I used the heads, then made us a cup of tea each. Gavin smiled as I put the two mugs through the hatch. 'Good morning.'

He sounded as alert as if he'd had a full night's sleep, but not, praise be, offensively cheery. I took the helm and narrowed my eyes into the greyness ahead. The moon had set, leaving only a faint gleam on the western horizon, and the sun was a pale streak of light along the top of the eastern hills, dimmed by the orange glow of the Scalloway streetlights. I'd put a waypoint in just before the channel through the islands, and I checked our heading to it: spot on. I nodded to Gavin, approving. 'Good course.'

'I have a GPS like yours on our wee boat. It's easy to use.'

He'd told me about their boat, a fibreglass dinghy with a small cuddy, which they used for visiting up and down the loch, and for transporting sheep from one part of the loch to the other. Dead stags were moved by pony.

We threaded our way between the islands, and ghosted into Scalloway harbour. It was light now. On the hill above us, the rain had darkened the heather flowers to auburn, lightened by a pink haze of wiry marsh-grass stems. The peat had taken up as much water as it could. The cut banks were black, and the rain lay in a sheen across the flat surfaces, the greff where years of peats had been cut out, the moor grass between burns.

In front of us, the water was mirror still, the tyres on Blacksness Pier doubling themselves, the image castle stretching downwards against its green hill. On the real hill behind, a hazy cloud rested on the hilltop as if it had got tired of sculling itself along in the sky. I switched the engine on and furled the jib. We putted forwards, a widening ripple vee behind us, while I took down the sails, then I added speed to go around the corner of the breakwater and into the shelter of the marina.

'Wait!' Gavin said suddenly. He lifted his binoculars. I throttled back the engine and let us drift.

He was looking at Burn Beach, the little corner of beach below the street of coloured houses. The tide was washing two feet up the wall below the car park, and there was a dark mass floating in the water ten metres from the shore. Two herring gulls were circling it, taking off from the sea to flap above it, landing for a moment, then taking off to curve round it again.

I put the engine in gear and putted slowly towards it, keeping an eye on the echo-sounder. In this high tide we should have plenty of water, but we'd have longer to wait to be floated off, should we run aground. Four metres – three point five – three – 'I can't go much closer,' I said.

'That's close enough.' His voice was grim. He fished his mobile from his jacket pocket and dialled. 'Macrae here. Can you organise the team to get a boat on the water here in Scalloway, as quickly as possible. There's what looks like a body in the harbour.'

gruli, grulik (n): a masked person, a person in disguise, especially at Hallowe'en

Chapter Thirteen

Sunday 28th October

Low Water Scalloway 01:46 GMT 0.6m
High Water 08:02 1.6 m
Low Water 13:59 0.6m
High Water 20:14 1.7m
Moon waxing gibbous

Moonset 05:47, 290 degrees
Sunrise 07:20
Moonrise 15:32, 67 degrees
Sunset 16:17

We couldn't see who it was. We stood guard for what felt like an hour, waiting five metres away from the dark form that just broke the glass-still water. It was only when the ebbing tide began to move it seawards that we were able to approach.

'We won't try to haul it on board,' Gavin said. 'I don't want to destroy evidence. My team will be here soon enough.' He unclipped the boathook from the cabin roof. I manoeuvred alongside, and Gavin leaned over, hook end of the pole reaching towards the water. He gave a surprised 'Oh!' and reached again, manoeuvering the hook. His arms tensed as they took the weight. He looked back at me and nodded. 'I've got him.'

I reversed us back into deeper water, switched *Khalida*'s engine off, and came to look.

I'd expected a starfish shape of dark arms and legs, but only the back confronted us, clad in a black hoodie, with long hair fanning out from the downwards-bowed head. The arms were drawn forward in some way that we couldn't see. Gavin had hooked the boathook round a serviceable leather belt, the sort that would have a large bronzed buckle on the front. The trousers were dark too, and the legs held together, slanting below the water to a blue rope around the ankles, and pulled down by heavy black boots. My heart felt cold.

'There's a stone below the Smiddy there.' I tilted my head at it. 'They used to leave the witches there at low tide. They'd bind them hand and foot, and wait. If they floated, it was the Devil supporting them, and then they were tried and burnt. If they drowned, it was a sign that they were innocent.'

Gavin nodded.

The dark hair swirled in the last wash from *Khalida*'s propellor, the head turned slightly, and with the movement I knew him. 'It's Nate,' I said. 'Isn't it?'

Gavin nodded again. 'It looks like it could be.' He turned his head to give me a sharp glance. 'Are you okay?'

'I'm fine.' It was a lie, of course, but I had myself under control now. I didn't want to think, couldn't help but think, of Nate being bound like this and put to the witches' test. The water licked *Khalida*'s hull in the silence, and the body swam on its hook beside her, in the middle of a flicking of little fish. The waves curled against the froth-bleached stone of the Smiddy wall.

The police came at last, one of Shetland's chevroned cars turning into the Blackness pier, and the other heading along the Port Arthur road. Presently there was a wreath of blue smoke from the marina. One of the aluminium salmon boats roared towards us. Gavin raised a hand, and it came alongside. Sergeant Peterson was aboard, and a couple of uniformed officers. I took the strain on the boathook, and Gavin climbed aboard the smaller boat, and took charge.

I watched in silence as they lifted Nate from the water and laid him on a polythene shroud. His arms had been bound at the wrists, and there was a gag in his mouth, what looked like a man's handkerchief tied at the back under the dark hood. His eyes were open, peat dark and staring in the white face. The little fish had begun to nibble at his nose and cheeks, scarring the skin as if it had been rubbed by sandpaper. I hoped the undertaker would be able to cover it, for the mother who didn't keep well, for his father, the minister. I didn't suppose that even the religious convictions of a minister would make losing your son any easier. The words from Genesis rang in my head: *You did not deny me your son, your only son.* Abraham sacrificing Isaac. Suddenly I was bone weary.

The salmon boat raced ahead of me to the marina. A white van was waiting in front of the boating club. I watched them trundle Nate to it. The van had headed up the hill towards Lerwick by the time I curved *Khalida* into her berth. It was very still, with no thrumming in the rigging, nor ripples knocking against my head. I wanted to lie down and sleep, sleep. I could have an hour before I needed to leave for Mass. I kicked off my boots, hauled off my outer layers, and collapsed into my berth.

When I woke, my watch said only half past eight, although it was bright daylight outside, and I had a moment of confusion before I remembered the changed hour. This time yesterday had been half past nine. Now we were into the sun's own time, what the old sailors still called Greenwich Mean Time. I splashed cold water on my face, brushed and re-plaited my hair, fed Cat, and was just about to set out when my phone rang. It was Maman.

'Cassandre?'

'*Salut, Maman.*'

She was offering me a lift to Mass, and lunch afterwards. It meant I'd need to leave Cat in the car during Mass, but I accepted, with the proviso that we'd go as late as possible to shorten his ordeal. It didn't worry Maman, who was well-steeped in the Catholic tradition of drifting into Mass as the priest finished the introduction. I kept an eye on the clock, and Cat and I were waiting, ready, for Dad's black Range Rover slide in beside the boating club. I lifted Cat's basket in, and clambered after him.

Maman was in between playing the Rameau equivalent of a fairy godmother in a *son-et-lumiere* production at some Loire château (late September) and the vengeful daughter of a Persian king in a indoor production at an equally magnificent château in the Auvergne (mid December). This meant that she was temporarily normal, instead of taking on the character she was about to sing, so that every small household accident became Greek drama. As normal, that is, as it was possible for her to be; the stage was her habitat, as the sea was mine, and even for Mass in our small church in Lerwick, she was dressed as if the press were lurking at the door: a cream hat with black felt flowers over one temple, a sweeping cream wool coat over a slim black skirt, seamed stockings above heeled black shoes. Her dark hair was parted in the middle, curved to a smooth bun at the nape of her neck, her powdered cheek was flawlessly smooth, her brown eyes darkened and lengthened by a broad line of eyeliner, Callas-style. This last month, she'd changed from burnt scarlet lipstick to frosted pink: 'It is kinder, at my age. And when are you going to start making the most of yourself?'

I regularly dodged the answer to that one. 'I put on make-up last night,' I told her now, 'at a party, with Gavin.'

She nodded approvingly. 'A very *eligible parti* who does not need a conventional wife. And a dress?'

'Your pretty one. It was the children's Hallowe'en party,' I added.

Her pink lips curved. 'So, you build me up, then deflate. Wicked Cassandre.'

I grinned.

'All the same, he is serious, that one.' Her dark eyes flicked a

114

sideways look at me. 'You do not think so?'

'Yes,' I agreed, 'but I'm not sure I am, yet.'

'Oh, you were serious even as a little girl. You thought about something, then decided, and after that you would not be diverted.'

We'd reached the houses now, and I remembered Shaela's talk of eggs. The teenagers had gone to town. There was yellow and white egg smeared everywhere, and the gutters crunched with broken shells. Outside one pair of houses, three men were gathered around their cars. The morning's sun had baked the egg onto the car bonnets, and you could see by the way they looked at it that retribution was being planned.

Past the Meat Co., there was no sign of this morning's find. There were no rubberneckers or police cars at the car park above Burn Beach, and Blackness pier was quiet, with only the occasional person working on a boat propped up with pallets. The tide was still retreating, the brown-pebbled shore giving way to layers of glistening kelp floating at the water's edge. Then I noticed that the boat workers lifted their heads from time to time to look at something to their right, and as we came up the road past Fraser Park I looked back. There were dark figures moving along Burn Beach, heads down, searching what had been the sea bottom.

Maman came round the curved road in a smooth swoop, and began climbing the hill to the quarry. 'But how can you fit him into your career?'

The heather hills here were rust brown. We passed the clay pigeon shooting range that had been made for the Inter-Island Games, littered with orange targets. On our right, the hills opened up to the south. A herd of ponies, red and white, came galloping alonside the fence, manes and tails flying. On our left, the hill with the post was Hollanders' Knowe, where the medieval Scalloway folk had traded eggs and meat for gin with the men of the Dutch herring fleet.

'I don't know,' I said at last. 'I thought I'd worry about it if he asked me.'

'He will ask,' Maman said. She shot a sideways glance at me. 'I thought, with your father, that love would make it possible to be in two places at once. You know how wrong I was.' We passed the Sandy Loch and the mustard-coloured houses that had once been Shetland's weather station, drove alongside the magnificence of Sound's 'Nob Hill' houses, Lerwick's most expensive real estate, then negotiated two of Shetland's four roundabouts, Maman's face set with concentration to cope with cars coming from her wrong side.

'But then,' she said, cheerfully, now that hazard was past, 'you are not me, and your M. Macrae is most assuredly not Dermot.'

She turned up King Harald Street to our church and parked behind the scarlet Range Rover with the gold dragons on the side. I poured Cat some water, set down a dish of catfood, and opened his lid, then we slipped into the church. As I'd suspected, the service hadn't yet begun. Father Mikhail was dressed in his robes, but still greeting the last straggle of Mass-goers. He shook my hand. 'Hello, Cass. What news do you have from the young man who was injured?'

He'd been with us at Voe Show in that awful moment when the bull had charged. 'Back to work,' I said, 'and getting bored. He's threatening to come back to Shetland.'

Maman's dark eyes flicked across at me. I was in for a lecture about making up my mind. She held her hand out to Father Mikhail and he bowed over it. 'Welcome back, madame.'

I usually lurked at the back of the church, but Maman swept me past the cluster of white-surpliced altar-children to the second-front pew, where we'd always gone as a family. We knelt together, her shoulder six inches taller than mine, white coat by navy jacket, dark chignon and dark plait. The marks on the hymnal shelf at my eyes were as they had been when I was a child: a spiral scrawl, a run of varnish in the shape of a feather, eleven jabs of a pen making a rough J. I'd always wondered who that J was. Beside me, Maman's dark lashes swept down over her eyes. I could not tell what her prayers might be now: for her and Dad, for me and Gavin, for that lost baby brother Dad had told me of, little Patrick who had never drawn breath. Or perhaps for her new production, for the homeless, the starving, for prisoners, for world peace. She was a book I was only learning to read.

My prayers were for Nate, and Annette, their parents and Rachel, and then for Gavin, that he would catch the murderer before more damage was done. I was just starting to assemble my wayward thoughts when the bell rang, the keyboard wheezed into life, the guitars strummed, and Mass began. I scrambled to my feet, and Maman rose gracefully beside me, as if she'd calculated to end her prayer at just that moment. A moment more, and her voice floated out in the hymn. When I was little, I'd imagined the angels sang like Maman, that clear soprano that even at its softest could ring across to the carved altar like the note of the ship's bell on a still day, its sweet tone enriched by the softness. When she gave it full volume, in tunes like 'Eternal Father, strong to save' it would ring round the whole church, and I'd fancy the birds in the trees outside stopping their cheeping in astonishment, listening for a moment to this human eagle, then joining her with renewed vigour.

St John was the church's eagle, who soared even to the throne of God in his visions. I wondered about the eagle we'd seen, floating on its great wings over the cliffs. Was it a solitary wanderer, or the harbinger of its species' return to Shetland, coming to spy out the land as the Vikings had come, thirteen hundred years ago? I'd visited the Lerwick school for some assembly once, and all I remembered of it was a wardrobe-sized case of stuffed birds, with the great erne in the middle of them, chestnut feathers and charcoal beak faded by the long incarceration in that glass coffin. It would be wonderful if the clock could be turned back, the sea eagles restored to their nests on the high eyries of Watsness cliffs, Maman and Dad celebrating Christmas together in our house on Muckle Roe –

In the name of the Father and of the Son and of the Holy Spirit ... I finished the prayer I hadn't realised I was making, and focused my mind on the Mass.

We came out in a blaze of stained-glass light, the glorious triptych at the end of the church. I'd called it the oily window when I was little, for its centre was an oilman in his orange overalls receiving communion, and the upper half of the windows showed a rig in a stormy sea and men straining at a pipe. The lower half showed scenes from my childhood: Lerwick, with the old *Saint Clair* ferry at the pier, a woman with a kishie, a man casting peats. Around were the creatures Maman used to encourage me to look for when I got bored, the peewit with its crest, the dinner-suited shalder, the seal on its rock, the Arctic tern.

We came through the knots of English and Polish conversations and back to the car. Cat uncurled his plumed tail and sat up with a welcoming yawn. I tipped his water out into the gutter, and we headed back up the twenty miles to Brae.

It was breath-still. The water of Laxfirth was so smooth that the salmon cages floated on replica black hoops, and each green hill that sloped down to the water sloped back again beneath the pebbled shoreline. Girlsta Loch was filled with grey clouds. Past it, the sheen of water stood on the hill, and a grey ribbon twisted in front of each dark peat bank. A diver sculled on Sand Water, slender beak tilted. Then we drew away from the sea, driving along between two of the three long hills where Dad planned to put his wind turbines. The Kames, they were called, the long spine of Shetland that had once been a part of the Caledonian mountain range around Loch Ness. Draw a line from the Kames and you'd join up with the Great Glen.

'How's Dad doing?' I asked.

Maman made a blowing-out sound. 'He is not. After everything having gone so smoothly, now it is all problems. There is the court case, and the delay on the interconnector, you have heard this?'

'Another five years,' I said.

Maman nodded. 'Five years, and Scotland will be filled with turbines who can produce their electricity much more cheaply than Shetland, with no long cables to pay for. And then – but do not mention this again, it is not public yet – the electricity company who was to be their partner in the business, well, they have just sold off their shares in another windfarm. The Shetland people would not like that, Dermot says. To have a company that is a Shetland one joined with another that is large and well known here, they can live with that. To risk an unknown business suddenly taking almost half of the shares, no.'

'No,' I agreed. I could just hear Magnie: 'What, hae folk fae south able to decide for more turbines or roads and us no be able to stop them? Na, na, bairns. We're no haeing yon.'

'So there would need to be an agreement that the firm would not do this, and Dermot is not sure they will accept such a limitation.'

'But is it possible for it all to be stopped now?' I asked. 'The impression I've got is that the Shetland Islands Council has got the wind behind them. They smell money and jobs.'

'It is not so many jobs,' Maman said. The village of Voe slipped past, its pier curving out into the mirror water, each yacht floating above a double with a mast twice as tall, each hill as green below the tide line as it was above. The freshness of the colours suggested rain to come, and the grey cumulonimbus curled like fleece across the sky. She swept one hand out, palm up. 'I do not know. Tourism, it is becoming important here, and if the windfarm makes the tourists stay away, then there will be jobs lost. Nobody has studied that.' Her mouth twitched downwards. 'I find it hard to agree with Dermot, but I am like you, I am the bird of passage. It is for the people who live here to decide.'

Now we were entering the world of my childhood again, but from land. The chocolate-dark island to my left was Linga, the heather island, and behind it were the hills of Muckle Roe, the big red island where our house was, and the passage from Papa Stour we'd sailed yesterday. Aith was down to our left. The water spread in front of me had been my back garden. I'd tacked my beloved *Osprey* from the pier up to the opening of adventure, the Atlantic rollers, beaching her on the pebble curve below the house. Suddenly, sitting here with Maman, I felt that world surge up again, the constant battle between Maman's wish for me to be a pretty girl and mine to be an adventurer. I asked now, 'Why did you always want me to be a girl? To be pretty, and read books, and play with dolls?'

She shook her head. 'It didn't make any difference what I wanted, you went your own way.'

'But why?' I insisted. 'Why did you think it was better?'

'It is always easier to be conventional.' She wrinkled her nose. 'I was not conventional either. I wanted to sing. Well, you can imagine – a farm

118

girl, in a small village – who did she think she was, they asked. But my mother said that I should have my chance, and she persuaded your Papy to let her save the money from the eggs and the goats' cheese so that I could have lessons with the music teacher in the village. He thought I had talent, and so I went further. Oh, it was hard work, and sometimes I regretted being separated from the other children. A child who has a talent has to sacrifice childhood. I wanted you to belong.'

'What you wanted me to belong to wasn't interesting,' I said. 'The idea of what girls ought to be, with a pretty dress, and playing with dolls. I could see that, even when I was only six. The older girls at the Brownies did craft and fashion shows, while the Boys' Brigade got to go camping.'

'You're a rebel.' She jerked her chin back at Cat and echoed Nate: 'In the olden days, with your independence, and your little cat following you, you would have been burned as a witch.'

'I don't get it, though. Are men so convinced this show is theirs that they can't let us have even a little piece of independence?'

'Yes,' Maman said. 'I think they are all convinced, deep down, and even in spite of their better nature, that they know best, and that a woman's true happiness lies in finding the right one of them to look up to.'

'In spite of nearly a hundred years of voting? In spite of women doing every sort of work?'

'Only seventy years of voting in France,' Maman reminded me. 'That is only yesterday. Every woman over eighty can remember her mother not being allowed to vote.'

They had taken the masts down in the Brae marina. Winter was on its way. We came past Busta House, where we'd staged a ghost to catch a murderer.

'Maman,' I said tentatively. It was easier to talk like this, side by side, with her expressive dark eyes on the road. 'Dad told me you'd lost a baby, my little brother.'

Her head turned quickly towards me. Her face was filled with wary hope. 'Did he indeed say that, that I had lost a baby?'

I shook my head. Her mouth drooped. 'No, I thought he did not. He will not believe – but I will tell you what happened, when we reach the house, and you will know the truth.'

We drove the last mile in silence, along the single track road with the verges overhung with rose-rust heather, and the sea burnished grey below us. Dad had built our house square, grey-harled, with a porch at the back, and great picture windows looking out over the sea. Cat leapt out and went off to investigate what other cats had been in the garden since his last visit, while Maman and I went into the kitchen. She poured us each a glass of *Légende d'automne* and we took it through to the sitting room. The sky was clouding over: rain before nightfall.

'It was my fault,' Maman said. 'It was my first big chance, you know, after I had married your father and come here, I had tried to keep in touch, and I had had little roles here and there, but this was a friend directing, from my days in Lille, and he offered me the role of La Folie in *Platée*. She has this aria – like the Queen of the Night in the *Magic Flute*, a real show-stopper. I could not bear to refuse it.' Her dark eyes held mine. 'You understand that, Cassandre. For you it would be the offer of captaining a four-master.'

I nodded.

'Dermot was against it, because of the baby. We argued. We both became more and more stubborn – you have inherited that from both sides.' Her face stilled; the dark lashes veiled her eyes. 'But he was right. It was too much, and I lost the baby.' Her long hands curved around her belly. 'It was my fault. It was not as your father believed, that I had had him –' the fingers clutched one another '– removed. I would never have done that, and your father should have known, but he was so angry, and grieving, *his boy*, and I was grieving too, but instead of clinging together, we took out our grief on each other, and found consolation apart. Oh, not that sort of consolation! He worked, and I sang. *Platée* was a mad success, and then there were other offers, larger roles, and suddenly every château on the Loire was doing its own son-et-lumière.' Her eyes returned to mine. 'Never do that, Cassandre. If a grief should come, however hard it is, share it.' Her eyes suddenly filled with tears. 'They let me see him, in the hospital. He was so little.'

'Have you tried to explain to Dad?' I asked. 'He might listen now.'

She shook her head. 'We are together again, and he has forgiven. That is enough. It was my fault, as much as he believes, only in a different way. I killed him with my ambition. Even now, when the audience are applauding to raise the roof, I remember what it cost.' Her eyes started straight ahead. 'I would never have thought that I defined myself by my ability to bear a child, but after I lost the baby I felt that I had failed as a woman. I should have nurtured him, mothered him, above all else. It took a long time to get over that. Even now, sometimes, I feel this – ' Her slim hand indicated the dark eyeliner, the smooth cheek. 'All this, is just a mask to make me look like the woman I do not feel I am any more.'

My son, my only son ...

She drained her glass, and rose. 'I have made a chicken. I put some aside, and poached it just a little. Your cat will eat that?'

He ate it with enthusiasm, and sat in the exact centre of the dark green Chinese carpet to wash his whiskers, purring like a jet-ski engine, while we ate at the oval table: chicken in a pot, with leeks and a wine sauce, followed by a Normandy apple tart. I told Maman about the mad people at my college course, and she countered with characters she had met in the world of Sun King music, and we both laughed a lot. As she cleared the plates away, she smiled at me. 'I am very glad to have a daughter.'

'It's good having a mother,' I agreed.

Chapter Fourteen

Maman drove us back to Scalloway just after two. Now the sky had clouded over completely, and the first drops splashed the windscreen as we came through the Kames, singly at first, gathering until the glass was flecked with them, and Maman had to clear them with a single wipe, then, by Tingwall loch, she needed the full sweep, sweep, sweep. The water ran at the roadside, and hissed under the car wheels. We came past the little grass isthmus where law-seekers had walked, in the days of the Norse foudes, to ask for justice. Shetland's oldest document showed a woman taking a high official to court because he was embezzling the rents due to the overlord. Like the witches three centuries later, she lost her case.

On the way, I told Maman of what was happening in Scalloway, and was surprised to find she knew the people. 'You would not remember, but we lived in Scalloway when we were first married, Dermot and I, while our house was being built. I do not know the children, of course, but the parents, yes. The Minister Halcrow and his wife – what was she called now? Maria. She worked in Lerwick, in the Port Authority. He was a good man. Although I was not of his flock, he would call in from time to time, just to say hello, and ask how I was. He liked music. We used to talk of that. A cultivated man, and kindly, to visit a stranger. Maria, now, I have a feeling she was ill. Not in those days, later. Dermot told me. Six years ago, perhaps. The illness when you are suddenly very tired. She had to leave her work, and now I think she needs a wheelchair to go out.'

'Rachel said she didn't like to leave her mam on her own.'

'He was an old-fashioned man, a family man. He was sorry they did not have children.' She smiled. 'Then the little boy came along, and they invited us to the christening. The parents were so proud, and he was very sweet, with big brown eyes, like a French baby. You don't remember? There was tea afterwards, and you ate a huge slice of chocolate cake, and asked me why I never baked in the English way.'

'What about the family dynamics?'

'What can you tell from outside? I think he would have liked a wife who was more traditional, who would have stayed at home, and run the women's guild and the baking circle – but she did that once the children were born. The last time I saw her – oh, it was long ago. It was the last regatta I saw you sail at. She had the children with her. The boy was spoiled, I remember that. He demanded attention as of a right, and wanted money for the shop. The girl, she had an unhappy, withdrawn look, that pale skin and smudged eyes. The boy teased her, and Maria did not stop him, just said, "Oh, Rachel, stop complaining," and gave the boy a five-pound note.'

'I think they grew up like that,' I said. 'How about Lawrence Ratter? He'd be about my age.'

'Ratter, Ratter – oh, he is exactly your age. He was born in the same week as you were. In those days, you stayed in hospital for a week with your first baby, and so his mother and I were in hospital together. Now, what was her name? Joyce. Her father was an elder of the kirk in Scalloway. He disapproved of me, as a foreigner and a Catholic. Her husband, John, he worked in the bank at the end of the Street, is that the Royal Bank?'

Peter's bank. Not that there was anything in that; everyone knew everyone in Shetland. Perhaps, though, that was how Peter had found out who Annette was entangled with; John Ratter would have heard any gossip going, and might have felt it his duty to pass it on to her father.

'Joyce was imaginative. She wrote short stories for the *New Shetlander*, but she had to do it under a different name, because her father-in-law disapproved. Has the son inherited that imagination?'

'Perhaps.' I visualised Lawrence's wistful look as I'd told him tales of tropical seas. 'He asked me, in college, about my voyages.'

'That could be difficult. To have imagination, and be made to give it up for a respectable career. What does your police inspector do with his imagination?'

'Goes fishing. Lawrence seems to have turned into his grandfather's boy. He was at the Hallowe'en party, and disapproving of everything. One last family: James Leask. He's a crofter family, on Trondra, I think.'

'Leask.' She shook her head. 'What age is the child?'

'Twenty, the same as Annette.'

'So young. It is very sad. Her poor parents.' Then she shook her head. 'I do not know this boy. There are too many Leasks, and we would not have known the people from out of town.'

I put Cat's basket aboard, then headed back along to Kate and Peter's house. Sunday afternoon was a good time to call, and I wanted to see when I'd be needed next week. We'd have our work cut out to finish all the undergrowth slashing for Bonfire Night. Their gate was the only one free of the egg-and-shell mess; even in their rioting, the teenagers had respected their grief.

I pulled my hood over my hair and strode briskly up the path, Cat bounding ahead of me with his tail fluffed out. The kitchen door was closed, but there was a light in Kate's workshop. I hesitated a moment, for I hadn't been there yet, and didn't want to invade her sanctuary. There wasn't a doorbell or knocker. I scuffled my feet, then called 'Hello.'

There was no reply. The door had four clear panes of glass in the upper half, as if it had once been the door between a kitchen and a back porch, so when I came up to it I was looking right at her, sitting with her back to me. This was a side of Kate I hadn't seen, so absorbed in her work that the world dissolved. Her chestnut head was bent over her easel. Beside her, an anglepoise lamp lit up a bird's skull. Her brown hand moved across the page with savage intensity, scoring the sharp line of beak, then became tender as a mother's, smoothing the charcoal curve of the delicate cranium with the side of one thumb.

Boannie pictures o' flowers, in bright colours, Magnie had said. Three paintings hung above her, and there was a monkshood flower in a jar, gentian-bright, but it was the intricacy of colourless bone that absorbed her now. If she had blotted out her own ache with her work, I didn't want to haul her back into the reality of loss. Just as I started to back away, Cat pushed past me, stood on his hind legs, and shoved the door open. He swarmed forwards as he made the gap. I took a long stride backwards, so that she wouldn't know I'd been spying, and called again, 'Hello?'

'Cass? I'll be out in a moment.' Her voice sounded fuzzy, as if she'd been woken from a deep sleep. The chair legs scraped back. 'Cat, hello. No cats in here.' She came out with him tucked under one arm, and closed the door firmly behind her.

'I'm sorry,' I said. 'I didn't mean to disturb you working. I just wanted to check when you wanted me this week, with bonfire night on Saturday.'

Her smile took an effort. 'And the bottom of the garden still to clear. Come and get a cup of tea and we'll see what hours you can manage.'

'I didn't mean to stop your work,' I repeated.

'It's time for an afternoon cuppa. I've gone stiff.' She flexed her shoulders, and gestured me towards the house. 'We had the police round all morning.' I should have thought of that. I was about to say something when she continued. 'Not the one who came yesterday, in the kilt, with the eyes that look as if he's sorry you're telling lies.'

I remembered that grave, regretful look from when I'd been a suspect myself. 'Did he get the fish-flies out?'

'Fish-flies? Oh, yes, he did that too. Got a battered tin box out of his sporran, and began tying a trout fly. Extraordinarily distracting.' She paused to stamp her shoes on the kitchen mat. 'Particularly to Peter – they launched straight into a discussion of something called a Greenwell's Glory, which Peter liked, but the inspector didn't.' She pushed open the kitchen door, and motioned me inside. I was taken aback to find Peter there, in the act of filling the kettle. He turned and smiled.

'Kate telling you about the Highland DI? Clever chap – well, you'll have met him. We got to talking about flies, not at all appropriate in the circumstances, but I suppose he meant to put me at my ease.'

He did it deliberately, he'd admitted to me, to stop a suspect thinking of his next lie: *Nobody watches their words when they're watching my finger.*

'The next thing I knew,' Kate concluded, 'he was showing Peter a different one, a Silver Invicta, he called it, which sounds just like a bike, an old-fashioned Raleigh the way they were when I was a child, with upright handlebars –'

This fast rattle of information was no more the real Kate than the numbed, incoherent phrases of Friday. Although they must be relieved knowing Annette's death wasn't murder, although they must be telling themselves Nate's death was nothing to do with them, this new casualty must have upset them. Peter flicked Kate a quelling glance as he handed her the filled kettle. She put it on the hot-plate, then gave a would-be casual laugh. 'Anyway, he said this Silver Invicta gave better results under what sounded a very precise set of conditions – a rainy evening the second Tuesday after a full moon, or something like that. He wasn't at all my idea of a hot-shot detective. I was just beginning to write him off as a country bumpkin when he flashed a look from those extraordinary eyes, and I suddenly felt as if I had no secrets left in the world.'

She paused for breath. I was annoyed to find my lips were curving into a stupid Mona Lisa smirk, just talking about him. Get a *grip*, Cass. I wiped the smile off, and fetched the mugs from the tree. 'Are you having tea, Peter?'

He nodded. I put the mugs down on the table, and warmed the pot, then occupied myself putting the tea in it, and fetching milk from the fridge.

Peter interposed quietly. 'Did you hear them too?'

I gave him a blank look. I'd suddenly lost the thread of this conversation. A police officer who wasn't Gavin had come to tell them about Nate – 'Hear who?'

'The teenagers. Of course –' his voice went sarcastic '– they maybe didn't bother coming as far as Port Arthur. It's a longer walk than any of them are used to, with parents running them everywhere.'

Memory stabbed at Kate, I saw it in her eyes, of the days when she too had taxied Annette, and Peter had lectured her for it, but she pushed it away, although her fingers clenched on the kettle handle, and the stream of water from spout to teapot wavered. She rattled determinedly on. 'The eggs, it was our local sergeant, asking about the eggs. Did you see the mess?'

Enlightenment dawned. 'Eggs everywhere,' I agreed. If Gavin hadn't told them of Nate's death, then I ought not to queer his pitch. 'They must have had boxes and boxes.'

'Such a waste,' Kate said, 'when there are people starving. They didn't come to us, which was good of them, but they ran riot everywhere else.'

'The sergeant thought I might have seen something, while I walked the dogs,' Peter said. 'The householders are furious, apparently. He wants to call on a few houses, you know, give the ringleaders an official ticking-off.'

Clever, I thought, and plausible. 'And did you see them?'

'Oh, yes. I'd just got out of the gate when I saw a group of them, ducking and dodging in and out of the houses, in dead silence. Rather sinister.'

'You were quite wild about it when you came in,' Kate said. She stirred the tea, pulled the cosy over the pot and poured at last. 'One of them threw an egg at him, Cass – missed, fortunately, otherwise he'd probably have got himself had up for tanning the brat's bottom.'

'I set the dogs after them, but they ran up the street by the Eventide Home,' Peter said. 'Then I realised when I got to the youth club that there was one of their infernal discos on.' He snorted into his tea. 'Assumed they were escapees from that. You know how they find ways to climb in and out of toilet windows, and mill around all over the street.'

The Meat Company was just along from Burn Beach, and the youth club ran behind it, parallel to the shore, with the entrance at the far side of the block from the beach. There was a car park in front of the YC, where the youngsters would no doubt have been milling around, with a sea wall to hide bottles of alcohol in. They would have spread further along that way, towards Kate and Peter's house, but the car park by the beach would have been deserted, and in darkness. The echoing shrieks of the disco-goers could well have masked the sound of Nate being overcome. Anyone looking out from a window on New Street – someone who'd not closed window and curtains against the thump, thump of contemporary music – would have taken any seeming argument for disco behaviour, unless they'd seen the moment of him being thrown into the water. I wondered how strong local feeling was against rumours of witchcraft, if a group of teenagers at a disco might indeed have made someone they believed to be a witch undergo the ordeal by drowning.

'Were there many of them?'

'Half a dozen.' His cheeks reddened. 'But by the mess when I went out this morning, it was the whole teenage population of Scalloway, egging each other on.' He smiled suddenly, a real smile. 'Forgive the pun. Swelled by cousins from other places, no doubt, all thinking it a great spree, and forgetting the damage they make has to be cleared up by other people.'

'Teenagers never think of that,' Kate said. Her face went bleak as she remembered that there would be no pile of towels on bathroom or bedroom floor, no clustering of mugs on window sills, not ever again.

'I'm surprised there weren't more householders out chasing them,' I said.

'They hadn't started the damage then,' Peter said. 'Just lobbed that one egg at me. I saw another two or three smashed on a door along the main street, but other than that it was all quiet. I was later than usual. We'd been watching TV. It was getting on for eleven.'

'I suppose the real rampage was later still, after the disco closed,' I suggested, and he nodded.

'I haven't been out to look,' Kate said.

'Eggs everywhere,' I said. 'On cars, and walls, and the pavement. But the disco must have ended at, oh, one in the morning? Wouldn't you think their parents would be starting to round them up, out that late?'

One in the morning, summer time. High tide would have been around eight o'clock the previous evening. If Nate'd gone over the low wall of Burn Beach any time before, say, eleven o'clock, the ebbing tide would have taken the body away. He had to have died after that.

Kate shook her head. 'We never did, with Annette.' She said the name determinedly. 'We knew she was safe enough, here in Shetland, coming home with her friends. We wouldn't have worried. Those parents didn't –'

'Until they saw the state of their cars,' Peter said. 'Tom Hawkins, up Ladysmith Drive, he was so furious he could hardly speak. A spread of egg all over the bonnet, cooked on by the sun. But I'm afraid I didn't recognise any of them. I told the sergeant so. Except –' He frowned.

'Except ...?' I prompted, when he remained silent.

'I passed one person, later, going round the end of New Street, just at the Castle. Said goodnight, of course, the way you do, and got a grunt back.'

'And you thought you recognised him?' I said.

127

'Well, not to say recognised.' He lifted his mug, drank several mouthfuls. 'But I thought it was that James Leask.' His voice was suddenly venomous. 'The crofter's boy with ambitions to be a sea captain.'

Dark came unexpectedly early. It was just after four as I strode back to the marina, collar turned up against the rain, yet the sky had already begun to dim, and in half an hour I'd need to light the lamps aboard *Khalida*. Lights lit before five ... winter felt just around the corner.

I was just unlocking the marina gate when I heard my name being hissed from the shelter of the boating club back door. I froze, peering into the shadows. 'Who's that?'

A small, black-jacketed figure eased itself off the wall. 'Me, Cass.'

'Shaela? Lass, you'll be starved, waiting around there. Come on board.'

She was wet through. I ushered her on board *Khalida* and passed her a towel to dry the rats' tails of hair that clung to her forehead and cheeks. I made us a cup of drinking chocolate each and waited till she'd stopped shuddering to sit down opposite her. 'Shaela, lass, what on earth's going on?'

'I canna bide long,' she said.

'Then you'd better tell me quickly,' I said, and passed over the tub containing the last few ginger nuts.

'You'll think I'm daft,' she said. 'Seeing things.'

'Try me,' I said, and told her the story of my blind-eyed mer-horse off Fiji. I took my time over it, and when I'd finished her near-panic was diverted into round-eyed wonder. 'Really truly?'

'Cross my heart and hope to die. I ken he's no' in the nature books, because I looked, but I saw him all the same.' The brass lamp cast comforting gold shadows across the cabin. 'Now you.'

'I wasna meant to be out,' she began, 'but I kent the older ones were planning a real fun, so I put clothes rolled up in my bed, and a lump o' jumper on the pillow, and pulled the covers up, then I crept out.'

A child after my own heart. 'Down to the disco?'

She nodded. 'It was an over-sixteens, and they had one of the youth leaders on the door, and she kent all our ages, so there was no way I'd get in, but I didn't want to miss the fun, so I just hung around, waiting. It was brawly cold, so I'd walk along one way for a bit, then back, then the other way.' She shivered. 'It wasn't as much fun as I'd thought it would be. One way was all streetlights, and I felt that exposed, as if all the neighbours were watching, ready to phone Mam and report me, but the other side was dark, all creepy shadows, and that made me feel worse.'

128

Her dark lashes came down over her eyes; her mouth quivered. 'And it was while I was at the dark side that I saw … *it.*'

I waited encouragingly, my heart beating faster.

'It was wi' Nate,' Shaela said. 'I heard these two men coming, and I hid in behind the skip, in case they were, you know, dodgy. Then I heared Nate speaking. I couldna hear the words, but I recognised his voice, so I kent it was all right, and I was joost coming out from behind the skip when I saw the other one.' She glanced around her and leaned towards me. her voice lowered. 'Nate was talking to a demon.'

'What did it look like?' I asked.

'It had a horrible, sneery face, an eyes that glowed red, an a smooth skull wi' peerie horns, an a hump on its back, and a tail, no just a piece o' string hanging, it was like it was alive by itself, it waved about, and I had this awful feeling it was like an antenna, sensing things, and when it swung towards me I was that feared it was going to tell the demon I was there.' Her face was white, remembering. 'I shrunk right back behind the skip. I couldna understand why Nate should want to talk to such a horrible creature, then I thought maybe he didna want to, and I wondered if there was anything I could do to help.' Her mouth turned down. 'But I was over scared o' it.' Her eyes met mine, beseechingly. 'Was I being an awful coward, Cass? I wish now I'd jumped out and said something, or just run for home and told Mam, whatever the trouble. Maybe Nate would still have been alive.'

I shook my head. 'I don't think it would have made any difference. I think you were very brave, to have stayed there, and noticed so much.'

The hand that clutched the mug of drinking chocolate relaxed a little. 'I felt safer in the dark behind the skip, but then I couldna bear no' kenning where it was either. I was just about to inch my head out again when there was this snuffling sound, like a dog, but I thought it was the tail, it was horrible, like it was alive, the way it moved. Then there was this grunt noise, not quite an "ouch", more surprised, then a thud, an I heard footsteps, coming to the skip. I was that feared I thought I was going to pee myself. I just huddled into the shadow, below the slanted end of the skip, and made myself as peerie as I could, but I could imagine that tail waving back and forward, seeking me. I heard the demon looking into the skip, and even looking under things, I heard them shift in the skip, but then it moved back again, and by this time I was over feared to move a muscle. I just froze, waiting for it to come back, only this time it would see me.' Her voice wavered; something glittered in her eyes. She blinked furiously.

'I'd a been terrified an all,' I said. 'It sounds like one of those horrible nightmares where you can't run.'

Shaela nodded. 'It *was*. Then there was this dragging noise, then a thud and chink of pebbles, as if something had gone ower onto the beach. Then the demon laughed. It was horrible, this cold laugh. I stopped even thinking o' running away then. I just screwed me eyes up tight and prayed it wouldn't see me. Then, when it had all been quiet for a bit, I opened me eyes. I stayed there for ages over feared to look an' see if it had gone. I thought it would just be lurking, ready to get me. An when I did stand up, I was that cold at I could only hobble, and I thought I was a goner for sure. But the stiffness eased off by the time I'd crossed the street, and I didna bother wi' the eggs, I just ran for home as fast as I could, and climbed in the window, and dived into bed and got my head under the covers.'

Her eyes had been round as a child's, as Cat's when he was frightened of a sudden noise outside the safety of *Khalida*. Now, abruptly, she returned to a teenager. 'It can't really've been a demon, o' course. It was stupit o' me to be so feared. I didna ken then that the dragging noise, the thud and the pebbles –' Her eyes were bleak. 'That was Nate. The demon was just a grulik.'

It was a word I'd never heard. 'A what?'

'A grulik. It's the old word for a guizer. He was just in a costume. The red eyes, that was some kind o' a torch. It was spooky, but that's all it was. Even the tail, I'm seen that meself at Hallowe'en pairties. It has a wire in the inside, to make it wave every time the person moves. There was no need for me to panic like yon – but I was on me ain, an' in the dark, an' no supposed to be out, an so it was the scariest thing I'm ever seen.'

'I'd have been scared too,' I said.

'But the thing is, Cass, what am I going to do now? I wasna meant to be out, and if me Mam learns at I was, she'll ground me for ever, mebbe even put the computer off bounds except for school work. I wondered if maybe – see, that man in the kilt, the other night, maybe you could tell him about it, without me needing to.'

I shook my head. 'You want whoever killed Nate to be caught, don't you?'

She nodded.

'Then I can't tell it. I wasn't there, you see. There may be little things you noticed that you haven't told me because you barely noticed them yourself, but the police will help you remember everything, and maybe in among it all will be the clue they need to catch him. The man dressed as a demon. It has to be you.'

She shook her head. 'Mam will be that mad.'

I tried to think myself back into the mindset of a thirteen year old, but it was too long ago, and by then my Mam had gone off to France, leaving a wardrobe of dresses behind. I gave it straight. 'You were old enough to risk your Mam being mad to have fun. I think you should risk her being mad to get justice for Nate.'

I managed to persuade her, in the end. I hoped her parents would be so glad she'd not come to any harm that they'd forget it, after the initial explosion, but it was a very subdued Shaela that I walked along Port Arthur road and back to the corner of her street. I watched her into her house, and set out back to the marina, walking briskly, the hood of my oilskin jacket pulled so far over my head that only the tip of my nose showed.

A man dressed as a demon, to keep spreading the idea of the Devil being loose in Scalloway … but who?

Chapter Fifteen

Gavin came round just after eight o'clock, phoning first to tell me he was almost at the marina gate. 'And have you eaten?'

'Ages ago.' I'd had a boiled egg, bannock, and apple at six. 'Have you?'

'I had fish and chips in Lerwick.' He didn't sound as if it had been an experience to savour.

'Frankie's is the best,' I agreed, and went along the pontoon to let him in.

The rain had settled down from drenching to that persistent mizzle that creeps into every crack in your oilskins, insinuates itself down the sides of your boots, and gets you just as wet as the hosepipe stuff in the end. Gavin was back in his usual green jacket, collar turned up against the rain, but he walked with his shoulders back and head high, obviously believing the old Scots idea that rain will only get you as wet as you let it. When he reached *Khalida*, he shook off the drops that had clung to him and hung his jacket under the sprayhood.

'It's not that warm inside,' I warned him, and put the gas on.

He hauled a jumper out of the inevitable carrier bag. 'I brought some biscuits.' They had a sticky puff outside and lemon icing. I decided I wasn't going to worry about the way he associated me with the tartness of lemon, and turned my attention to the sludge-green jumper he was struggling into.

'Did your Granny knit that for you?'

His face emerged from the neck. He gave me a sideways grin. 'She did.' He smoothed the misshapen sleeve. I'd forgotten how to do the three-colour Fair Isle knitting I'd been taught in primary school, but I could tell where someone had had trouble increasing the stitches. 'She wasn't fond of knitting, Granny Mharsailidh, but she knew it was something grandmothers did, so she persevered. This one was for my eighteenth birthday, the last she knitted for me.' He pulled the waistband down to hip level. 'The best fit, too. She was very pleased with it.' He grinned again. 'Our mother is beginning to say it's past wearing, so I bring it with me when I come away.'

My favourite navy gansey had belonged to Alain. The police had taken it to examine for bloodstains, in the film murder, but I'd got it back, and either had to wear it straight away or accept that I never would again. Perhaps I should have given it away, but it was one of the last links I had with Alain. I'd bought it for him in a Breton market, when we'd not been together for long, and were crazy with love and sea-fever, and planning our first Atlantic crossing together. It had taken me ten years to accept my guilt for his death. Now I wore his gansey in memory of the good times.

The kettle whistled, and I spooned the drinking chocolate into the mugs, added the water, and stirred. 'I have an eyewitness for you.'

His head went up, the eagle spotting a fish, then he brought out his black policeman's notebook, and waited, pencil poised. Above us, the rain pattered on *Khalida*'s fibreglass roof. I sat down opposite him, and Cat jumped on my lap.

'It was one of the guizers who came round the other night. Shaela, the one who was dressed as a witch.' His eyes narrowed, focusing, then he nodded. 'She didn't want to be left out of the egg-throwing fun, so she climbed out of her bedroom window, and headed down to the shore.' I gave Shaela's account, as much in her words as I could remember, and he scribbled, then closed his notebook and put the elastic around it.

'Is she in general a truthful child?'

I shrugged. 'She was frightened. Her eyes went like saucers when she was talking about it. Also, the way she described Nate's death and the body being thrown over, she said, *'this dragging noise, then a thud and chink of pebbles'*, it's not very dramatic. If she'd been making it up, she'd have put in a cry at least.'

Gavin nodded. 'She's described exactly what happened: someone hit Nate, then went to the skip for rope to tie him up.'

'I noticed the rope in the skip the night Annette died,' I said. 'I even pulled it out to see if it could be useful for something. It was too old, no strength left in it.'

'Strength enough.' Gavin's mouth set in a grim line. 'Don't mention this further. Nate was still alive when he was thrown in. We have to wait for the official PM, but all the signs were that he drowned.'

A cold hand clutched around my heart. *Thou shalt not suffer a witch to live.* The blow Shaela had heard had only stunned him. Then he'd been bound with rope from the skip, gagged, and thrown on the beach for the tide to take … I frowned. 'That was risky,' I said. 'It was after high water, so he wasn't taken off then, but just lay there on the shore until it came in at eight this morning. It might just have been that someone, a disco-goer, would have found him still alive. Nate'd have known who it was

133

that had left him there.'

Gavin nodded. 'Perhaps not, if the demon had kept his disguise on. It's more of a chance than I'd expect a murderer to take. On the other hand, how much would a non-seafarer know about tides? I'm like you, I'm used to seeing the tide ebb and flow each day, and knowing what state it's at without even thinking about it. A normal Scalloway inhabitant, now, would they know how much beach there is at low tide, or would they expect it always to have water over it?'

'It mostly does,' I agreed. 'And you're right, it always surprises me how even sensible children don't connect the moon with the tides, or know unless you tell them to look whether it's ebbing or flowing. But here in Scalloway I think an adult would know. It's a seafaring community. Maybe the killer just didn't care.'

'It was a long chance,' Gavin said. 'People nearby weren't looking out of their windows, because of the disco. They just shut their curtains and turned the TV up. The only person who saw anything was Mr Otway, and his bunch sounded like stragglers. We're trying to trace them, in case they saw someone around, but he doesn't know the local children of that age, so he couldn't help with names.'

'And the beach was in shadow,' I said. 'There are streetlights on the pier, and up on New Street, but nothing around there.' I swallowed. 'So Nate lay there, injured maybe, in pain, on the cold beach all those hours, with all the youngsters in Scalloway dancing and drinking and having fun, just a hundred metres away, until the tide came.'

'He might not have known anything about it,' Gavin said. His voice was gentle, as if I was a relative. 'Cold would have made him lose consciousness.'

I thought about that for a moment, and was comforted. 'If the rope was taken from the skip, does that mean the murder was on the spur of the moment?'

'The murderer could have spotted the rope earlier, as you did, and counted on being able to use it. It's interesting that Nate seems to have walked freely to the skip car park with his murderer – but we knew that. Some time after dark, according to his mother, there was a knock at the door, and she heard voices, then Nate taking down his coat and going out. A good while after she'd gone to bed, she thought. She's an invalid, and usually starts going to bed around nine.'

'"Ages after the disco started" was the best Shaela could do.'

'Ten o'clock. Mr Otway went out just after eleven, later than he would usually go, he said, because he and Mrs Otway had been watching TV.'

'Is that significant, do you think?' I asked. 'Peter's pretty well known in Scalloway, he walks the dogs every evening, and always along the same way. Up through the fields, to let them race, then over the fence opposite Fraser Park, across the roundabout, down Castle Street, New Street, along the sea front, and home. The murderer would have expected him to be well past by "ages after ten o'clock".'

'Especially if it was a murderer that was familiar with the household,' Gavin said. 'We're going to be interviewing James Leask tomorrow.'

'Peter told you he saw him?'

'Going up from the street, from the skip car park maybe, towards the castle. He was out on his boat when we called. I'll talk to him tomorrow.' Gavin drained his mug and set it down. 'We had to search Nate's room, of course. Do you know the family?'

I shook my head. 'Maman told me a little about them. The father was a minister, and the mother was in a wheelchair.'

'They're shattered. Mr Halcrow's been in post for over thirty years, but he's not originally from Shetland – he was brought up in Invergarry. My impression was of a good man, very committed to his ministry, and the elders speak well of him. Mrs Halcrow is a poor, tired soul. Nate was the apple of their eye, "the boy". They expected him to be a doctor or a university professor.'

'Maman remembered him. Spoiled rotten, she said, and Rachel neglected.'

Gavin nodded. 'I've spent the day talking to people. Several of his past teachers said he was lazy at school. He found the work too easy at first, then got out of the way of thinking. His English teacher said he had a passion for computer gaming. His reports go downhill. He skimmed through his Standard Grades then failed his Highers, spent his sixth year "discussing" ideas in the common room, but not producing any work. After that, three months in his mother's office, three months with a band, a year in computer programming at college, a year at art school – the same story in both of them, a lot of good ideas, genuine talent, but no self-discipline.' He paused. 'They had one of his paintings.' Another pause, then he said, with fastidious distaste, as if he was having to pick a stinking fish off the deck, 'I suppose it was powerful. There was a fire in the centre of the picture, with hooded figures crouched around it, and a great black horned man dominating them.'

I grimaced. 'The witches' Sabbat.'

'After that his father refused to bank-roll him, hence the job at the Fisheries College. Now there's a kind of armed neutrality at home. His parents still hoped he'd "find what he really wanted to do" but the mother at least knew they were just kidding themselves. As for his reputation outside the home, well, the chef at the college shrugged and said he worked well enough. The kirk elders wouldn't be drawn out. I got a wary, "Ah, well, he's gone now, poor boy" from two of them, and the others just shook their heads and said it was very hard on the family.'

It seemed very little for an epitaph. 'Did you find anything to link him to Annette's death?'

Gavin nodded. ' You know the house, the white one which stretches from the Spanish closs down to New Street. His room was right up in the top of the house, up a winding stair. We found a number of books on witchcraft, and folders of research on the witches here in Scalloway.' He grimaced. 'The room was sick with the stuff. The first thing you saw was a great goat-head poster, above a mantelpiece with black candles, an upside-down crucifix, and a ritual chalice.'

'Didn't his parents object?'

'His mother hasn't been able to manage the stairs for some years. His father can't remember the last time he was up there. "Letting the boy have his privacy." If they wanted him down for a meal, they just yelled from the foot of the stairs.' His long, mobile mouth turned down. 'I had to ask him to come up and look. I was sorry to be spoiling his illusions.'

I left a sympathetic pause. 'It's strange.' I tried to sort out my thoughts. 'If he was trying to impress people – ' The three hooded crows flashed into my mind. 'Girls, then he'd do that sort of thing, have stupid symbols everywhere. But if he was real – ' His sea-grey eyes were steady on mine, pupils wide in the dim light. He nodded encouragement. I looked around at *Khalida*'s cabin: the wooden fiddles, the row of pilot books, the polished wood of the bulkhead, the looped curtain shading the heads. There was no need of jaunty 'Captain' slogans on the mugs, or framed pictures of signal flags; anyone could see she was a working yacht. By the same token, I wouldn't be seen dead in the 'nautical chic' of southern yacht clubs, navy and white striped tops, white jeans and suede loafers. 'If he was real, surely he wouldn't need to draw attention to himself. He wouldn't need the showy trappings.'

'I thought that too.'

'So … he wasn't the head witch? He was just doing a DIY witch cult to show off? Compensate for being a failure?' I remembered the way the girls had gathered round him in the college.

'We found this.' He fished in his sporran for a Body Shop container, *Rose Hand Cream*. 'The container probably came from the Otway household. Mrs Otway uses this cream, and finished a jar recently. Inside – ' He unscrewed the lid, opened it. The circular box was half-filled with fine red ash.

'The ash from the museum?'

Gavin nodded.

'So then Nate was the person who was going to exorcise Annette. She'd got the ash for him – given it to him, all ready for the ritual. Except that they didn't manage to finish the ritual, because she died.'

Gavin nodded. 'Nate was the person who made the claw marks too. Rachel called in on her way home from the party, last night, to check her mother was settled for the night. She returned his werewolf suit. A nasty piece of work, with sewing pins inserted in the fingers to make claws that would scratch. Her story is that it was he who offered it to her, for the party.'

'To get it out of the house?'

'We'll get forensics to make sure, but I'm certain her scratches were made by those gloves.'

I thought about it. 'She went to visit him, because she thought he could help. If he'd been doing paintings of demons at college everyone would know that. He'd have a reputation. He told her he wanted the ash, and she wasn't keen.' I imagined them, sitting together in Nate's room. Annette had demurred, and he'd reached for his glove and pulled it on, then caught her by the throat. *You want rid of the witch who haunts you, you'll have to do as I say.* 'His story to me about seeing her with the claw marks, that was bluff. I did wonder if he could really have seen them at that distance. He knew about them because he'd made them. So, in the same way, do you think he brought her back to his house because he thought you wouldn't suspect him?'

Gavin shook his head. 'She died, and he panicked? I'm not sure. There are still factors that don't make sense. Why was she searched?'

'Maybe she died before she'd taken the ash out. That would have linked her to him – no, not to him, but to witches, so he had to find it.' Enlightenment flashed on me. 'No, he was looking for her keys.' I remembered Peter fishing them out of his pocket, with that blank look. 'Peter found them in the wrong pocket. The next day. Nate didn't want Annette's death to be associated with witches, so he hid the ash, and returned the keys. A pocket would be a safe place to put them. Everyone does it. You've got something to carry, so you shove the keys in a pocket, and forget to put them on their usual hook. You wouldn't be suspicious.'

I had a horrid picture of Nate sliding into the dark garden, making his way round past the lit kitchen where Kate and Peter were being comforted by the police, to the darkness of the front door. He'd ease the door open, drop the keys into the first jacket hanging on the row, and slip out again.

Gavin's grey eyes met mine; he nodded, then rose to wash the cup, and spoke over his shoulder. 'So he was involved in Annette's death. He was the werewolf who made the claw marks. If there was another person involved – this demon he met last night – then he'd have known who it was. There's the motive for silencing him. We'd seen the claws on the suit, we were going to question him about it. To get himself off the hook, he'd have told us who.'

'Lawrence knew I'd seen the claws,' I said slowly, 'and Rachel told me the suit was Nate's. She might have told him I'd asked.'

'Or there's a different scenario,' Gavin said. 'We've only Rachel's word for that. The parents wouldn't know, and Nate's dead. Maybe we're being given a scapegoat.'

Rachel, then, or Lawrence.

'The last thing,' Gavin said, 'was that Mrs Halcrow thought she heard Nate coming back in. Well, if your Shaela's story is true, that couldn't have been Nate. Perhaps the man dressed as a demon returned.' He stood up, rinsed his cup, dried it, slotted it back into its place, and sat down again. 'We took prints in the room, of course. The analysis has to come back, but we found a couple on the door that might be Annette's. As for the witchcraft things, well, they'd been wiped clean. All of them – the candlesticks, the chalice, the books. It looked as if the person wiping them had worn gloves, for extra security. There were just traces of a mark round the rims, as if someone had put them back with gloved hands.'

'So somebody was searching for something?'

'Perhaps. Or perhaps – well, as you said, it was all a bit stagey. Either he was trying to impress his visitors – though according to his mother he rarely had any – or someone else was trying to impress me. Maybe it usually lived in a box in the wardrobe, and someone set it all out.'

'Would Rachel know what his room normally looked like?'

'She said she didn't go into his room.'

Five knots on the cord that had been left on my berth: the three hoodies, Rachel, Lawrence. Scalloway's little coven, that excluded Nate. He'd kept his end up by showing off, and that had brought Annette to him. Rachel had reason to dislike Nate personally; if Lawrence was Shaela's demon, he'd resent Nate trying to usurp his lordship.

There had been a persistent, distant noise in my ear for the last few minutes, a motorboat coming from across from the other marina, at the other side of the castle. From the engine sound, it was a lightweight thing, maybe twelve or fifteen feet. Now, as it came to within a hundred metres of us, someone gunned the throttle and the hum rose to a whine. *Khalida* rocked to the wash as it curved around the corner, then there was a thud in the cockpit, as if something heavy had been thrown in, another, a third, and with each thump was a hissing noise, like hot iron being plunged in a bucket of water. I dived along the centre passage of *Khalida* into the forepeak and flung open the forrard hatch. I was out of it while the motorboat was still turning. It was a fibreglass dinghy with a small cuddy. It was too dark to see the face of the person driving it, but he – she – seemed tall, and dark hair whipped like tentacles around the face. Two other people huddled in the back. A voice shouted, 'Witch!' and a second cried, 'You were warned!' The voices were female.

There was the smell of burning peat, and a cloud of smoke swirling in the cockpit. I swung along *Khalida*'s side. Gavin had the washboards out, was standing on the steps.

'The fire blanket, quick!' I said. 'Above the cooker.' Already, I could smell the acrid smoke of scorched fibreglass. A glass boat would go up like a torch. Gavin turned and reached behind him. *Oh, God ... quick, quick.* There were three dark lumps in the well, rectangular-shaped, glowing orange in the breeze, too hot for me to pick up, although my fingers were curving towards the nearest, not caring about the pain. Then I heard Gavin behind me, and reached my hand back, and the metallic blanket pressed into it. I lunged for the first shape. It was twice the size of my hands, glowing, trailing sparks. I didn't wait to watch it fall. I was already saying to Gavin, 'There's a bucket in the heads' as I grabbed the second, and the third, and threw them overboard too. The water hissed, and gave a plume of steam. Gavin had dipped the bucket overboard for water by the time I'd dealt with the third. When I turned around, ribs heaving, heart thumping, he was pouring water over the cockpit floor. I ran my hands over where the peats had been, and felt the rough indentation where the hot peat had begun to melt the fibreglass.

'If I catch them,' I said, between my teeth, 'they'll be sorry they tried that.'

'You know who they are?' Gavin asked softly.

'The demon's little followers. The hooded crows.' My left palm was stinging where I'd reached out to the burning peat. '*Fuck.*' I went back below and pumped cold water over it, then reached for the lavender oil. 'Trying to set fire to *Khalida*.'

Gavin stowed the bucket and sat down again. 'Lavender?'

'Great for burns.' I was so angry that my hands were trembling. 'If I catch them anywhere near me again – '

'You tried to pick it up with your hand?' He said it calmly.

'A fibreglass boat can go up so fast you wouldn't believe it.' I wound some cling film around my smarting hand. 'I saw one once, in a marina. An electrical fault, they said later. There was a trickle of smoke, then suddenly the whole boat was ablaze. It was burned to the waterline in less than two minutes. There was nothing anyone could do.'

'When you get done for grievous bodily harm,' Gavin said, 'the victim's lawyer will suggest that the way fibreglass boats burn isn't common knowledge.'

'The victim,' I said, through gritted teeth, 'will be represented by her heirs if she puts so much as a finger on my boat again.'

'And speaking as a policeman,' Gavin continued, 'I'll be very happy to tell them how grieved I was to be aboard tonight and witness such an attempt at arson, and possibly manslaughter, and how very much more upset I'll be if you have any more harm done to you.'

I stopped scowling. 'Tempting.'

He leaned forward, grey eyes on mine. 'It was peats they used to burn the witches.'

I tilted my chin at him. 'I'm not a witch. You know that.'

'But they think you are, and the child said it the other night too. Where's the idea coming from?'

I shook my head. 'In the old days, the only reason they needed was that you were different. I've got black hair, I've got a scar, my cat follows me. Black Patie's ministers would have burned me for those.'

Gavin shook his head, unconvinced. 'We're not talking primitive villagers here. Someone's spreading rumours.'

'But who? Why? I'm a stranger here.' My hands had stopped trembling now. I began to unwrap the clingfilm. 'Look, don't have a word with them. That'll just make things worse. I'll promise not to wreak vengeance, if that will make you happier.'

He frowned. His hands sketched a perplexed curve in the air. 'Cass –' His soft voice was suddenly jagged, shallow water over sharp stones. I couldn't look at him, felt *Khalida* rock as he stood. 'Cass, I don't want to change you, not even a little. I don't want you to feel like *the policeman's girlfriend*.' He laughed, but there was no joy in the sound. His voice was like blood flowing over broken glass. 'The Cass I'm getting to know would go like a tigress for someone who laid a finger on her boat. I can't tell you not to. I don't have the right even to hope you won't, because of me.'

I turned then. 'I hope my own sense and principles will stop me going for her.' I looked him in the eye. 'I wouldn't expect you not to arrest me, if I did.'

He put his hand out towards me then. We stood there for a long moment in the flickering gold light. I felt myself beginning to sway towards him. The cabin was so quiet I could hear the flicker of the candle in its brass lantern. Seized with a sudden panic, I stepped back, rocking the boat in her berth. My heart was thumping in my throat, and I didn't want to think what he could read in my face. His hand drew back to his body. He turned to pick up his carrier bag. 'I'll leave you the rest of the biscuits.'

I wanted to say that I'd save them for his next visit, but it would have sounded crass, as if I was blowing hot and cold. I wanted to explain, but I couldn't think how to begin. 'Thanks.'

'Thanks for the chocolate.' He motioned me forwards up the steps. I lifted the washboards and slotted them into their stand, went out on deck before him. It was still raining, a sullen drizzle slanted in the orange circles of the streetlights. 'Don't get wet,' he said.

'I need to let you out.' Stiff, stupid words. 'It's not that bad.'

We walked along the pontoon in silence. At the gate he said, 'Phone me if they come back,' and I said, 'They'll not come back tonight, I don't suppose,' and let him out of the gate. He stood for a moment after I'd closed it, with the mesh between us, then nodded goodnight, turned, and strode off.

I went back to *Khalida* and sat down at the table. I must have sat there for a good half hour, gazing at the lantern swinging gently from its hook, before I roused myself enough to put the kettle on for my hot water bottle. *I don't want to change you, not even a little.* Bed felt like the best place for me … but it was a long time before I slept.

Auld Clootie, Auld Nick (n): Shetland names for the
Devil

Chapter Sixteen

Monday 31st October

Low Water Scalloway 02:19 GMT 0.6m
High Water 08:37 1.7 m
Low Water 14:34 0.6m
High Water 20:50 1.7m
Moon waxing gibbous

Moonset 07:02, 292 degrees
Sunrise 07:22
Moonrise 15:49, 59 degrees
Sunset 16:14

For a moment I wasn't sure what had woken me. The soft tapping of the rain on the cabin roof had given way to watery moonlight slanting in through the long windows. It was still, except for long ripples running along *Khalida*'s hull, and the purr of an engine breaking the silence. Then I felt *Khalida* sway to the wash of an approaching boat. I was alert instantly. I wriggled out of bed, hauled my mid-layer suit and boots over my sleeping thermals, and eased up the forrard hatch, shadow-silent, enough for me to see out, but not so much that they could see I was looking.

It wan't yet dawn, but there was the first hint of light to come silhouetting the hills on the eastern side, and it felt as though I'd slept just about enough. Five, half five. I reached for my thick jacket and slid my arms into it. I swung my feet on to the berth so that I was ready to spring out.

It was coming slowly around the corner of the pontoon, a sizeable motorboat with a tall cabin, railed around the top for sea-fishing. The dark water rippled away from the flared bow to rattle against *Khalida*'s sides. I couldn't see the person in the shadow of the wheelhouse, but there was someone on the foredeck, arms stretched as if it was holding something. My hand clenched around the long boathook.

The motorboat crept along my side of the pontoon. The figure at the front seemed to be looking for something. One arm came up, pointing at *Khalida*. My grip tightened on the boathook. But the arm remained extended as the motorboat slid past me, and fell as she turned into one of the vacant berths. 'Slow – slow –' a voice called in Norwegian, and the boat slid smoothly into position, the bow-thrusters creating a swirl of water that came to lap against *Khalida*'s bow.

I knew that voice. I swung myself out of the hatch and went along to the berth. The figure in the motorboat's bows flung back his hood to show short hair, silvered by the marina lights, and a neat Elizabethan beard. White teeth flashed as he grinned.

'Anders!' I said, and held out a hand for their bow line. 'Welcome to Scalloway.'

Anders jumped lightly down to the pontoon, and put a bight around the cleat before embracing me. 'Cass! I told Reidar you would be awake the moment we put in.' His arms closed around me. The familiar smell of engine oil and cinnamon shower gel stung my eyes. I clung to him for a moment, then stepped back, and he released me. 'Rat will be pleased to see you. Come on board.'

We fastened the motorboat up, lines fore and aft, with a bow spring for good measure, before I joined the skipper in the cockpit. 'Welcome,' he said, in Danish, in a bass rumble of a voice. 'Go below, it's breakfast time.'

Cat had slipped out after me, a grey shadow on the edge of the pontoon. I whistled to him. 'Come on, Cat, you've an old friend here.' He slid warily towards the boat and I picked him up and carried him below.

The motorboat was a third longer than *Khalida,* and twice her width, with a double settee and table facing the galley. Everything in the cabin was secured for sea: sleeping bags shoved into the locker ovals, the chart under an elastic net, a thermos held by bungee clips. There were two mugs and two plates in the sink. Anders hung his life-jacket and oilskins up and slid behind the table to reach the hanging lantern. It was an LED which bathed the cabin in silvery light, bleaching his hair and fair eyelashes, and casting sharp shadows on his hollowed cheekbones. There were no signs of injury now. His brown hands went confidently up to the lantern, one holding, the other adjusting, with no sign of stiffness. 'How's the shoulder?' I asked.

He swirled his hands extravagantly and smiled at me. 'As good as new. You're a sight for sore eyes, belle Cassandre. Rat, come out, look who is here.'

'You spoil that animal,' the skipper said, following us below. He was a great untidy bear of a man, forty maybe, and more like a Norwegian than a Dane, with a tumble of tawny hair above a square forehead, blue eyes below bushy brows, a wedge of a nose, and a beard that would have done for Up Helly Aa. He held out a hand the size of a keelboat rudder. 'Reidar. Are you hungry?'

'Cass is always hungry,' Anders said. Reidar nodded and reached for the kettle. The boat had some sort of power system for the taps, I noticed enviously, with hot water as well as cold, and a draining board beside the rectangular sink.

There was a scuffling noise in the berth forrard. Rat swarmed out of the forepeak and came forward to join us, whiskers forward inquisitively. He was still larger than Cat, nearly sixty centimetres from nose to tail-tip, and blotched black and white, with a glossy coat. He knew me, of course; rats are very intelligent animals. He leapt on my shoulder by way of greeting, whiffled round my neck, and slid down again, tail hooked, to touch noses with Cat, who stiffened warily as if he didn't quite remember, then jumped to the ground and turned to pounce. Within a minute they were chasing around the forepeak just as they used to on board *Khalida*, along the perimeter of the berth, round the back of the toilet, in through the chain locker, and up on the berth again. Anders nodded in satisfaction. 'I knew Rat would remember. Cat has grown, he's twice the size.'

'Rats on board a boat,' Reidar grumbled to himself. He put half a pat of butter in a frying pan whose weight would have made *Khalida* list to port, then began chopping onions so fast the knife blade blurred. 'Una tortilla.' He tipped the onions into the pan and began on potatoes. 'And hot chocolate, a special recipe from Andreas Viestad. You will like it.'

'I will,' I assured him. The hands chopping potatoes and whisking egg were delicate in motion as Cat picking his way through puddles.

'So,' he said, 'you are Anders' damsel in distress.'

I flashed a look at Anders.

'It sounded like trouble to me,' Anders defended himself, 'and my mother was beginning to drive me crazy, and the young man replacing me in the yard was doing well, so I decided to come and see what was happening. Life in Norway was very quiet after all the excitement we have had here in Shetland, these last months.'

Reidar turned to give me a long look. 'She is not distressed, no,' he rumbled, 'but she is worried.' He handed me a tall mug entirely hidden by a swirl of cream, with what looked like two marmalade strands for decoration. 'This will help.'

'It will,' I agreed. My nose tip touched the cream as I tried to drink from the cup. I gave up, and resorted to a spoon. It was delicious, chocolate with a tangy hint of orange, frothed to a smooth cream. A mug of this, and I'd take on a dozen covens single-handed. Warmed plates appeared from the oven, and Reidar slid a triangular wedge of tortilla onto each.

'Now,' he said, sliding in beside me at the table, 'we eat this, and then afterwards you tell us.'

This was my world, my people. Now I felt at home again, squashed behind the fold-out table, with a man in a thick sea jumper on each side of me, eating without polite conversation or worrying about table etiquette. The tortilla was deep yellow with the yolks of free-range eggs, and deliciously runny inside. Reidar hacked off a slice of bread and polished his plate with it, and I followed suit, mopping up the last of the eggy fluid. I washed the plates in the beautiful hot water that gushed from the tap, and Anders stowed them. It was only once we'd had two Ballerina biscuits each and a lump of chocolate, and Reidar had found, cleared, and lit a pipe whose smoke-colour suggested his own home-cured tobacco, that it was time for me to speak.

I did my best to explain clearly, but everything was too muddled in my own head. Annette, the devil who'd carried her, the glass that had broken on the canteen floor, the witches gathering heather for their Sabbat fire, Nate floating in the harbour, his hands and feet bound, the burning peats thrown into *Khalida*. They listened, nodding from time to time, then, when I'd finished, Reidar drew on his pipe again, blew an amber smoke ring, and said, 'I know only Danish tales. Witches almost sank the ship of our Princess Anne as she was coming to marry your King James, by sending small devils to climb the keel. They caused smallpox too, I think. I don't know what Scottish witches do. I think you need to go and find out.'

The way he said it, it seemed the most obvious thing in the world. 'Yes,' I said slowly. 'Yes, I think I do.'

'Do you know where?' Anders asked.

Nate had had a file on witchcraft, but I wasn't going to go back to Gavin. I nodded. 'Lerwick, the Archives. I'll bunk off class and go this afternoon.' I looked down at the heap of grey fur and black and white velvet sleeping together on the cushion. 'Could you maybe keep Cat? I don't want to leave him alone on *Khalida.*'

'He will stay,' Anders said. 'You can see, they have missed each other.'

I thanked Reidar once more for the wonderful breakfast, and headed back to *Khalida*, leaving them to sleep.

It was seven o'clock. Now the sky was flame-orange in the east, the clouds varying the intensity of the colour so that they were scaled like the side of a red gurney, trailing away to one side, and becoming paler as they went further from the sun. Even as I watched it, the sky brightened to fire-orange, then faded; in five minutes it was gone, leaving the clouds milk-grey.

Red sky in the morning. But there were no other signs of trouble; the sky was patterned lightly with those mottled clouds, with a thicker clump only in the north-west, arranged in long bands as a warning of wind or rain. The occasional drop made circular patterns in the mirror-smooth water.

I could see my decks now. I went round the three indentations where the burning peats had landed, tracing each with my fingers. The first, the one I'd lifted most quickly, was the shallowest, but the second was deeper, and the third had burnt almost through the fibreglass. I'd need to patch that. We'd been lucky, *Khalida* and I, lucky that the decks had been wet with rain, lucky that I'd moved fast, lucky that Gavin had been quick with the fire blanket. My tough little boat had been seconds away from burning. The three crows would regret this, along with the shadowy leader who'd sent them.

Witches. There was the display in the museum, here in Scalloway, and Peter had said that when the organisers had done their research, they'd kept a copy of everything they'd found out, so that other researchers could sit at a table in the glass café corner, and read through the sources. There would be a file on witchcraft, with photocopies of what was in the Lerwick museum. I didn't fancy looking through a witchcraft file here in the heart of Scalloway, framed in the glass, so that any passer-by could see that I was researching something, maybe even see from the colour of the file what exactly I was looking at. No; I'd head to Lerwick after the morning's gardening.

Peter's car passed me, coming out from the upper entrance as I opened the garden door. Kate was standing at the side of the house, looking towards the drive. There'd been an argument, I could feel that, though whether it was over his going back to work, or if he'd gone back to work to get away, I couldn't tell. Kate turned with her usual smile as she heard the gate clunk closed. 'Good morning, Cass. You're very prompt. I was feeling guilty about telling you to come so early.'

'I was up anyway,' I said. 'I had a surprise at dawn. My friend Anders, who used to crew for me, he arrived on a motorboat from Bergen, so we had breakfast together. Cat's stayed on board with him.'

'Peter's off to work,' Kate said. 'I thought it was too soon, nobody would expect him, but it's Monday, and he wanted to get back to normal.' Her voice made it achingly clear that there would never be a normal again. The circles under her eyes were bruise-blue. 'Well! Talking doesn't clear a garden.'

She flung herself into the work, hauling out the last suckers and pulling up handfuls of a silver-striped nettle-leaf and rust geranium stems, until suddenly we came on flagstones. We scraped and hauled, and revealed a path running between what had been two herbaceous borders at the sea end of the garden, under the overhanging sycamore branches. I saw at last what she'd meant by the garden's bones; cleared of the plants that had hidden it, the path was laid in a smooth curve that rested the eyes.

'This has been lovely,' Kate said, her eyes bright, cheeks flushed, so that for a moment she looked herself again. 'I can plant this with paeonies and old roses, and lilies, and clove pinks spilling over the edge of the flagstones. I could hang Chinese lanterns in the tree branches, like that Sargent painting. We need to cut these sycamores back to let the light and air in. You take that barrowful to the car, I'll fetch the saw.'

We spent the next hour lopping off jagged tree branches. Each one half-filled the car, and Kate had to make a dozen trips to the bonfire site, but by half past ten the tangle had become two long beds waiting to be dug properly. The clear morning light poured in like a blessing on the disturbed earth.

'Tea,' Kate said, dusting the sawdust and bark from her hands, 'and we've earned a chocolate biscuit.'

The kitchen was beautifully warm. Working so vigorously had kept me from feeling the cold, but soon my hands were tingling with the glowing heat of the Rayburn. Kate produced a packet of orange Clubs. We slumped into our chairs and drank our tea in silence.

'We heard, last night,' Kate said abruptly. I looked across at her, and saw Nate's face in her eyes. 'The place has turned rotten,' she said passionately. 'It's like this garden. It has to be rooted out, completely, all of it, so that there can be new growth. Slashed down – ' Her words choked to silence. She swallowed and looked straight at me. 'Do you think your policeman can do that?'

'I'm not sure,' I said. 'Someone has to.'

'You help him,' she said fiercely. 'If you set your mind to it, it'll happen. Don't worry about what you have to break.' She made a jagged, stabbing gesture. 'It killed Annette. She got mixed up in it, and it killed her. Whatever you have to do, do it for her sake.'

We spent the rest of the morning digging. The beds had become infested with a fresh, green leaf which Kate called ground elder. My first handful pulled up easily enough, but then I discovered that my fork brought up a tangle of bitter-smelling white roots. The earth was filled with them, and a metre of border had the barrow overflowing.

'Root it up,' Kate said. 'All of it, then in the spring I'll put poison on what's survived.' Her hands were trembling on her spade. 'Root it out – ' Her eyes were full of tears. She pushed them away with one hand, leaving a smear of dirt on her cheek. 'I think I've maybe done enough. Would you like some soup before you go?'

I shook my head. 'I'm going to skive college and head for town.'

'Then let me make you a sandwich – no, I insist. It's no trouble.' She packed an ice-cream tub with buttered bread and slices of roast lamb, and added a bottle of water. 'There.'

On the doorstep, she laid a hand on my arm. 'You'll remember? Whatever it takes.'

'I'll remember,' I promised, and set out along the road.

Chapter Seventeen

It had become a lovely sunny day. It could have been summer, except for the long shadows that magnified every hollow, bringing back the boundaries of long-gone croft houses. The heather hills were patterned like the coat of a tortoiseshell cat, swirls of fawn, chocolate, ginger, with the burns running down in a path of brighter green. Cloud shadows chased each other over the hills, and the sea was burnished silver.

I walked briskly out of Scalloway, past the school which was half occupied, half achingly empty, around the curve of the burn, and up past the quarry. I paused at the viewpoint to look over Scalloway and drink some water. From here I could see some thirty miles: up to the north, and the silver-red bulk of Ronas Hill; down the long coast southwards, with the islands of Trondra, Burra, the deserted South Havera; out to the west, where Foula floated on the horizon like my granny Bridget's Isle of the Dead, Tir nan Og. I wondered what sort of heaven Nate had believed in.

I felt a stab of pain behind my left eye, and realised that there had been a nagging pain there since last night. Stress; too much happening. This walk would clear it. Below me, Earl Patrick's castle dominated the town, taller than the modern cubes of ice plant and factory, doubled in height by its own reflection. The sandstone was a soft red in the autumn sun. From here I could pick out the close where Annette had lain, but the bay where we had found Nate was hidden behind houses. *Khalida* floated in her berth, with nobody near her, and Reidar's high-bridged motorboat just two berths down. I screwed the top on my water bottle, took out a sandwich, and strode on.

This was one of the narrowest parts of the island. Just two hundred yards further, the curve of the road hid the Atlantic, and gave me a view up Dales Voe to the North Sea, with the Out Skerries on the horizon: the Viking sea-road which Anders and Reidar had travelled last night. I kept on the north road, rather than turning to the eastward. These heather hills were darker, as if the sun didn't shine within the valley, to bleach them to rust. A herd of Shetland ponies galloped towards me as I walked by their fence, little legs pounding, then wheeled at the last moment in a tossing of manes and tails, and stopped, as if that was quite enough exercise for one day. A few early golfers were out as I came over the Brig of Fitch and alongside the last hill before Lerwick. A couple of ravens wheeled above them, waiting for the chance to snatch a ball. One capped golfer waved a club at them, but they just glided lower, unimpressed. I plodded steadily up the hill, around the last curve and onto the downwards stretch into Lerwick.

The best way to come into Lerwick was by sea, straight into the harbour at the heart of the old town, where grey-stone houses still stood on their strong foundations, gable-end to the sea, their wooden unloading doors fastened now against the rising water. Between them, under the street, were smugglers' tunnels where Lerwick merchants had hidden gin and schnapps brought by Dutch fishing boats. The oldest part of the town dated from the 1660s, just after the downfall of Black Patie. Cromwell's troops had used his castle as a headquarters for a while, then built a new fort here during the Dutch wars. Naturally the inhabitants of Shetland kept on trading with the herring fishermen in the harbour below the guns. Then the tollbooth had been built here, and the town house, and Lerwick had become Shetland's administrative centre. It had boomed in the herring years of the late nineteenth century, and the enterprising Victorian merchants expanded the pier, built the square-towered Town Hall that dominated the skyline just as Earl Patrick's castle had ruled over Scalloway, and laid out the broad streets and flower parks between their substantial villas. Now the mackerel went to the factory at the end of town, and the villas were mostly flats or B&Bs, but the Town Hall clock was still the clincher in any exact-time argument, and the gardens were filled with colour from the first crocus to the last rose.

Coming from the north brought me through the industrial end of town. I came past two garages and tarmac filled with chrome-winking cars to the Gremista turn-off, the area up to my left, with *The Shetland Times* printing factory, the Shetland College, and the Tyre and Exhaust centre, hidden behind a roog of tyres. The Bod, where P & O's founder Arthur Anderson had been born, was preserved in nineteenth-century stone among a cluster of modern sheds: the marina, McNab's fish, and the Shetland Heat Exchange building that took the refuse from all over Shetland and burned it to create central heating for Lerwick. The marina was behind them, four double lines of boats floating comfortably in the arms of their rock wall. The blue building at the back of the marina was Shetland Catch, one of Europe's largest fish-processing factories.

My feet were getting tired. Briefly, I regretted the little white Citroen I'd bought for the longship film, but as I didn't need it at college, and didn't have a licence anyway, I'd sold it before coming to Scalloway. I'd got away with driving in the country, but it didn't seem worth risking illegal-driving in Lerwick just to get to Mass once a week. I plodded on past Lerwick Power Station, a cavernous brown building with a spike of a chimney, and at last I was at the outskirts of the town, with the first council housing schemes on my right, and the ferry terminal on my left. The blue and white North boat was at sea, leaving the passenger walkway sticking out into space. Cargo boats, a clutter of cargo cages, the Co-op. I was almost there. I cut alongside the Peerie Dock with its rowing boats lying on the shingle shore, slipped through the timber mill of Hay and Co., and came out on the path around Hay's Dock.

The new museum (it would be new for another thirty years at least) had been built where Hay and Co., the island's main fishing agents for three centuries, had had its boatbuilding sheds. Three of these sheds had been incorporated into the museum. One was still used for restoring boats. The new building was impressively tall, with its gables shaped like the brown sails of the herring drifters that once filled the sound. It was sited right on the waterfront, with a little walled harbour in front of it, and a shingle shore, where the museum's own fleet of boats was pulled up. Moored at the pier were fishing boats like the ones I could just remember seeing in the country in Ireland when I was a child, dark hulled, with a small white wheelhouse, and names like *Pilot Us* and *Nil Desperandum*. A couple of seals were sculling in the harbour, popping their noses up, then turning over to show pale bellies. I came past the murmuring speakers of the Modern Art Installation (a babble of recorded Shetland sounds that intensified depending on the wind speed) and into the museum.

I hadn't visited it yet, and suspected that it would take more than the half hour I could spare from witch research, but I couldn't resist a scoit into the boat hall I'd heard so much about. I crossed the flagstones to the start of the exhibitions, and found I couldn't go slowly: there were stones to run a finger over, smooth axe-heads to curve in the hand, a model broch, a display of Pictish silver, Norse combs, and a scratched drawing of a young man with a tight head of curls and Anders' straight nose. After them was the cramped room of a croft house, with a wild-boar pig tied by its leg to the settee, a bannock on the fire, and a lady singing to her cradled baby in the ben room. Past that was a stuffed Shetland cow, black and white, with long horns, then a display on fishing, with a turtle caught off Unst suspended above me – and then I came into the boat hall, and was transfixed. On the ground was a great 'flit-boat', tarred black, almost the length of *Khalida*, used for shifting peats or sheep. Above it, suspended in the air for three storeys of height, were the elegant hulls of Shetland models, our own class of racing dinghy: shallow and double-pointed, like miniature Viking war galleys. I admired the hulls from below, then went up the stairs to lean on the balcony and enjoy the man with his lunch in the motorboat, the elegant lines and set sails of the racing Maids. They'd been moving towards obselete on the west side when I'd been growing up, so I'd never sailed in one of these three-man flyers, but I was determined that if I was still here next summer, I'd get a crewing berth.

I didn't have time to dream about next summer. I needed to find out about witches now. I threaded my way through the glass cases of Victoriana, Up Helly Aa costumes, and knitting, dodged round a circular display about the oil era, and came out into the upstairs corridor.

There was a stern notice on the Archives entrance: no food or drink, no mobile phones. I checked mine was switched off, took a last swig of water, and opened the heavy door. Instantly, silence surrounded me – that working hush that you get in the control room of a ship at sea, with the navigator intent on his chart, the steersman looking forward. There were half a dozen people in the room, spaced along long central tables, heads bent over their work. The far side of the room had computer terminals, and this side was lined with books. A man looked up from the reception desk. 'Can I help you?'

I sat down on the convenient chair. 'I'm looking for information about witches.'

He pushed a sign-in book towards me. 'You'll be wanting Marion Perdone. That's Hibbert.' He unfolded himself up from his chair, went straight to one of the shelves, picked out a large, black book, and brought it to me, looking in the index and flipping to the page before handing it over. 'Here you are.'

'Thank you,' I said, and took it to the tables. There were holders of sharpened pencils and homemade notepads. I took one of each, settled myself in the black net chair, and bent my head to the book.

'Hibbert' turned out to be Samuel Hibbert, *A Description of the Shetland Islands, 1822*. The book's paper was browned the colour of weak tea, with the edges nibbled as if by mice, and he'd given Marion Peebles *alias Perdone, spouse to Swene in Hildiswick, AD 1644*, a whole section to herself. It seemed to be some sort of accusation, for it was given as 'you' – *that you did send sickness on Janet Robertson, saying she would repent what she had done to your daughter and good-son* – and so on for a four-page list of malice. The first account was of her having sent sickness on Janet Robertson, but when Janet's husband threatened her, she transferred the sickness to a cow, which died, while Janet recovered. She did the same in the next account; the next charge was spoiling beer, and the fourth had her casting madness on Madda Scuddasdoughter *until she drew blood of you, biting two of your fingers whereupon she came to her ryt senses.* There was more trouble with animals – two cows which gave strange milk, a herd of horses which she was supposed to have cursed, a calf that ran mad and died. By the end of the first account I was left wondering why the local folk hadn't run her over the banks, if she'd really been that malevolent. Then there was a second set of accusations, dated Scalloway 15th March 1645. The first concerned an Andro Brown; she'd set sickness on him *frae the crown of his head to the sole of his fute* and it was only when the neighbours came round and prayed *in God's cause* that she would cure him that she consented to come. This surprised me. Surely if she was a witch it should be the Devil's cause. She uncovered his leg, put her finger on it, then put the finger on the ground three times, *where immediately his pain was dissolved.* However, he'd obviously blamed her for causing it in the first place too publicly, for she told the neighbours she'd heard what he was saying, and *said emgrace on them that bewitched you* whereupon Andro fell back into the sickness. Eventually Marion sent him a bannock, which he ate, and recovered, the sickness going into a cow, which died.

The second one was stranger, and involved another quarrel between Marion, her husband Swene, and Edmund Halcrow, over shifting a 'knot' in Andro Brown's peat back. On her husband's advice, Marion transformed herself into a *pellack quhaill* and overturned Edmund's boat while he was at the fishing. He and four others were drowned, and when the bodies were found, Marion and Swene were sent for. When Marion laid her hand on the body, blood gushed from its hands and fingers – a sure sign, apparently, that she'd caused his death.

'Very Shakespearean,' the librarian commented, coming over to see how I was doing. 'Romeo says something about that when he's in the tomb with Tybalt that he killed.'

My education had let me miss out on Shakespeare. 'Do you think they really believed that she'd done all this – putting sickness from people to cows and back, and changing into a whale?

'A porpoise,' he said. 'A pellack whale. They believed it enough to burn her for it. She and her husband were executed on the Hill of Berry, in Scalloway, in 1645.'

I looked back at the place where she'd cursed Andro for calling her a witch. 'There doesn't seem to be anything here about calling up the Devil, or meeting in covens.'

'Keep reading.' He pointed to the last paragraph. 'She was seen walking from Breckon to Hildeswick, accompanied by the Devil, disguised as two corbies.'

'Corbies? Crows?'

'Ravens. The hooded crows are just craas.' He considered the short entry, then went back to the shelves, and came back with a buttercup yellow book. *A Source Book of Scottish Witches*, it was called, and someone had kindly written a list of all the Shetland ones at the front. There weren't very many of them, an appropriate baker's dozen, but the book didn't give any actual information, just a reference where you could find more. 'Dal.,' the helpful librarian said. 'That's Dalyell, he's online.' He fired up a computer for me, and found a scan-in of an ancient tome, with writing where the shorter letters linked up to the taller, and an erudition of footnotes on each page. 'The source book will give you the page numbers.'

I got to work. Each of the witches had several page references, and there was more folklore here. I found the knotted thread, called a 'wrestling thread', but here it seemed to be a cure, to be given in 'the name of the Father, Son, and Holy Ghost, with the words "Bone to bone, synew to synew, and flesh to flesh and blood to blood", which would make any man or beast haill.' However another account reckoned 'casting knots' was supposed to control the elements. From what the hooded crows had said, my knotted cord had been a warning. A Katherine Jonesdochter had wished her husband's infirmities might be transferred to a stranger, and grasped the hand of the intended sufferer, who became sick while her husband got well ... the sickness transfer thing again. I remembered Annette reaching out a hand to stroke Cat. *He looks a very healthy peerie cat,* she'd said. I understood now that strange look she'd given me, part defiance, part apology. Dan had been sick, and the three crows had claimed it as their work. She was going to transfer the sickness to Cat, except that he wouldn't let her lay hands on him ... so, my brain went on, she'd agreed to pay them instead. The £100 she'd taken out that day, which Sergeant Peterson couldn't account for by purchases in Lerwick, had been intended for them. Had been given to them? Except that I was sure 'he' had done the ritual without them, and Annette had been home all evening. That would be something for Gavin to follow up. *Whatever it takes ...* I was going to have to swallow my pride and phone him.

Sickness, curses, none of these seemed any help to my situation. The only double trials were Marion and her husband, and a mother and daughter couple fifty years later. There was no suggestion in any of these records of pacts with the Devil, or covens, or gathering at midnight on the witches' sabbath. Whatever records the shadowy leader had consulted, it wasn't these. I gathered up the books and went back to the archivist's desk.

'Where might I find something on covens?'

He gave me a doubtful look. 'I trust you're not thinking of starting one up.' It wasn't quite a joke. I shook my head, and glanced around. Nobody was listening to us.

'I want to stop one,' I said softly. 'I need to know what they do. No, I need to know what other people think they might do, someone who's researched them a bit.'

'You could try Isobel Gowdie.' His fingers rattled over the keys. 'Here, yes, tried for witchcraft 1662 … the library has a book on her.' He picked up a pencil and scribbled the title and author. 'It sounds like this will include her confessions. They're startling stuff. Here, I'll phone them.' He had the number in his head, and in half a dozen words established that yes, they had the book, yes, it was in, and I could go along now, it would be at the front desk for me.

'Thanks.'

He wished me good luck, and I headed off to the Shetland Library, up King Harald Street, and past the playpark where the galley was burnt each Up Helly Aa. Today it was full of shouting children, and toddlers being swung by a parent. Opposite it, in the the flower park, the last coral astilbe plumes mingled with purple poppies and sharp-petalled dahlias. The scent of the climbing roses spilled over the wall. I climbed up King Erik Street to the war memorial and the Town Hall, where I could see the stained-glass figures from Shetland's past in reverse: James III and his reluctant-looking bride facing away from each other (tradition had it they'd installed the two windows the wrong way round), the Maid of Norway, St Magnus and St Olaf, Floki with his raven on his shoulder. The old library was opposite, a sixties cube used for admin. now, and the books were in St Ringan's Church, refurbished with a ramp for wheelchairs. Inside, it wasn't as hushed as the archives had been, with a nurseryful of toddlers gathered around one of the librarians for story time, and a cluster of teenagers on a computer. I filled in a form, got my ticket, and took the book upstairs, to where a stained-glass Madonna presided over several squashy couches. I loved this window, because of the Madonna's individual face; I was sure it was the artist's wife holding her first child. I bagged a corner couch and contemplated my doom. *The Visions of Isobel Gowdie*, it was called, by Emma Wilby, a stout paperback heavy enough to make a serviceable anchor, with a picture of stormy clouds on the cover. A quick look at random showed the prose was academic. I braced my shoulders and launched in.

If I was looking for malevolence, it was here in spades. There were four confessions, given roughly a fortnight apart, and attested to by various local worthies – a long list of them, headed by the minister, the sheriff, the lairds. The list ended with a statement that the confession had been 'without any compulsitoris.' I took that with a pinch of salt. Isobel's words were given as she'd said them, and I'd have had difficulty deciphering them if it hadn't been for my school friend Dodie, now working on the Yell ferry, who spoke exactly as she did. I imagined him reading out to me, and worked my way through each, taking notes, then paused to consider it all.

It was a weird mixture. The picture of these high-up and presumably intelligent people listening with serious faces to this garbage was testimony to their belief in the Devil. If they hadn't – and, as the author pointed out, there were places where you would hear the ring of the omitted questions 'Where did you meet the Devil? What did he look like?' – they could never have taken this seriously. Jaunts to fairyland, meetings with the elf king and queen, flying on a docken straw … and in among it all, the black malevolence of shooting elf-arrows at the 'Laird of Parkis' bairns', and making a clay model of the Laird himself, and roasting it at the fire. She claimed to have killed several people, but only admitted to regretting one. There was none of the messing around with animals that Marion Perdone had been accused of. She and her coven went for people.

The account of the coven had me thinking. She'd met with the Devil on the road between 'the town of Drumdearin and the headis' and covenanted with him. They'd met again at the church, and she'd put one hand on her head and the other on the sole of her foot, and sworn everything in between to the Devil's service. He'd bitten her on the shoulder, then he'd twisted the bite in his hand 'till the blood spurted out', and he'd sprinkled it over her in baptism. Then there'd been an orgy, with the Devil going at it 'like a stallion among mares'. There had been thirteen in the coven, with the 'Maiden' sitting at the Devil's side.

It could have been the Devil, of course. But reading it, I began to think how someone of imposing stature, someone quick-witted, with a presence, maybe someone with knowledge of hypnotism, a conjurer, a charlatan, could have had a lot of fun imposing on a group of simple village women. People were more sophisticated now, of course, but they also had more time to spare, because they weren't working every moment of their lives just to make food for their bellies, clothes for their backs. They had time to get bored, and the restlessness to seek something new. I reckoned you could sell this coven idea to daft teenagers as a laugh, something to do on a dull Sunday evening … and then you could appear among them, looking very imposing in your devil suit, and whether they believed that was what you were, or whether they went along with it and took you as high priest for their high jinks, either way, you could have fun manipulating them, if that's the way you got your kicks. Post-hypnotic suggestion could account for the wild rides over the countryside, or creeping inside people's houses as they lay sleeping.

I flipped on through the book, rubbing my stabbing temple. This author seemed to take the confessions as evidence of a Scottish shamanistic tradition, where women (generally, though some men were mentioned too) took dreams as messages from another world, and through sharing them came to believe they attended these covens as an out-of-body experience while in a trance state. But I didn't see the three crows reading the whole book. They'd have ploughed their way through the confessions and found the recipes for witchery: beating a wet rag to raise the wind, knotting threads, making a clay model of an enemy and roasting it before a fire. I could see the three of them on their knees together, hair loose around their faces, chanting Isobel's charms 'in the Devil's name', and glorying in the theatricality of their mischief.

I closed the book, returned it to the desk, and headed back out into the sunlight. The Town Hall clock said it was almost five. I wanted to get back to *Khalida*, to safety. I felt exposed here in Lerwick, as if that old woman leaning on her stick, or that pair of young lasses walking past the playpark, phones glued to their lugs, were liable to turn on me and mutter a curse that would bring me to my knees on the pavement in front of them. Superstitious rubbish, all of it. I passed the park and came into church. I sat quietly in the back pew, with the greens and blues of our 'oily' window falling on my shoulder, and contemplated the carved high altar in its curve of gold wall. If God was real, so was the Devil, but I didn't believe in him stalking the streets of Scalloway. Just as God had no hands but ours to do good, so the Devil had no hands but ours to do evil. It was human hands which had bound Nate with rope and thrown him over the sea wall to die. Curses, though … if prayers to God could do good – and I believed that they could – then did it follow that prayers to the Devil could do harm? I wasn't sure I was prepared to follow logic that far.

I shouldered my bag again and headed out onto the north road. Either way I'd have to head through houses, but the north road got me into the country quicker, rather than the long walk through Sound, with the rows of council-estate houses on one side, and Nob Hill on the other. I'd just come out of the old North Road onto the new one when a police car passed me, indicated, and drew up. Gavin got out. He was formally dressed this afternoon, in his red kilt, with a claymore pin glinting among the folds of cloth. His voice was as remote as his dress. 'Can we give you a lift to Scalloway?'

Damn it, I wasn't going to apologise or explain, especially not with Sergeant Peterson sitting there, mermaid-indifferent, with her hands at ten to two on the steering wheel. 'Thank you,' I said. He opened the front door for me, gestured me inside, then got into the back himself. 'Hi,' I said, across the front seat. The car was spotless. Even the dashboard was dust-free. Sergeant Peterson's doing, I'd have betted.

She gave a nod. 'Ms Lynch.'

'An afternoon in town?' Gavin asked, leaning forward to my shoulder.

I caught the sense of him, a clean smell, Imperial Leather soap, no aftershave. It didn't take a DI to see I hadn't been doing a weekly shop, and he knew I wasn't the window-gazing type. *Whatever it takes* ... I offered an olive branch. 'I've been looking up witches.' Sergeant Peterson made a snorting sound. 'Great minds thinking alike?' I asked.

'I spent most of the morning on Wiki,' she agreed, 'working through Nate's files.'

'Did you find Isobel Gowdie?'

'Along with Margaret Aiken and Janet Wishart and several hundred others. It just shows how stupid people were in the past, that they believed such rubbish.' She shot a look backwards at Gavin, indicated for the Scalloway turnoff, and retracted that sweeping statement. 'But I suppose people now are believing it too.'

'I don't know if they do really believe it,' I said. 'Don't you need to believe in God before you can get all excited about the Devil? Or are they just having fun spreading rumours and feeling a shiver down their spines, like watching a scary film?'

'I think they didn't believe it,' Sergeant Peterson said, 'and now they're afraid it might be true. Scratch any human being and the cave dweller's just under the surface, scared of the dark and propitiating any evil spirits going.'

'When people believe in nothing,' Gavin said, a half-metre behind my ear, 'then they'll believe in anything.' It sounded like a quote.

'Oscar Wilde?' I guessed.

'G. K. Chesterton.' His voice had warmed a touch. 'To be exact, his Father Brown said, 'The first effect of not believing in God is that you lose your common sense.'

I considered that for a moment. 'It's against modern thought,' I said at last.

'Definitely,' Gavin agreed. 'Go on then, tell us about Isobel Goudie.'

'Nate had quite a lot about her. Tried as a witch in Auldearn, 1662,' Sergeant Peterson said briskly. I shot her a sideways glance. Gavin had been talking to me, but she had only this short while to impress him. We saw a lot of that on board ship, guests arriving for a week, picking this holiday's flirtation, and moving in fast. It was an occupational hazard of being a crew member, particularly if you had gold braid on the shoulder of your jumper. Even I'd suffered from it, in spite of my scarred cheek. 'Gave a detailed confession of witchcraft, including coven activities, spell rhymes, harming the Laird's children, and going on night rides with the Devil. There's no record of whether she was eventually executed.'

'That's the one,' I agreed. The car swept down the curve into Scalloway. The water below the castle was summer blue, the reflection ruffled to a brown block. When it was built, it had stood at the water's edge. In the 1850s, the fishermen of Scalloway had used the stones of two ruined brochs to create the pier where now the ice plant sat, and the salmon-processing factory. Shetland's prosperity depended as much on fish now as it had then. The witch with the strange name, Jonka, her husband had been lost at the fishing ...

We came round the roundabout and along the street front. Monday tea-time shopper heads turned as it passed. I could see them recognising me, and turning to each other, could almost hear the whispers: 'Do you think she's under arrest?' 'No, she's ower thick wi' that policeman in the kilt. She'll be telling him aathing sho hears ida village.' My name would be mud in college tomorrow.

'So?' Gavin said, ignoring them. I gave him a blank look over my shoulder. He was smiling, an enigmatic curve of his lips. 'What did you find out?'

I reverted to five-year-old mode. 'Just the same as Sergeant Peterson.'

'The same sources,' he agreed. His voice hardened to a note I'd not heard since the longship murder. 'What was your take on it, Ms Lynch?'

War had been declared. The car slowed along the sea front and stopped at the marina. His hand was resting on the door button. I wasn't going to entertain Sergeant Peterson with an undignified struggle. 'I thought that it would be easy to impersonate the Devil at a coven meeting, especially with modern theatrical effects. I thought some unscrupulous person could have a good deal of fun with naive women out for a thrill.'

'So he could,' Gavin agreed. 'And have you any ideas about who that unscrupulous person might be?'

I turned my head to look him straight in the eye. 'Nate seemed the obvious person.' My gaze moved to his hand. 'And now, if you'll excuse me.' His hand moved back, with a ceremonious swirl. 'Thank you for the lift.'

He got out to open the door for me. 'Thank you for the information.' A jerk of the chin towards the marina. As luck would have it, Anders had just come up into the motorboat's cockpit. 'You didn't mention that Anders is back.'

'He came over last night,' I said. So that was what this coldness was about. Well, be damned to the lot of them. I shouldered my bag and stalked towards the gate, without turning to look back. Anders was just coming through it, and I was tempted to greet him with more enthusiasm than I otherwise would have, and knowing it wouldn't be fair, only to be taken aback by a casual nod, as if to a pontoon aquaintance. 'Fine day,' he said, face expressionless, and passed by without a further word.

I heard the soft whiff of the police car's engine, then the scrunch of gravel under the tyres as it moved off. Let Gavin make what he wanted of that little exchange. I hoped it puzzled him as much as it puzzled me.

There had to be a reason for it. Then I looked along the shore road and saw the three crows strolling away, their grey clothes merging into the dimming buildings. That made it obvious. Anders had gone along the street, made connection with them – now I thought of it, I'd told him they could be found hanging about by the Shetland Bus memorial, wreathed in smoke – and thought he was getting somewhere. I'd text him later.

Besides, I wanted to be alone. I could have groaned aloud when I heard a Shetland voice call my name. A dark-jacketed figure lounging in the boating club doorway straightened and came towards me, head twitching over his shoulder, as if he was afraid of being overheard. James Leask. I was sorry for his loss of Annette, truly I was, but I didn't feel I could do sympathy right now.

He came straight to me. 'Cass, I was hoping to catch you. Listen, I can't speak right now, but I need to talk to you urgently. It's about Annette.' He looked over one shoulder, back at the college. His eyes bored into mine. 'I *know.*'

'You know who killed her?'

He almost put a hand up to cover my mouth, then realised how obvious it would be and let it fall again. 'Ssssh. Don't say it. Can you meet me later? After dark.' He gave the already-dimming sky a haunted look. 'Half past six. No, seven. Seven o'clock … in Mary Ruizland's garden, in the little hut at the back. Nobody will see us there. Come alone. Will you come?'

'Why all this secrecy?' I asked.

His head twitched to his shoulder again. 'Seven, in the shed in the garden. I've got to go.' He hurried back into the college.

Melodramatic idiot. It was the detective story classic. Man who has discovered the murderer won't tell the inspector, and the next you know, his body turns up. Girl is given mysterious appointment and is abducted. I made a disgusted noise and kicked a pebble across the road and into the far gutter. Above me, the sky was covered by mottled clouds. The moon had not yet risen above the north-eastern hills, but her silvery light glowed in the sky behind the sentinel wind turbines.

I walked along the swaying pontoon, clambered down the

companionway, and put the washboards back up. Home at last. The warmth from the sun lingered in the cabin, and it was still light enough not to need the lantern. The kettle had just boiled when Cat slipped in, with Rat behind him. I made my tea and sat down, patting my lap so that he'd jump up. Rat swarmed up onto the fiddle and whiffled his whiskers at me. He hadn't forgotten *Khalida*. I stroked Cat as I drank my tea, trying to forget my curiosity over what Anders was up to, and the cold ache in my heart. I couldn't blame Gavin, after all; I'd jumped back when he'd seemed to think of kissing me, and now Anders was here, without me mentioning he was coming. Maybe it would be easiest to go for the devil I knew, and become a Norwegian girlfriend. 'With,' my inner voice pointed out, 'a hostile mother-in-law, and only a small boat to start living-together life in. *Your* boat too, turned into our boat.' My *Khalida*. We'd managed to live aboard together for a summer in reasonable harmony, but she was too small for long-term. We'd have to sell her, and buy something bigger. Anders was one of the black-clad Lutheran persuasion too. That wouldn't cause difficulty at first, but later I knew it would come to haunt us. The gulf between that and my own Catholicism was too wide.

Yet how could I explain to Gavin without seeming to blow hot and cold? Oh, I could describe how Anders and Reidar had arrived last night, out of the blue, but that in itself didn't mean anything. What I had to explain was that even though on paper Anders was right, and Gavin wasn't, in practice, with Gavin in front of me, he felt right and Anders didn't. Why had I dodged, then? Because of the paper; because I was afraid it wouldn't work, and then we'd both be hurt. I didn't know how I could begin to explain that. I knew that if I wanted to take a step towards having a relationship with DI Gavin Macrae I'd have to try. Otherwise, this wall would remain, because it had been I who'd rejected him. The Highlanders were a proud race. I understood that.

I was dozing off when there was a light step on the pontoon beside us, then on *Khalida*'s side. A dark shadow blocked the companionway window. I tensed; Cat sprang to the floor. Then a hand knocked on the sliding hatch, a bass voice rumbled, 'Cass, are you home?'

Reidar. I got up and let him in. He had two cups of drinking chocolate in one of those moulded mug holders, and several homemade biscuits, crumbly ones that smelled of orange peel. The man was a genius. We sat companionably sipping in silence for ten minutes before he got down to business.

'Anders spoke to your chief witch,' he said at last, when both cups were empty, and Cat had finished licking the finger of cream I gave him off his nose. 'He went along to the shop, and saw them hanging about there, so he poured on the charm. He told her that he was on a boat on the pontoon here, and then he hung around, you know, sat with a fishing rod in the sun for an hour on the pontoon, and they came along to talk. Now he is meeting her after work. He said she was excited. She was not exactly dropping the hints, but he said she was all lit up, jumping with that "something exciting" feeling.'

'It's Hallowe'en,' I said.

'I do not know this word.'

'The evening before All Hallows, that was the old name for All Saints' Day.' In France, my cousins would be buying chrysanthemums. 'I have information too. I found out about Scottish witches.' I told him the story of Isobel Gowdie, and he nodded, and made rumbling noises in his beard. 'Then perhaps there is a coven meeting tonight?'

'Perhaps ... I don't know. It depends if Nate was their Devil.'

'You think that he was?'

'I suppose I do.' That feeling of unease swept over me again. 'If the werewolf suit was his, he was the one who clawed Annette. But someone else wore the Devil costume, to kill him.'

'That someone else would have to be stupid, to hold a meeting this night, with the police everywhere.'

'I'm not sure if he could help himself. That kind of power, it'd be addictive.' Skippers knew about power. You held the safety of the ship and the life of its crew in your ability to read the pattern of isobars that meant fair weather or foul, in your navigation towards a clear passageway or a rocky shore. Power was lonely. However much you consulted your officers, in the end it was your orders which counted. Skippers found it hard to adjust to life ashore, with a thousand petty checks to each move. 'Without his coven he'd just be an ordinary person again. Besides, he doesn't know that Shaela saw him, that he's linked to Nate's death.'

'So if it is not this Nate,' Reidar said, 'you are looking for someone overlooked, someone who feels that he is special, except that the world does not recognise this.'

'Or someone who had power and has lost it,' I said slowly. An idea was struggling to the surface of my mind. Claws ... snatching, holding. Rachel saying that Lawrence didn't like her to be out. She'd been independent, then become part of a couple, her wings clipped. Nate was of slight build; a suit made to bulk Rachel out could have been left in his room. It would have looked a fit for Nate – and who could come and go more easily in the house than the daughter who'd lived there?

I liked Rachel. I didn't want her to be mad. 'I've been asked to meet someone,' I said abruptly. 'James Leask. He says he knows who killed Annette.' He'd kept looking over his shoulder at the college, as if he'd been afraid of being overheard. Rachel? Lawrence?

163

'Where does he want you to meet him?'

'In Mary Ruisland's garden.' I looked out of *Khalida*'s port window into the dusk. 'It's over there, the garden with the flowers, just above the little roundabout.' Above the shore where Nate had died. 'There's a shed in one corner. I've to meet him in there.'

Reidar voiced my thoughts. 'It is the classic chapter in the detective story. The heroine is lured to the lonely place to be murdered.'

'I'm not anyone's heroine,' I said, 'and I'm not going to be murdered if I can help it. But I need to talk to him, and he said to come alone.'

'Then I will go there first,' Reidar said. 'When have you to meet him?'

'At seven.' I glanced down at the little clock attached by velcro to the bulkhead just by my berth. It was quarter to five.

'Very well. I will go at six and a quarter, somewhere I can see his approach, and yours. Then you can learn what he has to tell you, in safety.'

Chapter Eighteen

The moon was above the eastern hills by the time I set out towards Mary Ruisland's garden, a silver penny with a twisted smile smoking the clouds with light. A full moon gave a full tide, but not quite yet; it was two hours to high water, three-twelfths still to come in, pouring into every bay and voe and geo on this side of Shetland, then swirling around to fill each inlet on the other side. The sea below the pavement was molten mercury washing up the beach. Every little stone had a bright summit, a magnified shadow. Darkness and light …I'd thought Cat would want to stay with Rat, but he came up the cabin steps with me, and trotted before me along the pontoon, the moon glinting on the silver underside of his plumed tail. He'd stop and go home when he thought he'd gone far enough, or wait in the ditch, out of sight, until I returned.

Hallowe'en. The guizers were out. There was a group clustered in front of the sheds where the men of the Shetland Bus had repaired their boats. They were dressed in a bizarre assortment of costumes left over from Up Helly Aa: a fur fabric parakeet, a Spanish dancer with a high mantilla, an inflated sumo wrestler, a long-nosed witch, an Elvis in a silver poncho. His false head had a high rubber quiff. They'd stopped under the shadow of the sheds to raise their bottles, and the Elvis was drunk already, staggering between two of his mates. If I'd been on the mainland I'd have dodged into a side street until they'd passed, but there was no side street here, just the long promenade, and this was Shetland, so I had nothing to fear from gangs of young folk out for a spree. Cat pressed closer to my heels.

I stepped into the road to pass them. Suddenly I was surrounded. The Spanish dancer flung her shawl over my head, and the parakeet grabbed my arms, and before I could yell or strike out my wrists had been bound with thin cord. The shawl was pulled away. The witch stuffed a handkerchief in my mouth, and held it there with claw-fingers, while the dancer pulled a false head over my face. A blanket dropped over my shoulders. A woman laughed. There was a growl from Cat, and a hiss, then a cry of pain, another voice that could have been young man or woman. 'It fucking bit me.'

165

Good for Cat. I was trembling with fury. Whoever this was, whatever stupid joke they'd decided to play on me, they'd be sorry. It wouldn't just be Cat who bit and scratched, once I got my hands free.

'She'll no get out o' that in a hurry,' a voice said, with satisfaction. It was the girl who had worn the dog-collar. Her drawled, flat voice was like a bucket of ice water poured over me. Not my college mates being stupid, but the hooded crows, the witches. There had been five of them in the road, and five knots on the piece of string I'd found under my pillow. The coven … and its master? There was a cool intelligence behind this. The way they'd caught me had been thought through, efficient. I didn't see the lead hoodie craw working like that. She was too emotional. No, this was done under the master's orders. James Leask, I fumed, making sure I'd be on the road at the right time. A pretty piece of acting that had been, the artistic glances over his shoulder towards the college. Damn and damn, letting myself be taken in like that. Reidar had worried about me being grabbed at the meeting place, but we'd neither of us thought of the dangers of the road there. *Worry about me, Reidar, when I don't turn up. Phone the police.*

An arm each side of me linked through mine and pulled me forward, swaying me as if I was drunk, and they were supporting me. A passer-by wouldn't look twice at me, any more than I'd looked at the drunken Elvis. If I fell, they'd have to drag me, but there were enough of them to be able to do it, and they wouldn't do it gently. I'd just have my hands and knees scraped to ribbons on the gravelled road. I was better to stay upright, and save my strength for when I could use it to help myself. If the sandpaper scrape on my wrists was baler twine, then the little multi-tool in my pocket would cut through it in seconds, once I got my fingers to it. The cloth in my mouth tasted of fabric softener, the sort that would be called 'Summer Meadow', and the intense floral taste made me want to gag. The head over it was one of those uni-size plastic affairs with wider cheeks than mine. I might be able to work the cloth out of my mouth and into the pouch of its cheek. The head would muffle a scream, but I'd still be able to make enough noise to attract attention. If we kept moving forwards, we'd arrive at the street.

I darted a glance each side of me. Trying to see through the eyeholes was like looking through a letter box. I turned my head left, then right. It was the parakeet and the Sumo wrestler who were holding me. I could hear footsteps behind me: the Spanish dancer, the witch, Elvis. I focused on the cloth in my mouth, working it forward with my tongue and lips. We'd be at Norway house in fifty yards, the start of the people zone –

They'd not mentioned Cat any more. I hoped that meant he'd bitten and run into the safety of the ditch, where his grey would blend into the shadows, where he could slink safely home to *Khalida*. I hoped he wasn't following, with some dog-like instinct of sticking with his mistress. He didn't usually; once we started meeting people who were likely to want to stroke him, he headed for home. *Girly stuff* ...

My captors turned left, dragging me with them. Now we were facing the burn up the hill, the traditional route for witches to be marched to the gallows on the summit. Kate had said once that she'd been working in her studio later than usual, on a black night with no moon, and she'd heard the chinking of chains, and the roaring of the crowd. She'd been too afraid to move, she'd said, but had stood there, paintbrush poised in her hand, as the crowd growled past. When silence had deadened the night once more, she'd slipped out of the door and run like a hare for the house. She'd put her head under the pillow, she said, but she didn't sleep. Kate would have heard if I'd yelled her name, but it was too early for her to be in her studio. She and Peter would be in their dining room on the other side of the house, eating their roast lamb with silver cutlery, chatting across the white tablecloth. My captors hustled me past the garden wall, as if they'd thought of that too. I felt the tarmac of Ladysmith Drive under my feet, then a gravel track between the last pair of gardens, and finally there was grass underfoot. We'd reached the foot of Gallow Hill.

Now there was nobody to hear me if I screamed. I was cold with anger at being man-handled like this, a stranger on each side with a rough grasp around my arms, forcing me onwards. The multi-tool in my pocket bumped like a talisman against my thigh. Just thirty seconds with these heavy hands off my arms, and I'd have this baler twine cut, and my hands free. The false head wouldn't let me see what was underneath my feet, but I'd seen it in the daylight, a rough earth path a foot back from the burn banks. I stumbled upwards between my captors, my shoes slipping on the uneven ground. They were less fit than I; the parakeet's breathing became laboured before we were half way up, and the wrestler's pace was slowing. I'd soon give them the slip once I was able to run. Someone shoved me from behind: 'Get on, hurry up.' It was the lead hoodie crow's voice. I looked behind. She was the witch. Five of them ... the three crows and two unknowns. I was pretty sure Dog-collar was the parakeet, and wouldn't have been surprised if the sumo wrestler was the third one, who'd worn the sea-green corset. I tried to visualise Rachel's height and built. Yes, she could be the Spanish dancer or Elvis behind me.

'We're going as fast as we can,' the wrestler retorted, her voice raggedly breathless. I recognised it: Sea-green Corset. I'd be able to outrun these two, even on a path as bad as this. If they would let go of me, I'd make a run for it. I jerked forward suddenly, as if I'd stumbled.

The parakeet let go, then grabbed my arm again, but the wrestler overbalanced, and went down on her hands and knees, pulling me with her. My knee hit a stone with a painful crack, making me spit a cry of pain into the mouth cloth. I was glad they didn't hear it. The parakeet gripped my arm with both hands while the wrestler sorted herself out, then they hauled me to my feet again. Someone jabbed me in the back. 'Keep moving, you.'

It felt as though the walk would never end. My face was wet with sweat under the stifling mask. Up, up by the burn, then into open ground at last, where the moonlight poured like silver on the heathery moor. Now I was stumbling over ankle-deep tussocks of heather, fumbling forward with each foot to make sure I wasn't going to break a leg in a rabbit-burrow. How far had the Gallow Hill been, when we'd looked at it from the boat? An hour's walk, maybe, but that would have been a brisk walk with swinging arms, not this stumbling progress. The frost sparkled in the air, and my captors breathed ragged smoke. Left foot, right, left, right. The drudgery of putting one foot in front of another was stopping me from thinking, and I had to think, to keep my brain alert. What time was it now? I could calculate that. I turned my head to catch the moon in my letterbox, then looked downward at the black islands on the shining sea. The silver penny was over the hills of Quarff, sailing through the clouds like a full-rigged ship. Once I got through this, I'd be away on a ship myself, and having no more dealings with land people. The island of Trondra was due south. I visualised the map in my head and laid a compass rose over it. The moon was around 120 degrees. She'd risen around 1600, in the north-east, say 60 degrees, and she would set at 0700 just north of west, say 290 degrees. 230 degrees divided by fifteen hours, fifteen degrees an hour. If she was at 120 degrees now, she'd moved 60 degrees, 60 divided by fifteen, four. Four hours on … around eight o'clock. An hour for Reidar to realise something had gone wrong, and for the police to start looking. I hadn't mentioned the witches' sabbat this evening, just kale-casting, but the children who'd come guizing had mentioned meetings up on Gallow Hill. Gavin would know that Hallowe'en was the night of the dead. Help should come soon, however annoyed he was with me. Anders too, he'd had been talking to the chief hooded crow. She might have told him where they were going that night.

This was far too much trouble just for a quiet chat. They'd been gathering their heather roots and berries on Saturday, ready for their big celebration, their Hallowe'en Sabbat. Somehow, I was to be part of it. Either I was to be menaced into joining them, or I was to be eliminated. I remembered Nate, bound and floating. It was all very well for Wiki to say modern witches were harmless sacrificers of berries and other produce. These ones had taken the malevolent Isobel Gowdie as their model, Isobel who'd shot elf-arrows to kill her neighbours' children during her wild night rides with the Devil. My bound hands were dangling tantalisingly close to the back pocket where I kept my penknife, but each time I tried to stretch them downwards, the hands jerked my arms up again. Once I had my hands free, I'd yank this mask off and run.

It couldn't be far to the burning site now. The cloth was soggy in my mouth, but I would leave it be; they'd check my bonds before they got on with their chanting, leaving me, I hoped, to work on escaping. One foot, then the other, sliding on the uneven heather until each found the soft peat underneath. My captors were beginning to lean heavily on my arms, and the wrestler was puffing like the pellack whale Merion Perdoun had turned herself into. My legs were aching, my bare ankles scratched by the tough heather stems, my shoulders needled with pain, but I'd still be able to outrun her. That left only four, I thought grimly. The night wasn't in my favour, this lovely silver that would show me up clear as day. There had been a dyke, though, no, two, running north to south along the crest of the hill and swooping down to the shore. If I could get on the shadowed side of one of them, I could reach the shore and get back to *Khalida* that way. Home, sanctuary.

We came at last onto more level ground, with soft grass in place of the heather. I remembered what Dorothy had said, back in *Khalida*'s cabin: *Jim o'Shalders'Ayre ploughed it over. He said it was a superstition and a shame* ... The wrestler paused. I could feel the hand that clutched my arm jerking as her chest heaved. The parakeet's grasp was slack on my other arm, and I was tempted to make a break for it now, while I had the advantage of fitness over them, except that my arms were still fastened, and my vision limited by the mask. Surely, surely, they would dump me somewhere for a moment while they prepared their bonfire or cauldron or whatever. Thirty seconds, twenty, to get my knife out and use it.

The dark shapes surrounded me. I was pulled and pushed into a particular spot, then my arms were forced upwards until my bound hands were level with my shoulderblades, then scraped down rough wood that was cold with frost. A last yank set my shoulders aching once more, then I felt a rope being passed around my waist and forearms, once, twice, three times. The third loop tightened as one of the witches tied it in a knot at my wrists. Then they stood back and looked at me. I slumped against the rope, making my breathing heavier, as if I was exhausted.

'That'll fix her,' said Dog-collar. Her voice oozed malevolent satisfaction. 'Learn her a lesson she winna forget.'

'Don't light the fire yet,' the leader said. 'We dinna want to draw attention to ourselves until it's over late for rescue.'

They turned away and moved together to the far side of the level silver field. I heard wood scraping against wood, saw a flap of dark fabric. They were setting up their communion table. Now! I twisted my fingers in their bonds, and felt the pole that held my arms backwards. It was a strainer post, 20 cm across and just below my shoulder height. At the least it'd be buried two foot deep in good hill earth, at worst – I scraped my foot sideways, and felt the hardness of concrete. I wouldn't shift this in a hurry. On the plus side, something fixed firm as this wouldn't make any noise as I freed myself.

The rope first. After years messing about in boats, there wasn't a knot I couldn't undo with my eyes shut, and these were the rankest of amateurs. I turned my hands upward and felt the rope with my fingers. Yes, a bonny granny knot, and they'd used almost all of the rope to wind around me, so the rope ends were usefully short. I had all but the last knot undone in twenty seconds, and flexed my forearms in relief.

Now to get my hands free. Without the rope, I could twist my fingers forward enough to reach the top of my pocket … into it … my first two fingers wormed down and curled round the lanyard. Carefully, gripping it between them, they pulled the knife up. I caught the little tool with my other hand, then used both to open the blade. I curled my right hand back and back upon itself, and achieved a vertical stroke down the baler twine between my wrists. The scrape of blade on string echoed like a saw stroke in my head, but they were busy over at their table, laying out dishes that glinted in the moonlight. The binding loosened straight away. Another stroke, and my hands were free. I tucked the multi-tool back in my pocket, and returned the hand nearest them to the 'tied' position. My eyes fixed on that dark group, I eased the false head up from my chin and pulled the poisonous cloth from my mouth. Blessed air rushed into my lungs.

The dyke was less than fifty yards from me, across smooth grass. They gave me one glance as they moved to their triangle of fire-wood. I pulled the false face off, and slid away from the post. No heads turned. I kept sliding, like a game of Grandmother's Footsteps, my eyes on the huddle around the fire. There was orange smoke puffing around them now. Soon the moonlight would be challenged by a blaze. I'd gone only five metres from the post when there was a sound like a thin horn, an eldritch wail, and a black figure loomed out of the silver heather. The witch nearest me gasped, and froze for a moment, hand rising to her throat, then she turned around to face him. Behind her, the others were straightening. A panicky murmur ran round them: *It's him, it's him.* Then they all dropped on their knees.

170

I hadn't seen him coming, for all the watch I'd kept. He was just there, taller by a head than any of the witches, with horns outlined by the moon behind him, just as Shaela had described him, with a thin, lashing tail with an arrow at the end of it, and slanted almond eyes as red as fire.

I was getting out of here. I ran for the dyke, placed one hand on it on the top stones, vaulted over, and landed in a tumble on the other side. I didn't know if they'd seen me move, but they'd be wanting to show off their captive, so I had to be fast. Downhill, shorewards, was safety. I was running, running, bent double in the shadow of the dyke, stumbling on the heather tussocks, before I realised that they'd be able to run faster than me on the other side, with the smooth grass under their feet. I paused, and heard a shout behind me, a yell of rage, followed by the confused clamour of hounds set on a hunt. They knew I'd come this way, and they were after me.

There were no peat banks breaking the silvery moor with darkness I could hide behind, but the moor itself was uneven with natural banks of heather above areas of soft peat. There was one not far from me. I threw myself towards it and rolled into the blessed darkness. My scarlet sailing jacket was striped with high-visibility reflector strips, but the blanket they'd slung round my shoulders covered those. Only movement would betray me.

They were searching for me downhill, so I'd go up. I'd pass their bonfire again in the shadow of this dyke and keep behind it to where the dyke joined another, at right angles, and straight down into Scalloway that way. Their trampling feet sounded a cable-length down the hill. I eased my head up to look and saw the dark figures moving on the other side of the dyke. I slid slowly upwards, moving from shadow to shadow. Then, in front of me, a shadow bulged and moved, and a dark figure stood up in front of me, one hand stretched towards me.

I skidded to a halt, and was swerving away when he caught me. A hand went over my mouth, and before I could bite a familiar voice hissed 'Cass!' The moonlight shone on silver-gilt hair.

'Anders?' My heart was thudding like a piston.

He tugged me back into the shadows. We collapsed together on the heather. 'Cat came back to the ship, just as I arrived,' he breathed in my ear. 'He was running, with his ears flat, as if he had had a fright. I thought it was odd, so I looked. I saw them hustling you up the hill. I could see your sailing jacket under the poncho.' He patted a pair of binoculars that hung against his chest. 'Night vision, they are excellent. So I followed, and waited for a chance to free you.'

Jeg ventet på en sjanse til å frigjøre dere. That was the second time he'd used the Norwegian plural 'you'. 'Us?' I asked.

He jerked his chin towards the level ground over the other side of the wall. 'They have another prisoner.'

I eased my head above the dyke to look. On the far side of the crackling blaze, tied with rope to a strainer post, was another figure, hooded as I had been.

Whoever had tied him, her, up had been more efficient than my captors. The dark figure was backed up against a post, as I had been, but with hands in front, and the rope around the waist was knotted behind the post. Trussed up like a chicken, ready for cooking. They would be back soon. I gave a hurried glance downwards and saw that the first of the witches was only half a cable away. They were coming uphill in a little bunch, with the devil following more slowly, head turning from side to side. I saw the red eyes flash. We weren't going to be able to release this other prisoner without being seen. Yet we couldn't run for safety and leave them here.

I ducked behind the dyke again and sat down beside Anders, back to the dyke, shoulder to shoulder. I turned my head, and our eyes met in the moonlight. We didn't need to speak. We'd come through some tight moments together, in *Khalida*, and he was a fellow sailor. He understood about responsibility, about instant action or waiting for orders.

Here, in the heart of their coven meeting, was the last place they'd look for us. We'd wait here for our chance to free the other prisoner. Or should one of us go for help while the other waited? Then I remembered my mobile. I could summon help, if there was a signal here, and there should be, with the red light of the Weisdale Hill mast glowing over to the right. I eased my mobile out of my pocket, praying I'd left it at standby. I wouldn't dare risk the little tune it gave when it was switched on from cold, or the bleep of a new text coming through. I gestured it at Anders. 'Have you phoned the police?' I breathed in his ear.

He shook his head, his lower lip jutting out stubbornly. *Men …* This wasn't a 'save the heroine' game. We needed cohorts of policemen in a car with lights and sirens, as fast as possible. I opened up 'new message' and typed in: 'witches up on gallow hill'. It didn't matter how annoyed Gavin was with me, or how little I wanted to ask for his help. I didn't know what they planned to do with this prisoner, but it had to be stopped. Then I remembered how often I'd received a text several hours after it had been sent, even though my mobile had been on and within signal.

This was too urgent to risk. I flashed a look at the nearest witch, climbing steadily towards the bonfire, found Gavin's number, and pressed the green button. There was a ringing tone, horribly loud in the silence. I clamped it closer to my ear. *Pick up, Gavin –*

Three rings, then I heard his voice, briskly neutral. 'Cass.'

The witch was only thirty yards from me. 'I'm on the Gallow Hill,' I breathed into the phone. 'The coven – up here. They have a prisoner.' The sss of the whisper was too loud. 'Thend help.'

He didn't argue or demur. 'How many?'

'Five. Don't phone back, they'll hear. We'll keep with them. *Hurry,*' I breathed, then cut the connection. I wondered for a moment if I should switch the phone off altogether, but it took ages to warm up, and I might need it again. I slipped it into my pocket and crouched down to wait and watch.

There was a glint of orange light shining through the dyke some twenty metres forward of me. I gestured to Anders. 'Going to look,' I breathed. I squirmed forward on elbows and knees, and found a place where the stones had fallen in, leaving a gap big enough to peer through. To my right, the first of the witches was panting into view. The fire was flickering in the centre. The hooded figure was tied to the post on the left, slumped over the ropes, as if in exhaustion or despair. How quickly could Gavin muster his troops? If he was in Lerwick, they'd have a ten-minute drive to Scalloway, then the climb up the hill, although where a tractor had gone, a police car could probably follow. It depended too on whether he decided to surround the coven with police before pouncing, or whether he'd just send the cars in with sirens blazing, to scatter them.

'She'll be back,' the chief hooded craw said. Her witch false-face was pulled up on the top of her head, giving her a double-faced deformity; her voice trembled. 'As soon as she gets down the hill, she'll be back wi' the police.'

Anders had come forward beside me. Shoulder to shoulder, we looked through the wall.

The devil laughed. Theatre, I reminded myself, *theatre.* Maman in her goddess costume, with platform shoes under her lengthened Grecian robe, and an angled spot hidden among the paste jewels in her piled up hair to make her face glow with divine light. I saw the firelight glint on his horns as he tipped his head back. The red eyes glittered. LED lights, I thought, sewn into eye-holes in some sort of padded mask, with the real eyes down below, hidden by black net, so that he looked at us all through a black veil. His tail moved like the carved snakes you could buy in India, where you held the tail and the trembling of your hand made the head strike and retreat. There was some sort of voice distorter sewn in his

173

costume, for the laugh echoed round the open hill, and his voice rumbled and reverberated. 'You think I need fear the police?'

To my astonishment, the chief hoodie backed away from him, and bobbed a curtsey. 'No, Majesty.'

The man in the devil suit laughed again, contemptuously. 'We will conclude our business here before the representatives of the law arrive.' He stood up straight, tall. A piece of dried grass flared up, letting me see his great cloven hooves. Whoever had created this disguise, it hadn't been cheap. The shining horn of the hooves was a platform, with the toes of the real foot in the last fur over the top of the hoof, and the heel in the fetlock. No wonder he walked mincingly on this uneven ground. He went over to the prisoner, pulled off the Elvis mask, and threw it into the fire. The flames hissed and flared. His head tipped back in a parody of laughter, then he turned back to the witches. 'You who tied up the escaped prisoner, come forward.'

The clawed hand rose, and now I saw that what I'd taken for a stick was a carriage driver's long whip. He flourished it above his head, with a noise like a pistol shot. *Smoke and mirrors*, I reminded myself, as I jumped. An actor in a costume.

Dog-collar and Sea-green-Corset shuffled forward, heads hanging. I turned my head away, gritting my teeth. I'd read it all in Isobel Gowdie: *sometimes when the Devil was displeased with us he would whip us and buffet us all about.* The whip cracked. There was a yelp of pain from one of them, a growling of insults from the man dressed as the devil. I was flooded with such anger that my body shook with it. I wanted to leap up and shout at them all for a bunch of fools, letting this man mistreat them for his own ego-trip. I wanted to grab his mask and hurl it away, let them all see who he was. My hands were clenched so tight that I felt my nails in my palm, and the pain steadied me. They couldn't believe he was the Devil, these street-wise girls in their steampunk clothes. For their own reasons they were colluding in his fantasies. I gritted my teeth as the whip writhed on their backs, and looked away from them. When would the police come? Ten minutes from Lerwick, the time to find someone who could lead them up the hill –

The whip cracked a last time, then stopped. I turned my head to look through the gap again. Dog-collar and Sea-green-Corset were sobbing with a horrible pleasurable excitement. Their faces were flushed in the firelight. If this was all it had been, fools playacting, then I would steal away and leave them to it, but Annette had died, and Nate, and the still form tied to the post was listening and watching and waiting. The man dressed as the devil caught the thong of his whip with one easy movement, and thrust it into his belt. 'As for the sailor-woman – ' His voice curled around the name. ' – where would she go but her boat? I can put my hand on her any time I choose.'

The threat hung in the air. Anders' hand stole to my arm, a warning. *No*, I mouthed silently at them, *you won't catch me a second time. I'm not afraid of you.* It was true. I wasn't afraid of this play of demons and disciples. I was afraid of a murderer. Who, *who*, was under this mask?

'Well, Maiden,' the voice rumbled, 'have you no cup for your lord and master?'

The chief hoodie bobbed her stupid curtsey again, and scurried to the table. She lifted a silver cup shaped like a communion chalice, and a bottle of wine. I gave an inward snort of derision, imagining her in the wine aisle at the Co-op. '*That's a little light, I need something full-bodied ...*' Someone must have been busy today, bringing all these props up the hill. The cloth was black, embroidered with twisted symbols that caught the moonlight. Dog-collar placed an Oriental dagger with a curved blade beside the chalice. If the police didn't arrive soon, we'd have to act.

The man dressed as the devil came behind the table, with the chief hoodie at his side, and the others knelt before it. The chief hoodie filled the goblet, then the man raised it, in a horrible parody of Mass. The words echoed the ones I was accustomed to hear each Sunday. It was blasphemy, with the crowning moment being when the man dressed as a devil took the dagger and made a slash across his palm, then let the blood drip into the wine. The cup was passed ceremoniously around them.

There was still no sign of lights below in Scalloway, no sound of sirens. I turned my face to Anders, leant towards him till my mouth was at his ear. 'This could be our best chance,' I breathed. 'You draw them off, I'll free the prisoner.'

He thought about it, and nodded, eyes on that curved knife. 'I will go over there.' His hand pointed across the hill. 'Get as close as you can. I'll make a noise, as if you have fallen.' His breath was warm on my face. 'If too many of them stay there, do not take any risks. Look, there are cars moving down in the village now.'

Two cars, three, but there were no blue lights. Gavin wanted to catch his murderer, not scare him off. Anders' hand gripped mine, warm and strong. 'Good luck.'

He began creeping across the hill, from shadow to shadow. I slipped along behind the dyke until the fire was between me and the coven. There was a wire fence right beside the dyke, to keep it sheep-proof. I set my foot on the wire and let it take my weight, then swung over. The knot of people were still at their blasphemous table, passing their cup around. Then I heard a scrabble two hundred yards away, a slithering of feet, a smothered cry of pain. Nice acting, Anders. The heads around the table turned. 'That's her,' Dog-Collar snapped, 'over there.'

In the moonlight, a dark shadow moved, limping away, desperate fear in every step. The witches gave an inhuman howl, and poured like a dark stream towards him. The man dressed as the devil remained at the table, watching, head turned to the chase. The tail moved as if it was searching for me, a nasty, sinister piece of trickery. *I had this awful feeling that it was like an antenna, searching for me* ... Shaela had said. But the red eyes were turned towards the hill, away from me. I slid up to the prisoner, flattening myself behind the post. 'Quiet,' I breathed, and snicked open my little knife. This close, I could feel it was a woman, taller than me. I slid an arm around to her front, blade poised, feeling my way down her arm, her wrists, to the twine. 'Hold still.' One slash freed the bound hands. I dropped the knife back in my pocket, and began to work on the knotted rope. A reef-knot, glory be.

The man dressed as the devil must have sensed me, for his head turned. He gave a shout then came hobbling towards us, short steps that still carried him over the ground faster than I liked. My fingers pulled the last piece of rope through and let it fall. 'Run!' I said.

She didn't hesitate. Quicker than thought, she was pelting over the silver-washed grass towards the dyke that ran downhill to Scalloway. I threw the rope in the devil's face, and ran in the other direction, towards the burn. Divide and conquer. Then the night split open with the sound of engines, a glory of light, as one of those Landrovers with flashlamps on top came bumping over the hill, spilling out dark figures. Help had arrived.

I turned and ran back towards the shouting, towards the burn, where the running woman had gone. I couldn't see her, in the deep shadow cast by the burn gulley, but she couldn't be more than twenty metres ahead of me. 'Wait!' I called. 'It's Cass.'

There was a long pause, then a noise behind me. I spun round as the dark figure came up out of the ditch, and tensed, ready to run or scream.

'I kent it was you,' she said. It was Rachel's voice. 'Thanks for freeing me. I saw you get away, and thought you'd call the police, but I was faered it would be ower late for yon craetur wi' his knife.'

'I was faered too,' I admitted.

Her eyes glinted in the firelight. 'Wha' was yon, wi' the mask?'

I shook my head. 'I couldna see.'

She drew a shuddering breath. 'I'm sorry I didna stop them catching you. I kent what they were going to do, but I couldna shout out to warn you. That fause face, and there was a handkie in me mouth. I struggled wi' them, but it just looked as if I'd been drinking.' She clasped her arms round her body. 'I'm that cold.'

Away from the smoke, I could smell the frost in the air now, and see the first glitter on the heather.

'Let's leave the police to mop this lot up, and get you into the warm,' I said.

She looked up at the hill. The scatter of people had gathered into one knot now, with the witches in the middle. I could see the swirl of Gavin's kilt in the moonlight, and the glint of the pin that held it. His head was up, and he was looking round the group, speaking slowly, as if he was reading their rights. 'I assume you phoned them.' Now she sounded like the college lecturer again, in command, with a touch of wry amusement. 'You're brawly resourceful.'

'I'm just a sailor with a knife in her pocket,' I said. I jerked my chin over at the bonfire. 'I need to tell the police we're safe. Once I'm done that, there's a guy who makes the most incredible hot chocolate down at the marina.'

'Sounds good.'

We made our way back over the silver-washed hill to the group of police. Gavin turned as we approached. The moonlight highlighted his cheekbones, shadowed his eyes. 'Thanks for the cavalry,' I said.

'You're unharmed?' It sounded like he was preparing a charge sheet.

'A good number of bruises,' I conceded, 'from being marched up that hill with my arms tied and part blindfolded by the mask. You should be able to do them for breach of the peace, at least.' I gestured. 'Rachel was my fellow-prisoner. Can I take her down to *Khalida* to warm up?'

He nodded. 'I'll join you as soon as I've dealt with these.' He looked over at the huddle of witches, surrounded by burly police officers. 'It may take some time.' He added, so casually that it sounded like an accusation, 'I explained that Anders was with you.'

'I wasn't playing detective,' I said. 'They kidnapped me. He saw, and followed. Then, when I freed myself –'

His mouth curved in the moonlight. 'You're a most discouraging heroine. Don't you ever need to be rescued?'

'You should be grateful,' I retorted. 'There's a dirty great carving knife on that table, and it looked most horridly as if they were planning to use it on Rachel and me.' I looked over at the prisoners. There were the four witches, with an officer beside each, and the moon glinting on Anders' blond head – 'The devil? Didn't you catch him?'

Gavin's head jerked up. 'The coven leader? Was he here too?'

'A man in a devil suit.' My breath caught in my throat. 'Did he get away?'

Gavin spun on his heel, and strode over to the police officers. 'There's one more. Spread out. He's in a devil suit. He could have ditched it. Stop anyone on the hill.'

Within seconds, the hill was criss-crossed with torch beams, in the best *X-files* tradition. Beside me, Rachel was shivering. I looked over to Anders. 'I think we should get Rachel home.' Gavin knew where to find me. *Where would she go but her boat?* I didn't like the idea of the devil being loose.

Anders pulled off his jacket and put it around Rachel's shoulders. 'You are unharmed?'

Her voice was shaky, but determined. 'I'll have a touch o' the spaigie come the morning.'

'We'll head for *Khalida*,' I said. My home, my refuge. 'We've both had a shock. D'you suppose Reidar would make us a pot of his hot chocolate?'

'He's waiting for us, with the heater on,' Anders said. 'I phoned him, as soon as I saw you heading down.'

'Bliss,' I said, and led the way towards the burn. Our feet slipped and stumbled in the dark hollow. Above us, the lights crossed and re-crossed the hill, but there were no shouts to tell us that the devil was found at last. I bit my lip. *I can put my hand on her any time I choose –*

We reached the road at last. There were lights on in Reidar's motorboat, and I could have sworn I smelled the drifting odour of baking biscuits. The man was treasure-trove.

He was on deck as soon as he heard the clang of the marina gate. 'Come in,' he boomed. 'All is ready for you.' He gave me an expansive hug. His jumper smelt of food, and warmth, and comfort. 'When you disappeared behind those sheds, and did not appear again at the corner by the memorial, I began to imagine all sorts of horrible things. I thought it must be an ambush, and then Anders phoned, and the man you were to meet turned up too.'

'James Leask – he came?'

Reidar nodded. 'Five, seven minutes before seven. He waited, then left. Now, he has just arrived here, looking for you. He is below.' One large hand gestured at the motorboat's cabin.

So it hadn't been James Leask who'd set up the ambush. Someone had overheard. All they'd had to do was wait for me to leave *Khalida*. From their point of view it was safe enough, even with Rachel captive in the middle of them. Nobody was going to notice a group of guizers hanging around on Hallowe'en night. I gestured Rachel into the cabin before me, and followed her down.

It was blissfully warm inside, and smelling of cinnamon. James was sitting in the corner behind the table, his face anxious and relieved at once. He half-rose as we came in. His eyes stopped on Rachel's face, then his cheeks began to burn scarlet. He gestured Rachel past him, into the corner. 'I can't stay. I just wanted to make sure you were safe. I felt it was my fault, leading you into an ambush.'

'That occurred to me too,' I said. 'If thoughts have any power, your ears should have been burning around ten to seven.'

'Sit down,' Reidar said, behind me. He brought out a plate of biscuits, golden and crumbly at the edges, crowned with curls of steam, and put it in the middle of the table. 'Eat.' I sat down. Cat slid out from under the shelf and onto my lap. Reidar set out mugs, and poured the frothing chocolate into each, then topped them with cream, sprinkled cinnamon on top, and added two curls of orange peel to each. 'There. No talking until it is all gone, or I will be insulted.'

I wasn't going to insult anyone who could produce food like this. I launched in, and after a moment's hesitation James sat down beside me. There was an odd irresolution about his movements, as if he wanted to go, yet felt he should stay until – until what? Until he'd told me what he'd asked me to meet him for?

The biscuits tasted as good as they smelt, with a rich buttery texture like the best shortbread. One day, I promised myself, I'd buy an oven for *Khalida.* The drinking chocolate was piping hot through the cold cream. Reidar was a genius, and if he wanted to stand for Prime Minister of Denmark, I'd vote for him. I scooped a fingerful of cream and let Cat lick it. Two sets of tiny claws squirmed onto my lap, followed by two more, and a tail: Rat, wanting a share too.

'So,' Reidar said, once the plate was empty, 'tell me what happened.'

I made a 'you first' gesture to Rachel. She shook her head, and gave John an uneasy look. 'Cass first.'

It was quickly told. Reidar made a popping sound when I described the devil. 'You see, Scottish witches.'

'It was horrid,' Rachel agreed. 'They caught me the same way they caught you, Cass. I went out for milk, and I saw this group of guizers at the foot of the lane, then they surrounded me. Then they came for you, and I couldn't shout or warn you. And then that horrid devil –'

'Costume,' I said vehemently. 'Cloven-hoof shoes, padded shoulders, LED eyes.'

Rachel shuddered.

'They didn't expect him,' Anders said. We stared at him. 'The witches,' he said. 'Taking you was their own idea. They didn't expect him to come. I saw their faces when he appeared. They were shocked.'

I re-ran the scene in my mind. 'Yes,' I agreed. 'They had their stuff ready for their own ceremony, and he just appeared among them. The thin horn noise – they all froze, and looked at each other, as if they didn't believe it.'

'They were afraid of him.' Rachel said.

I remembered chief hoodie's bobbed curtsey, the trembling in her voice. 'But they knew him. He'd come before. The coven ritual with the Maiden, all that, they'd done it before.'

'If he was really the Devil,' Reidar said, 'then I would be afraid too.'

'He wasn't the Devil,' I insisted. 'He was a person in fancy dress. Smoke and mirrors.'

'It is what they believe that matters,' Reidar said, 'and they believed he was the Devil.'

'If they believed in him, why didn't they expect him?' I argued.

James pushed his mug into the centre of the table, and rose. 'I'd need to go. Rachel, I'm going your way. Would you like to walk wi' me? You'll no want to go on your own, after this night's experience.'

'That's fine o' you,' she said. She smiled at Reidar. 'That was wonderful. Thanks to you.'

James waved her up the stairs to the cockpit, and leant over me to pick up his jacket. His voice breathed in my ear: 'Don't trust her. Rachel. I saw Lawrence that night.' He pulled the jacket on. 'Thanks to you, Reidar. That's set me up now.' His blue eyes fixed me earnestly. 'Don't trust her!' he mouthed, then turned to go up the steps. 'See you later.'

'Phone me,' I said.

He nodded, and closed the washboards behind him. Reidar, Anders, and I looked round at each other. 'Don't trust Rachel?' I said. 'But she was a prisoner too – '

'Are you sure?' Anders asked.

I stared at him.

'I did not see the prisoner's face,' he said. 'Not to recognise. At first, there was the mask on, and then when the devil threw it away, the fire flared up, and the light was in my eyes. I could not say for sure that it was Rachel.'

'You think she was one of the witches?'

He shook his head. 'The police caught the witches. I saw them – they were pursuing me, remember. They caught them all.'

'Wait,' I said. It was falling together in my head. 'They didn't expect the devil, because they thought they knew who it was. The person who played the devil, the witches thought they knew. They thought it was Nate.'

'Nate is the young man who died,' Reidar said.

'Yes,' I said. '*Yes.* That explains why they were shocked – because they were shocked, when the devil appeared. They thought their devil was Nate. They were having their own ceremony, maybe even like a memorial. That explains why they took me. They blamed me for Nate's death. The other day, they cornered me, and told me to keep away from him. They thought I was a witch too, but a different sort from them. They were out for revenge.'

'Except that they had it wrong,' Anders said. 'Because Nate wasn't the devil.'

'Maybe he had been, earlier,' I said. 'But not tonight.'

Rachel had come from the wrong direction. The prisoner I'd freed had run towards the burn, run with the devil at her heels.

When the witches had run in Anders' direction, the devil had stayed behind. It would take less than a minute to kick off cloven-hooved overshoes, pull off tailed trousers and a mask with LED eyes. If the devil had been wearing normal clothes under the costume, then he – or she – could just mingle with the rest of us. She could thrust her disguise into the shadow of a rock, then come out at my call, diminished, ordinary, pretending she'd been the prisoner I'd freed.

Perhaps Nate had been the devil earlier, but for tonight, I'd bet any money that the black figure with the red eyes and brandished whip had been Rachel.

at faat (n): at fault, guilty

Chapter Nineteen

Tuesday 1st November, All Saints Day

Low Water Scalloway 03:51 GMT 0.6m
High Water 10:11 1.7 m
Low Water 16:14 0.6m
High Water 22:31 1.6m
Moon waning gibbous

Sunrise 07:30
Moonset 10:26, 315 degrees
Sunset 16:06
Moonrise 17:14, 45 degrees

It had been a cold dawn. The windows were laced with frost when I awoke, and the wooden floor was icy under my bare feet. My breath smoked in the air as I grabbed for my jumper and jeans to go out and switch the gas on. *Khalida*'s fibreglass curves were furred with white, and the pool of water on her stern was glazed with ice. My fingers were numbed before I'd done more than raise the hatch, pump the bilge, and turn the gas switch.

Now, at nine o'clock, a dazzle of sunlight poured in through the port window and slanted onto the gold wood of the fiddle above my head. The sky was clear and blue, milky at the edges, the near hills the pale gold of long grass, the far hills dusted with morning light. The sea was blue as summer, dancing ripples that sparkled with light. Through the starboard window, I could see the silver-pale moon descending on her arc towards the west hill, her leading edge dissolving into the blue sky.

Anders and Reidar had insisted in chorus that, for my own safety, either I slept aboard Reidar's motorboat, or Anders returned to his forepeak berth in *Khalida*. I settled for Anders aboard, as the lesser of two evils. Rat had come with him, of course, and he and Cat had slept on the middle berth, a curl of black, white and grey fur. My neck had been cold without my little companion snuggled up to me. Now Anders was looking at home in his old corner, hair gleaming gilt against the mahogony bulkhead, a cup of coffee in his tanned hand, his navy shirt open at the throat, when there were steps on the pontoon, a knock on the cabin roof, and Gavin's voice calling, 'May we come aboard?'

I got up from the table and slid the hatch back. There were dark shadows under Gavin's eyes, as if he'd had no sleep. His hair was damp from a wake-up shower. 'Good morning.' I suddenly realised I'd never called him Gavin, directly. I wasn't going to start now, with Sergeant Peterson standing at his back, her feet at ten to two. I lifted out the washboards and stowed them in their slot. 'Come aboard.'

'Just a few questions about last night,' he said, swinging over the guard rail in a swish of green pleats. I motioned him down the steps. Sergeant Peterson followed him, notebook in one hand. Her green eyes slid across to Anders. 'It's good to see you on your feet again, Mr Johansson.'

He gave her a blank look.

'I was there,' she explained, 'when the bull attacked you, in the summer.'

A tide of pink swept up his neck and coloured his jaw. Maybe I could foist him off on the mermaid. They would make a bonny couple, I told myself, ignoring the twist of jealousy that curled in my belly, except that she wasn't a sailor – but she could learn. Women were good at taking up their men's hobbies, and a police lifestyle with odd shifts might complement a gamer apt to disappear into interplanetary warfare for several days.

Gavin looked at Anders in his corner, and his face took on that blank look of someone who's not going to say anything. In this case, attack was better than silence.

'Anders wasn't happy about me being alone,' I said. I nodded at the tumbled sleeping bag in the forepeak. 'He and Rat came back to their old berth. Have you had breakfast?'

'Tea is always welcome,' Gavin said. He sat down opposite Anders. Sergeant Peterson settled for squishing herself into the awkward seat beside the chart table. 'When did you come over from Norway, Mr Johansson?'

'The day before yesterday,' Anders said. He frowned, and re-thought. 'No, it was just before dawn yesterday.' He gave Gavin one of those men-ganging-up-together smiles. 'Life is exciting with Cass around. Each day feels longer.'

'I don't see,' I said frostily, 'how I can be held responsible for what idiot women decide to do up on the hill on a moonlit night.'

Anders grinned, and made a winding motion with his hand. I scowled at him and got on with boiling the kettle, setting mugs out and fishing the milk out from below sea-level.

'Samhain,' Sergeant Peterson said, flipping her notebook open. 'The Night of the Dead, and their principal celebration of the year.'

'Tell me your side of it first,' Gavin said. 'We haven't charged them with anything so far, because they're consenting adults.'

'I suppose you could try breach of the peace,' I said, 'but I escaped before they could do me any harm, so you might have difficulty proving they intended any. That nasty looking knife could have been for cutting their bread.' I told him the whole story, beginning with James Leask's phone call, my capture, the walk up the hill, the arrival of the devil, the horrid ceremony, as neutrally as I could, pausing in the middle to make a pot of tea when the kettle whistled at last. 'And then you arrived,' I ended, 'and I brought Rachel down here.'

'They all clammed up the minute I mentioned you,' Gavin said. 'The one I took to be the leader said she didn't know what I was talking about, there were the four of them up on the hill, and that was all. No prisoners, no devil, and anyone who said different was just trying to cover up the fact they'd been sneaking about watching, and hoping they'd take their clothes off.' I could just hear her saying it.

'Who was the fourth?'

Sergeant Peterson didn't need to look at her notebook. 'Sarah Cheyne, 23 Ladysmith Road, works at the college café with Nate.'

I nodded. 'I should have thought of her. I saw her with Nate and the other three a couple of days ago.'

'They began their rituals about six months ago after listening to Nate telling them about what witches used to do, because they thought it sounded cool.'

'We thought Nate was at the bottom of it,' I said, and explained our thinking that they'd believed Nate was the devil, and been shocked by the appearance of someone else in the devil suit. Gavin nodded, considering it.

'As for your idea about the £100,' Sergeant Peterson said, 'they denied it. The one with the spider on her cheek admitted that they'd given the dog something to make it sick, "just an emetic, nothing harmful", then told Annette they'd put a curse on it, to frighten her. The local SSPCA man will be having a word with them about that. They denied having asked her for money, and they all insisted she'd never given them any.'

'So where did it go, then?' My head was closing in again. I rubbed my temple. I'd take an aspirin after Gavin had gone.

'They were frightened of the devil,' Anders said. 'They enjoyed the whippings, but they jumped to do his bidding.'

'Yes,' Gavin agreed. 'I picked up on a genuine fear, although I'm not sure they really believed he was a supernatural devil. What description can you give me of the person under the costume?'

I shook my head. 'None. Height and walk, build, voice, they were all altered.'

Gavin looked over at Anders. 'Mr Johansson?'

'Nothing. You could see only the costume.'

'Then we'll try to trace that,' Gavin said. 'If we don't find it on the hill, I'll send Sergeant Peterson back for the fullest description you can manage.'

'You didn't find it last night?'

Gavin shook his head. 'We couldn't search every rock shadow in the moonlight. I left a man up there overnight, and sent a party up this morning. I can't say I'm hopeful. It sounds too distinctive to be left where we could find it.'

'Too expensive too,' I said. 'Unless it was homemade – and if it was, you're looking for someone who's inventive, handy with a sewing machine, and able to fix electronics.'

'From what you've said, I'd guess a theatrical costumier.' He looked at Sergeant Peterson. 'If we don't find it on the hill, Freya, you might need to spend the afternoon phoning round as many as you can find.'

That was a move-on from his earlier brisk 'Sergeant': . Freya, the Queen of the Norse goddesses. I checked my lower lip wasn't pouting like a sulky child's, and put my own oar in. 'Something that cost that much to make would have to be signed for. Are we looking for someone without a family to say "What was that large package, dear?"'

Of course it could have been delivered to the college, along with a dozen other packages each day: books, chemical supplies, lobster eggs for their breeding programme marine equipment. Perhaps a glimpse of a black suit in a brown parcel, or a costumier's name blazoned above the address, was what had told the chief hoodie their devil was Nate.

'He couldn't have walked up the hill in those hooves,' Anders said. 'He must have climbed the hill in ordinary clothes, with his costume in a backpack. He crept up on them, changed, sounded his horn, then bounded into their midst, as if by magic.'

Gavin nodded. 'Yes. When we arrived, he could have done the reverse: stuffed the disguise into the backpack, put on different shoes, and strolled away, mingling confidently with the police. We had a lot of men up there, not all in uniform, and we were focused on the ones who were running away.'

'We had an idea,' I said diffidently. Sergeant Peterson straightened in her space. Gavin's sea-grey eyes narrowed. 'We thought it might have been Rachel. I released the prisoner, and Rachel said she'd been that prisoner, but I didn't see her face. She could have run out of the firelight, ditched the suit, and re-appeared behind me.'

'Interesting,' Gavin said. 'Sarah Cheyne denied she was one of them. She said she'd been kidnapped and marched up the burn with you, and tied to a post – until you freed her.'

I stared at him. 'Sarah did? So if she was the prisoner, do we have an escaped witch? Rachel …?'

'The others said she was lying,' Sergeant Peterson said. 'She said they had it in for her because she'd called their games 'a lock o' bruck.'

'If Nate was the devil before,' I said, 'then Rachel would have had access to his suit.'

'So would the person who killed him,' Gavin said. 'Maybe that was the reason he called on Nate – to borrow the suit. He made a joke about wearing it out, and Nate came with him – to his death.'

'You don't think Rachel might have been the devil?'

Gavin shook his head. 'You said the devil last night seemed to know the ritual?'

'He said about the Maiden offering him a cup … he seemed to be at ease with it all.' I looked across at Anders, who nodded.

'I did not have any sense that he was feeling his way,' he said.

'Then Rachel couldn't have hoped to impersonate him.' Gavin stopped looking at me, and focused on swirling the last of his tea in its mug. Under his tan, his cheeks reddened. 'They based the ritual on the confessions of a woman called Isobel Gowdie, who was the best known of the Scottish witches.' His voice was matter of fact. Sergeant Peterson was looking at her sensible shoes, but I thought there was the twitch of a smile at her mouth. 'After the pretence of a Mass, then there was an orgy.'

A hot tide of scarlet flooded my cheeks. Stupid, stupid! I had read it myself. Of course the devil had to be male, and from the sound of it, he'd have needed a hefty dose of Viagra beforehand.

'All the same,' Gavin said, in a much easier tone, 'that's an interesting idea, that they'd expected no devil because they'd believed it was Nate.' He looked across at Sergeant Peterson. 'Then, when someone turned up, it gave them the fright of their lives. That'd explain their reactions, don't you think?'

She nodded. 'It's possible, sir.'

'Backtrack,' Gavin said. 'Do you think James Leask set you up?'

I shook my head. 'He was here when we got down to the boat. He'd been really worried about it all.'

Sergeant Peterson gave me the kindly look reserved for the weak-minded. 'Had he been with your friend Reidar all the time?'

'No,' Anders said. His fair brows drew together in a frown. 'He came to the meeting place at seven, waited for a bit, then left. He would have had time to climb the hill and appear as the devil. Then when you escaped, yes, he would have had time to come down before us and get to the marina. It was very odd that he should ask you to meet him like that. If he really had seen Lawrence on the night Nate died, why should he tell you? What is it to do with you? It was the police he should have told.' He added, fatally, 'I wish you had consulted me before setting off to meet him like that.'

'Or the police,' Sergeant Peterson said.

I sat up straighter on my box. 'I'm accustomed to making my own judgements,' I said. 'Reidar was there as guard at the meeting place. You don't expect to be kidnapped in the middle of Scalloway. Especially,' I added, for good measure, 'when it's crawling with police cars.'

Gavin laughed out at that, looking suddenly younger. He was smiling at me, eyes warm, the companion of the sail to Aith, my fellow-judge and fellow-dancer in The Grand Old Duke of York. We were friends again. I wouldn't analyse the rush of gladness that filled my breast, not right now. 'But if he was telling the truth, and he did see Lawrence the night Nate died – '

'He was at the Hallowe'en Party,' Gavin said.

Memory returned. Yes, he'd been at the Hallowe'en Party, wearing his furry suit with the claws which had made the indented marks I'd seen around Annette's neck.

'But he and Rachel were back in Scalloway by half past nine,' Gavin said. 'Nate was attacked around eleven.' He rose, took Sergeant Peterson's mug from her, and rinsed both in the sink with the last of the hot water from the kettle. I watched her clock his familiarity with the boat and her habits, the way he reached for the dish towel without looking at it, and set the dry mugs back in their slot above the cooker. Mentally, I descended to a three-year old, sticking my tongue out at an annoying rival, and was well served for my petulance when Gavin said, turning, 'I was going in to the 1.15 Mass. Can I give you a lift?'

I looked blankly at him.

'All Saints,' he said.

Of course it was, and a Holy Day of Obligation too. I'd completely forgotten. That meant Mass at either 1.15 or 7.30, in Lerwick. 'Yes, please. I'll meet you at the old museum.'

'One o'clock?'

'That'll be fine.' I glanced at *Khalida*'s little clock, velcroed to where

I could see it from my berth. It was half past nine already. 'My mercy, I'm late.' I grabbed my jacket. 'Come on, Cat, we've a garden to clear.'

Everything was bright outside: the blue water, the coloured houses, the red-brown stones of Scalloway Castle. The great turbines on the hill blinked white light as the sun caught the slow turn of the blades. At ground level, each grass had a thin blade of frost, each curled leaf was outlined with ragged white. In Kate's garden, the newly turned earth was glazed with silver. Kate was standing on the doorstep waiting for me, a mug of tea cradled in her hands, the barrow parked beside her. The fork and spade lay in it, and two pairs of thick gloves.

'Good morning, Cass. Isn't it cold? I was beginning to wonder if you were okay, then I saw the police car at the marina.'

'Just more questions,' I said.

'They caught them, didn't they? The witches. Last night, on the hill. You can't see the flames from here, but I saw the light of the bonfire in the sky, and then there were all the police cars going up past.' She set her mug down, face earnest. 'Did they catch them? Will it be stopped?'

I couldn't answer that. 'They got the girls. It was those ones in grey and black who hang about by the shop, smoking and trying to be cool.'

Kate's eyes filled with tears. 'Playing at witchcraft … Their stupidity killed my child. Can they be held to account for that?'

'Maybe,' I said. 'If what they did led to her death.'

Kate stood up, moving slowly, like an old woman. 'Peter wants to leave here. He's asked for a transfer.' Her eyes went slowly across the cleared garden. 'But it'll take time. Maybe I'll still see this garden in spring.'

'Do you want to go?' I asked.

She shook her head, spilling the tears down her cheeks. 'Annette's grave will be here.'

My heart wrenched with pity. There was nothing I could say. I was glad when she picked up the handles of the barrow and headed down towards the broad border.

We worked in silence, digging up forkful after forkful of the tangled, bitter roots, whacking them free of earth and flinging them into the barrow. The earth was cold as death. The crisp brown sycamore leaves fell around as us as we worked.

I was still trying to make sense of it all, my brain teasing at the deaths here in Scalloway. It had begun with Annette's dreams of being a witch. She'd gone to Nate to ask him for help, for exorcism, and he'd said he would help, if she would steal him the ash of the burned witches from the museum, using Peter's keys. They'd set Wednesday night for the ritual. Annette had waited till Peter had taken the dogs out, then she'd gone to the museum and got the ash and the castle keys. She'd met Nate in the castle – no. No, Nate had been the werewolf whose claws around her neck had shocked Annette into the seizure that had killed her. *Someone* had been the werewolf, and there'd been the devil that Kevin's nan had seen, who'd carried her.

I started again. Nate had been the demon of the witches' sabbats up on the hill. He was strong enough to have carried Annette; I'd seen him lifting the chief hooded crow in the college, and he'd 'carried her off' in that play they'd done. Someone else had done the ritual, and he'd appeared behind Annette – no, that didn't work either, for it had been claw marks from the werewolf on her neck. He'd made them earlier, when she'd first demurred at getting the ash. He'd stretched out his gloved hand, and caught her neck, and said, 'Get it for me, or you'll never be free.' I could see that. It fitted in with the way she'd spoken to James. She didn't want to do it, but she had to.

Hang on! We didn't know for certain the suit had been Nate's. Rachel said it had been, that she'd borrowed it from Nate for Lawrence; but suppose it had been Lawrence's all the time? I tried that idea out. Annette went to *Rachel* and asked *her* to exorcise her, and Rachel said she would, if Annette got her the ash. Lawrence was there too, and he did the clawed intimidation. Then, at the castle that night, while Rachel was bending over the cauldron, Lawrence appeared from behind, and shocked Annette. And then … no, I wasn't going to believe that they ran in shock, and the real Devil appeared in a cloud of sulphur, with the hounds of hell at his back, and carried the body to Spanish closs to accuse the murderers.

'Kate?' I asked. She turned and wiped her hand over her brow, leaving a smear of earth. 'Kate, that last day of Annette's life, just as I was going out, Peter said he'd found out who Annette had got herself entangled with.'

Kate nodded. 'Nate. John Ratter, he works at the bank, he'd seen Annette going into Nate's house. He knew the boy's reputation, so he had a word with Peter, that maybe he should try and discourage that friendship.'

'He saw her going into the house, he didn't see her with Nate?' That left Rachel still in the frame.

'It doesn't matter now,' Kate murmured. She flung her handful of roots into the barrow. 'He's dead too.'

A rhyme from an Agatha Christie swam into my head. *Mrs McGinty's dead, why did she die?* I watched unseeing as Kate picked up the barrow and trundled it off up the garden. Why had Nate died?

Because he'd seen the murderer. He hadn't been part of the ritual. He'd been watching from behind the window, the shadow I'd seen, and he'd seen the murderer dropping Annette's body at his door. And then ... and then ... I saw it suddenly, as if I'd been there. He'd gone out with his clawed glove and made fresh marks on her throat. I heard his voice in my mind, the day she'd died: *The Devil's loose in Scalloway.* Nate had started the three hooded crows on the idea of witchcraft, that had turned into the satanic rituals up on Gallow Hill. He'd enjoyed spreading ideas of devilry. Malice or just mischief, he'd gone out and made those marks, then slipped back into the house as he heard me approach. I remembered the closing door.

Now I didn't need an unlikely combination of Nate, Rachel, and Lawrence – because having seen them together, I didn't believe that they'd have been co-conspirators. I needed only two, Lawrence and Rachel. Rachel the witch, Lawrence the devil. They'd done the ritual together, and Annette had died. Lawrence had carried her body back to throw suspicion on Nate. Rachel had gone into the house to watch what happened, Lawrence had returned Peter's keys. Lawrence had been the demon who'd called Nate out of the house that night, the frustrated writer in a nice, safe job measuring lobsters all day, the anti-Hallowe'en kirk-goer who turned four times a year into the devil, with power over a group of silly girls. Gavin had caught only three girls, but there had been four, two with each prisoner. In this new scenario, the prisoner I'd released had been Sarah from the canteen, being punished for laughing at them. Rachel had been the fourth witch, enjoying her reputation for eldritch behaviour, and the only one who knew who the devil really was. The other girls thought it was Nate, and she'd encouraged that to keep Lawrence's secret. They'd taken me up there in revenge for Nate's death, and she'd hugged her knowledge to herself with glee, waiting for their shock when their devil was still alive.

We finished the border by midday. Kate straightened her back and looked along at the black earth, then up through the cleared shrubs to the house. 'Work done. Well done, us.' She smiled at me. 'A last cup of tea together, Cass, in celebration.'

My hands smelt of the bitter roots. I'd scrubbed them twice over, but the earth-tang clung to them still as I lifted the mug to my mouth, and made my tea taste bitter. We drank in silence. I'd hoped for more work planting bulbs and shrubs but if Peter and Kate were leaving, there was no point. As I left, Kate handed me the usual envelope. 'There's a bit extra in there.' She made a movement as if she wanted to take my hand, then, suddenly, awkwardly, she leant forward and gave me a brief hug. 'This last week, you've been such a support.'

'You're welcome,' I murmured. She stepped back, cheeks red.

'Now remember to drop in for a cup of tea anytime.'

I knew she didn't mean it. I'd seen her at her most vulnerable, and she wouldn't want reminded of that. I thanked her again, patted the dogs goodbye, and headed off, ashamed of my relief at escaping from Kate's agony.

I'd said I would meet Gavin at 13.00. I went back to *Khalida* to leave Cat, and tidy myself up, then headed off along the shore road. I had lamb for tea still, or maybe I could join forces with Anders and Reider. *Stick to your own, Cass.* I'd get a couple of onions and make a stew. The shop was busy, with mothers and pushchairs blocking the fast-food aisles, older folk contemplating the saucermaet in the meat counter, and a group of primary pupils, along with their teacher and several assistants, doing some kind of survey among the sweeties. I'd just squeezed through to get a pint of milk and a bag of bannnocks when I came nose to nose with Rachel. She smiled, and waved a carton of milk at me. 'The milk I didn't get last night.'

Her dark eyes were clear, meeting mine squarely. She was wearing her schoolgirl jumper once more, the round collar neat over the neck rib. I tried to imagine her with tangled hair, hunched over a cauldron. Her colouring fitted, and the high, bony nose, but her eyes dispelled the picture. They were good eyes, honest, and I felt my picture of Lawrence and her acting together dissolving.

'How are you feeling this morning?' I asked.

She made a face. 'Sore.'

'Me too.' I gave a quick glance round to make sure the school assistants were intent on helping their pupils. 'My calves are used to climbing the rigging on tall ships, but not to scrambling up burns at night, with my hands tied.'

'It was horrid.' She shuddered. 'I was so afraid. I haven't said "thank you" properly yet.'

'Yes, you did.' We squirmed our way to the till together. Kate had been extra generous, I realised, when I saw the sheaf of twenty-pound notes in the envelope, Cashline crisp. I'd write her a note of thanks. We paid, and set out into the bright day.

'We had the police round this morning,' I said. She nodded.

'They were wi' us too. I didna ken what to say to them – how to explain. The inspector, the one with the nice grey eyes, he was asking why they might a taken me away like yon, why they would want to harm me.' She stopped, and drew away from me, towards the sea wall. We were in the widened part of the pavement, where the memorial for the men of the Shetland Bus bisected the nose-in line of parking. Rachel leaned against the waist-high walling and drew a long breath of sea air. I came forward to join her. The smell of seaweed was strong in the air, a fresh crop washed up by the tide, with the curls of wave just receding from it. Two hundred yards away, Cat was a small grey blob on *Khalida*'s roof. Reidar was scrubbing his fibreglass decks. The froosh, froosh of the brush carried across to us. Beside me, a strand of Rachel's dark hair whipped free from her bun, and curled free in the wind, like a ship's banner.

'When I was peerie –' Rachel began. She shook her head, and started again. 'Do you have brothers an' sisters?'

Little Patrick who hadn't lived to be born. I'd have been a good big sister. I'd have taken him sledging, and helped him sail siggie boats down the burn. I'd have protected him from bullies in the playground, listened to his reading, helped him do his sums. 'No, I'm an only child.' I realised, suddenly, that I wouldn't get a confidence unless I was prepared to give one. Cool Cass, who stood outside the world and watched. I leaned forward, resting my forearms on the wall, gazing out at the sandy curve of the bay, and found that I wanted to tell someone about it. 'But I have a half-brother or sister. Over in America. It'll be born soon, I think. My Dad had this affair, and I knew the girl was pregnant, but they quarrelled. That was probably good, she was my age, and Dad and Maman, I think they'll make a go of it again. Dad doesn't know about the baby. But I want to keep in touch. I can be an exciting big sister who just blows into the harbour, takes the child out for the world's largest icecream, tells stories of whales, then wafts off again.'

'You canna make the brother or sister you want,' Rachel said. The corners of her mouth drooped. 'I aye looked up to Nate, from when I was peerie. He was my big brother, and our folk were that proud of him. He was clever, doing well at the school, so I worked that hard, to keep up wi' him. Then, one year – you went to the Brae school, didn't you? Did you have commendations?'

The word brought memories flooding back. 'Blue card, wi' a list o' all you'd done well at through the year.' I'd always got commendations for English, Maths, and PE – French of course – Geography –

She nodded. 'Well, I was in primary three, and Nate was in primary five, and I got one more subject than him. He was that mad. He stormed back to the house, and when we got home, and Mam put both certificates up on the the mantelpiece, he waited till she'd gone back in the keetchen, an ripped mine up and fired it in the stove. I gowled, and telt Mam, and she just made shooshing noises, and didna tell him off. But at teatime, Dad went on about what a clever lass I was.' She took a deep breath. 'It was after that it started.'

She left a long pause, looking out over the dinkling waves. I didn't hurry her. 'I started to get clumsy. Things would fall just after I passed them. I smashed Mam's best vase, and she was the mad. It came a joke in our family – Mam wouldna let me touch valuable things ony mair. Nate stuck up for me against her, and said it wasna my fault. Even at school, it happened, because I'd lost faith in myself, and expected to drop things, and so I did. I got teased about it. Then, this day, I was in the parlour, and looked in the mirror, and I saw Nate arranging a cup so that I'd catch it with my elbow as I turned again.' Even all these years later, her voice hurt. 'My big bridder, that I'd aye thought was so clever. He was the one doing it all. He'd pulled me down to feel I was clumsy and stupid. He'd never forgiven me, you see. I'd dared to be cleverer than him.'

She straightened up. 'Well, I decided I'd show them. I worked hard at the school, and the better I did, the more turned he got. There'd be accidents, and aye blamed on me. When I went into secondary, that was Scalloway school then, I decided I was going to get away from here, an I did – college, then a job south. It was six blissful years. I had me ain flat, and you kens this, there was no even one piece o' lem smashed, no' in that whole six years. I even began to get me confidence back.' Her voice dragged down into defeat. 'Then Mam came ill, and I had to come home, back to where I'd been. Only it got worse. There was this whispering running round, that I was a witch. Nate's work, I have little doubt. Then – well, you saw, that day in the canteen. I wasna near that glass. I couldna have pushed it from where I was. And you saw how he reacted. I thought I couldn't bear it all over again. I went round that night – it wasna to see Mam, like I said, though I did help her while I was there. It was to have a blazing row with Nate, to tell him if ever he did anything like that again I'd walk out o' there and leave him wi' Mam, on his own, to make nothing o' his life if he wanted. I'd leave him to it. I said it aa' and it hurt more than anything I'd ever done, because he was my brother, an' yet I'd tried all I could to keep the peace, and there was nothing more I could do.'

'And that was why they took you up there,' I said. 'They took me because they believed I'd ill-witched him, and you because they'd heard about the quarrel, and they thought you might have killed him – killed their devil, the leader of their ceremonies. Except it wasn't him after all, because the devil was still there.'

Rachel looked quickly, left, right, then leant her head close to mine. 'Who was it in the devil suit? Who was it?'

I looked her straight in the eye. *Rachel or Lawrence* – 'Don't you know?' I asked.

194

'No,' she said. Her breathing was ragged. Her chest rose and fell, there was panic in her eyes. 'No! I don't know, I don't!' She turned away from me and half-walked, half-ran up the road.

Chapter Twenty

I considered that one all the way to the temporary police HQ in the old museum. If Rachel was innocent, if she had been set up as a witch by Nate – and I was inclined to believe that – then my whole scenario for Annette's death was wrong. Then I had a sudden inspiration. I didn't need Rachel. If Nate had been the witch Annette had approached – and everything we knew made that likely – then all we needed was for the real devil to have found out that someone was taking his name in vain. Nate held his ritual, and then, just when he was least expected, the devil arrived in his frightening costume. Nate ran for it, and so the devil returned the blame to his doorstep. Simple, plausible. All I needed to know now was who could have found out. Who might Nate have told? Not the hooded crows, his closest confidantes; certainly not Rachel. Annette, then. I knew who she had told: James Leask. James, the crofter's son who'd wanted to be a sea-captain. Someone who lacked power in their life … I was just considering the implications of that when Gavin came out.

'All set?' He opened the passenger door for me, then went round to his own side. He was in his scarlet kilt now, ready for church. 'How's the garden clearing going?'

'Finished,' I said. I stretched my hands, which were still ingrained with dirt, in spite of a third wash aboard *Khalida*. 'I was hoping the work would last a little longer, but Peter's put in for a transfer, so there's no point in doing all the planting work Kate had planned. Someone else will get our clean slate. According to Kate, they'll still be fighting the ground elder a decade on.'

'It's nasty stuff,' Gavin agreed. We swooped smoothly round the curve, came above Scalloway, and left it behind the hill as we headed north. There was a police van parked in lay-by, and a line of black-clad figures spread out along the lower slope. Gavin didn't comment, so I didn't ask. 'My mother got it in her flower garden from some root she'd bought at a plant sale, and she ended up having to leave the whole border under old carpet for a year.'

'No weeds at sea,' I said cheerfully. 'Well, except the ones that grow on your ship's hull.' Round-the-world sailors had to stop several times to careen their hulls, or, if they were non-stop, to swim round on a calm day, and scrub.

'Once you've finished your course, you'll be free to set off again.'

'If I finish it,' I said. Sitting side by side, with his eyes intent on the road, somehow made it easier to drop back into the friendship we'd found over the phone. 'It's driving me round the bend, being in a classroom. I'm going to miss my gardening. At least that got me outside. I'm going to have to take to long walks, or start climbing cliffs.'

He smiled. 'You'll finish it.'

'I will,' I agreed, 'but I don't have to like it.'

'I have something for you.' His voice was constrained. 'It was one of the things we found on the hill. It's in the glove compartment.'

I opened the pocket in front of me, and found a little package, rolled in a handkerchief. It was the size of my hand, and heavy. I unwound the wrapping and found a little figure. My heart choked within me. It was of clay, roughly made, and painted with blue jeans and a navy jumper. The hair was black, with what looked like real hairs among the paint, and there was a fingernail score across one cheek. A thick sewing-needle jutted out of the forehead. I held it in my hands and felt sick.

'I'm sorry you have to see it,' Gavin said, 'but I thought you should decide how to get rid of it. We don't need it as evidence. No court is going to convict them of witchcraft these days.'

I looked at the jutting-out needle and remembered the stabbing headache I'd endured these last few days. All my commonsense said this obscenity couldn't harm me, yet I understood why Gavin didn't want to just destroy it. I closed the handkerchief again, and shoved the nasty thing into my pocket.

He parked round the corner from the church, and we walked back together in silence. There was a fair sprinkling of people already inside. Gavin motioned me ahead of him, and I slipped into a pew halfway down. The sun smoothed diamonds of green and white through the window and over our shoulders, so that we knelt together in a rectangle of light. He brought that still concentration here too, hands clasped on the wooden pew, russet head bent over them. I looked away and focused on my own prayers, but the words wouldn't come. The little figure was too heavy in my pocket. I ended up reciting the 'Our Father' slowly, then took it out. I eased the needle from its head, then wrapped it up once more.

Father Mikhail swept in, in his best scarlet. We murmured the entrance greetings and the Gloria together, then there was a pause. The readers' rotas only covered the Sunday masses. Gavin gave a look around, then stepped forward. I took a deep breath, then followed. It was only standing-in as readers, but it felt like some public declaration, to walk together down the aisle, and bow our heads to the altar before standing at the lectern. Gavin motioned me forward, which gave me Revelation and the psalm: the multitude of people robed in white, the psalm that began *The Earth is the Lord's*. 'Who shall stand in his holy place,' I heard my voice read out, and the answer, '… those who do not lift up their souls to what is false.' The hooded crows and the fourth woman, who'd worshipped the devil up on Gallow Hill.

Gavin took over from me for a reading from St John, the reminder that we are all God's children. 'Sin is lawlessness,' his voice read gravely, and I wondered if that was his policeman's viewpoint. Breaking the law was a sin. No, St John had it the other way round, sin was breaking the law. '… little children, let no one deceive you …' They'd had charlatans and con-men in Biblical times too, people who worshipped idols.

The Gospel was the Beatitudes: blessed are the peacemakers, blessed are those that hunger for righteousness, blessed are the merciful …

When it was time to come forward for communion, Gavin stood back and motioned me forward. I tried to forget him behind me, to focus only on the blessed Presence I was about to receive. There was a cluster of small children ahead of me, with their mother. The first was old enough to receive communion, and the others each got a blessing. The mother was busy mustering them, so it was only I who noticed that the little boy who'd gone first had dropped his communion wafer on the floor. His neck and ears went scarlet. He stooped quickly to rescue it and put it in his mouth, then he turned to make sure his mother hadn't seen. His eyes met mine. I looked away, but not before I'd seen the guilt and shame flood his face. I wanted to say to him, 'It's okay, it was an accident,' but he was already scuttling back to his pew without looking at me again.

I didn't have time now to think where, or when, but I was filled with a sense of déjà vu. Somewhere, I'd seen that look of guilt, of being at faat: 'You caught me.'

At the end of Mass, I gave the handkerchief-wrapped figure to Father Mikhail. 'It's a witch figure. Maybe … maybe you can think of a way of destroying it so it does no further harm.'

'Cass,' he said, and shook his head. 'I have been hearing stories from Scalloway, but that you, a practical sailor, should listen to such nonsense!' He unwrapped the figure and let it drop on the concrete path. The black head cracked and lay aslant to the body. 'Will you jump on it first, or will I?'

I felt his common sense blow away the atmosphere that had gathered like a black mist around me. 'Me first,' I said, and landed squarely on it. I was wearing light sandshoes, so I did more damage to myself than I did to the figure, but the relief was enormous. Father Mikhail's black shoes pounded it to fragments. Behind me, Gavin was laughing.

'There,' Father Mikhail said. 'Please give my regards to your dear mother.'

'I would like to meet your mother,' Gavin said, as we walked back to the car, leaving the clay fragments to blow with the wind and dissolve with the rain. 'After the summer, I bought one of her CDs.'

I'd forgotten that he hadn't interviewed her, in the longship murder. Another policeman had crashed his shiny shoes into her fragile reunion with Dad, when she'd dropped everything to come and help us. I tried to imagine how they would get on, Gavin's sturdy country aura and Maman's Callas elegance. 'I think you'd like each other,' I decided at last. 'You're like my French family. They're very proud of being paysanne, country folk. Their roots are in the earth. Maman's are too, in spite of the way she looks. When I needed a dose of French common sense, I phoned her.'

'And a glorious voice.'

'When I was little,' I confessed, 'I thought the angels must sing like Maman.'

I sat into the car beside him, and we set off. 'Straight back to Scalloway,' Gavin said. 'I have a murder to solve still.'

I watched the houses of Lerwick slide past, the grey fishermen's houses, with the net sheds still behind. 'That reading you did,' I said. 'Sin is lawlessness. Surely it's the wrong way round?'

His grey eyes sparked. 'I thought that too, the first time I read it – oh, nine years ago, it must be. I'd done seven years.'

'Like Jacob.'

'In policing. Then I realised it was the right way round. Do you remember your seven deadlies, from the catechism?'

I wouldn't have, except that the Mariakirchen in Bergen had their opposites, the seven virtues, carved around the pulpit. The church also did organ recitals, and I'd spent several lunchtimes listening to the wonderful music and trying to work out which virtue was which. *Temperance, charity, patience, kindness, diligence* with her spindle. 'Gluttony, greed, anger, envy, sloth.'

Gavin nodded while I was trying to remember the last two. 'Gluttony, not knowing when to stop drinking, for a start. That's ninety per cent of our weekend work. In a broader sense, taking your own desires at the expense of others covers practically all of our criminal work. Greed, not sharing with others, wanting it all to be yours. There's whole raft of laws against theft, from the financiers wanting another million to the petty thief wanting a newer iPad. Anger takes us back to pub brawls and domestic abuse. What was your last one? Sloth creates all sorts of difficulties when someone expects another person, or the state, to carry them instead of pulling their weight. Benefit fraud for a start.'

I hadn't thought of it like that. I imagined a world, Gavin's world, spent battling against the consequences of people indulging in sin. He glanced towards me. 'Last two?'

I ran through the ones I'd done. 'Despair?'

His mouth curved in a smile. 'Comes under sloth. Not one of your failings.' His eyes shadowed. 'The number of criminals I've arrested who've just stopped caring. They've been brought up on a minimal income in a broken home.' His voice sparked into anger. 'They don't expect life will ever give them more, so why bother about the laws?'

I'd seen them on a tall ship, through the Tall Ships Youth Trust, where they'd done special rehabilitation voyages for young offenders. 'Send them on a tall ship,' I said. 'Oh, some don't respond, but so many do. They have a fun job to do, and rules that make sense, and they have to discipline themselves. They can spend their energy climbing the mast.' Of that team of thirty, we hoped twenty would go on to make good. I visualised the last two virtues now, Chastity, with her veiled face, and Humility. 'Lust and pride.'

'Lust's easy. All the laws against rape and child abuse. And the last one.' His profile was remote against the green hills speeding by. 'Pride. By this sin fell the angels. The belief that you're more important than anyone else. The murderer's sin.'

Suddenly I remembered the expression of the child who'd dropped the host. 'Annette's expression,' I said. 'It was guilt. "You've caught me".' His head turned quickly towards me, returned to face forwards, but not before his thought had flashed into my head. 'You know who it is,' I said.

Now I was looking at a policeman. 'I'm waiting for proof,' he said. 'Once you're sure of who, it can be found.'

If he wasn't at liberty to tell me, I wouldn't force his confidence by guessing. I'd had the clues that he had. I sat considering, as we passed the golf course, slid between the hills, came around the corner to see Scalloway spread below us, and arrived at last in the car park where Nate had been attacked. Gavin came to open the door for me.

'Thank you,' he said. For not asking, he meant. I put a hand on the rough tweed of his arm.

'You'll phone me when you can? To tell me – '

He nodded, and I let my hand fall. I had no part in this investigation now.

But I wanted to know. It wasn't quite two o'clock. Instead of heading to college (*Safety at Sea part II*), I walked up New Street, between the coloured houses, and stopped just short of the lane leading up to the museum, the castle – the lane with the opening to Spanish closs, where I'd found Annette. I'd been here when I'd heard someone shout. I'd assumed it was a drunken person at the Chinese takeaway, but the police hadn't traced any customer at that time.

I turned and walked slowly up the lane. This was the way the murderer must have come, with Annette over his shoulder, a humped, misshapen beast, with his horned head and swinging tail. I turned my shoulder to the red-painted wood of the museum, and went downhill to the castle. The heavy, black-studded door was open. I climbed the re-concreted steps of the broad stair, and came out into the Great Hall.

I stood in the middle of the floor, turning slowly, looking. The Great Hall was a rectangle some thirty metres by ten, with the main staircase at one end, and the little spiral stair which would once have led to the laird's bedroom at the other. There were two small rooms at the head of the main stair, and another opposite it. The placard on the end wall showed this hall as it once was, wood-panelled and painted, with bright tapestries, and a blazing fire in the wide chimney. Here, Black Patie would have sat in his carved chair, and pronounced judgement on the miserable women charged with witchcraft that had been dragged before him by a howling crowd.

Now it was a roofless box. The red-brown stone was hazed with drifting snowflakes. There were two rows of windows, for this floor and the missing floor above, unshuttered and uncurtained. The flagstones were hard underfoot, with pools of water where they were worn. I went to look up the spiral stair, barred by a grill, then returned to the chimney. There were the blackened remains of a fire in the hearth: ash, darkened to brown with water, and fragments of charred peat. Had Nate crouched over a fire here, with Annette waiting and watching, hoping to be freed of her demons?

I had the place to myself. I went to one of the windows that looked out over Scalloway, and considered. Practical Cass. Forget this miasma of witchcraft, of devils, and think of how Annette's death had come about. Annette had asked Nate to help her, and in return he'd asked for the witches' ash. She'd taken her father's key when he'd taken the dogs for their walk, and come to the museum below me to steal the ash. The container of ash, and the ash on her hand, made that certain. They'd come into the castle, for their ritual. I frowned here. Peter's dogs' walk, up the hill, out through the fields, and back down past the swimming pool into Scalloway, took an hour. It didn't seem a lot of time for a witch-banishing ritual. Annette would know, too, exactly how long it took. Maybe she'd counted on his not needing his keys until morning.

Leave that aside for the moment. The demon had materialised, and Annette had fallen. It had been a man who'd shouted – Nate or the demon. I looked doubtfully at the thick walls, the diamond-pane windows. Would I really have heard a shout from inside the castle all the way round the corner?

Annette had fallen, and Nate had run for it. The demon had picked up Annette and followed. I looked down at the path winding round the castle and coming out in front of the museum, opposite Kevin's nan's house. It kept him off the street slightly longer, bringing him out directly opposite this end of New Smiddy Closs, but it seemed to me a good bit further, with the weight of a dead girl to carry. He had gone that way, though, for Kevin's nan had seen him crossing the road here. That was a third unlikely thing, and while there was no accounting for people's reactions, I didn't like it. It felt like a tangled rope, twisting this way and that, instead of pulling in a straight line.

Think again, Cass. If Nate wasn't the demon, with his diary filled for the eve of All Hallows, then why was he doing this all-important ritual last Wednesday? Surely Hallowe'en was the big night, the night for hocus-pocus mumbo-jumbo, the perfect night for summoning long-dead witches. In which case –

My heart stopped for a moment as it all began to make sense, then thudded into life again. In which case, the only thing Annette had been doing on Wednesday was *stealing the ash*. Peter's hour up on the hills was plenty of time to do that. She'd phoned ahead to Nate to tell him, and he'd been waiting for her to bring it to him, ready for the big ritual on Monday night. She'd gone into the museum, taken the ash, come out again – and she'd been caught, caught locking up the museum she'd no business to be in late at night like that. The person had come up behind her, shouted angrily, put his hands on her shoulders. The wind had swirled the sound down the closs to me. Annette had dropped like a stone, and the person who'd caught her was left standing in front of the museum with a dead girl at his feet. He knew what she was up to, and for whom. He put the keys in his pocket to slip back at the first opportunity – I remembered Peter's look of surprise as he'd found them in his old dog-walking jacket, which he never wore when he was driving the car or walking to the museum. Then the person who'd caught her lifted Annette on his back and carried her to Nate's door. Nate had come out and searched Annette's pockets for the link to him – the witches' ash. In mischief or malice, he made the claw marks, and slipped back inside his door as my shadow crossed the lane towards the closs. Now my rope was running true. Then, when the police had announced that Annette had died of natural causes, the person who'd killed her had taken the law into his own hands. Nate had been morally responsible for Annette's death. He'd die like the witch he'd pretended to be.

My rope had paid out until I had only the bitter end in my hands. Now I needed to see the face. Somebody who knew what Annette was up to, and for whom; someone who loved her enough to kill for her. I looked out of the window and saw him, just as Kevin's nan had described him, the words I'd taken as vivid imagination: 'tall, he was,' she'd said, 'and black as the inside of a chimney, with a misshapen hump on his back, and a cloud of evil around him, and the hounds of Hell at his back' and at last I knew who she'd seen.

He was striding towards the castle path, his head smooth between the two pointed horns of his ear-flap hat, the tail of his dog-leash swinging around his legs. He looked up and saw me there in the window. It seemed an endless moment that he stood there, staring up at me. I saw in his face that he read the knowledge in mine. Then he began to move again, pace quickening, towards the castle gate. He'd be at the door before me, and I was alone in the castle with nowhere to hide.

I had two possibilities – to hide downstairs, and hope he came up first, or to hide upstairs and run while he searched downstairs. I began moving towards the stair, then stopped dead. Below me, the door downstairs was being eased open. Soft footsteps went into the antechamber where the witches had been held, whispering on the flagged floor. I heard my name being breathed up the stairwell: 'Cass! Where are you?'

I wasn't going to stay and be caught like a rat in a trap. The echoed 'ss' was still dying as I slid backwards from the main stair towards the far end of the hall, where the little spiral stair led upwards. It was barred now with a grill, but the stones to each side were worn enough to give me toeholds. I wedged one foot as high as I could reach and thrust myself up, clinging like a lizard to the rock. There was a doorway to the stair just above my head, from the long-gone bedroom floor. I got my forearms over the doorstep and hauled myself up onto level ground, legs flailing.

Years of mast climbing had given me a head for heights. I glanced down at the flagged stones of the hall twenty feet below, then flattened myself behind the door arch to listen. My follower was coming up the main stair now; I heard the pad of feet on stone, the echo of breathing. I dodged into the spiral stair and began climbing. It had been solidly built, but the next curve had lost stones, and I had to chimney up it, pressing the flat of my left palm against the cold, rough wall, gripping the last of the central pillar with my right, and wedging my toes into what step remained. My hands would hurt later; the sharp edges of stone clawed the skin off. *Claws* ...

I reached the end of the staircase and paused, looking up. The last step was a flat landing stone, beside what had once been an attic doorway. The start of the inverted V of the gable was only three feet above the last step. I could go up onto the gable, four storeys above the ground, sixty feet, less than the height of the second platform on *Sorlandet*'s mast. I could see the double wall construction from here, filled between with rubble and earth. I'd go over the top of the gable and lie between the walls on the other side. If this devil was determined enough to come after me there, he would be the one in a vulnerable position. I would be lying securely, ready to grab at his ankles if he came too close.

'Cass! Cass!' The whisper came from below me now. I couldn't move yet. I sent up a quick prayer that the stonework above my head was sound, and the stones and earth between the two walls packed down firmly.

There were steps across the hall. I could hear ragged breathing and checked my own, drawing air steadily in through my nose and out again, silently, silently. The steps came to a halt by the spiral stair, as I knew they would. The person stepped back to look upwards. The voice came again, impatiently: 'Cass, are you up there? Come down.'

I wasn't coming down to an empty building, with thick walls between us and the friendly outside world. Below me, I heard the person place a foot against the wall, then come up as I'd done, with a thrust and scrabble on the lime-faced wall. Now!

I grasped each side of the gable. The stone blocks felt firm enough. I pushed up with my legs and scrambled up onto the gable. There was a rattle and scurry in the ledge between the walls, then three starlings flapped up from among the stones, wings rattling like an unsecured sail. Instinctively, I flung my arm up in front of my eyes, and flinched backwards. Birds around your face was one of the things I didn't like about shore life. Furthermore, they'd made it clear to the person below that I was up here. I had to get into safety, and fast.

It didn't matter about noise now. The faced crowstep blocks under my left hand felt less secure than the inner gable. I put my weight more towards the hall side, then went down on hands and feet, scarlet jacket shrieking (I hoped) like an alarm signal, and scurried upwards to the squared-off top. The stones were slippery with ice. A long way below me, the grass of the castle courtyard glittered silver.

I could hear the footsteps coming faster up the stair, then pausing. The person had found the broken stones. The voice came again: 'Cass, don't be stupid!'

At the top of the gable, I let myself down into the gap between. To my relief there was no further flurry of wings. The stone in-fill wobbled as I put one foot on it, but it had been packed down by four centuries of weather, and gave no further. I crouched down between the walls for security, and waited, arms spread on the stone blocks, head high. The view was spectacular: the dark ring of stone that marked the Althing, the Viking parliament, outlined in snow, with the grey Manse above it. The hills on my right were the colour of dark chocolate, sprinkled with snow like the frosting on a Yule log; on my left, the hill had been reclaimed and re-seeded for grazing, short green grass where the snow lay smooth as icing. The five wind turbines stood proud over their kingdom.

The voice called again: 'Cass!' Then suddenly there was noise from below, a car stopping, the gate slamming open with a click, running feet, and when I looked over my shoulder there was a squad of police officers swarming below me like more starlings. Before I could say anything, three had begun coming upstairs, the tramp of their shoes echoing up the wide staircase, while two came round to the gable end, directly below me, leaving the door unguarded.

My pursuer heard it too. I heard feet skid and clatter on the spiral stair below, the iron rattle of railing, then he raced across the great hall and dived out of sight. He just made it into the anteroom before the policemen got into sight on the stair, then, as they charged into the main hall, I saw him slip out behind them.

The first officer stopped half way along the hall, tilted his head back and called up in a friendly, reasonable tone. 'Now, son, you're not very safe up there. How about coming back down?'

I recognised his face from the murder aboard my longship *Stormfugl*, when we'd had most of Shetland's police force swarming around for a week. He was the one who wouldn't let me aboard my own ship. I smiled sweetly down at him. 'The view's fantastic from up here. Come and look.'

He did a classic double-take. 'Miss?' Then he recognised me. 'Ms Lynch, isn't it?' The voice slid from friendly encouragement to scepticism. 'What are you doing up there?'

I looked over my other shoulder, at four black-clad figures converging on one in navy, sharp outlines on the grass sward four stories below me. Gavin had brought the cavalry.

'Oh, just keeping an eye on events,' I told the officer. The figures below me became six, as Gavin joined them, scarlet kilt clear against the green grass. I watched as Gavin gave the official caution, and then he and his squad led Peter Otway away.

Chapter Twenty-one

The sky was dimming as I walked home from college, with the first frost-blue stars blazing above the dark outline of the Scord. I paused at the marina gate, looking onwards to where three rectangles of orange light shone out from Kate's kitchen. I hadn't expected to visit again soon, but things were different now. If she'd been alone after Annette's death, she'd be even more alone now. I turned my back on the gate, and began walking towards the lighted windows. I wasn't much, but I was better than no one. If she didn't want me, I'd go away again. My steps grew slower and slower as I approached the gate. I'd have turned back if the dogs hadn't come barking to greet me, and escort me up to the house.

She was sitting at the kitchen table, a mug within her curved hand. I slid into the other side and sat, waiting. The oil flame hissed in the Rayburn, and Dan's tail thumped against the side of his basket.

'I knew,' she said at last. She lifted her head, and I saw that she looked more like herself than she had since Annette's death. The worry lines, the grey skin, had smoothed away. She didn't have to fight between instinct and loyalty any more, now the truth was known. *The truth shall make you free ...* 'Oh, not that he'd killed Annette! I'd never have thought of that in a million years. No, I knew about the coven. I think he got a kick out of knowing I knew. He didn't tell me himself, but he'd look at me, the nights he was going out, and say, 'I'm just going for a long walk. I'll leave the dogs behind.' Then I'd know he was meeting *them*. Those teenage girls who got a kick out of their stupid ceremonies. And Peter strutting about in that idiotic costume.'

She sighed, and turned the mug in her hands. 'I can tell you when it started. It was the financial crisis, when suddenly bankers went from being "somebody" in the town, the person you'd ask to be on committees, or guarantee loans, all that, to everyone seeing them as the people who'd ruined the country. He couldn't bear that. He liked being important. Back in Gloucestershire, we'd been in the county set, so he was Duneton's son-in-law.' Her accent mocked itself. 'You know, nice little place just out of Cirencester, some cousin of the Spencers. He had his own status here: Mr Otway, the manager of Shetland's largest bank. Then there was the crash, and he lost the status. Oh, he was still a member of the Lodge, and the Rotary, but people didn't treat him with respect any more. They lectured him about what banks had done to the country.'

She picked up her mug, took a sip of cold tea, made a face, and set it down again. 'It was all bad timing. Annette went from being Daddy's princess to the teenage rebel stage, and once she'd left school she wanted a life of her own. And me, well, I'd been the older woman, and he'd liked that. Liked me being in charge of the home. Now he couldn't bear it. He wouldn't let me contridict him over anything. He wanted me to give him the respect he wasn't getting any more, and I just couldn't do it. His world was falling apart, and our marriage with it.'

'Then, one night, he saw the coven. He was up walking the dogs, and saw their fire. He went and looked, and told me about it when he came down: "Stupid girls playing at witches!" Then he broke off, and I saw him thinking about it. He was in London not long after that, and then this box turned up with a costumier's name on it.' She shuddered. 'I remember his manner when it arrived – gloating, nervous, and that horrid "I know I shouldn't do this, but I'm going to" look. I asked what it was, and he wouldn't tell me.' She blushed. 'So, naturally, the next time he went out, I looked. He meant me to. Then, the next full moon, he went out, and when he came home I could smell it all on him, the smoke, and the adrenalin, and the sex. I challenged him with playing the devil, and he just laughed and said it would make a good story for the divorce court, if I wanted to lose my home, and studio, and income. How would I support myself, he sneered, untrained and middle-aged, when young university candidates like Annette couldn't get a job? And I thought about this house, and the garden, that I'd just started to restore, and my studio, and I was *damned* if I was going to throw it all up, just like that. I decided to stay. He got a kick out of that too, pretending in front of people what a devoted couple we were.'

'And then Annette got this idea of being reincarnated,' I said.

She pushed the mug away, covered her eyes with one hand. 'If only she'd talked to me about it. I should have explained to her, but I didn't want to give Peter away. When she was little, you see, we had this old spaniel, Hector. He wasn't very fond of her, he saw her as a usurper, but she loved him, she'd try to pick him up and pet him. Then he got a septic paw, and Peter was afraid he would bite her. He told her she had to stay away from Hector, and she just wouldn't listen, and one day he lost his temper and took her by the shoulders, by the throat, and shook her. She almost lost consciousness. I was so angry. I told him if he ever did anything like that again, if he ever laid hands on her, I'd leave him and take her with me, and he'd never see her again. But that was when it started, that fear of having something around her neck. She'd wake in the night, saying she was choking. I suppose that once we came here, and they did witches in school, then that linked up with something in her head and that's how the reincarnation idea started.' She stopped, shuddering.

'I can tell you the next bit,' I said. I kept my voice soft, as if I was trying to talk a child to sleep. 'She did that Hallowe'en play with Nate. She told him about the reincarnation idea. He was like your husband; he'd lost status too. He'd grown up his parents' golden boy, and turned out nothing. He had all these ideas and ambitions, but not the application to make anything of them, so he saw others succeeding where he'd failed. As a child, he'd made himself big by bullying his clever little sister, but he'd ended up having to be grateful to her for getting him a job, waiting at tables and running after a temperamental chef. The teenage girls who used to hang around asking him about occult stuff had gone off to do their own orgies. They didn't know their devil was Peter; they thought it was Nate. They stopped talking to him about the occult, because they didn't want to spoil their fun by admitting they knew it was him. Here was his chance to have some fun again.'

But the witches hadn't liked it. They thought Annette was taking their devil away from them. So they started to hassle her, and they told her they'd put a spell on her dog, make him sicken and die if she didn't leave Nate alone; but Nate persuaded her he was the only one who could help.

'Nate told Annette they'd have a session in Scalloway Castle, where the witches had been condemned, and raise the ghost of the witch she'd been. But he wanted to get a hold over her. So he asked her to steal the ash from the museum. It was a little, stupid thing, not valuable, but symbolic. She'd have to take Peter's keys, betray his standing. Peter'd sneered at Nate, and disapproved of the Hallowe'en play. It was Nate's revenge.'

'They were on his key ring,' Kate said. 'I worked that out. She couldn't get at them during the day, because he had them, so she had to take them while he walked the dogs.'

That had been where it had gone wrong. Dan had been ill, so Peter hadn't been able to take the dogs out on Tuesday night. He'd gone on Wednesday, as usual, and Annette had seized her chance. She'd phoned Nate and told him she'd bring him the ash that night ... except that Dan was still a bit shaky, so instead of going the great circuit around the hill, Peter just went through the town, up the back of Fraser Park, round the roundabout, and down towards the castle. He'd arrived at the museum, the dogs padding along behind him, just in time to see Annette coming out out of it, and locking up behind her with what had to be his keys. He'd grabbed her shoulders, like he'd grabbed her when she was little, and she'd gone into shock and died. I didn't want to think about how he must have felt then, nor to talk about it to Kate, with her white face and ghost-seeing eyes.

'The keys were in her hand, and he just shoved them in his pocket. He found them there, later – that day I came round, and he was on his way out.' I remembered his look of surprise. For a moment, he'd forgotten how they came to be there. He hadn't known, though, what she'd been doing at the museum. He didn't trust Nate. I think he was afraid she'd been stealing from the museum – money, I mean. He searched her bag and found she'd got £100 in her purse. It was the money for paying off the witches, but he didn't know that. So he took it, and as soon as he could he went down to the museum to check there was nothing missing from the till or the cash float, or money waiting to be banked.'

He'd have behaved as though he wanted something to take his mind off, and the staff would have been too sympathetic to say anything. He checked the till and the float and there was nothing wrong. It had just been money she'd taken out after all.

'He put it in our money jar,' Kate said. 'I just thought it was useful petty cash, so I gave it to you. I told the police that.' She frowned. 'It didn't get you into trouble? The police didn't think you stole it from Annette, did they?'

I shook my head. 'They didn't know I've had it.' They would probably want it back, for evidence, I thought, with regret. 'Have you eaten?'

'I'm not hungry.'

I rose and searched in the cupboard for tomato soup, comfort food, poured it into a bowl and microwaved it. There was a packet of cheddar biscuits too. I put them in front of her, found a soup spoon and gave it into her hand, then sat back in my place. She drank half a dozen spoonfuls without interest, then hunger kicked in, and she finished the bowl. The warm spiciness brought the colour back into her cheeks. She laid the spoon in the bowl and took a deep breath, bracing herself. 'Now I know it was him, I can imagine how it happened. The museum was the last thing he had left, his bit of status. He'd enjoyed it so much, steering the committee, being there at the opening, shaking hands with Queen Sonia of Norway – it was the way things used to be. Then he saw Annette there. This red mist of rage just came over him, and he did what he did before, when she was a child: he went to shake her.' I remembered that look on her face. Guilt, the shock of being caught. The shock killed her. 'He hadn't meant to kill her, but she was dead all the same, and nothing he could do would bring her alive again. He was still half out of his mind with grief and rage, and it was all Nate's fault. So he decided to take her to Nate's house, and leave her there, with her hand pointing to the guilty person. He didn't think about how it would affect me –' A spasm passed over her face. She took a moment to fight the tears, then continued, her voice steady. 'The police would punish Nate. He lifted her the way he'd learned in the fire brigade, and carried her down that short passage from the museum to the Spanish closs.'

'That's when Kevin's nan saw him,' I said. 'We should have listened to her more closely.' *The Devil, with his horns and his tail, and a misshapen hump on his back, she'd said, and the hounds o' Hell at his heels.* I'd seen him myself, with his ear-flap hat making two horns, and the dog-lead swingling like a tail around his legs, and Dan and Candy following behind him. A man walking his dogs.

But Nate had seen him. He'd known Annette was going to try for the ash – she'd phoned him as she left – and he was waiting for her. He saw Peter drop her in the courtyard. He didn't know if she'd managed to get into the museum, but if she had, then he was afraid the witches' ash would lead them to him. He dived out into the courtyard and felt in her pockets, and there it was, a little container of ash. Then he heard someone coming down the close, and got back in again just in time to lurk in the shadows behind the curtain, and watch me find the body.

Kate rose to set her bowl in the sink. Now she had said the worst of it, she could move again. 'Nate. Poor Nate. Those phone calls, those people saying your computer was upsetting the Microsoft mainframe. Those were Nate, the police said, trying to get hold of Peter. Your policeman explained. Blackmail. Peter went up to the house, and Nate came out with him, and – Oh! they didn't put it like that of course, just "reason to believe" he might have been involved.' She turned away from me. Her voice sounded as if she was far, far away. 'As soon as I heard about Nate's death, yesterday, I knew. I didn't want to believe it, but inside me I –' The bowl clattered from her hands back into the sink. She picked it out, rinsed it, and began drying it, rubbing the cloth round and round as if it was the most important thing in the world. She'd just set it back in the cupboard when the front door bell jangled. Kate jerked her head round. Her eyes were filled with dread. '*The Shetland Times* has phoned already.'

'I'll get it,' I said, and went through the wood-lined hall, with Peter's jacket still hanging nearest the glass-paned door, ready for him to reach out a hand and pick it off the hook. Already it looked like something from another time. The outline through the door was a woman's. She held her hand out when I opened the door.

'Mrs Otway?'

I shook my head. 'A neighbour.' Her suit and briefcase looked more like a lawyer than a journalist. 'You are?'

She had her business card ready. *Kerr and Newby*, it read, *Solicitors*. 'I'm Peter's lawyer.'

I stepped back and waved her in. 'Kate's through in the kitchen, the door on the right.' I saw her into the room. 'Kate … if you'd like, I'll call back over later.' We could have a drink together, just before bedtime. If ever a woman needed a goodnight brandy, Kate would, this night, though I didn't expect it would help her to sleep.

She nodded, and I nodded back, and left them to it.

Now the sky was blazing with stars. The air was crisp on my face, cold and clear as well water in each breath. The police car was drawn up in front of the marina, so I wasn't surprised to find Gavin sitting below in Reidar's warm cabin, a cup of drinking chocolate in front of him. Anders was tucked into the opposite corner, with Rat on his shoulder, and Cat on his lap. There was a scatter of lethal-looking hooks on the table, each tied with jewel colours, as if Gavin and Reidar been comparing their lure of choice, and a heavenly smell of some kind of stew. I realised I'd missed lunch.

'There you are,' Reidar said. He poured the last portion from a little saucepan into a mug, added the cream and set it exactly in the centre of the table. Suddenly I realised how awkward this simple act of sitting down was. The settee around the table was U-shaped, with Gavin on one side, Anders on the other. Reidar was standing still, in the centre of the passage, with no indication of where he'd been sitting. Gavin was nearer to me, but the space beside Anders was slightly larger, and Cat was on that side. I could slide in beside either with equal naturalness, and one'd take it as a commitment, the other as a rejection. I longed for *Khalida*'s neutral engine box steps … and then Gavin moved into the middle section, as naturally as if he'd never seen the hesitation, giving me the whole of the side he'd been sitting on. 'Have a seat.'

I put my mug on the table, and sat down. His cushion was warm. 'I went to see Kate on my way home. Her lawyer's with her now, but I said I'd go back.'

Reidar indicated the oven. 'I have a stew cooking. You may take her some of that. She will need to eat, poor lady.'

They obviously knew all about it. 'I went to the shop,' Anders explained, 'and the people in the queue were all full of gossip. They had seen you up on the castle roof, and Peter being taken away.'

I looked at Gavin. 'You knew, didn't you?'

He nodded. 'Almost from the start. Ignoring the witch trappings, the people to look at were the victim's family, so he was right in the frame, and on the spot too. The old lady mentioned dogs, and there he was, walking the dogs. When we found that her death had been accidental, I was certain, and the link with the ash from the museum clinched it. He'd caught her coming out, using his keys, and grabbed her, with tragic results. We could have left it there if it hadn't been for Nate.'

Least said, shunest mended, was an old Shetland proverb. He couldn't have told me, of course. I understood that. I'd been too close, working with Kate daily. I wouldn't have been able to react naturally to Peter, and that would have put me in danger.

'Will you get the proof you need?'

'For Annette, no. He was wearing gloves, so there are no fingerprints, and no eyewitnesses now. But we have a simple chain of suggested events which hangs together plausibly, so the jury should take that into account.' He gave me an apologetic look. 'Have you spent much of the £100 Kate gave you?'

I shook my head, and fished in my pocket. 'Evidence?'

'Make-weight support.' My envelope went into his sporran. 'Come along tomorrow and Sergeant Peterson'll give you a receipt. The bank's working on tracing numbers, and it can be fingerprinted. It's the strongest link we have to Annette.'

'What about Nate?'

'We have a number of phone calls from Nate's mobile to his house, all short, all roughly agreeing with the times Mrs Otway thought she'd had phone calls from the Microsoft scam people. Nate's actor friends agree he could do a convincing Indian accent. Then there are two at times when she was out in her studio, and Otway was in.'

The status Peter had prized so much was gone now. Gavin used his surname curtly. 'Otway's admitted to two anonymous phone calls saying "I saw you" but says he knows nothing of what they were about. He would have known it was Nate – who else could it be? And so he went up to see him, the next time he took the dogs out. He knew about the mother's illness, he knew their father was away. If he went late enough, Nate would answer the door. He's got a firearms certificate, and a .22 rifle. My guess is that he took his gun with him, pressed it against Nate's side, and said he'd shoot him if he didn't come with him.'

I'd forgotten Peter's rabbit shooting. 'And Nate didn't dare risk arguing.'

'Otway took him down to the skip. Bullets are traceable, and Otway knew that. He hit him over the head with some improvised sandbag, like a sock filled with sand. We found grains of sand in his jacket pocket – harder for Otway's lawyer to explain than the sand in Nate's hair, which could have come from the beach.' His mouth curved in a grim smile. 'We also found a sock at low tide, at the distance of a good throw from the car park. It had builders' sand inside, held in by a knot, and it hadn't been there long. It's Marks and Sparks, black, sold by the thousand, but it just happens to be the sort that Otway wears. He hit Nate with it, then threw it as far as he could. He tied Nate with the old rope from the skip, accessible to anyone here, threw him over onto the beach, and left him there to drown.'

Nate's face swum again before my eyes, floating, with the scarring from the tiny fish on his cheeks.

'Otway's a landsman. The sea was usually there, so he expected it would be, or would be soon. I don't think he felt guilty. Annette's death was Nate's fault, and he'd got exactly the punishment he'd deserved. His pretending to have magical powers had killed Annette, so he got a witch's death.'

'But that is what you think he did,' Anders said. 'You cannot prove that he did it.'

'Not yet,' Gavin conceded. 'The phone calls, the sock, and the sand are all we have so far, and we can't hold him on those. His lawyer's pointed out that he admitted to being in the area that night, and that he had the dogs with him, so he was hardly likely to commit a murder.'

'They're very well trained,' I said. 'If he said "sit, stay" they'd have done it. Shaela heard a snuffling noise, like a dog. Is there any chance she can identify the devil she saw talking to Nate?'

'She'll recognise the suit, once we find it. He's denying all of that, and from his confidence it's not at his house. I presume he ditched it, after us nearly catching him last night. We'll find it. Rolled up in a black bag and shoved under a stone or overhang of peat bank somewhere on the road between Scalloway and Lerwick, is my guess.'

I remembered the officers on the hill as we drove to Mass. 'Was that what they were searching for?'

Gavin nodded. 'Every officer we have. The suit's distinctive, custom-made, delivered to him at his house. If we find it, if Shaela can identify it, that's strong evidence. If we don't, we may trace it from the maker's end, and show her a photograph. Of course his lawyer will say he hid it because he didn't want the ridicule of being known as a fake Satanist.'

'Was it Peter who went back to Nate's house, the person his mother heard going in?'

'Naturally Otway says it wasn't. I think he was pushing the witchcraft motive. It's like you said: there was no need for Nate to display all the trappings. There was an empty cardboard box in the bottom of the wardrobe, and I think that's where the chalice and black candles and all the rest of it normally lived. The last person to handle them was someone with gloved hands, and there'd be no reason for Nate to wear gloves, in

213

his own house.' He stood up, and I stood too, to let him pass me. 'It's all paperwork now. They won't need to pay my B&B here in Shetland for that.' He picked up a cardboard tube from the shelf and looked at Reidar. 'Thank you for the drinking chocolate. I'll try that fly of yours next time I'm after sea trout in bright conditions.'

'It will lure them from under a metre of weed,' Reidar promised.

I went up the steps ahead of him, and we strolled along the pontoon together. Gavin had the tube tucked under one arm. I wondered what it was, but didn't want to ask.

'I don't think you'll have any more trouble with your witches,' Gavin said. 'They're just bored girls with fevered imaginations and not enough to do. We leaned on them pretty heavily about their hocus pocus up on the hill. Your local officer has his eye on them now, and he'll make it obvious they need to keep their noses clean.'

'I'm going to have to re-laminate one piece of my deck, where the peat lay longest,' I said. 'It's an excuse to see if I can still remember my fibreglass skills – but they needn't think I'm happy about it.'

'They don't,' Gavin said. 'I told them I'd been on board, and recognised them. That quietened them down. You'll get it paid for, and I wouldn't be surprised if you see them scrubbing the pontoon come spring, as their community service.'

'I'll avoid dark alleys, all the same.'

'You should.'

'And the fourth witch was Sarah from the canteen?'

'She knew Rachel had run, and thought it was worth trying to pretend she'd been the other prisoner, rather than have her mum find out what she'd been up to when she was supposedly at her pal's house watching teen movies.' He smiled in the moonlight. 'The others set me right on that one, with emphasis. She'll have to keep clear of them for a bit, which will do her no harm.'

'So Rachel wasn't anything to do with any of it?'

'Nothing at all to do with any of it. The lead witch told us all about it in the end, when the Lerwick constabulary told her she wasn't leaving the cell until she'd made a statement we believed. You and Rachel, the rival witches, according to Nate's gossip. They thought they'd lost their devil. They got the shock of their lives when he turned up. She said they weren't going to hurt you with that nasty-looking knife, just give you a bit of a fright.'

'Of course.' I unlocked the heavy gate for him, and swung it open with a clang. 'When do you go back to Inverness?'

'Tomorrow. Like I said, it's all paperwork now. The Lerwick men will take over.'

He was going, and I didn't want him to, yet I didn't know what to say to stop him. I left the gate open, and came through it with him. 'Thanks for the crewing job, last Saturday.'

'Thanks for taking me. I enjoyed it. One of the other Inverness officers has a boat up in Fortrose, and he keeps saying I could crew for him. I'll maybe try it.'

'It might clash with fishing days.'

'Still days are the best, for fish.'

'No use for sails,' I agreed.

'How's your headache, now you've destroyed their figure?'

I rubbed my temple. 'Still there. I think the college central heating is going for me.'

My heart was thumping like a single-cylinder engine. My throat felt as if it would choke any words I tried to force through it. 'Gavin,' I said tentatively. The name hung in the air between us. He didn't turn his head, but I knew he was listening. 'I was wondering if your offer of Christmas was still open.'

He turned towards me. The moon poured silver on the curve of his brows, his cheekbones, the long, rather wooden line of his mouth. I thought for a moment he might try to kiss me, and I braced myself not to panic this time. But he didn't. He took the card roll from under his arm, and handed it to me. I looked a question at him, but he still didn't speak, just nodded and got back into the police car. I was still standing there, the tube in my hands, staring stupidly as he turned the car and drove off.

I watched the two cones of white light run smoothly along Port Arthur road and disappear behind the shed the Shetland Bus men had used. Their women had had to wait at home, not knowing if they'd ever see them again. That was the life of a seaman's woman. A policeman might be an easier bet, if he was willing to be a seawoman's man. The car reappeared again at the monument, slipped behind the shops, then the headlights lit up the pink front of the Old Haa, the withered vegetation of Mary Ruisland's garden, and turned to two red lights as it went up the hill. I turned and waited, watching the road by the Scord, until I saw the lights again, travelling up, round, and dwindling into the darkness.

The tube was featherweight in my hands. A poster, for their police Christmas Ball? I wasn't going to open this in front of Anders. I took it aboard *Khalida*, lit the hanging lantern, and put two fingers inside to coax the paper out. It was much larger than a poster, and stiff, stiff paper, like a chart. I rolled it out under the flickering golden light, and found that that was indeed what it was: a proper seaman's chart, hand-drawn in black ink, with every rock and headland marked, and the depths of every bay. I put a weight on each corner, and leaned over it. It began half way down his loch, with the three islands and the Barrisdale Narrows. A child had marked a solitary house by the point labelled Caolas Mor, and drawn a little picture of a man and woman beside it. The man wore a deerstalker and carried binoculars, and the woman had a fishing rod. There was a narrow passage to the head of the loch, then another little drawing: a building marked 'Farm', and a father with a bale of hay, a mother in an apron, feeding hens, and two boys, both wearing the kilt. The smallest one had red curls.

There was a wider bay before the farm, with the contours running smooth round it. A pier was marked, but it would dry out at low tide. In the bay there were ten metres of water at the centre, sloping to three.

It was an adult hand that had drawn a little anchor symbol for 'good anchorage' in the centre of the bay.

Glossary

Shetland has its own very distinctive language, *Shetlan* or *Shetlandic*, which derives from old Norse and old Scots. Magnie's first words to Cass are,

'Cass, well, for the love of mercy. Norroway, at this season? Yea, yea, we'll find you a berth. Where are you?'

Written in west-side Shetlan (each district is slightly different), it would have looked like this: 'Cass, weel, fir da love o mercy. Norroway, at dis saeson? Yea, yea, we'll fin dee a bert. Quaur is du?"

Th becomes a *d* sound in *dis* (this), *da* (the), *dee* and *du* (originally thee and thou, now you), *wh* becomes *qu* (*quaur*, where), the vowel sounds are altered (well to *weel*, season to *saeson,* find *to fin)*, the verbs are slightly different (quaur <u>is</u> du?) and the whole looks unintelligible to most folk from outwith Shetland, and *twartree* (a few) within it too; so, rather than writing in the way my characters would speak, I've tried to catch the rhythm and some of the distinctive usages of Shetlan while keeping it intelligible to *soothmoothers*, or people who've come in by boat through the South Mouth of Bressay Sound into Lerwick, and by extension, anyone living south of Fair Isle.

There are also many Shetlan words that my characters would naturally use, and here, to help you, are *some o dem*. No Shetland person would ever use the Scots *wee*; to them, something small would be *peerie*, or, if it was very small, *peerie mootie*. They'd *caa* sheep in a *park*, that is, herd them up in a field – *moorit* sheep, coloured black, brown, fawn. They'd take a *skiff* (a small rowing boat) out along the *banks* (cliffs) or on the *voe* (sea inlet), with the *tirricks* (Arctic terns) crying above them, and the *selkies* (seals) watching. Hungry folk are *black fanted* (because they've forgotten their *faerdie maet*, the snack that would have kept them going) and upset folk *greet* (cry). An older housewife like Jessie would have her *makkin*, (knitting) *belt* buckled around her waist, and her *reestit* (smoke-dried) *mutton* hanging above the Rayburn. And finally... my favourite Shetlan verb, which I didn't manage to work in this novel, but which is too good not to share: *to kettle*. As in: *Wir cat's joost kettled. Four ketlings, twa strippet and twa black and quite.* I'll leave you to work that one out on your own... or, of course, you could consult Joanie Graham's *Shetland Dictionary*, if your local bookshop hasn't *joost selt* their last copy *dastreen*.

The diminutives Magnie (Magnus), Gibbie (Gilbert) and Charlie may also seem strange to non-Shetland ears. In a traditional country family (I can't speak for *toonie* Lerwick habits) the oldest son would often be called after his father or grandfather, and be distinguished from that father and grandfather and perhaps a cousin or two as well, by his own version of their shared name. Or, of course, by a *Peerie* in front of it, which would stick for life, like the *eart kyent* (well-known) guitarist Peerie Willie Johnson, who recently celebrated his 80th birthday. There was also a patronymic system, which meant that a Peter's four sons, Peter, Andrew, John and Matthew, would all have the surname Peterson, and so would his son Peter's children. Andrew's children, however, would have the surname Anderson, John's would be Johnson, and Matthew's would be Matthewson. The Scots ministers stamped this out in the nineteenth century, but in one district you can have a lot of *folk* with the same surname, and so they're distinguished by their house name: *Magnie o Strom, Peter o da Knowe*.

For those who like to look up unfamiliar words as they go, here's a glossary of some Scots and Shetlan words.

aa: all

an aa: as well

aabody: everybody

ahint: behind

allwye: everywhere

amang: among

anyroad: anyway

auld: old

aye: always

bairn: child

banks: sea cliffs, or peatbanks, the slice of moor where peats are cast

bannock: flat triangular scone

birl, birling: paired spinning round in a dance

blootered: very drunk

blyde: glad

boanie: pretty, good looking

breeks: trousers

brigstanes: flagged stones at the door of a crofthouse

bruck: rubbish

caa: round up

canna: can't

clarted: thickly covered

cowp: capsize

cratur: creature

crofthouse: the long, low traditional house set in its own land

daander: to walk slowly, in an uneven, wandering fashion

darrow: a hand fishing line

dastreen: yesterday evening

de-crofted: land that has been taken out of agricultural use, e.g. for a house site

dee: you. **du** is also you, depending on the grammar of the sentence – they're equivalent to thee and thou. Like French, you would only use dee or du to one friend; several people, or an adult if you're a younger person, would be 'you'.

denner: midday meal

didna: didn't

dinna: don't

dis: this

doesna: doesn't

doon: down

drewie lines: a type of seaweed made of long strands

duke: duck

dukey-hole: pond for ducks

du kens: you know

dyck, dyke: a wall, generally drystane, i.e. built without cement

ee now: right now

eela: fishing, generally these days a competition

everywye: everywhere

fae, frae: from

faersome: frightening

faither, usually **faider**: father

fanted: hungry, often **black fanted**, absolutely starving

folk: people

gansey: a knitted jumper

geen: gone

gowled: howled loudly, like a child

greff: the area in front of a peat bank

gret: cried

guid: good

guid kens: God knows

hae: have

hadna: hadn't

harled: exterior plaster using small stones

heid: head

hoosie: little house, usually for bairns

isna: isn't

joost: just

ken, kent: know, knew

kirk: church

kirkyard: graveyard

knowe: hillock

lem: china

Lerook: Lerwick

lintie: skylark

lipper: a cheeky or harum-scarum child, generally affectionate

mair: more

makkin belt: a knitting belt with a padded oval, perforated for holding the 'wires' or knitting needles.

mam: mum

mareel: sea phosphorescence, caused by plankton, which makes every wave break in a curl of gold sparks

meids: shore features to line up against each other to pinpoint a spot on the water

220

midder: mother

mind: remember

moorit: coloured brown or black, usually used of sheep

mooritoog: earwig

muckle: big – as in Muckle Roe, the big red island. Vikings were very literal in their names, and almost all Shetland names come from the Norse.

muckle biscuit: large water biscuit, for putting cheese on

na: no, or more emphatically, **naa**

needna: needn't

Norroway: the old Shetland pronunciation of Norway

o: of

oot: out

ower: over

park: fenced field

peat: brick-like lump of dried peat earth, used as fuel

peerie: small

peerie biscuit: small, sweet biscuit

peeriebreeks: affectionate name for a small thing, person, or animal

piltick: a sea fish common in Shetland waters

pinnie: apron

postie: postman

quen: when

redding up: tidying

reestit mutton: wind-dried shanks of mutton

riggit: dressed, sometimes with the sense dressed up

roadymen: men working on the roads

roog: a pile of peats

rummle: untidy scattering

Santy: Santa Claus

scaddy man's heids: sea urchins

scattald: common grazing land

scuppered: put paid to, done for

selkie: seal, or seal person who came ashore at night, cast his/her skin, and became human

shalder: oystercatcher

sho: she

shoulda: should have, usually said sooda

shouldna: shouldn't have

SIBC: Shetland Islands Broadcasting Company, the independent radio station

sixareen: double-ended six oared boat, around twenty-five foot in length

skafe: squint
skerry: a rock in the sea
smoorikins: kisses
snicked: move a switch that makes a clicking noise
snyirked: made a squeaking or rattling noise
solan: gannet
somewye: somewhere
sooking up: sucking up
soothified: behaving like someone from outwith Shetland
spewings: piles of vomit
splatched: walked in a splashy way with wet feet, or in water
swack: smart, fine
tak: take
tatties: potatoes
tay: tea, or meal eaten in the evening
tink: think
tirricks: Arctic terns
trows: trolls
tushker: L-shaped spade for cutting peat
twa: two
twa-three (usually twa-tree): a small number
vee-lined: lined with wood planking
voe: sea inlet
voehead: the landwards end of a sea inlet
waander: wander
waar: seaweed
wand: a fishing rod
whatna: what
wasna: wasn't
wha's: who is
whitteret: weasel
wi: with
wir: we've – in Shetlan grammar, we are is sometimes we have
wir: our
wife: woman, not necessarily married
wouldna: would not
yaird: enclosed area around or near the croft house
yoal: a traditional clinker-built six-oared rowing boat.

DISCOVER MORE BOOKS IN

THE SHETLAND SAILING MYSTERIES SERIES

Available now from

ACCENT